THE PHILOSOPHER
AND THE GOLEM

The Philosopher and the Golem

A Novel By

JERRY LEVY

Adelaide Books
New York / Lisbon
2018

THE PHILOSOPHER AND THE GOLEM
a novel
by Jerry Levy

Copyright © 2018 by Jerry Levy

Cover design © 2018 Adelaide Books LLC

Published by Adelaide Books LLC, New York / Lisbon
adelaidebooks.org

Editor-in-Chief
Stevan V. Nikolic

For any information, please address Adelaide Books
at info@adelaidebooks.org
or write to:
Adelaide Books LLC
244 Fifth Ave. Suite D27
New York, NY, 10001

ISBN13: 978-1-949180-09-1
ISBN10: 1-949180-09-3

Printed in the United States of America

Chapter One

It started with the call. If only I had let the phone ring through to the answering machine, I might have thought about the request more carefully, perhaps declined. I just know this: the phone was insistent, ringing shrilly like the cry of a hungry baby. I had no choice, it was driving me mad. As I ran to pick it up, I contemplated all the swear words I could utter to a telemarketer; the truth of the matter was that I hardly got any calls other than from people who wanted to sell me things I had no interest in.

"Hello!"

"Is that Karl Pringle?"

"That depends."

"Depends on what?"

"On who's calling. Who the hell are you anyway?"

"My name's Ruth and I'm the landlady for Rivka Howard."

"So?"

"So, she's dead. I'd like you to come get her things."

I barely knew Rivka Howard; I had met her a few years earlier in a group therapy program and to the best of my re-collection, she attended all of three or four meetings, barely saying a word throughout. Which to me seemed positively ridiculous; why come to group therapy if you won't speak? I do recall that the facilitator prodded her but it was all for naught. She was as closed as a clam. What else? Ah yes, she was close to my own age, mid-thirties or so. And a cutter. That's what I remember most. During a break in a session, when we had both stepped outside the building for a smoke, I saw a series of ugly zig-zag scars on one of her arms. Her long sleeve shirt had somehow ridden up as she took a drag, revealing the misfortune. And as she swayed nervously from foot to foot, I also learned from her that she had a passion for books, her favourite writer being Virginia Woolf. It was during that brief encounter that I had given her my phone number, one book lover to another – but she never called.

The apartment building Rivka lived in was the kind you passed by quickly; the doorway was without a door and the smell of roach spray permeated the halls. The balconies stood like impenetrable fortresses into the lives of the inhabitants, protected with laundry lines of clothes, mattresses, and rusting bicycles. Three young toughs loitered in the lobby and eyed me suspiciously. "You got a smoke?" said one. His N.Y. Yankee hat was on backwards and his oversized black jeans hung halfway down his bum, revealing a pair of Looney-Tunes cartoon underwear. I snuck a quick glance at Daffy Duck and handed over my entire pack of Du Mauriers.

"Here," I said. "I'm trying to quit anyway." I wasn't.

I recognized the name – *Zisturn* – on a wall plaque. The *Zisturn Buildings* were once part of a government-sponsored initiative to provide lower income housing for those in the arts. Rent was geared to income. But through mismanagement and cuts in provincial funding, the project fell apart and now housed impoverished immigrants and those on the margins. The newspapers sometimes had stories of deaths in the buildings. Guns. Knives. Gangs. Drugs were prevalent. So was prostitution. Most of the artists had moved out.

I met Ruth as planned. She had some sort of blue dishrag around her head, thin strands of mousey brown hair sticking out. Her eyes were beet-red, like she hadn't slept in days. She was terribly overweight. As a first impression, she was terribly, horribly, miserably, that's what she was and more, with legs peeking out from the far reaches of a dirty paisley smock like mottled balloons.

As we walked the length of the long, dark corridor with its peeling paint and frayed carpeting, I wondered how Rivka fit into the equation. Artist? Immigrant? Misfit? Surely not a moll or hooker. I only knew one thing: I felt I was marching to my execution — there was something terribly depressing and ominous about the place.

"The cops told me to look for a relative," said Ruth.

"I'm not a relative," I countered.

"Yours was the only phone number I could find in her address book. Somebody has to remove all the crap and it sure as hell ain't me."

When the door was opened, an indescribable smell wafted out, causing me to gag. Ruth held her nose. "She killed herself, maybe it was an accidental overdose. We found the tenant lying on the bed. There was an open bottle of sleeping pills next to her."

The tenant?

"What exactly do you want me to do here?" I said.

"Simple. I have to rent this place out again. I need you to clean it, take her stuff. Capiche?"

"What about the police?"

"Their investigation is over. It wasn't much of anything. They only asked a few questions: How long the tenant had lived in the apartment, did I know of any friends or relatives. That sort of thing. They didn't search the place, just went through her wallet. They looked at all the pills on the bed, saw how dirty the place was, and said 'we're done.' What did they call it? Oh yeah, *death by misadventure.*"

"So how long did she live here?" I said. "And, what about any friends?"

"A few years. Like I said to the cops, I keep to myself. I don't want no trouble. In this building, people come and go. What they do, who they know...that's none of my business."

"Interesting."

"Maybe to you but not to me. It's a big hassle, that's all. Anyway, don't ask me nothing no more. Just get her things out."

"Excuse me. The woman died. Doesn't that mean any-thing..."

"So?" interjected the landlady. "Is that *my* fault?"

For a second, I thought about telling Ruth to stuff it...she was a real piece of work. But I realized that if I helped out, that I might come to understand the mystery that was Rivka Howard. How, I wondered, had a bright woman in what should have been the prime of life sunk so low? Why had she lived in such decrepit circumstances? The other thing that caused me to keep my mouth shut was that I realized the endeavour might do me good – I needed a distraction from the circumstances of my own life.

Ruth took out a pack of Kleenex from her smock and gave it to me. "You'll need this for your nose."

I wandered through the apartment, a kleenex covering my mouth and nose. The wallpaper was peeling in spots and the wall-to-wall carpeting was spotted with stains. Cigarette butts were everywhere. On the bathroom floor, I found a solitary razor blade. It was streaked with dried blood.

As utterly filthy and disgusting as the place presented, it was the smell that nearly caused me to double over. To say it was of decay would be too generous; it was as sharp and cutting as a garbage dump – a malodorous swamp of vomit, food, booze, cigarettes, and of things I couldn't name. It was nothing less than the sad refuse of life long since abandoned.

"Oh God, what is that?" I said.

"I don't know," answered Ruth. "But whatever it is, I need it cleaned."

I pried open a jammed window with a butter knife I found in a kitchen drawer and stuck my head out for a breath.

There were stacks of newspapers and magazines piled everywhere, and unwashed plates and cutlery littered the sink where a family of roaches reveled amidst the food remains. A furry brown mouse scurried along a countertop, causing a fright in me.

"Are you going to pay me?"

Ruth rolled her eyes.

"I'll do what I can," I said, "but it might take a week or two to make this place look presentable. Maybe even longer."

"That's fine. I'm going to give you some boxes so you can put stuff away. After that, I don't want to see your face until this place is spic 'n span. Got it?" Her index finger was inches from my nose.

"Don't point, ok? And yes, I got it."

Stupid twit. "I'll need some gloves," I said. "There's no way I'm touching anything."

Ruth left me alone and I waited in the hallway for her to return. The three dudes from the lobby passed by. "Hey man, anything else for us?" said the Yankee fan.

"What do you mean?"

"Don't play dumb, man. Money."

I gave the three of them the once over. Black, late teens or early twenties, tattoos galore, some snaking up the necks. I took the request seriously, they didn't appear to be people you could fool with. One of them, wearing numerous gold chains around his burly neck, spit pistachio nuts at my feet and smiled ironically. I saw that he had front gold teeth, which matched the chains.

"I might have something in the apartment," I said, recalling the various pill bottles I had seen on a table. "Stay here."

The spring-loaded front door began closing but the Yankee stuck his foot in the crack. Suddenly all three squinted their eyes and a look of alarm invaded their countenances.

"Hell man, what is that?"

"Yah, man. Fuck."

The door closed slowly on my nemeses but I thought it best to open it and explain.

"You live here, man?"

"Yah."

"We don't want your shit, asshole." The punks walked away, coughing and gasping for deep breaths.

I was now alone in the apartment, grateful that I had drubbed my assailants. Even Superman wouldn't have stood a chance against the smell. It was nothing less than decaying kryptonite. I quickly held a Kleenex up to my nose.

When Ruth walked back in, I was never happier to see someone. Although I knew that the three idiots were not to be messed with, I had the same impression about Ruth. If I needed an ally against the punks, she was it.

"Here, put these on."

I slipped the latex gloves on and tied a surgical mask around my face.

"Now I'm leaving," she said. "Here's the keys. I'm in 1A. I expect you to check in next Tuesday. One week."

I wandered through the apartment, surrounded by rot and feeling much like a zombie walking amidst the dead. I had hardly slept the night before, beset as I was with recurrent insomnia. I felt like passing out and briefly rested on one knee.

In a kitchen cabinet, I saw a myriad of pill bottles – *Ativan, Xanax, Serux, Vulium, Celexa, Zoloft* – too many to get my head around. From my own bouts with depression, I recognized them as anti-depressants and anti-anxiety medications. Years earlier, during a particularly stressful period in my life, I had taken Celexa. I must dutifully admit that it improved my mood considerably; I felt happy all the time. Almost euphoric. So much so that I couldn't sleep; I'd go for long walks in the middle of the night, venturing to parks to lay bird seed on the ground. And while my brain's happiness quotient greatly perked up, my other mental faculties did not. I walked around like the village idiot, a perpetual grin on my face...and I couldn't think. After a few weeks on the drug, I wasn't able to muster up a single cogent thought; a thick fog shrouded the analytical side of my brain and the best I could do was repeat what others said. My school grades dropped precipitously and watching TV became a favourite pastime. Mind-numbing game shows mostly. After six months of this zombie-like behaviour, I packed the drug in.

As I looked through Rivka's pharmaceutical collection, what immediately stood out was that they had all been prescribed by different doctors. Multiple doctors, multiple medications...it was a recipe for disaster.

In another cabinet, I found vitamin bottles. I recognized the most common ones – B's and C's, *Calcium/ Magnesium* – but there were many others that I had no knowledge of: *TG-100, Rhodiola, TAD+, Ashwaghanda*. I conjectured that Rivka had probably tried to balance the pharmaceuticals with natural herbs and vitamins, that seemed the most logical explanation. In the fridge were at least half a dozen bottles of a vitamin formula called *E3-Live*. No real food, unless two tins of half-eaten sardines could be counted. That and cans of cat food.

The apartment really was a pigsty. Things were flying about, grey, moth-like creatures that I gobsmacked between my gloved hands. I slumped down into a tattered reclining chair in the living room and put my feet up. I reached for a small bottle on a coffee table and held it at eye-level. Chanel No. 5 perfume. Classic. 0.50 oz, the price tag clearly visible

– $160. I lowered my mask and took a whiff. Mystical. Gossamers of exquisite flowers and herbs wafted to my nose, effectively blocking the horrid smell of my surroundings. Instinctively, my eyes closed momentarily as the scent descended upon me. The woman had taste, I couldn't deny it. I sat there motionless and stared at the bottle. If only she had said something to me. If only...

I searched the drawers in the kitchen for a pack of cigarettes and found a carton of

Gitanes Brunes. My lucky day. The Spanish gypsy woman on the black, blue and white cover was playing a tambourine. It wasn't lost on me that such an uplifting act was in sharp contrast to the bleakness of Rivka's apartment.

I sat back down in the chair and opened a slit in the mask for my lips. I lit a match and took a drag. The cigarette had a real bite. My entire body relaxed at once as I exhaled. I didn't stir, didn't blink. I simply sat and wondered why I was such an idiot for agreeing to clean the place. Chances were that I wouldn't uncover anything in Rivka's junk pile that would shed any insights into her. Even if there were, it struck me that I didn't really care. Hardly about anything and certainly not about some drug-crazed woman I didn't know. I had gotten myself into a stupid mess and now there was no backing out.

I stood up, walked to the sink and seared a distracted roach with the cigarette. It glowed like a red-hot ember and made a mad dash to safety behind the sink. I discarded the cigarette into a pot of murky water and left, the carton of *Gitanes* safely ensconced beneath my right armpit.

Chapter Two

I returned the following day to Rivka's apartment, armed with two gym bags filled with cleaning utensils, disinfectant, and bug spray that I had picked up at Canadian Tire the night before. I liberally sprayed Mandarin Orange and Sprightly Lemon from odour eliminator cans throughout and opened all the windows. I considered lowering my mask but decided against it, the air was still putrid. The perfume was where I had left it and I sprayed that too – undoubtedly Coco Chanel would not have approved of such blatant use but I needed every wonderful scent for my arsenal.

It was impossible to work with all the flying moths. They buzzed around my face like mad kamikaze pilots. The night before, I brought home a solitary one that I had squashed and compared its appearance with ones I found on the 'net. There was no question, these were pantry moths. I put up sticky moth paper on walls and shelves, on kitchen counters. In no time at all, the papers started filling up, the moths attracted to the pheromones. It was utterly disgusting and all that was more than enough for one day.

I returned each day after that, always with a single daily project in mind. On Thursday and Friday, I worked on eradicating the vermin, roaches and mice. Saturday was set aside for the bathtub, which had a terrible black ring encrusted in the enamel. Sunday and Monday was for sanding the floors, and so on. I figured that if I set aside each day for just one task, that the whole affair might not seem so onerous. Dividing the tasks in such a manner seemed to work; once the smell abated somewhat and the mask was no longer necessary, I actually looked forward to visiting Rivka's apartment. It gave me something to do.

My inclination though, was to do a half-assed job. I hated anything to do with cleaning and rarely lifted a broom in my own apartment. But I surprised myself. I'm not exactly sure why. I surmised that it probably had to do with Newton's Second law of Thermodynamics, the one that states that all things in a closed system tend toward maximum disorder, toward entropy, unless worked upon. And Rivka's apartment certainly embodied that chaos. So I would be the force that contravened the natural universal progression. I liked that, it made me feel somewhat powerful. A silly argument in favour of cleaning, I realized, but I always gravitated toward postulates.

I set wooden snap traps for the mice using bits of peanut butter as bait. I could hear the pop as the metallic spring came down hard on their necks; I didn't mind one little bit. I found in a local hardware store more humane mousetraps – box traps as they were known – complete with one-way doors that allowed the mice to enter but not escape. Unlike the snap, crackle, and pop traps that I preferred, these could be used over and over again. But I wanted no part of them. It meant madly shaking boxes and taking the mice outside for release. That was a waste of my time: these were only vermin, after all.

Likewise, I set up motels of death for the roaches all throughout the apartment…it was too easy. They crawled in and were stuck for all time. Just to be on the safe side, I also went through three cans of roach spray.

With the vast majority of the insects and such out of the way, working in the apartment became easier. The smell, although much improved, continued to linger on and so each morning the first order of business was to give the place the once-over using a can of scent – Jasmine, Cinnamon, Green Apple. There were the more exotic ones too – Crisp Linen, Spring Waterfall, Ocean. And when I started washing the floors and countertops and threw away the stale food, the smell began dissipating even further. It improved dramatically when a week later I checked in with Ruth and she gave me permission to rip up the wall-to-wall carpeting. Little did I realize that when I did so, I would unearth even more creepy-crawlies…long and black, they were centipede-like things that were inordinately speedy. With their home exposed, they began darting to safety but in a mad scramble, I did my best to step on each and every one.

On the Tuesday, Ruth gave me cardboard boxes into which I could place all of Rivka's clothes. I had no use for the apparel of course and so my intention was to cart them over to *Goodwill*. But when I started sorting through her clothes closet, I noticed something highly unusual: some of the dresses and a few blouses had anti-shoplifting tags still affixed. Plastic bits molded together, looking like graham cracker sandwiches. There were quite a few broken pieces littering the floor of her closet too. Unless Rivka had a clothes shop of her own and the items in the apartment were part of her inventory, this made no sense whatsoever. But that possibility disappeared altogether when I started scrutinizing the clothes further. For they had come from a variety of upscale stores. Certainly not Zeller's or Walmart. No, these were all designer labels from clothing stores Holt Renfrew, Prada, and Hermes. A Dolce & Gabbana jacket hung forlornly in the closet, never having seen the light of day, the price tag of $1295 still attached. A Gucci brown silk scarf with gold embroidering around the edges was tied around a military green Prada purse, looking like they were ready for an evening out. The scarf $129, the purse $1,234. I found a handbag called the *Hermes Birkin* with the astonishing price tag of $14,500.

It was evident that Rivka had been a shoplifter. A high-end one at that. How she had beaten the system was a complete mystery. My knowledge of pilfering was non-existent – I was many things but definitely not a thief. To further complicate matters, I realized I couldn't take the goods to Goodwill. There might be security cameras in the store, or someone might see me drop the clothes off. I just didn't need the hassle, trying to explain away what I was doing with stolen clothes and accessories. I suppose I could have dumped garbage bags full of the stuff into the building's garbage bins but again, I was concerned that something might go wrong. And as strange as this might sound, I also didn't want to implicate Rivka in any way. Now that I was aware of her proclivity for thieving high-end goods, I developed a new-found respect for her. She had bested the uber-rich, the 1%. Good for her.

Still, something didn't add up. All these beautiful clothes and accessories in a roach-filled apartment? It was true that the enigma of Rachel Howard was now crystal-lizing. A cutter and a shoplifter. Nonetheless, it was all rather vague. How had this disaster come about? Why did she feel compelled to risk stealing? And was it really a suicide? Maybe she had accidentally overdosed. Death by misadventure, as Ruth had been told by the police...maybe that was the best answer.

While I couldn't take all the clothes to Goodwill, I did drop off at the store goods that contained no anti-theft devices, a small black and white TV, a stereo, and numerous CD's. Many of the CD's were still wrapped in plastic; perhaps they too had been stolen. But I was hardly concerned about $14.99 CD's, nor did I suspect Goodwill would be.

As interesting as the clothes had been, I still needed to concentrate on the apartment itself. Sure I had made some dents in getting it ready for Ruth to rent out, but there was no question but that the place still required a lot of work. The bathtub, for instance, had that black concentric ring and try as I might, I just couldn't get rid of it. In fact, the more I scrubbed away at it, the blacker it became. Left with no options, I visited the same hardware store where I had purchased the mousetraps and ended up renting a palm sander. A sand palmer, no less, something I had never even heard of before this Rivka caper unfolded! But once I got started restoring the apartment, I knew there was no point in taking shortcuts. So I used cheesecloth and a spray bottle to apply a chemical adhesive to the surface of the tub, and then painted on an acrylic polymer coating. In no time at all, and much to my utter amazement, I had actually restored the tub to a white, pristine condition.

I did something similar with the wood flooring. I rented another piece of equipment of which I had no knowledge, a hand-held drum sander. Once I explained the situation, the hardware store manager was kind enough to throw in some knee pads and safety glasses free of charge for the job.

The flooring had enormous potential, even a lay person such as myself could see that. But it was all badly scuffed and nails were sticking out in spots. I swept the floor clean and pulled out the protruding nails. As I had been instructed, I then attached coarse sandpaper to the sander and began the operation. Once I got started, it was like manoeuvering a Zamboni machine over a piece of ice...the sander just slid along the grain. Once the first go-round was complete, I had to change the sandpaper to a finer grade and go over the entire flooring once again. Despite the ease with which the sander moved, it was nevertheless a daunting job. I worked in small squares and it took considerable time to finish. But finish I did, and then the floor was down to its natural wood. I might have then stained it but that in itself was a big job and as I had already spent a day and a half with the drum sander, I let it be.

Each day the place looked better and better. After every task I would sit in the recliner and reach for a smoke. Although I would never have imagined it, there was great satisfaction in completing a job. It made me feel somewhat competent, something that had been missing of late in my life. Sometimes though, a solitary moth would flitter by or I would spy a cockroach and that feeling would dissolve...

I sifted through the stacks of newspapers to see if there was any reason or rhyme behind Rivka having kept them, but there was nothing. At least nothing I could determine – they were just yellowing pieces of newsprint horded by a mad collector. I bundled the entire collection and took them to the incinerator. I had no idea if you were allowed to throw paper into it but I didn't care…as long as I got rid of the lot.

On one occasion I passed one of the three amigos. Unlike the Yankee fan or the gold man, this was the quiet one, who hadn't said a word in our last encounter. He had on an oversized pair of Sony headphones and was bopping down the hallway, mouthing the words to imaginary songs. When he got within ten feet or so, he backed up theatrically against the wall to afford me a wide berth. Arms and legs dramatically apart, a look of sheer horror was etched into his face as he watched me pass. I nodded, what else? I could now hear the staccato thumping of the music; it sounded curiously like the explosive booms of gunshots. The dufus was a complete asshole but I was glad for his mocking me; it was obviously better than being confronted.

Back in the apartment, I found something of real interest: In the top drawer of a desk was Rivka's diary. Page after page of woe. There was great confusion about her health: she had been sick with some form of chronic fatigue that the doctors couldn't treat…or wouldn't treat, suggesting it was an imagined illness. There were money concerns and worries about her future. Loneliness. Boredom. Insomnia. Heart palpitations. A solitary quote from T.S. Eliot's *The Waste Land* – *"I can connect / Nothing with nothing."* Throughout there was no mention of any family or friends, no talk of trips or anything joyful. Bleakness.

On one page, I found mention of her excursions into back alleys to feed feral cats, many of whom she had given names...Oscar, Sonia, Luther...Early each morning she would slip out of the apartment to feed and water the homeless felines. That explained the many tins of cat food in the kitchen.

There was something else, a number of flyers neatly folded in the pages of the diary. They were taken out on the letterhead of a group called *The Underclass* and the message seemed to be devoted to a philosophy of sorts. Dime-store variety philosophy. I myself had a graduate degree in the art of reasoning and wondering and so could speak with authority. Still, the flyers piqued my interest.

"The world is run by psychopaths fueled by greed," it was written on one. "Bankers, lawyers, stockbrokers, investors, venture capitalists. Money-grubbing pigs. They play power games, manufacture weapons, and by carrying a large footprint, divest the world of its resources. They are interested in one thing and one thing only: accumulating as much wealth for themselves as possible. In earlier times they were considered 'robber barons.' But is the term any less apt today? They exploit the underclass for their own gain by paying nominal wages, enslaving those in need. They drive small companies out of business and build monopolies. They are today's counterparts to the medieval German feudal lords who charged exorbitant fees on ships to traverse the Rhine River. This country, this world, needs a cleansing. We need to clean out all the capitalists and not give them sympathy." The flyers were all the same – anti-capitalist rants. Diatribes against big business, oil barons, the very wealthy. Some quoted Karl Marx, citing capitalism as being the "dictatorship of the bourgeoisie." They all contained verbiage about the oppression of the exploited working class – the proletariat, wage slaves, workers alienated from the fruits of their own labour.

I had heard this type of 'philosophy' a million times before. While it always made some sense on a grassroots level, I discarded it. The fact of the matter was that despite the ascent to power of certain money-hungry individuals, no other economic system in the world had ever worked. Certainly not communism, which is what Marx espoused. Besides, I had studied true philosophers like Georg Hegel and Friedrich Nietzsche in depth and so couldn't abide by this pseudo-philosophy. It was too easy... extractions from Marxist doctrine manipulated and chopped into palatable bites for the unsuspecting twenty-first century masses. Ted Kaczynski, the *Unibomber*, had a similar manifesto that was all drivel. Thirty-five thousand words that called for a worldwide revolution against the effects of society's industrial-technological system. The guy should have stuck to the mathematics he was schooled in.

The one thing that struck a deep chord in me is that one of the flyers culminated with a paragraph that read thusly: *"Do not be afraid to take what is rightly yours. Beat the pigs at their own game. Steal when you can, what you can. You have the right."*

I sat at the kitchen table, appraising the damage such a doctrine can have on someone, especially someone vulnerable like Rivka. If she felt overwhelmed by life – as she surely must have been – then reading these words would have fueled in her the notion that the world was inherently unfair and that she deserved better. Moreover, she was at liberty to do something about it. That explained the shoplifting.

I returned to reading Rivka's diary. Suddenly, within all the doom and gloom, I saw the slightest glimmer of hope. It was a brief mention about her writing and how it brought her solace. That she thought she had talent and hoped to write more when she felt better, if she ever would feel better. Considering that I found in a box Rivka's unframed degree in English Literature from the University of Toronto, it was perhaps not too surprising a revelation.

But it was only a brief respite. For on the page following, she spoke of the cuttings.

"It makes me feel better," she wrote. "Especially when I'm sad or depressed, which I am much of the time. It's a release, not only of blood but of endorphins."

And then, on the very next page, there was a final note: "It's over. My fate is sealed."

So the diary ended.

Chapter Three

Fortunately, I had many days available in which to restore Rivka's apartment. I was...well, temporarily unemployed. In between jobs, as they say. But in sales, there are always jobs to be had. It's just that I didn't want any part of them.

My last job was selling lighting fixtures for a company in mid-town Toronto called The Lighting Emporium. It wasn't much but did give me an opportunity to get a piece of writing published – 'Replacing the Ballast in a Fluorescent Lighting Fixture.' It appeared in *National Lighting & Fixtures Magazine.* Not exactly the kind of writing I wanted to be known for but it was a start. In fact, it was my only piece of published material. My other work, the material I toiled on almost daily, was good prose. Short stories mostly but I had also finished a novella and a couple of non-fiction pieces. I wasn't exactly James Joyce but considered myself a decent writer; it was too bad the literary magazines didn't think likewise. They rejected everything I submitted. If there was one good thing about my temporary state of unemployment was that I could get down to writing without distractions.

How exactly had I come to write prose? How had I come to the pinnacle of all jobs – selling lighting? Even to study philosophy? The questions are worthy, deserving of answers. It started when I was a child; at least, that's how I look upon it. My parents were *Roma* from Hungary, gypsies as some people like to say. *Thieves* and *witches* yet to others. They were heavily persecuted and fled to Canada but that perpetual outcast label remained etched in their psyches, an attitude they passed on to me. I was the outsider throughout school, never making any friends. It was my parents and I against the world. Sure, they settled into jobs in Toronto and tried to fit in. The jobs though were menial cleaning ones in office buildings, bringing only the basics of food to the table and shelter over our heads. We could afford no luxuries of any sort, had no car, and certainly there were no trips. Even taking public transit was not feasible – I rode my rickety bicycle everywhere, even in the winter. My nose froze, my hands froze, my feet too; it didn't matter though, there was no choice. Besides, once my Dad showed me how to patch a flat tire, I felt a sense of autonomy...nothing could get the better of me if I needed to be somewhere.

I suppose things might have been different if my parents had reached out to the various Canadian social service agencies set up to help refugees, but that didn't happen. They had an innate distrust of institutions and regarded any such governmental agency as a thing to be avoided, just like in Hungary where the government often perpetrated violence against the Roma people.

As might be expected, my parents argued constantly about money. With her old-world views, my mother believed that as the man of the house, my father should be the one to keep the family in comfort. But with no real skills to offer and with language an issue, he was at a vocational dead-end. He did the best he could but with the constant nagging and with my mother's tendency to shop for goods we could not really afford, his heart gave out at the young age of 49.

Very soon after his death, my mother passed away. She lost the will to live, that was evident: she would be beset with crying spells, eat only sparingly, and would often fail to show up at work. She had always been prone to bouts of self -pity – which might have explained why she felt inclined to shop at the higher-end of the spectrum – and now with her husband gone, she probably realized that there was no escaping her menial life.

It didn't help matters that we lived in Parkdale at the time. It was becoming more gentrified each year, with young urban families professionals buying and restoring some of the grand old houses. New commercial shops and cafes began opening on King Street and some of the parks were being swept clean of vagrants. Amidst all this change were my very guarded parents. They were uneducated, without means, and while my father seemed to not be bothered in the least by the opulence that was springing up around him, my mother was a different story. She would gaze wistfully into the windows of pricey dress shops or else deliberately take walks by the refurbished Victorian houses, with their prim gardens and terraced brick exteriors. On occasion, she would even dare to walk up to the front door and spy through the windows. I know this because she often reported to both my father and me about what she saw inside – magnificent chandeliers, spacious living rooms with leather furniture, accent tables, curio cabinets, pine book-cases. It ate at her, being so close to such luxury, and yet so far. My father begged her to stop but she would hear none of it, satisfying her desires temporarily with buying a blouse or dress or pair of shoes that was beyond our means. Sometimes she stole the flowers that dotted the lawns of the homes she so coveted.

After the death of my parents, I continued on at school, eventually studying Philosophy at the University of Toronto. I was a good student and drawn toward the subject. I was a *thinker*, so my parents had always said. To go even one step further, I could offer up a conjecture and say that philosophy lies within the domain of the perpetual outsider. It provides for no directly-related employment opportunities in the world at large, of that I am certain. I did however once read about a pub in London that employed philosophy students to engage patrons in friendly discourse about ideas, but suspect that type of thing is rare. Moreover, it seemed to me that the management was simply trying to get its customers to linger longer, and thus buy more beers and food. Putting aside those somewhat dubious motives, to those who embrace it, philosophy offers the opportunity for a rich inner life. A life of the mind. Where one is encouraged to examine concepts in detail, think, and question.

Let me say that it's not that I didn't try other pursuits. Like football. Well, soccer to North Americans. I dreamed of being a great player like Pele or Messi, but it wasn't to be. My hand-eye co-ordination was especially bad. I just couldn't run and kick a soccer ball at the same time; I'd those experiences, I'm convinced. Eating a wonderful meal, making love,case, I couldn'toften trip and skin my knees. And the times I tried heading, I only succeeded in mashing up my nose. Which was all too bad because Toronto now has a Roma soccer club, and it would have been a great way to meet others. Even to get out of my own head and be involved in a more experiential life. While I have always been attracted to affairs of the mind, I had long been aware that certain things in life should not be contemplated. *Just do it,* as the Nike ad says. Too much thinking harms romping in the ocean…they're all better left to the senses. But in my kick the damn soccer ball while I hotfooted it down the pitch, so what are you going to do?

Throughout school, I supported myself with student loans and working at odd jobs – sandwich maker at Mr. Submarine, security guard at a senior's home, and dishwasher at a Chinese restaurant being amongst the least memorable. Not knowing what else to do and with my stated predilection for matters of the mind, I had fully intended to continue on with school and obtain a PhD. I knew it was a massive undertaking but I also realized that doing so suited my nature. In writing my dissertation, I would be on my own, which, to me, would feel normal. And the end result of all my labour would be a position in academia, a professorship.

The path was charted, the route made clear by my advisor Aaron Feldstein. I had known Aaron during my undergraduate years, when he taught a course I was enrolled in called *Philosophy after 1800.* Essentially a discourse on social and political currents in 19th century philosophical thought. I studied Hegel, Schopenhauer, Nietzsche, and Bertrand Russell.

Later on, I took yet another course with him entitled *The Existentialists*. We delved into aspects of identity, absurdity, and alienation, and read from the works of Kierkegaard, Dostoyevsky, Tolstoy, Sartre, and Camus. Oh, and lest I forget, Kafka. I could never forget my first encounter with Gregor Samsor, the protagonist in *The Metamorphosis* who turns into a bug and withers away. A bug no less! Still, it was a very effective tool to emphasize the absurd nature of man, one locked into a world of drudgery, a world of meaningless repetition. Gregor became the manifestation of what he always was, a small and inconsequential entity.

I looked upon Aaron as a kindred sprit. He too was a loner, never quite fitting in. He was overweight, a bit of a slob (there were always food stains on his shirts), and would carry his books to school in paper shopping bags. He seemed to show little interest in women, sports, politics, fashion, movies, food, cars, business...anything really. Anything other than philosophy, that is. He authored many papers on diverse philosophical subjects ranging from Logical Empiricism to Hegelian Dialectic to the Greek Sophists to Epistemology.

The very last course with Aaron was the *Philosophy of Law*. It made sense for me to take it since I always considered, albeit half-heartedly, a career in law as a *Plan B* should the professorship in Philosophy fail. If truth be known, being a lawyer seemed remote for the very opposite reason that drew me toward matters of the mind – one had to interact with clients in the everyday world. So while I enjoyed a certain affinity for the logic that is associated with the law, a career in the field did not seem overly viable. Nevertheless, as I needed a credit and given that Aaron was teaching the course, I enrolled.

For all of Aaron's accomplishments, there was one thing that stood out as being amiss: no student had ever asked him to be their advisor for the doctorate program. I was the first. In hindsight, I should have taken more heed of that fact. In *The Symposium*, Plato said that one of the highest human privileges was to "be midwife to the birth of the soul in another." Aaron never succeeded on that front. As time elapsed, I became aware that he was perhaps jealous of me, that he viewed my burgeoning academic career as threatening to his own. That was my impression. He appeared remote and provided very little in terms of mentorship. Once again I was alone. Since I believed I was too far along in the program to switch advisors and also because I viewed Aaron if not exactly as a friend then at least an ally, I confronted him.

"I have to know your commitment level with me," I said.

"You have a persecution complex," he said without missing a beat. If there was one thing about Aaron that could not be denied, it was that he was brutally honest. "So that makes it hard for me to be there for you."

"I don't know what you mean," I countered.

"It's your background. You've changed and anglicized your name from Gabor Wallachia to Karl Pringle but you still haven't shed the inferiority complex that Hungarian Romas have always exhibited. Until you do, you'll never succeed. Not only in Philosophy but in anything."

It had been a long time since I had heard my birth name uttered. Not since my parents were alive. Aaron knew of my background only because I had trusted him. It now seemed as though that trust was mislaid.

Those caustic words elicited in me emotions that I had long ago suppressed – fear, anxiety, confusion, hopelessness. We continued talking, arguing, and in doing so, it became abundantly clear that Aaron wanted out of our professional relationship. He wanted to go back to being the absent-minded professor that he always was, the one without any real obligations to his students. The professor who gave lectures students complained about as being too obtuse and unrelated to the subject matter. The one who seemed to exist in his own intellectual bubble.

"There's one more thing," said Aaron.

"What's that?"

"You might want to rethink your commitment to the program. You've been mucking around in graduate school for eight or nine years now. And you've only shown yourself to be a mediocre philosopher at best."

It was all falling apart. Rage supplanted the primary emotions of fear and terror and blinded me. I lost all control and reared back, clapping Aaron with my closed fist at the side of his head. He collapsed at once to the ground in a crumpled heap and blood spurted from his ear. For good measure, I kicked him hard in the ribs.

That one punch, of bare knuckles against pudgy flesh – which felt so good – ended my academic pursuits. I was banished from the university and made to account for my actions before a magistrate of the courts. I threw myself upon his mercy and was grateful that I wasn't imprisoned. Instead, I was ordered to serve two-hundred hours of community service and told to attend anger management classes. Those anger management classes eventually morphed from one-on-one sessions with a psychologist to group therapy with upwards of twenty people, many of whom had a multitude of issues. And it was in that group therapy that I met Rivka Howard.

Despite this abomination, this descent into the bowels of academia and the legal system from which I barely managed to escape intact, there were some positives that emerged. From one, philosophy taught me think for myself, to argue, and to reason. No one can suggest these are less than worthwhile traits. And my readings in Existentialism opened up doors for me into the world of literature – Camus, Dostoyevsky, Kafka, and other masters. From them I learned not only the tenets that emphasized the isolation of the individual experience in a hostile or indifferent universe, but their works also fostered in me a love for the written word. Of prose. And so it was because of that that I tried my own hand at writing. Not very successfully as I have mentioned but nonetheless it has been a beneficial pursuit, allowing me to move away from the philosophical doctrines in which I had so long been immersed into other worlds. Imagined worlds. And, if I am to be honest, the brutal descent forced me to seek out work in the labour force. Something that I had long thought of as worthless. I saw my parents struggle with work and I always suspected that if it were not for the possibility of a career in academia, that I too would face those same struggles in the workforce. Work was unimportant, overrated, and able to give meaning only to those who lacked the rigorous discipline to think for themselves. An army of automatons. I would often see them debark at the St. George subway station early in the mornings, preparing to head southbound on the subway. While I was going to the university to engage in matters of the mind, they were going to their sad and pathetic nine-to-five jobs downtown to shuffle papers, to photocopy, to make ridiculous phone calls, to sell their souls for money. Now, I would be forced to covet those same work opportunities that I had long eschewed. And I would have to deal with it, move far from my comfort zone. Despite my revulsion, I realized that that might be beneficial for me in some ways. I would just hold my nose and bite my tongue. And so we have *The Lighting Emporium* – that's what *the punch* did for me.

Chapter Four

I now understood that Rivka was a sensitive soul who had somehow lost her way. To get caught up in all this anti-capitalist stuff surely could not have helped her. Nor could the cuttings. But what came first? It was the old chicken and egg dilemma. Was Rivka sad and depressed because of her illness and perhaps for other reasons **and then** listened to all those rants? Or had The Underclass' theorizing thrown her headlong into some deep chasm of doubt and darkness from which she could not emerge? I would likely never know, I realized. Furthermore, I came to the conclusion that it didn't matter. Not really. She was dead. I decided one thing though: that I would do my best to treat anything I found of hers with reverence and dignity and try to find homes for anything of even the slightest value. While fully admitting that I didn't have a complete handle on all aspects of her being, the more I came to understand certain things about her, the more I started to respect the woman. It was her intellect of course. That and because I sensed she was an outsider, much like me.

If there was one thing that Rivka possessed in abundance, it was books. Serious books. Dickens, Coetzee, James, Woolf,

D.H. Lawrence, Borges, Richler, Auster, Doyle, Orwell, Byatt...a large library of important writers. With my interest in Existential writers, I recognized Camus and Sarte and Bukowski. I opened Sartre's *No Exit* and read his most famous of lines: "Hell is other people." I returned the book to the shelf and shook my head in agreement. There was no question, Rivka was one learned woman of literature.

I contemplated what to do with all the books. By my rough count, there must have been close to two thousand. They were on book shelves, in kitchen cupboards and crates, baskets, and on window sills. There was not a cranny left in the apartment where a book had not taken up residence. Anyone could see that they provided her with comfort, that they must have been constant companions during times of strife. It seemed to me then, that these keepsakes deserved a better fate than to be carted off to Goodwill, where they would sit on shelves next to self-help and popular fiction books.

So I decided to hold a book sale. Right in Rivka's apartment. It seemed fitting that in death, her place would be host to lovers of literature. There would be people and life within those four walls, if even for a very short time. I think Rivka would have appreciated that. The likelihood was that while she was alive, no one had ventured into the apartment for a very long time.

As had been my habit, I worked in Rivka's apartment throughout the day and returned to my own hovel in the evenings. If I looked upon Rachel's place as being abysmal and decrepit, my own apartment wasn't much better. I had moved there following the death of my parents, living in the apartment throughout my undergraduate years and continuing to do so after I was summarily dismissed from the philosophy department. It was a small one-bedroom above a variety store in Kensington Market. I loved living in the Market, surrounded by vintage clothing stores, fragrant cheese shops, an African hand-drum store, and even the fish market where live crabs clamoured over each other in aquarium tanks. It was a cornucopia of diverse humanity, where this century's newly-ordained hippies mingled with Italian grocers and Portuguese sausage makers, and where everyone fit in perfectly. Well, almost. Until that megalithic food giant Loblaws decided they would attempt to muscle in and set up shop a stone's throw away on Bathurst Street. While family-run store owners and activists organized a petition that drew nearly 8,000 signatures, the food chain remained undeterred. Despite that battle, the apartment served my needs well. It was cheap and close to the university, functional. Other than that, not many more attributes could be said of it. Roaches were prevalent and oftentimes the smells from the butcher shop next door wafted through my window, causing me to gag. Bloody animal innards. There was a simple solution, I discovered – keep the window closed year-round.

Down the hall lived the tenant from the adjacent apartment. A seventy-seven-year-old woman, crippled with rheumatoid arthritis and with a touch of dementia, was my flat mate. If the woman could've cooked like my mother, it might have been alright. Instead, because she seemed to constantly keep her door open, when I went into the hallway I had to endure the smells – open cans of mackerel and tuna mixed with chopped onions and some monstrosity called blood pudding, a sausage made with dried pig's blood and oatmeal as a filler. The slaughtered remains of the goats and cows next door sometimes seemed like exquisite perfume in comparison. If all that weren't enough, my flat mate, who went by the unlikely name of Brenda Bumblegate, would try and regale me with tales of her life in show biz, where she once worked as a B movie star. Apparently, she had once worked with Buster Keaton, so she said, which I highly doubted. With Brenda's appetite for deep-red lipstick, copious amounts of mascara and face powder, a beehive hairdo, it was like living down the hall from a half-baked Betty Davis.

So it was to this glorious apartment that I retreated every night and it was there that I was able to indulge in my favourite pastime – playing the online game *Dark Age of Camelot*. I don't recall the exact moment when I started Camelot, only that I have been immersed in the wonderful online fantasy gaming world for many, many years. Certainly all throughout my undergraduate years. I do know that when I read Amazon's summation of the game as being perfect for those who "do not play well with others," I was hooked. Aristotle said that "excellence is an art won by training and habituation." Of course! Of course! I had to excel and could only do so by playing constantly.

I suppose much of my interest in Camelot rests in the fact that the game resides in fantasy. I have always needed a break from the real world. But it's more than just that: the game speaks to me in ways people cannot. Everywhere I have run into forgers and shiftless people, rogues like Aaron Feldstein, but not so in Camelot. Yes, yes, I know King Arthur is dead there and with him the force that holds the three realms rests in a precarious state of peace. But no matter, I have examined these realms in detail and know which suits me best. For the uninitiated, the realms are known as Albion, Hibernia, and Midgard. Following the good king's death, they waged war against each other, vying for control of keeps and towers, relics, and the entrance to Darkness Falls. Ultimately, they tried to preserve their homelands. Why not? Wouldn't anyone of sound mind do the same?

My actions in Camelot have always had a tangible result, that's what I'm saying. In this other-world, I can reclaim power and work toward the enhancement of mankind. I can advance a new generation of beings, bigger, stronger, and more astute. Supermen. I can be Nietzche's *Ubermensch.*

Chapter Five

I packed Rivka's vitamins and pharmaceuticals into a large box and brought it all home, thinking I might have some use for them. When I studied the various pill bottles, it struck me that Valium might actually be handy to have when the rejections from the literary magazines arrived, as invariably I knew they would. Moreover, I realized that in a more general sense, I could use some psychotropic drugs. All this working in Rivka's apartment without any clear benefit to myself was getting me woozy. Sure I had nothing better to do and it was making me feel somewhat useful, but so what? What good was it really doing? I was finding it hard to sleep, tossing and turning half the night. So I devised a plan to start taking some of the pills, only when I needed them. Which seemed to be quite often. I knew that if I stuck to a rigorous routine, that nothing bad would happen. So I started with 1/2 Ativan in the mornings followed by an entire Xanax in the evenings. It seemed to work out just fine. I had considered starting Paxil but realized that it might be foolhardy to do so; I knew that antidepressants took a full six weeks or so for their effects to set in and I figured Rivka had a supply of about three months. Not a happy equation. But the benzos kicked in at once, taking the edge off, and my sleep was restored.

I brought home from Rivka's place other items that I had yet decided what to do with. There was a jewelry box filled with bracelets, rings, earrings, brooches and such that I wasn't ready to part with. Many had prices still affixed. As she had done with clothing stores, Rivka ripped off jewelry shops. I saw a sterling silver bracelet with a Birk's tag –$495. A heart pendant from The Bay – $45. Many other pieces. It seemed that only death was able to stop the kleptomaniac.

I counted the total of the price tags – $4,625. A virtual gold mind. I couldn't in all good consciousness give the stash to Goodwill. I didn't think Rivka would have wanted that. So I kept it all, figuring I might one day pawn the items on Church Street.

It struck me that the only thing that Rivka's nimble fingers hadn't lifted were some exquisite paintings, the kind one might find in a fine art museum. In fact, the apartment had no art whatsoever. The walls were threadbare, not only of original painting, prints, art photos, or what have you, but also pictures. Family pictures. Of parents, nieces, nephews, kids, family pets, friends. There wasn't a solitary picture that showed that Rivka had any connection to others. Nothing to make the world familiar. It was as if she had retreated into her tiny, decrepit apartment, reading, taking pills and vitamins, counting her looted goods…then waited for death. And no one, not a single soul, would have cared. The tenant, as Ruth had said, the tenant was alone.

I suspected it couldn't have been exactly like that, but the more time I spent in the apartment, the more I was aroused to the profound sadness of Rivka's life. Her missing life. And the most unusual thing, the dichotomy that was not lost on me, was that within the very books that Rivka so loved, was a rich, magical world. Perhaps then that was the answer: it didn't matter to her that she had no one in her desultory real life for she had everyone and everything in fiction.

I brought home a couple of plants that were barely hanging on, determined to nurse them back to health. There were brown leaves amongst the foliage that simply flaked off at the touch. They all needed water, and repotting, and I worked diligently to make sure they would survive. I even went to the trouble of going to a nursery to get the best advice about proper food and soil. I also took away a collection of small stuffed animals – bears and cats mostly,... Rivka's extended family, I suppose. I couldn't drop them off at Goodwill. No, they were much too personal and I didn't at all mind having them with me – they somehow made my own place look more cheerful, homey. There was even a solitary doll amongst the lot. Tufts of light brown hair were missing as were three fingers. Clearly it had seen better days. But I found it in Rivka's bed, under the blankets, and right away realized that this too I could not give away, especially when It looked up at me with its big, glassy eyes. So I brought it home and placed it in the washroom, just above the toilet.

I still had some of the stolen clothes to deal with, the ones with the anti-theft devices attached. On the floor of Rivka's clothes closet, I found one of the devices smashed to bits. It looked as though a hammer had been used. I suppose

I could have done the same but instead decided to simply get rid of all the clothes. I ventured down to the Bloor Street Viaduct with two full green shopping bags, where I knew a group of homeless people lived under the bridge. Deep into the night, in the bowels of the city. I approached a group of men hovering over a bonfire.

"Can I burn something here?" I said.

"What's it worth to you?" said a man from the shadows, his face lit by the flames. He was small, emaciated, and frail-looking. In fact, the whole colony of six men looked grizzled, worn to the bone.

I produced two bottles of red wine from beneath my coat. I suspected, quite rightly, that I might need them. I pulled out one piece of clothing after another and tossed the lot onto the fire. I lingered to watch the crackling of the fire as the garments shriveled down to nothing. Then I joined the men in drink.

After about two weeks of cleaning, the apartment was presentable and I was ready for the book sale. I priced all the books and then set out to place flyers advertising the event. I returned to the university that had so wantonly booted me and ventured to the English Department, where I found a suitable bulletin board. After, I made my way to a number of coffee shops along Bloor Street – Second Cup, Starbuck's, Paulo's Espresso Bar – where I posted the flyers. Then to the very bohemian Kensington Market where I lived, which is always ripe for artsy events such as the one I was promoting. The Moonbeam Café was my first stop, followed by the

Baldwin Café. I stood on the corner of Baldwin Street and Kensington Ave, handing out the flyers.

"Please come," I urged. "It's for a good cause."

While some people were congenial and asked questions about the sale, even going so far as saying they would show up, others were outright rude.

"What you selling, boy, I have no interest," said one man, giving me a dismissive wave with his hand. He had long dreads and wore a multi-coloured knit cap. "Don't give me no shit papers." He was walking alongside his bike and steered it dangerously toward me, veering off at the last possible second.

I called CIUT, the university's radio station, and pleaded with them to find some air time to promote the sale. I told them that all proceeds would go to Sick Kid's Hospital. I wasn't exactly sure that that was the case; I hadn't worked out all the details. But I thought saying as much would elevate the occasion to a charitable event and bring in more people.

At 9 AM on the day of the sale, knowing full well that I would have to interact with a bunch of strangers, I took an entire Ativan. I made two pots of coffee and set out a few boxes of chocolate chip and Oreo cookies onto the table. I took one last look around the apartment and opened the door at 9:30, where a line of customers had already formed.

"Come in, come in," I enthused. "I'm so glad you're all here."

Glad you're all here? It didn't matter, I was just trying to be jocular, convivial. It was not lost on me that those were words not normally found in my vocabulary.

I was approached by a particularly pretty thing with multi-coloured hair. She was perhaps twenty-five or so and wearing Ugg sheepskin boots, ones I knew all the fashionistas of the world wore and which I detested. "Any Harold Robbins here?" she said.

"You've got the wrong sale, honey."

"How about Sidney Sheldon?"

I shook my head.

"Nora Roberts?"

I walked over to a bookshelf and plunked out D.H. Lawrence's *Lady Chatterly's Lover*.

"This is for you," I said. "I think you'll like it. It's full of sex and intrigue."

"Rad, how much?"

"For you, it's free. Have an Oreo."

People sat in chairs and read. Dawdled and munched on cookies. I didn't mind. The Ativan had set in and my mood was light, almost ephemeral. Even when I was approached by those who wanted to haggle over the prices was I not particularly bothered. I merely explained that the listed amounts were cheap enough and that the proceeds meant to help children in need. Cancer patients. Everyone quickly relented.

It was mostly the usual suspects who attended. Owners of second-hand book shops, students, a few professors wearing worn tweed jackets. "You've got good taste," I was told numerous times. To which I simply replied 'thank you.' It was too complicated to reveal Rivka's story.

I recognized the owner of an antiquarian book shop – John Fraser. Our paths had crossed on many an occasion when I purchased philosophy books at the store. Sometimes we met at university lectures that had been open to the public. We also knew some of the same people.

I felt uncomfortable seeing John and would have preferred to avoid him. But needless to say, the apartment was too small and so we swaggered slowly toward each other like gunslingers meeting at high noon. I extended a friendly hand. "John Fraser," I said. "It's been a long time."

"How are you, Karl? I didn't know you had such a collection. Philosophy, yes. But literature?"

The jig was up; I revealed a version of the truth. "Selling these books for a friend. She moved to Amsterdam and won't be coming back. She wanted all the proceeds to go to the hospital. She's got a heart of gold."

"Would I know her?"

"I don't think so. Her name is Joan Roland. Went to Concordia and then York. Not U of T. She had an interest mostly in Victorian literature. Dickens, Bronte, Jane Austen."

"Austen was really pre-Victorian."

"That's true. That's true. Anyway, I think you get the idea. Great collection of books, don't you think?"

"I'm quite interested in a couple of first-editions. Atwood, Isherwood, and Orwell." John waved the books in front of me. "How much?"

"I hadn't priced those, John, simply because they were first-editions. What do you think is fair?"

I accepted John's first offer, telling him that we were old friends. Really, I just wanted him out before he started delving into my now non-existent studies at the university.

Fortunately, it worked. John took the books and walked out the door. "Drop by the shop," he said as parting words. "I've got some rare David Hume and Plato books you might be interested in."

The sale went on all day. By four o'clock I was bushed. Not only had I sold almost the entire library but I had also chatted with numerous people. I even exchanged phone numbers with a few. At five o'clock, I ushered the last of the people out the door and slumped into the reclining chair. That was it, the deed done. I counted the loot – $964. I grabbed a coffee and a handful of chocolate chip cookies, which I downed with great satisfaction. I thought about what I would do with the money and decided upon a new computer. There would probably be a few bucks left over to purchase more time on Camelot. It truly had been an amazing day.

Chapter Six

After two complete weeks in which my normally placid life was turned upside down, the onerous task of getting Rivka's apartment ready for the next tenant was done. The only thing left was to paint the place, but I was no painter. Someone else would have to finish the job. I took one last stroll around the once-dismal apartment and realized that despite my hard work and good intentions, I had to get out of there. The apartment still radiated sadness, as if the walls had absorbed the worst of Rivka's broken life. I turned the keys over to Ruth.

"Find any treasures?" she snorted.

"Hardly. Mostly junk, as you said. Lots of books though."

"I know. I always told her it was a fire trap but she didn't listen. You have to be a little nutty to keep that many. What are they, trophies?"

"Definitely weird."

It really was weird. But not for the reason I portrayed to Ruth. I had spent two weeks sifting through another person's belongings, trying to put the pieces of a life together. In some ways I had done so but in some other, more fundamental ways, I was no closer. The window into what had catapulted Rivka to the brink of darkness was closed. And probably would remain so for all time. And yet I had been a voyeur into her life. Yes, a voyeur, one who surreptitiously spies on another. It reminded me of a book I had once read – Hell by Henri Barbusse. Because the novel dealt with solipsism and existentialism, it had been part of the curriculum in a Philosophy class. Even to this day, I can recall great chunks of it – the protagonist who resides in a Paris boarding house and who peeks through a hole in his bedroom wall to the room next door, where he observes the various lodgers who come and go. Not only does he witness birth and death but so too adultery, incest, lesbianism, illness. A wide swath of humanity. And only after he feels that he had uncovered all of life's secrets does he decide to leave the room for good. But, as he is about to depart, he is overcome with blindness. Voyeurism, obsession, loneliness – at this time, the book spoke to me like no other.

In the bottom drawer of Rivka's dresser was the very last thing I would take from the apartment. Hidden under socks and underwear, I had only found the shoebox after the book sale, when I was making my final rounds of the place. I tucked it tightly under my right arm and exited the apartment.

The sides of the box had been sealed with scotch tape and I felt certain it contained more stolen goods. I was brimming with excitement all the way home and barely contained myself from slipping a peek in the subway. But I resisted, thinking some nosy person in an adjoining seat might see the treasure trove as well. But when I got home and ripped the box open, I was startled to see that it only contained papers.

I sifted through the find. These were Rivka's written works, what she had referred to in her diary. There must have been thirty or so short stories along with a half-completed novel.

Rivka had been a basket case and I suspected that her work could only be garbage. But there might have been something in it that would shed further light on her plight and so I decided that I would read at least a few pages, maybe an entire forgettable story. But a most curious thing happened as I read – I continued. I read not one but many stories. They were so intriguing, so well-written, that after I began reading them, I neglected to play Camelot for a time. I was floored.

Now I understood why Rivka had mentioned in her diary that writing had brought a measure of happiness – the woman had talent; she was very, very good. One story concerned an aspiring writer who takes a most unusual job, posing as a patient with a debilitating illness. In another, a woman who can't find a job with her liberal arts degree decides to rob banks. There was a riveting piece that dealt with a man giving up his conventional life in Toronto to go live a more bohemian lifestyle in Paris. The winners kept on coming. I particularly liked the one about an anarchist who finds peace after nursing a sick animal to health, and yet another that profiled a woman who pines for the poet she once was. Perhaps most striking of all was a story that had aspects of the type of magic realism one would find in the works of South American writers like Gabriel Marquez and Jorge Borges. It was the tale of a Jewish man who is so devastated by the death of his fiancée, that he enlists the aid of a rabbi schooled in Kabbalah to help him erect a golem in her image.

When I started the story, I hadn't been exactly sure what a *golem* was and so did some research. It turned out to be a Jewish mythological creature brought forth from the earth to help Jews in time of need, usually during pogroms. Furthermore, the most famous of all the golem stories is the *Golem of Prague*. In that tale, Rabbi Judah Loew brought forth the entity from the mud and clay of the Vlatava River to help vanquish the oppressors of the Jews. Which is what happened. There was a pogrom going on, initiated by the emperor of Bohemia, Rudolf II, and it was quickly quashed by Rabbi's Loew's creation. Unfortunately, the golem, whom he had named Josef, became drunk with power and had to be put down. Which I suppose happens when one is born with a body but no soul. Interestingly, while the golem was of course fanciful stuff, there actually was a Rabbi Loew. He was a Talmudic scholar of note in the 16th century who wrote some twenty-seven books. Moreover, his teachings helped inspired Hasidism, the ultra-orthodox branch of Judaism that has its basis in mysticism. Mysticism, mythology, a very strange melange.

It was the very first time since the entire Rivka affair began that I realized she might have been Jewish. Certainly her first name suggested as much. And perhaps the golem story was an attempt to reconnect with her heritage. It was just an assumption but like almost everything about Rivka, I only had assumptions to go on. As dim as the situation still appeared, I felt I was making some headway into understanding what may have happened to her. It had to do with the very nature of being highly creative, in Rivka's case, a writer. I had read many an article over the years about the propensity for writers to suffer from various mental disorders. Edgar Allen Poe, for instance, suffered from depression, grief, and delirium at various times in his life and his writings are replete with themes of madness, disease, death, necrophilia and entombment. And although I was no big fan of poetry (I considered poets to be second-rate writers who couldn't write real prose), I knew that many of the same afflictions possessed Sylvia Plath. I had read her book The Bell Jar as a freshman in university and vividly recall she suffered a mental breakdown that led to a suicide attempt. During that time, she wrote that she hadn't washed her hair for three weeks, hadn't slept for seven nights. Her rational for keeping her hair in a state of decrepitude was that it seemed silly to wash it one day, only to have to wash it again the next. Although her initial suicide attempts failed, she finally succeeded by gassing herself to death in her own kitchen. And lest I forget, Rivka's favourite writer, Virginia Woolf, had mood swings throughout her life, eventually filling her coat with heavy stones and walking into a river, never to be heard from again.

Of course, the list of philosophers who were similarly afflicted is quite long. I knew them all from my studies. Friedrich Nietzche, for one. In the late 19th century, he collapsed on a street in Turin and, it is said, never returned to full sanity. It may be solely anecdotal, it may not, but the collapse that precipitated his downfall was caused when he witnessed a coachman whipping a horse and threw his arms around the animal's neck. Syphilis and a hereditary stroke disorder, even a suspected tumour, may all have complicated the picture, but there is no denying that he was unbalanced.

Another philosopher that exhibited mental health issues was the father of existentialism, Soren Kierkegaard. He could never overcome his tendency toward depression, although indications are that he wanted to. He considered his black moods as a failing, saying that individuals in that state had the possibility of something greater if only they could get rid of the albatross, the very one that followed Kierkegaard everywhere. He was quoted as saying, *"My depression is the most faithful mistress I have known..."*

Michael Foucault was tormented with acute depression, Martin Heidegger had a nervous beakdown. John Stuart Mill suffered from melancholic depression. And so it goes.

So maybe that was the answer. Rivka Howard was a writer. One with an interest in philosophy. She was a depressive, and suicidal. No surprise there.

I returned to my own life, somewhat buoyed by the entire Rivka experience. It actually left me with the impression that I could be useful if called upon, that I wasn't a complete washout. Despite that realization, I still had concerns. My mood was erratic, swinging from optimism to despair. I had no real friends, no job, and very little disposable income as a result of only a small stipend from Employment Insurance. Plus my ambition to become a writer was floundering –

every story I submitted to literary magazines had been summarily rejected by editors. Many had the nerve to offer suggestions, which I ignored. Why would I listen to some hack editor who never made it as a writer in their own right? Still, those hacks ruled the literary scene. It made me want to puke.

When I reviewed Rivka's work, there was no indication that she had ever tried to get any of it published. She probably wrote as a catharsis, something she could hold on to as the rest of her life went astray. Besides, there was probably one very good reason she never submitted. The risk in doing so is rejection. And from what I now understood of Rivka, that would have been intolerable for her.

The stories were all fairly short, under five thousand words for the most part. As might be expected, many of them dealt with alienation, people who were outsiders. I concluded that the central theme that permeated throughout was the idea of loss. Loss of a spouse, of integrity and ideals, loss of innocence and soul. Wide ranging, it ran the gamut of the subject. It also focused on strange decisions the protagonists took to deal with those losses. When the Jewish man lost his fiancée, he insisted on the construction of a golem in her image. The job-applicant who was turned down for a position in a law firm decided to steal a Hermes scarf from that firm's cloak room. And the woman who could not find a job with her newly-minted liberal arts degree made an unusual career move by becoming a bank robber. Wonderful flights of fancy all, with unexpected twists.

What a shame, such a waste. If only Rivka had had the nerve to send her work out, she might have had some success. No, she would have had success, the material was that good. I felt certain of it. And success was exactly what her miserable life needed.

I thought long and hard what to do with the collection. I considered just tossing it but that seemed foolish. I contemplated self-publishing the stories into a booklet: 'Rivka Howard: The Collected Short Stories', but realized that was just a dream. Even vanity publishing was not inexpensive and as it was, I had barely enough money to live on. Despite the fact that I earned a good sum from the book sale, those funds were earmarked for my own pleasure. Perhaps one day if I were to hawk the jewelry…

I did turn over the notion that I might approach big-name authors to help out with the publication of the stories. Someone like a Margaret Atwood or a Nino Ricci. I had heard that they sometimes championed novice writers. I could have done the same with book publishers, simply approached them on my own with details of Rivka's harrowing life; the story would have been compelling, I had no doubts.

But I didn't do any of those things. I simply couldn't go through with it. Dead was dead and so who really cared if the stories were published or not? Rivka had no friends, no relatives that would take great comfort from the publication of her gems. I had to admit it, not even I cared. Not really. Why would I? She was a virtual stranger. Besides, no one can deny that to the living go the spoils.

Chapter Seven

I decided I would find out exactly who The Underclass was. I felt that they should be made aware of how damaging their words could be. It was one thing to put out misleading flyers spouting all sorts of nonsense but quite another to have that material fall into the wrong hands.

I found them easily enough in a small office above an Afghan carpet store on St, Clair Avenue. The wooden stairs creaked beneath the weight of my feet and sure enough, there before me on the third floor, adjacent to a weight loss clinic, was the front door for The Underclass, Inc. A sign said to take off your shoes so I carried them through the chiming door. No one was at the front desk, which was piled high with Underclass flyers. Next to the flyers was an open box of donuts from Tim Horton's. And next to that a bell. Please ring, the sign next to the bell said. So I did.

A man came shuffling out of the back room. "Yes, can I help you?" he said.

I pulled out the flyer I had found in Rivka's diary.

"Is this your work?" I asked.

He took the flyer from my hands and read through it. "Yes, it's from our organization," he said.

"And can I ask you what sort of organization you actually are?"

"You can, but I'm not necessarily going to answer you. I don't even know who you are."

We were at a stand-off – he didn't know who I was and I sure as hell didn't know who The Underclass was. I surveyed the wretch of an individual standing before me. He was in his late forties or fifties, with only a smattering of fine wispy hair, and an ample girth that extended out his ill-fitting shirt and over his belt. The dark sweat from his armpits was clearly visible against the white of the shirt. I summed him up in one word – failure.

I quickly understood that if I told the truth about why I was there, that the guy would clam right up. So I lied.

"I'm a friend of Rivka Howard and she gave me this flyer. Said I might be interested in what you have to say. So here I am and I'd like to know what exactly it is you have to say."

"Rivka Howard…hmmm." *The Failure* put his stubby fingers to his chin and stroked it in contemplation. "Yes, I know her. She came to some of our lectures." He looked at me quizzically. "If she gave you the flyer, then why didn't she fill you in on our organization, what we're about, what we espouse?"

I chuckled. "You know these crazy academics. Smart as a whip but so scatterbrained."

The man took a seat behind the mahogany desk and told me to take my own chair.

"You know anything about philosophy?" He said. "Like Marx and Engel?"

"Not much. I think they were commies, right? You know, I took an undergraduate course once in Philosophy but that was ages ago." I motioned with a sweep of my hand over my head that the material had been above me anyway.

"No worries. I can fill you in. What's your name anyway?"

"Joseph. Joseph Briden."

The man extended a hand across the desk. "Michael Watson. Good to meet you, Joseph." He grabbed a jelly donut from the box and placed it on the desk in front of him. "Hope you don't mind. I haven't had lunch yet. Can I offer you one?"

"Sure." I selected a chocolate glaze and gently squeezed. The thing was stale, as hard as a rock.

"Coffee?"

"Great."

While Michael went to get the coffees, I held the flyer out in front of me. "It says here that you should *Steal when you can, what you can.* You have the right. Is that what you believe?"

"We sure do," said Michael confidently, handing me my mug. "Sugar? Cream?"

"Two sugars, no cream."

Michael settled into his seat and took a bite of his donut. Blue jelly squirted onto his hand that he promptly lapped up with his tongue. "Ever hear of that old adage *Cheaters never prosper?*"

"Of course."

"It's not true. Cheaters and liars do prosper. In fact, those are the people who run society."

"They run society, huh?" If I was to get anything from the fat pig sitting in front of me, I knew I had to play as dumb as possible.

"Yup. And they're psychopaths. Psychopaths are the heads of corporations, political and military leaders, you name it. They have their filthy hands in everything. The only difference between a psychopath who kills people and the ones who run companies is self-control. Killers are very impulsive. Corporate moguls aren't. But they're both the same. Both the same." Michael reflected on those last three words as if he were sipping a fine cognac. His eyes closed languidly and he took a deep breath.

"So what about the stealing part?" I said, returning to the question I had posed.

"The psychopaths have direct control over all the assets. But they didn't earn them, they stole them from the people." Michael used his index finger to point to his chest. "From people like me. So by stealing, you're only taking back what rightly belongs to you."

"And uh, what are the characteristics of these people?" I asked.

"Good question, Joseph. I'll tell you. First, they're all high achievers. Oh sure, they get things done but they leave people strewn in their wake. People are nothing more than commodities for them. Chattel. And very disposable." Michael went on to say that these people were able to work their way up the food chain because they were not only ruthless and devious, but charming as well. "No one can resist a charmer," he sighed. "They're the best actors." *Vladimir Putin, George Bush, John Kennedy, Charles Manson, Leonarda Cianciulli, Idi Amin, Winston Churchill –* according to Michael, they all displayed psychopathic behaviour. He went on to name many others, CEO's of Fortune 500 Companies, famous politicians, military leaders. A toxic brew of predators.

I had heard of many but not Leonarda Cianciulli. I asked him about her.

"She was known as the *Soap-Maker of Correggio*," said Michael, slurping the last of his coffee. "She was the most famous of Italian serial-killers. Between 1939 and 1940, she murdered three women and made them into soap."

"What kind of soap?" I said, laughing.

"Ha. Good one again, Joseph. I don't know what sort of soap. But I can tell you that she took the leftover blood from her victims and mixed it with flour, sugar, chocolate, milk, eggs, a few other ingredients, and kneaded the dough into tea cakes, which she served to her neighbours. A true psychopath."

"That's really sick," I said.

"Well, that's what you can get when you deal with these type of people, "Michael said. "They take great pleasure in the misfortunes of others. They plunder and pillage others for their own gain. Given a choice, they would rather plagiarize and steal than do an honest day's labour. And you know, they can't be rehabilitated. Their pathology is hardwired into their genes."

The funny thing is that after listening to Michael's diatribe, I didn't necessarily disagree with what he had said. He still was a lowlife in my books but did have some valid points.

"So how do you survive?"

"You mean me personally?"

"No, I mean your organization."

"Donations. We have a lot of support."

I was now more intrigued with Michael. *A lot of support?* People were naïve, drinking cyanide-laced, grape-flavoured kool-aid a la Jim Jones. Following modern day faith healers like Jim Bakker whose only supernatural powers involved lining their own pockets. Still, the fact that Michael had that support and made some sense was an interesting mix. Nonetheless, I wanted to move the conversation away from psychopathic behaviour back to my home field, back to philosophy. Then I would expose him for the cad he was.

"So Michael, just getting back to that Marx and Engel stuff, are you a communist?"

"I hate labels. So no, I'm not. But if you're asking me whether I know about their philosophy, I can tell you that I read the *Communist Manifesto* many times."

So had I. Little did The Failure know.

"Marx may have been wrong about Communism because he didn't foresee the tyranny that enslaved Eastern Europe and the old Soviet Union," said Michael, "but he was spot-on when it came to Capitalism. I'm sure I don't have to tell you that the middle-class is vanishing in this country. In many countries. Communism used the practice of a centralized economic management and redistribution of income. Of course there were problems of abuse. There was no equality. The Manifesto talked about overthrowing the bourgeoisie and allowing political power to be managed by the proletariat. It didn't happen. The question becomes, is capitalism any better?"

Michael took another bite of his donut and a long sip from his coffee. Good, he was collecting himself. Soon I would pull apart his ideas and the massacre would begin. I had heard all the arguments, both sides. Why Marx had it right. Why Marx had it wrong.

"Do you want to know why Marx wanted the proletariat to have political power?" Michael said in between bites.

I didn't want to go there. It all had to do with avoiding the worker alienation that Michael and company had written about on one of the flyers I found in Rivka's diary. Have the proletariat overthrow the capitalist system of private property, have them share the wealth they produced through a communist economic system, and, like the proverbial rabbit popping out of a magician's hat, interest in one's own labour would be restored. I knew Michael knew that and I didn't need him to lecture me.

"Nah," I said, waving my hand over my head as I had done earlier. "Just tell me about why capitalism stinks."

"Ok, let's talk about that. But first, I've noticed that you haven't eaten your donut."

I looked skeptically at the hard shell that I held gingerly in my hand. Under no circumstance would I take a bite.

"I'm saving it for later. Mind if I take it with me?"

"Here, have the whole box," said Michael, flipping the lid shut and passing it to me.

"Okay, thank you," I said slowly.

"No, thank you," said Michael. "I'm trying to cut back."

"Huh."

Michael licked his lips. "Under our capitalist society," he said, "big business today is said not to be concentrated in the hands of a few. These aren't feudal times, right?" He laughed and continued. "Some people say that because you can…get this…buy common shares in those big businesses. So you can own a piece of the pie. Isn't that nice?"

Michael banged his fist onto the desk, creating a small tsunami of coffee waves that nearly escaped his cup. "It's not true!" he yelled, the veins in his neck looking like they were about to burst. "The concentration of economic power is still in the hands of a few. Tell me, how many people do you know that own shares in corporations?"

I didn't know any, but then, I knew very few people.

"The fact of the matter is that there are not many possibilities these days for poor men to become rich men. Even middle-class men. Students are coming out of university saddled with mounds of debt, job security is non-existent. Even if you have a job, very few have defined-benefit pension plans anymore."

The quizzical look on my face did not escape Michael's attention.

"So, let me explain the defined-benefit pension plan," he said. "At the end of your working days, you know exactly how much money you'll have in that pension. Defined-contribution, and you don't. Your pension is governed by market forces. But just try and earn a good interest rate on your capital these days. You can't. Prices of goods and services are rising all the time and in effect, your capital is being eroded."

Michael wasn't finished. He asked me for my impressions of the 2008 financial debacle.

The only thing I remembered about 2008 was that it was the year I got booted from the Philosophy program at the university. I didn't think that was what Michael had in mind so I simply shrugged my shoulders.

"In 2008, stock markets around the world crashed. In the U.S., thousands upon thousands of people defaulted on their mortgages because the value of their homes tanked;

they were now worth much less than their outstanding mortgages." Michael went on to talk about credit default swaps, reckless lending practices by big banks, subprime mortgages, and how the big companies were complicit in all this. I knew nothing about any of this, only vaguely having recalled the incident. Why would I? Just as I had no money now, I had no money then. There was nothing on the line for me; it was just another news story.

"And the worst part," continued Michael, "is that not one CEO associated with the biggest banks and insurance companies has ever been arrested."

"Well, you would need some proof," I said. "You can't just stand in front of a judge and say, 'Hey Your Honour, throw the book at this guy for causing a market meltdown.'" It was a low blow, a groin punch, and I knew it would rile Michael up. I felt a little undermanned talking about all this financial stuff and wanted to even out the playing hand. It did the trick. He gritted his teeth and furrowed his brow. For a second, I thought he would create another tsunami. But much to my surprise, he maintained his composure.

"There is proof," he stated emphatically, grimacing. "But it's covered up. Everyone at the top is involved. The Fed, Justice Department, the banks, insurance companies… no one will squeal on anyone else because they all grease each other's palms." Michael sighed and the tone of his voice cranked down a notch or two. "People are tired of getting shafted. Joseph. They're tired of seeing the psychopaths at the top get away with murder. Everyone's fed up. That's why the Occupy movement started in 2011. It was a worldwide protest movement against social and economic disparity."

I could see the man was tired of talking. Maybe he was simply tired of fighting the battle. I felt for him. He wasn't such a bad guy, after all. So I shifted the conversation once again, throwing him a softball.

"And you said you have lectures, right?"

"Usually once a month."

"Large turnout?"

"The last lecture there were over four hundred. We scrambled to find some extra seats."

I lowered my head and stared at Rivka's flyer, lost in thought.

"Anything else, Joseph?"

"No, I guess not."

Michael stood up, signaling the end of the conversation. "By the way, how did you say you knew Rivka?"

"I didn't."

"Well, I hope to see you both at the next meeting," said Michael, clapping me on the back.

As I walked down the steps and out the door, I broke into a run. I just wanted to get as far away as I could from the place I had just been. My expectations were all wrong – I had been anticipating some punk, an anarchist without a single brain in his deluded head. Someone with a basket full of puffball ideas between the ears that I got easily pull apart like taffy. Instead I got Michael, a slob, but a coherent one. Someone whose logic I couldn't take issue with. I hadn't said a single thing that I had intended – not that he, Michael, was a piece of shit, not that The Underclass flyers had contributed to the demise of a very sick woman, not that the message was inferior philosophy. Not a single bloody word.

Chapter Eight

I set up shop at the Second Cup on Eglinton Ave. It was far enough away from my old haunts near the university that the likelihood I would run into someone I knew was remote. There, I carefully studied each page from the stories, checking for spelling mistakes, punctuation, and grammar. I made sure that the every storyline made sense and was consistent, the protagonist not having brown hair on page three and black hair on page eight. I also changed a few words here and there. And I wrote; the novel that Rivka had started deserved an ending. It was more golem stuff, but so highly interesting and entertaining that it was certainly worth a second look at the same subject.

The story was surreal, about a bookish lawyer in N.Y. who yearns for a daughter and instead erects a golem. She does so by upending her house plants and molding the earth, then saying prayers in Hebrew. With the creature's help, the lawyer's love life, previously non-existent, improves dramatically. Of more significance, she is now able to ascend to the position of mayor of the city. ~

There was no question about it: buried beneath all the depression and pills, Rivka had a highly-imaginative mind. What a story! My research indicated that traditionally, as was the case with the Golem of Prague, that the creatures are constructed from the mud and clay of riverbanks. But never from the earth of houseplants! The story though certainly worked for me. All the stories did in fact because I spent many hours at the coffee shop, churning out page after page of prose as a follow-up to hers. I had never found writing to be an easy undertaking but it became more fluid riding shotgun on Rivka's pen, simply because she was so talented.

After a few weeks of editing and writing, I was ready with the short stories. I picked a few of the top literary magazines in the country as my targets and packaged off to each one of Rivka's stories – Urban Legend – the one about the bank robber. In the cover letter, I said that the story had not been previously published and that I hoped it was suitable for the magazine. I made no mention of the fact that I had not written it. I still had vague thoughts that I would rectify that omission should the need arise. I suspected however, that that would never become necessary; getting published was no small feat and as good as the story was, if my own stories were turned down, there was no reason to believe Rivka's would fare any better.

After I sent Urban Legend on its way, I decided to experiment with Rivka's pharmaceuticals. There were so many I had no knowledge of that my curiosity was piqued. I had also done exceptionally well with the Ativan and Xanax. The use of those drugs caused me to come to a rather startling conclusion – I was a much better writer while on them. Freer and more fluid, and that allowed my imagination to flourish. I was then able to easily slip into character for Rivka's esoteric novel.

I wondered whether that same experience accounted for the many famous writers who were drunks. There was no soft-pedaling it, some of the most famous prose writers were out-and-out alcoholics. Dylan Thomas, Jack Kerouac, Raymond Chandler, Truman Capote…the list was quite long. Boy, could they write: drunk with words, as it were. But not only with words. I had never given the matter much thought, why they felt that necessity, but quickly concluded that it may have had to with writing itself – the loneliness, the isolation involved with putting words to paper. Maybe that or else there was some lack that caused them to gravitate toward writing.

I was looking for some happy pills. Not anti-depressants though. Something else, with a quicker starting point. I didn't want my euphoria to take weeks, I wanted it to right away, preferably without any mind-numbing side effects. I found a bottle with a label MDMA. But the label wasn't the kind normally seen in pharmacies – the pharmacy's name wasn't listed and there was no indication of dosage or side effects. Rather, it was a simple white label attached rather awkwardly at a slightly tilted angle. Aside from the MDMA lettering, there were no other markings.

There was another bottle, this time with the name of the pharmacy listed. The drug was called Supeudol and the instructions said to "take 1-2 capsules every 4 hours as needed." A narrow, bright yellow label was affixed to one side of the bottle: "Drink plenty of water. Don't take alcohol."

Being nobody's fool, I did some research into the drugs. It turned out that MDMA was also known as Ecstasy. Of course I had heard of it, mostly in conjunction with teenage deaths at raves. And Supeudol was another name for Oxycodon, the infamous pain-relief drug that was widely sold on the streets. I read that a 40 mg capsule prescribed from a doctor would have an approximate selling cost of $4, but the street price ranged from $25 to $40. Those were good margins by anyone's standards.

I began with the Supeudol. I took it not as per the instructions on the label but three capsules every hour. After two hours when nothing much happened, the effects came on dramatically fast and I was swamped by a great rush of energy. I had no choice –I ran to a corner café and ordered a cappuccino and an egg salad sandwich to go, but forgot the sandwich as I left. I became nearly hysterical, with fear, with anxiety, with something unspeakable, and as I dodged in and out of slow-moving traffic, tears streamed down my face. I held my hands up like a traffic cop and stopped a screeching car by smashing my palms onto the hood. "Yo, whassa matter?" I yelled. It was a bad idea. The driver emerged, his red face engorged with anger. "You're dead, asshole," he screamed. I couldn't think straight, it was all about the velocity of my neurotransmitters, which were spinning wildly through the stratosphere. He gave me a good hard shove which knocked me to the ground, but somehow I had the wherewithal to get up and run. Around and around the car we darted until I made a mad dash down the street.

Back in the apartment, I became dizzy and incredibly weak, as if someone had injected my muscles with silly putty. I could barely lift my arms and walking was a problem – movements became more viscous. Slower. It was like I was existing in a slow-motion dream state, some weird alter-reality. I simply had to lie down and wait until the effects passed, there was no other choice. After a time, they did. Or so I thought. I seemed to nod off, but I wasn't quite sure. I was on the couch one minute and then walking around the next, or so I thought. A somnambulist. Reality became a bit confusing and I gave up trying to make sense of it all. Which was a wise move. For as soon as I let myself go, I fell into a true deep sleep from which I could not possibly arise.

The following morning, I was blocked. Constipated. I took an Ex-Lax. Then a second. Sitting on the toilet, I reflected upon the previous evening's journey and concluded it had been an abject failure. While there was something to be said about the altered state of consciousness and the inability to distinguish wakefulness from sleep, the truth was that I was so out of it I had put myself in peril. At my best, I was all mind. The philosopher king. To take that away put me in a state of powerlessness, something that was simply intolerable.

Perhaps the MDMA would work better. Whatever better meant. At least it would be different. For now though, I had work to do. I really wanted to concentrate on finishing the novel Rivka started. It struck me that there was a possibility she had written herself into it, that in fact she was the female lawyer. This protagonist was an insignificant bureaucrat, without a love life, who pined away for a daughter. Of course I couldn't be sure if any of that pertained to Rivka but there was one fact that was beyond dispute – my dead friend could have used a golem of her own! And now that I thought of it carefully, it seemed to me that each of Rivka's short stories had as a lead character someone who closely resembled her – the liberal arts grad who robs banks, the anarchist who nurses a sick animal to health, the woman who yearns to be the poet she once was, the man who steals a high-end Hermes scarf. Although I didn't know every aspect of her debauched life, it all seemed to fit. I realized there was a very good possibility that if I studied the stories in depth, that I could uncover exactly who Rivka Howard had been. Someone once said that all prose writing is autobiographical to some extent; perhaps, at least in Rivka's case, it was true.

I returned to the Second Cup on Eglinton Ave. and began work in earnest. I tried to imagine how Rivka would have written the remainder of the novel and was determined to remain true to that. In other words, I tried to write more like Rivka Howard than Karl Pringle. It wasn't easy. She was a wonderful writer but I felt she had veered off course a number of times, putting in superfluous scenes and characters. Nonetheless, I didn't delete those and instead molded them a tad so that they fit right into the gist of the story. In *The Anarchist*, for instance, the protagonist finds a very strange animal in a ravine and, as a result of nursing it to health, turns her life around. The animal Rivka had chosen was not able to be identified, there was some magic realism associated with its lack of clear identity. I didn't think that was necessary, and so changed it to read a dog. Your ordinary household poodle. Something everyone could identify with.

On one occasion, I noticed a woman at the coffee shop staring at me. She was quite pretty, with sumptuous plump lips, a light-café-aux-lait complexion, and a smattering of child-like freckles dotting her aquiline nose. Her braided light brown hair was piled impressively high on her head, seemingly defying the laws of ordinary gravity. By contrast, with the exception of a cowlick at the very top of my head, my own black hair was flat, lifeless, no matter how I combed it, which wasn't very often.

I tried to not meet her eyes but she kept at it and so I offered a half-smile, no teeth. It turned out that was impetus enough. She sauntered over to my table and stood above me. "Are you a writer?" she said chirpily.

"Yes."

"What do you write about?"

"Fiction."

"You're very dedicated."

"Why do you say that?"

"Well, I see you here quite often, scribbling away."

Scribbling away? I had never in my entire life heard anyone use that phrase. What exactly did it mean? Scribbling entailed writing in a careless way, in a meaningless way. Was she trying to make fun of me?

"I'm actually writing," I said.

"Of course you are."

I would have preferred to be left alone at that point but the woman asked politely if she could join me. Please and If *it is no bother* followed. I really had no choice.

"And what fiction is it you are working on?" she continued, bringing her coffee to my table. "Writing on, je m'excuse."

There was something a bit off about the woman's diction. She was French, no question.

"You have an accent," I said, pointing out the obvious. "Parisian?"

"Yes, very smart you are."

That was it, the extent of my social skills. I was still feeling the lingering effects of the Oxycodon and in no mood for chit chat. "I have a deadline for this manuscript," I said, positioning my pen above the notepad I had been writing in.

"Yes, of course, you are a busy man. Please, I will sit here and drink my coffee and not bother you as you scribble."

"Not *scribbling*," I said. Writing. Writing."

"Of course. Writing."

I returned to the project at hand but couldn't concentrate, feeling the woman's eyes burning holes through me. I put the pen down and crossed my arms. "Ok, so you want to talk. Why don't you tell me your name."

"Solange."

"I'm Karl. Anything else?"

Solange took a sip from her coffee. "You are...how you say it? Ah...intense...yes, very much."

I could tell there was no winning with this woman. So I gave up. "I'm finishing a novel and I have a deadline. My publisher is waiting for it. But I can talk a bit."

"How come you are not using computer? Everyone uses computer to write these days. Your pen and paper is very old -fashioned."

"I don't have a laptop," I said derisively.

"And what is this novel about, Karl?"

OK, she asked for it. I started to tell the woman the premise of the lady lawyer and her golem, but got bogged down rather quickly. Solange's face gave it away, as if she had tasted a scoop of horseshit. It became all contorted upon hearing the word *golem.* Her forehead wrinkled, her mouth puckered, and her eyes opened wide with incredulity.

She had no idea what I was talking about. It was painfully obvious that in the telling of the story, I would first have to explain what a golem was. Fortunately, because I had done so much research into what these creatures were all about, I felt confident enough to talk about them: "Adam, from Adam and Eve, was initially considered to be a formless creature, in effect a golem," I said. "You understand? He was made from dust, and you know, all these beings are. Some arise from mud or clay but they're all conceived from the earth, that's a given. Actually, there are biblical references to golems but much of the literature regarding them seems to have come from the 13th century, mostly from Spain and Provence."

"Oh my, this is so interesting."

"You think?"

I thought she was pulling my leg, that she would mockingly stick her finger down her throat. Instead, she seemed interested. "Yes, very unusual," she said. "And I also know this Provence very well. I have a friend who lives there."

"Do you want to hear more?"

"*Porquoi pas?*" I shrugged.

"Ah, I mean, *why not?*"

"Very good. So it was in these regions of Provence and Spain that there arose something called the Zohar. It's also known as *The Book of Splendour.* It's not one book but a number of books and it is these books that are the foundational texts for the Kabbalah, which is the mystical aspect of Judaism."

"And this Kabbalah I know too. Movie stars wear such red strings around the wrist for protection against evil."

I had not heard of this and did not answer.

"*Je m'excuse*, **not only** movie stars," added Solange.

I took a hard bite from my bran muffin and continued. "The Zohar speaks of very strange things. The relationship between ego and darkness, the nature of god and souls, cosmology. So you can understand how something as bizarre as a golem might come from such writings."

"Again, very interesting, Karl. You speak of this strangeness very well."

"As I said, the Zohar was crystallized in the 13th century. But, it was written much earlier. According to legend, it was written in the 2nd century by a Rabbi. The Roman government was executing all Torah teachers and so this rabbi, along with his son, hid in a cave for 13 years. It was there that he studied the Torah and, it is said, received divine inspiration from the prophet Elijah to write the Zohar."

"I think he would study so much because there is not so much else to do in a cave."

Solange's petty comment was irksome. Especially as she laughed when saying it. I had done so much research on golems that I felt my treatise deserved something better than an inane pun. Of course all this golem stuff was hokum, but as the words flowed from my mouth, it made me realize that I really did want to tell someone about the creatures. Someone who would listen quietly though and not feel inclined to spit out ridiculous comments. Once I started to tell the old bag down the hall from me but she only ogled

me like I was the devil himself. Now here was an opportunity to reveal the full extent of my knowledge, and yet I
was being constantly interrupted.

"Look, if you would like me…"

Solange interjected. "Yes, please continue. *Je m'excuse
une autre fois.*"

I went to the counter for a refill on my coffee. When I
returned, Solange was silent so I started again. "Anyway,
between the 2nd and 13th century, the Zohar seems to have
gone missing. Nothing was heard of it. That's simply a
mystery. I should say though that perhaps the most famous
golem story occurred in the 16th century. It was called *The
Golem of Prague.* The Rabbi in the city – Rabbi Loew –
constructed a golem from the mud of a river. There was a
pogrom going on in Prague at the time initiated by the Holy
Roman Emperor Rudolf II and the golem was brought forth
to help vanquish the oppressors of the Jews."

Solange held up her right index finger.

"Yes?"

"*Qu'est-ce-que c'est 'vanquish'?*"

Aside from the words 'bonjour' and 'allo,' my French
was almost non-existent. Given the context however, I
surmised that Solange wanted to know the meaning of the
word 'vanquish.' I asked and was right.

"'Vanquish' means 'to beat down' or 'conquer.' I think
that's the best definition. Usually we refer to this term when
talking about war."

"I understand."

"Good. Now, the golem in Prague…"

"And what is 'pogrom,' please?" Solange interrupted. "I
have not heard of such a word."

So I explained the meaning. How it referred to an ethnic cleansing of Jews. Then I continued with the tale. "So in effect the golem was able to vanquish the oppressors. But, as is the case with such creatures, they become too powerful and are then difficult to control. So they have to be put down."

"You mean killed?"

"One might think so but remember that golems are constructed from the earth. So when they are 'put down,' we refer to the fact that they are returned to the earth from where they arose."

"Adam was made from this dust, as you say. And we are from Adam. Eve too. So that means that people too are not killed, only 'put down.'"

Solange's running commentaries had reached their zenith and I closed my notepad and stood up. "I really must be going," I said.

"And why is there not some magic academy that can track these monsters to see where they are at all times? In Harry Potter, there are many wizards who can do this."

"Goodbye. It's been a slice."

"Will you come back for more scribbling, Karl? I am here very often at this time."

"We'll see. No promises."

"And just one more thing."

"Yes?"

"These golems, they are part of Jewish history, no?"

"Yes."

"Are you Jewish?"

"No."

"Then why are you writing about such a thing?"

I didn't bother answering. I just picked up my things and left.

★

It turned out that that was not the last I saw of Solange. I could have easily picked another coffee shop to write in but something brought me back to the Second Cup. That 'something,' I knew, was that despite the fact that she had been able to push my buttons, I actually enjoyed being in her company. It had been a long time since any female was interested in what I had to say. It didn't hurt that she was slim and busty. And oh, that face. So we continued seeing each other every day during the week at exactly 12:30 and it we started becoming friendly, a concept I wasn't overly familiar with.

I learned that Solange was a kindergarten teacher in Paris. "Pour les petites," she said. I also found out that she was on a nine-month sabbatical here in Toronto, specifically to improve her English. She attended an ESL school near Yonge Street and Eglinton Ave. and lived with a family in the area.

To say that I actually did any work on the novel during the visits was an untruth. I never picked up my pen. It was simply two people to getting to know each other. Well, that was only partially true. I can't in all good conscience say that I revealed everything about myself to the woman. Some parts I made up. I told her I was a grad student working on my PhD in Philosophy but that I was also a successful writer, having published roughly thirty stories in literary magazines. Furthermore, that the novel I was working on was a distraction from the rigours of my doctoral studies; because I was fairly well-established in literary circles, a publisher had requested that I pen a novel. The golem story.

I did realize that our friendship was 'running on borrowed time,' to coin an idiom Solange was probably unaware of. She would be leaving Toronto sometime in the next few months and that would be that. I wasn't exactly sure what I wanted from her but could say with certainty that I felt the pull of attraction. She was perhaps in her mid to late thirties, slim with light blond hair and matching skin, of average height, and possessive of a nature one might certainly call 'joie-de-vivre.' I had almost felt that perhaps some of her joyfulness could rub off on me if I hung around long enough. The other thing is that it had been many years since I had slept with someone. I knew it was a long shot with her but at least there was that possibility.

One day, I invited Solange to my place for dinner. She accepted. But there was a problem – the apartment was terribly unappealing. I had crappy furniture picked up from garage sales and exactly four dishes, all of which had cracks.

I took three of Rivka's stolen rings to a pawn shop on Church Street. I knew how much they were worth because the price tags were still on. I was owed exactly $950 for the lot, not a penny less. Turns out it was less. Considerably less. The pawnbroker, an old man of seventy if a day, used a small, hand-held lens to scrutinize the rings.

"Where did you get these?" he inquired.

"They're from my mother. She died and left them."

"Are they hot?" he asked, now inspecting me.

"Look, if you don't want them…"

"Didn't say that. I'll give you $575 for all three."

"No way. They're worth more."

"Then take them back," he said, pushing the rings at me.

I relented. I figured it was better not to wander through the downtown core with stolen jewelry, looking for the best price.

★

I did what I could to make the apartment look presentable. I bought a set of dishes from a bargain-basement department store along with drinking glasses, coffee cups, pots and pans, cutlery, towels. I called an ad on Craig's List and struck a deal for a brown faux-leather sofa and two corduroy chairs. They were a bit worn but considerably better than the furniture I had. At Goodwill, I lucked upon an embroidered bedspread and a crystal vase. I also biked around to garage sales. At one, I purchased three framed Van Gogh posters and four wool area rugs. And at another, three narrow black bookcases made of pressboard and which easily disassembled. The couple who sold them told me they had stored CD's and VHS tapes in them. Dinosaur relics. Moreover, they had purchased the bookcases from Sam the Record Man back in the 80's! Sam Sniderman and his flagship store on Yonge Street. That was the mecca for all audiophiles in Toronto for decades. I wasn't one of those but appreciated the artistry with which he ran the store. There was really nothing like it. On those rare occasions when I ventured past the kitschy neon signage on the outside and wandered inside, I was amazed at the sheer volume of product— records, CD's, tapes – Sam had it all. So now I had a little piece of all that. If nothing else, it would be a talking point for when Solange came over.

I borrowed two cookbooks from the library. I had no culinary skills, eating almost every meal out. Shawarmas, samosas, hot dogs, burgers – those formed the bulk of my diet. There was a Vietnam place on Spadina Avenue called Bun Saigon that I frequented quite often. The best bowls of pho. Good shrimp dishes also. Cheap. And a Hungarian Restaurant on Bloor Street called *Country Style Hungarian Restaurant* was also on my radar. But on this occasion, I thought it best to try and cook something up for Solange.

With all the running around I was doing, it was a lot of trouble. Almost as much as when I had cleaned Rivka's place. But after I set everything up, I was quite please with my efforts. As I looked around the apartment, I realized it looked quite fine. And the expectation that Solange would come over seemed to dissipate the monotony of solitude that I normally felt and buoyed my spirits.

Chapter Nine

My hands shook as I cradled the envelope from The Nashwaak Review. My experience with literary magazines is that when they rejected stories, they sent them back in the large manila envelopes I normally included in the package. This was different. The envelope I now held was a simple 8 ½ x 11 regular-sized one. It meant that my story had not been returned.

I ripped the envelope open.

Dear Karl:

Thank you for your short story submission to The Nashwaak Review. We have accepted for publication your story entitled Urban Legend and it will be published in a forthcoming issue.

Thank you for your interest in our magazine.

Yours truly,
S. Solomon
Editor

Obscene! I bolted from my apartment. I absolutely had to tell someone so I hustled to Book City on Bloor Street. "Do you know this magazine?" I said to the clerk, showing her the letter.

"Yes, we carry it. It's in that little alcove," she said, pointing, "where all the literary magazines are kept."

"I just got my story published in it."

"Congratulations."

I was a tangle of nerves and a cauldron of simmering, mixed emotions. I could blow at any second. Everything was at one with the world and yet...Walking along Bloor Street, I became giddy and pumped my fist. At the corner of Spadina Ave., while I waited for the light to change, I jumped in place. Up and down, up...

At Starbuck's I paused to collect myself. Why shouldn't I take credit? I had edited the piece, changed a few words. You are not taking me down with you, Rivka Howard. I silently mouthed the words as I waited for my coffee.

I would tell the one person who cared. It was nearly 12:15 and if I hurried, I could meet with Solange. I decided to cab it.

Unlike the other occasions when we had met, this time Solange was not alone. She was surrounded by a group of people whom I immediately took to be her fellow classmates. It was the United Nations Assembly, with delegates from the Philippines, China, Japan, Mexico, what I perceived to be Eastern Europe, and a host of other countries that I couldn't readily identify. Solange waved me over and kissed me on both cheeks. I sat down.

"This is Karl," said Solange, turning to her mates. "He's a writer. Almost a famous one."

Every person in the fifteen-member panel proceeded to tell me their name. A Chinese woman offered a raisin oatmeal cookie which I waved off.

"Wow, what you write?" asked a young man whose name I could not recall but whose accent clearly placed him from South American. Peru or Argentina.

"His best story is about a golem," said Solange.

"A golem?" said the South American.

Solange went on to explain, which was just as well since I had no intention of doing so. "It's a little like Frankenstein," she said. She stood up and walked robot-like in a small circle, her eyes closed and her arms stretched out in front of her. Gales of laughter followed her every jerky movement.

"Such a creature we call a 'troll' in my country of Norway," said a perky blond woman. "Actually, they are very big and hairy and stupid. They live at the bottom of a lake and sometimes have nine heads."

"No, I think these are more like Frankenstein for Jewish people," countered Solange.

"And when I was a little girl, my father wanted me to be a mermaid," said yet another woman, whose accent I couldn't place. "He loved them and took me to the swimming pool and made me hold my breath underwater. Each day longer and longer. I thought my lungs would explode. And he made me swim very far. Very, very far. Also, he wanted to buy for me the bottom half like such a creature...flippers. We were going to be famous, he would say he found me on the beach."

"Is that true?" said Solange.

The woman smiled brightly, obscuring her eyes with the back of her hand. "No, I made it up."

The group went on laughing and laughing. Amidst the hysteria, I showed Solange the letter I had received from The

Nashwaak Review and she kissed me on both cheeks once again. Air kisses, like being kissed by a sibling.

"This is many published stories for you now, Karl," she said.

"Yes, about thirty or so. I lost count."

Solange passed the letter throughout the group. "I am getting more coffee," she said, standing up. "Can I get you another, Karl? I see you only have a Starbuck's one."

"No, it's ok. I'm fine."

I was left alone with the others and realized I had nothing to say to anyone. They went on giggling, uttering jibber-jabber, and generally acting infantile. I thought it best to go. I passed Solange at the counter and touched her arm. "I have a lot of work to do today," I said.

"You can't stay?"

"I can't. Sorry. I just wanted to show you the letter. Your friends seem delightful."

Sarcasm. My French friend could not yet decipher it.

"Ok, a *bientot*. And let me know when is a good time for the dinner."

Solange's soft voice rattling in my ears, I took one last lingering look at her, the sexy woman I now realized I had nothing in common with, and walked out of the Second Cup on Eglinton Ave. for the very last time.

Chapter Ten

I didn't really understand how Rivka had trumped me. She was a depressed, drug-addled deadbeat. How could she have written such good prose? It didn't make sense but then, I didn't care. It was simply my opportunity to get some work into print, that was the most important thing. And I felt I deserved it. I had lived dangerously by pursuing a doctorate in Philosophy while those less intellectually gifted had turned to the safety of traditional 9-5 jobs. Life had given me a raw deal – I had been born a Roma after all – and this was a golden opportunity to make up for some of it.

I looked through Rivka's remaining stories and decided to send out Paris is a Woman. It was a delightful tale of a man who leaves his middle-class trappings – his traditional office job, his house, even his wife – to travel to Paris where he settles into a bohemian lifestyle.

I scrutinized the story carefully and looked for a few passages I could read aloud. Throughout my sojourn in academia, I had often found that doing so gave me a fresh perspective on material I had written. I selected a few passages toward the end of the story, where the protagonist – Sidney – comes to realize that his new life in Paris is fraught with angst:

A small geyser erupted and subsided on the Seine's dark surface. A little girl stepped forward, her face contorted.

"Monsieur, pourquoi vous avez jetez votre bicyclette dans l'eau?"

Sidney snuck a glance. She was six, maybe seven. Pale watery green eyes set on a wide forehead. Blonde pigtails. Tiny hands and feet. A pink cotton dress with frilly trim.

He wanted to say something that would assuage her tears but could think of nothing and turned away. The child tugged on his shirt. He could see the girl's mother a few feet away and nodded sullenly.

"Only my bike is gone," said Sidney.

The girl gave him a brief look of confusion and then flashed a gap-toothed smile.

Sidney grinned. His heart was still thumping.

The child's mother came over and took her hand. "Elle est très précoce," she said to Sidney. "I'm sorry, my Englis…"

"Je comprends et c'est pas un problème. J'aime des enfants. And your English is fine."

As the girl was led away, she continued looking over her shoulder at Sidney. That face: sweetly peaceful, borne of endless possibilities.

Good for her, he thought. But it doesn't help me.

Sidney put one leg over the railing and straddled the bridge. Such a dismal grey day, overcast and drizzly. The late afternoon light refracted through raindrops.

Sidney looked at the people who had gathered close by. Shocked, concerned faces. He signalled with a slight movement of his arm. "It's alright," he wanted to shout, but no words came out.

A light mist accumulated on his head. He gazed once more at the worried faces on the bridge; where had they been all these years? Actors. Actors! A performance intended to show him he was important. And just then, just as he was contemplating the falseness of those around him – he had slid his body onto the river's side of the railing and made up his mind to jump – Sidney realized he had been falling a very long time. He took deep, laboured breaths.

After a minute or two, he shook his head, sighed, and laconically pulled himself over the railing onto the bridge. A few people came over to talk but he paid them no heed, walking away as if in a reverie. An hour later he found himself at Fabrice's, stocking the shelves with a new shipment of travel books.

That evening, he removed his laptop from his backpack. In the five months he'd lived in Paris, he had rarely used it, only occasionally checking e-mails and surfing the 'net. But now he began composing an e-mail:

My Dearest Sharon:

Paris is so beautiful, a true city of lights. But my time here has taught me that no matter where I go, I can't escape from my issues. I just have to work them out and do so in the company of people I love and who love me. I guess what I'm trying to say is that I'd like to come back. I don't have to go anywhere – Toronto has everything I need, especially you. It took me coming to Paris to understand that.

He put the computer aside and began leafing through two of the books that had come in that afternoon. One was on Budapest, the other Prague. The inside sleeve of the latter said: Prague is unquestionably one of the most picturesque cities in the world, with its historic centre designated as a Unesco World Heritage Site. The poet Goethe once said of it that it is the "prettiest gem in the silver crown of the world." Whether it be sculpture, literature, film, video or installation, the city's art scene is a vibrant one. It has often been called Paris of the East...

"Hmmm," Sidney mumbled. "Paris of the East, Paris of the East." He repeated the words over and over again. Then he saved the unfinished e-mail as a draft and dreamily shut the lid of the laptop.

I loved the Sidney character. I could relate to him. He took a major chance by leaving it all behind and going to Paris, just as I had done by leaving the study of Philosophy. Just like the irrepressible Mavis Gallant who left her career in journalism in Montreal to pursue creative writing full-time in Paris. And now, Sidney was paying a major price for his indiscretion. But perhaps he would come out the other end a better person. A more enriched person. Just like me. Just like Mavis had been.

Rivka's work was great. Exquisite. There wasn't one word I needed to change. As much as I hated to admit it, Rivka had been one fine writer. I knew that I could not have written prose on a par. But it didn't matter – I had, in effect, assumed her writing persona and negated the writer within me. That was a hard thing to do, push aside my ego, but I thought that sublimation of my essence would win me acclaim. I felt certain of it.

The only question now was where to submit the story. I perused the various literary magazines to see which might be a good fit and settled on Lowestoft Chronicle. It was an online magazine originating out of the U.S. and had as its focus stories dealing with adventures in various countries. Travel writing but with a slant toward fiction, heavy on storytelling. While it seemed like a very good fit for the story, it had the added benefit of being online, which meant I could save on stamps, envelopes, and photocopying. I downloaded Paris is a Woman onto the magazine's website and felt as happy as I had ever been.

Chapter Eleven

Generally, literary magazines do not respond quickly to submissions. Waiting for an answer from the *Lowestoft Chronicle* was killing me. Time seemed to pass achingly slow. I realized too that part of the problem may have been that I had nothing to do. Of course I still had Rivka's novel to work on but on a grander scale, no one was waiting for me, I had nowhere to go, no papers to write. My arrival anywhere was not anticipated. Suddenly, I felt a bit envious of all those dunderheads that I had seen mornings at the St, George subway, the ones hurrying to work on their way to the downtown core.

As part of my ongoing collecting of Employment Insurance, I was required to actively pursue employment. But looking for work was the very last thing I wanted to do. So although the nights were reserved for *Camelot,* the days were there for nothing at all. I came to dread them and it was all I could do in the mornings to remove my face from the coolness of the bed pillows. Lying there, the stillness of the room enveloped me, pressing down hard on the pulse of my existence.

Naturally, I felt sluggish, dull. I found myself sneezing a lot and my throat was constantly sore, like my immune system was half-asleep. I thought perhaps I could use a vitamin or two and considered trying some from Rivka's grab-bag, but knew my lethargy owed itself to more than that.

I would try the MDMA though, the pharmaceutical name for Ecstasy, or simply 'E.' Various handles but they all led to the same questions: where exactly had Rivka gotten hers from? And, what exactly was in it? I had read on internet sites that street Ecstasy, manufactured in clandestine labs, could contain just about anything. Aspirin, caffeine, and other over-the-counter medications were not un-common.

The tablets had a pink butterfly embossed on them. What did this mean? Was it a good sign or bad? Perhaps it meant nothing. But I was willing to take the risk. I needed something to help get motivated and to kick start my metabolism. Reaching a heightened state of nirvana, a state free of worry, would be an added bonus. I had to admit that of late, I was feeling more and more that I was retreating into a cocoon. An insulating cocoon from which I might not emerge.

I liked the idea of taking a drug called 'Ecstasy.' Having read the mystic poet William Blake, it seemed he had somehow reached a heightened state of inner consciousness that allowed him to see angels in trees and the head of God through a window. His unique state of ecstasy was unparalleled; how else could he have seen a "world in a grain of sand?" He was called mad and maybe he was, but in my opinion, joyous exaltation by way of visions with a deity shouldn't be sneered at. Maybe, as in Blake's case, madness was a label foisted onto him by those who were envious of his creativity, his writing abilities. Certainly no one criticized the three shepherd girls who claimed to see the Virgin Mary in Fatima. And the same could be said of Thomas Aquinas, the theologian and philosopher whom I had studied in university; he was no less a mystic. He was honoured as a saint by the Roman Catholic Church. Frequently abstracted and in ecstasy, unconscious of his surroundings, toward the end of his life he had a vision of Heaven and decided that compared to the wonder of God, his vast array of writing was unworthy, 'like straw' as he said. So he put his pen down for good and became silent. I had no idea how Blake and Aquinas had reached the perceptions they did. I knew one thing though: if they were my forerunners, I was in good company.

I prepared for the taking of Ecstasy by trying a few of Rivka's vitamins and minerals three days in advance. B vitamins, Calcium/Magnesium in a 2:1 ratio, Vitamin C, Multi-Minerals in an ionic solution. In actuality, I was preparing my body as best I could, viewing the entire Ecstasy experiment as though I were training for a prize fight or even running a marathon. Because as much as I knew my life needed some fixing, I did not want to die. Certainly not. And I had read plenty of stories about people who died taking Ecstasy. Yet others were rocked with brain hemorrhages, heart attacks, blood clots, kidney failure, elevated body temperature, dehydration – these were all possibilities. I had also read that the drug could seriously deplete one's body of vital nutrients. Long-term users were even known to suffer memory loss.

When the day of my reckoning arrived, I made sure I didn't eat anything. On the 'net, a few sites said that taking

Ecstasy on a full stomach blunted its effects. I also made sure I was sitting on my bed in case I felt like passing out.

There was only one final hurdle that I faced – the dosage. My research suggested that 75-125 mg was the optimal dose for an 'average-sized' person to experience the other-worldly effects of the drug. I fit into that category and made an educated guess that any single tablet, regardless of its source, would contain that many milligrams. Without the dosage being written on the pill bottle, I had no real way of knowing if I was right. Still, I hoped I was. So I took one capsule with a full glass of water. Then I waited. And waited.

Twenty minutes, half an hour.

I stood up and turned on the radio, settling on a pop music station. It was exactly the kind of music I normally detested but figured that dancing might "open me up" and allow feelings of warmth and connectedness to enter. I never danced, I found it next to impossible to prance about without appearing like a complete fool. Yet on this one occasion, being completely alone, I took my socks off and bopped around the room barefoot to the sounds of Katy Perry and Lady Gaga. Aside from tiring myself out, I felt nothing at all. So I took a second pill.

When in university, I had read an interesting paper penned by a biologist that said that animals in the wild were programmed to procreate. Their doing so ensured the survival of their species. According to the author, there was no other reason for these animals to exist. If for some reason there were those amongst them who didn't, then they were shunned by their peers. The paper, read by philosophy students such as myself to discuss Darwin's 'survival of the fittest' doctrine, said there were solitary animals like tigers and lions walking the savannahs and jungles by themselves, not attached to any pride or group. They were in a word, 'failures,' and without the benefits associated with running in a pack, doomed to die early. The contents of that paper always stayed with me. Was I any different than those ostracized animals? After all, aren't people merely evolved animals? I had for so long been on my own, closed, that I longed to open my heart and feel the flow of love between myself and others. I was hoping the Ecstasy would allow me not only to experience that higher state of consciousness that Blake and Aquinas did, but also that insouciant flow of an easier mindset.

The pills weren't working. I shut the radio off and listened to my heartbeat, my breathing. Was anything different? Was I becoming dehydrated? Was the room spinning? Did I see anything unusual, like an angel? But there was nothing. A big fat zero.

I looked at the bottle, the one marked 'MDMA.' Whoever sold Rivka the pills had ripped her off. To make absolute sure, I bit into a pill and chewed it. If there was a chemical taste…but it tasted sweet. Like icing sugar.

Chapter Twelve

The wait was interminable. I couldn't just sit around doing nothing while the literary magazine took its sweet time, so I decided to send out for consideration yet another short story. And there was no question that it had to be the *The Golem of New York City*. I felt that Rivka would have wanted that one, especially, to be published. My suspicion was that she had been Jewish, and so the story, especially if it were to be published, could be seen as reaffirmation of her roots. No one other than me would know that of course, but it didn't matter. I knew, and that was plenty.

I considered the story to be amongst Rivka's best. It was fantastical, no question, but it dealt with the type of issues everyone faces – loss, revenge, longing. And at its heart was a love story. I only had to decide where to send it. Literary magazines that catered to Jewish themes seemed appropriate, if in fact there were such a thing. But I would have to do research.

It was something I was good at anyway, research that is. I had done it throughout my university years. But there was no question that Rivka was similarly inclined. When I read through her golem story, it struck me that she had either read Kabbalistic writings concerning the construction of a golem or, had picked up ideas by reading other writers who dabbled in the subject.

Whatever she had done, she certainly illuminated the intricacies of bringing forth such a creature to life. I sat in my new second-hand corduroy chair and read passages from the story. I wanted to change something, a word, a sentence, so that I could more authentically claim ownership to it. But I couldn't. It just seemed as though there was no way to make it any better. It was as good as complete. I did however, practice reading it in front of a mirror:

Early the next morning we set out to the Allegany State Park. The Rabbi explained that the park had sixty-five thousand acres of land and was quite isolated in parts. Moreover, it had numerous primitive forested areas and the soil there, if extracted from the right area, would be perfect for preserving the highest ethical nature of the golem.

As we moved through the park, Rabbi Gerschem seemed to know exactly where to go. It was apparent he had been here before. We finally stopped next to a swamp, at the base of a tree that had huge twisted roots growing out of the ground, like giant tentacles. All around were thick clouds of fog. They rose up from the swamp like shrouds of vapour and enveloped everything. As soon as I stepped out of the car, I was damp with sweat. I tried to catch a breath but the steamy air was suffocating hot.

The Rabbi donned a pristine white robe he took from the trunk of his car and provided one for me as well; a third was for the golem. "For purity," he said. We set to work, but in truth it was the Rabbi who laboured away on his hands and knees. I mostly watched in awe but every now and then wondered what a rational, educated man like me was doing in a remote area of a national park, playing in the mud. If anyone happened upon us, I have no doubt that with white robes that cascaded to our ankles, they would have thought we were part of some cult. It didn't really matter though – I just wanted to see Rachel again, to tell her I loved her.

The surface of the swamp was very still as Rabbi Gerschem worked away, every now and then an insect skittering across. I touched the water with my hand; it was strikingly warm and I could see to the bottom where all manners of green plant growth resided. A short distance away, a brightly-coloured yellow and black salamander rested on a moss-covered rock that jutted from the water and at my feet, two brown-spotted frogs plopped through the mud.

The Rabbi used his hands to form the figure, whispering in Hebrew, not a word of which did I understand. "I'm praying for success in this endeavour," he explained. "Over here," he said, motioning to me. "The fingers." I got down onto my knees and formed them as best I could but they looked less like fingers than spindly tree branches.

"It's o.k." assured the Rabbi. "We only need a general outline."

After an hour, the mud figure had been carved. It lay there like an alien being, brown, bloodless.

"This can't work," I said in desperation.

The Rabbi was not through. He layered on more mud onto the forehead and using a twig like a master craftsman, carefully shaped a word with Hebrew lettering – 'EMET.' He turned to meet my disbelieving eyes. "It means 'truth.' Hebrew letters have substance within the world," he said. "In the right hands, they can be harnessed to create great power."

He covered the creation with a piece of cloth. "We must let it harden in the sun."

As we waited, nary a word was exchanged between us. We sat in the front of the car and rested, mud and earth from our robes falling onto the floor.

"Constructing such an entity is a way to cleave to God," he said, breaking the silence. "It's a way of understanding God's plan."

I closed my eyes and tried to relax but couldn't. Despite the great faith I had in the Rabbi as a learned person, for the very first time since this whole episode began, I wondered whether the man I sitting next to was a bit demented. I even considered leaving.

But Rabbi Gerschem left the car just as I was about to voice my doubts. He stood above the mud figure and removed the cloth. The mud had hardened sufficiently but there was a large crack running down the middle of the breastbone and the Rabbi set about repairing it with water. Then he got onto his knees and bent down low to his creation, blowing into the nostrils.

What happened next will sound unbelievable but as God is my witness, it took place before my disbelieving eyes: The inanimate shape began to glow like the embers of a red-hot fire, and the fingers and toes started to sprout nails; the head, black hair.

I took a few steps backwards. This was black magic, the devil's work. The Rabbi ordered me to get a bucket that was in the back seat.

"Last night after you left I took some earth from Rachel's grave. I knew you wouldn't have been up to it."

He told me to sprinkle the earth from the bucket onto the glowing figure. With each handful of dirt, the thing started writhing, moving more and more, coming to life. Remarkably, Rachel's face started to form...her lips, eyes, ears. Even her arched eyebrows. It was Rachel, there could be no doubt.

We each grabbed an arm and dragged the figure through the mud onto solid ground. The creature kicked a number of times, as if trying to get a foothold in the fetid, swampy earth. We then helped the golem to its feet, or rather I should say that the Rabbi helped her up. I moved a good distance back, completely in shock and quite afraid.

Not only was I supremely confident that the story would be picked up by a magazine, but I also suspected that I would be called upon to read at the edition's launch. I continued talking into the mirror: "Method acting, my boy. Method acting." I darted to a small dresser where I kept a few washcloths and put one on top of my head. "Yes, yes, a yarmulke. Now I'm in full character." I cleared my throat and returned to the mirror. "Let me tell you my dear fellows, what it is like to lose a beloved," I said, throwing my arms slightly apart for emphasis. "Everything darkens. You know you should take care of yourself but you can't. You feel living is impossible. Everything seems meaningless." I took a deep, measured breath. "The protagonist in my story is just such a person. He is so distraught upon the death of his fiancée that he is at a loss to know what to do. All he can think of is that he wants...no, needs, to see her once more. So he seeks out a rabbi with an understanding of the Kabbalah to help him construct a golem in her image. And yes, for those of you who are not aware of what such a creature is, I can tell you that Jewish mythology is steeped with stories of golems…"

I sat down, exhausted. It seemed like I had been speaking a long time. I slowly removed the washcloth from my head and read Rivka's story once more, from beginning to end. It acted like an anesthetic for I barely made it through before falling into a very deep sleep.

Chapter Thirteen

I came to the conclusion that a world stoked up on Ecstasy would be inhabited by blissed-out simpletons professing undying love for one another. It would be a fool's paradise. Maybe Blake and Aquinas were just deluded. My experiment ended with the pills in the trash can, which is where they belonged.

Still, I wondered why Rivka would have wanted the drug. Did she really believe – as I had, at least temporarily, – that Ecstasy would be the answer to her misery? It may have been that her continual tension caused her to try and grasp at anything. Sure she had her writing but evidentially it wasn't enough to save her. And while she did have her affiliation with The Underclass, she more than likely came to see that it wasn't the entire answer. One thing was beyond doubt: Rivka's life had been multi-layered, with each being covered by a different grainy texture. I tried to unravel and decipher them, like a detective searching for clues in a mystery novel, but I couldn't know it all. What I did know, what I felt with a peculiar mix of trepidation and relief, was that her death signaled the beginning of something new for me.

I had kept many of the literary magazines I found in Rivka's apartment and searched them to see if any were oriented toward Jewish-themed writing. There was one, affiliated with a synagogue in Seattle and possessing the rather odd name *Drash*. I discovered that in Hebrew it meant 'search', 'a word,' or even 'a telling.' There was no consensus. It didn't matter. I discovered on the magazine's website that they took four months to respond to submissions, too long for my purposes. Moreover, Seattle was a world away. I wanted to read at an opening, which meant that the magazine had to be located in Toronto. I settled on one called *Pilot Pocketbook* and mailed them the story. It wasn't a Jewish-themed magazine by any stretch but I felt that the story was good enough to warrant inclusion, irrespective of the orientation. Response time was a few weeks, unusually fast for literary magazines.

While I waited for Pilot to get back to me, I had a most encouraging bit of news. Paris is a Woman was accepted by Lowestoft Chronicle. They would publish the story, without any edits, in their next edition. The acceptance came via e-mail. I was extremely happy, but curiously not as enervated as when Urban Legend was picked up. Was it possible I had become just a tad blasé? So soon? If so, perhaps it was because I knew that the Paris story was too good to reject. I expected nothing less than an acceptance.

As the weeks passed, I started to let go of conflicting emotions. Getting published was a signal to me that I was capable of almost anything. For so long I had toiled diligently in vain, never able to get my work recognized. Now that it happened, I realized that with the exception of sending the stories out, I had to do nothing at all to them. It was all there at my fingertips, Rivka's entire works. Strangely, being idle conferred power, which was initially confusing. But then, slowly, I divested myself of this seemingly inherent contradiction. After all, what did it matter who had written the stories? Life was full of deceitful people who had made their way to the top. I had once read a line by Emile, the great Roman poet: *Audaces fortuna iuvat.* He was right, fortune does favour the bold. I was beginning to realize that nothing else was really important.

I sold more of Rivka's jewelry to the same pawnbroker as previous, this time netting $1,745. Again I was short-changed but it didn't matter much since I looked upon the proceeds as a major windfall. It was easy and this time the man behind the counter didn't ask if the goods were stolen.

I needed the money. My three-month subscription plan for Camelot was ending and required renewal. It was only $14 a month but still, combined with certain other costs, it all added up. Those other, more expensive costs, were incurred to satisfy my, ahem…'urges.'

I was thirty-nine and quite frankly, tired of satisfying myself. Now that I had money, getting a woman would be easy. I knew exactly what I wanted – blond, slim, about 5'7". A little like Solange but without the mamby-pamby demeanour. Lily white and bustier too. I checked online for escort agencies in Toronto and was overwhelmed by the choices. A smorgasbord of human flesh. Every conceivable yearning could be satisfied for a price. I had no desire to be whipped or spanked or to grovel but thought it might be fun to have someone in a nurse's outfit cater to me. Pretend to take my temperature and start me off with warm compresses. That is, until I realized that really, I only cared about one thing.

I settled on an agency called *Come Girl*. They catered to 'discriminating gentlemen' and that was fine by me. They also had in their fold a wide variety of woman from different regions of the world – Russia, China, Japan, the Middle-East, Scandinavia, the U.S; curiously though, none from Canada. Perhaps Canadians were simply not in high demand. Just too familiar perhaps, I had no idea. It wasn't of any importance though as I quickly settled on a statuesque blond from Sweden. Ingrid, what else?

I told the agency that I preferred if Ingrid came to my place, which was fine, except they needed to meet with me first. "Too many weirdos out there," I was told.

I showered and shaved and put on my best cardigan, my only cardigan. I then bought a $10 bottle of white wine and made my way to Come Girl. It was on the third floor of an industrial warehouse in the west end of the city and the sign on the front door said: 'Orion Casting and Modeling.' I met with Mrs. Kelly, a rather skinny, unattractive woman with an unruly mane of jet-black hair, who ran the place.

"You look like Russ Meyer," she said.

"I don't know Russ Meyer."

"He made pornographic movies in the 1970's. He had a thing for large-breasted women."

"Is that bad?"

"No, I'm just saying."

I removed the wine from a brown paper bag. "Here, this is for you."

"I don't drink but I'm sure one of the girls will enjoy it. Thank you."

I explained that I was a PhD student in Philosophy and lonely for female company. My schedule was grueling, non-stop what with helping to tutor undergraduates, writing my thesis, attending lectures.

"You look a little old to be a full-time student."

Again with the looks. I simply shrugged my shoulders.

"I have two questions for you," continued Mrs. Kelly. "First, do you have a record? And, do you like to hurt women?"

"No and no."

"We can't be too careful. The girls that work for me are my employees and I have to look out for their well-being."

"I understand completely," I said. "Don't worry, I'm completely harmless."

"Good." At that point, Mrs. Kelly explained how business worked. Condoms were a must. Ingrid could stay the night but there was an extra $50 charge. I had to pay her cab fare back to the office and that cost $25. No pals were to be hiding in closets when Ingrid got to the apartment; that is, no threesomes, no orgies. No anal sex. No drugs. Money had to be paid up-front. Cash only. Those were the rules. Everything else was negotiable.

I left Come Girl with a list of written prices. It was a little like a restaurant menu except that all the food was human flesh. And because I was a full-time student, able to show my University of Toronto library card that had long since expired, there was a 20% discount. That was good, better still was that Ingrid would be over three nights from now.

★

Unlike when I had prepared for Solange's dinner visit, with the exception of a quick cleaning of the washroom and picking up clothes from the floor, this time I made no special effort to get the apartment ready. I just figured that

Ingrid had probably seen a lot worse. I was also busy with the writing of the golem novel. It occupied my every waking moment and wherever I happened to be, I often found myself writing down words and sentences that I wanted to incorporate.

Rivka had left off at the part where the protagonist, with the help of her golem, wins the coveted position of mayor of N.Y.C. I had taken the story steps further, incorporating a complicated plot that implicated the newly-elected mayor in a corruption scandal. Even the golem was unable to extricate her from the mess. In the golem stories I was aware of, the creatures were all-powerful. I wanted to try a different slant, one that had the golem more human-like, even frail. It was impossible to know if Rivka would have approved of that direction. So for a time, I kept rewriting, not really advancing, trying to imagine what she would have done with the situation. But after I adopted the attitude that it was now my novel, the story moved along of its own accord as I constructed an alter-mythology for the mayor's golem.

★

Ingrid showed up at my front door, looking exactly as her picture. Stunning. There were no surprises. In order to get the evening started on the right note, I gave her a Birk's Sterling Silver chain necklace. I purposely kept the $165 price tag on, so that she would know it was new and that I was the real deal, no tightwad. I told her if things went well, there would be more. No drugs, I remembered that, but Mrs. Kelly never said anything about wine. So we each had a glass of Chardonnay. Then it was straight to bed, I couldn't hold off any longer.

There was no foreplay, as Ingrid had suggested. A little nibbling, a little kissing, a little holding – all of it was out of the question. It was my money I told her, so my rules. Besides, I just wanted in very badly.

Ingrid left that night, I had no desire to spend another $50. I felt fabulous, why spoil things? I never really liked sharing my bed with someone else. It had always been too complicated. In general, relationships were too complicated. I had had many over the years, but they all faded. Women offered pleasure but instilled fear, which I could not shake. My uncertainty about self-image, career choice, goals – these drove a wedge between me and my lovers. I couldn't risk being judged. My parents had been judged all their lives – *dirty Roma, lazy Roma* – and it drove them into early graves. So university became my haven, philosophy my mistress. It was better that way. Much easier than getting involved with women. Affairs of the heart were not the *sin qua non* of my world. On the one occasion when I did let someone in for a longer look-see, it was an unmitigated disaster. Michelle Lambert was an English major that I met in the school's cafeteria. I was enchanted with her looks as well as her smarts, but we ended up arguing all the time. Probably on account of those very smarts, she wouldn't acquiesce to my own intellect and we seemed to one-up each other all the time. She would lift an incredulous eye above the rim of her glasses whenever I said something she disagreed with, and I knew then I was in for a major fight. If she said Dickens was a great writer, I would say Dostoyevsky was better. Or if she talked about Robert Browning, I would say that poets were simply writers who didn't know how to write prose. You see what I mean? One-upping each other. These arguments, which I never did win, served to bow my straight and purposeful resolve, leaving me limp with anger.

Chapter Fourteen

In relatively short order, eleven short stories were published in literary magazines and anthologies. And just as I had hoped, I got to read from The Golem of N.Y. at the launch of Pilot Pocketbook VII. One of my stories – *The Anarchist* – about a rebellious young woman who finds peace after nursing a sick animal to health, made it onto the longlist for the CBC 'Canada Writes' short story contest. Considering there were upwards of four thousand entries from across Canada, I considered it a major accomplishment. Yet another story rose to even greater heights, placing second in the prestigious Toronto Star short story contest. It netted me $2,000, a princely sum in the literary world. A photo of me accompanied the piece, which was called *Starchild*. Of all of my stories, it was perhaps the quirkiest, about a young boy who believes he is from another planet. In order to stay remote from humans, he communicates solely by singing, never talking. He learns the words to over six hundred songs and the doctors devise a new medical label for him – Lyric Savant. Essentially it meant someone who can't speak in normal language but is so gifted and disordered that he can learn hundreds upon hundreds of songs by rote. The protagonist was exactly like that – he finds styles of music for every occasion: rap and hip-hop provide all the fuel for his anger, country music the words for when he is hurting, folk for revealing his maudlin side, pop and easy-listening for virtually everything else. And while he waits each night in the backyard for the mothership to take him back to his planet, the reader comes to understand the genesis of his disorder – his father has abused his mother and him for years.

While my writing soared to new heights, I began to make significant improvements with other matters. There seemed to be a corollary of sorts: As 'A' (my writing) improved, then 'B' (the rest of my life) followed suit. It was as if I didn't have a say in the matter. Under constant badgering from employment counselors at EI, I even landed a job selling frozen meats from the back of a van. I wasn't particularly suited for most selling jobs – which is why I never lasted very long at any – but this one allowed me to make my own hours and offered the incentive of three weeks paid vacation, a rarity in the world of sales. In addition, I was given a list of steady customers residing in Forest Hill, Toronto's hoity-toidy enclave of the rich. For some reason, the people there tolerated my aloofness. They weren't much different themselves, simply buying the meats and avoiding chit-chat. As jobs go, it was a good one.

When the money allowed, I saw Ingrid. It was the perfect relationship. We rarely spoke, it was all about the sex. I kept her in jewelry and cash and she kept me sated.

I had long ago run out of Rivka's Xanax and Ativan but it didn't faze me. I was healthier, eating and sleeping better, and didn't feel the pressing need for the pharmaceuticals.

Nor did I feel the need to masturbate to the point of ultimate frustration. That frustration came because of a realization that I might never be with a real woman again, that my right hand was to be my sole companion for the rest of my life. I also did something that I would have previously abhorred – I took out a profile on Facebook. I had always considered social networking sites the domain of the very narcissistic; imagine, with the click of a keystroke, you could become 'friends' with people you had never met nor spoken to. Still, despite my distaste for it, I slowly came to the realization that artists should probably have an online presence. The entire world was connected digitally, there was no denying. So I sent out 'friend requests' and quickly amassed two hundred and seventy five cyber-friends, all of whom were in one way or another connected to the Canadian literary scene. What was equally interesting was that I started to receive some 'friend requests' of my own; it was becoming abundantly clear that people knew who I was. Yes, there could be no doubt, I was morphing into someone of note in this world, an Ubermensch.

Chapter Fifteen

One rainy and cold day, just about ten months or so after I received the phone call from Ruth that was to change the course of my life, I received another unusual phone call.

"Is that Karl Pringle?"

"You've got him."

"This is Jeff Charles. I met you at that book sale you once held."

"I can't place the face, I'm afraid. It was some time ago. But of course I remember the book sale very well. Good cause."

"We exchanged phone numbers."

"I did that with quite a few people that day. Anyway, how are you Jeff?"

"Look, I just wanted to tell you that I read Starchild in the Toronto Star. It was a great story."

"Thank you. I try my best and sometimes luck runs my way."

"That's my story," said Jeff. I could hear the anger rise in his voice.

"Umm, I don't know what you mean."

"Sure you don't. Well let me refresh your memory. That story appeared in a British magazine called 'Bonfire' about three years ago. I guess you figured that you could get away with it because it's in a British magazine that's now defunct."

I was trembling and couldn't speak.

"OK, well. I'm not sure exactly how to handle this. Maybe a lawyer would know better. But one thing I will do right off the bat is contact the Toronto Star. I'll tell the organizers of the contest they were duped. Shame, Karl. Shame."

The phone went dead.

I ran my hand back and forth through my hair. Every fibre in my body felt taut, on edge. I had no reason to disbelieve Jeff; why would he lie? I would have to check it out for myself. I sorted madly through the pile of Rivka's literary magazines I had kept.

Bonfire, Bonfire.

I found three different editions and looked in the Tables of Contents for *Starchild*. When I found it, my hands turned clammy and I felt light-headed. I turned to the story, the author was clearly stated as *Jeff Charles*. To add insult, I saw tiny notes written in the margins. From her diary, I recognized Rivka's handwriting.

How could I be so stupid? How could I think that a severely depressed woman juggling copious amounts of pharmaceuticals would write brilliant prose? I now realized that all Rivka had done was copy the story word for word from Bonfire onto her computer, put her name down as the author, and downloaded it. The whole act had undoubtedly served to pacify her angst. And that was why she had never submitted the story to literary magazines. As loopy as she was, she knew better.

My mind raced. What about the other stories?

I had to leave the apartment. I walked in a daze from Bloor Street up to Eglinton Avenue, a distance of four or five kilometers, and stopped at the Second Cup. But it was nearly 3 PM and of course Solange wasn't there. Exhausted, I then took the subway back to Bloor Street and made my way to Book City, where I spoke to one of the sales clerks.

"Do you know much about golem stories?" I said, my voice shaky and my hair sticking to my damp forehead.

"Oh sure, those are the Jewish mythological creatures. Are you looking for a book of fiction that features them?"

"It's kind of complicated."

"We get complicated requests all day long."

I explained that I needed to know if she had ever heard of a novel wherein the protagonist, a lowly bureaucratic lawyer living in NY, constructs a golem and then is able to rise to the position of mayor.

"That sounds so familiar! Let me ask my colleague."

The two women consulted behind the counter. Watching them, I couldn't help but think about the scene in Kafka's *The Trial*, where the protagonist Josef K. is accosted by two policemen who advise him he is under arrest, but don't reveal the nature of the charges against him. I gave my head a shake, this was all craziness. Still, the women's laughter made me realize the news was bound to be bad. I walked slowly to the front counter.

"We've decided," said the clerk I had initially conferred with, "that the book you're looking for is called *The Puttermesser Papers*. It was written by Cynthia Ozick, who's a very well-known American writer. The lawyer that you mentioned, the one who brought forth this golem and who then becomes mayor, her name is Ruth Puttermesser. She actually constructs the creature using the earth from her houseplants. Anyway, we have it in stock. Would you like me to get a copy?"

I walked out of Book City without responding and into a bar that was musty and dark. I needed the darkness. I needed a drink. Whiskey neat.

Back in the apartment, I shredded all of Rivka's short stories and threw them down the building's garbage shoot. Then I focused on the novel, The Puttermesser Papers. Such gall, that woman. Methodically, I took a pair of scissors and cut the thing into tiny shreds. I unplugged my phone and searched for some hypnotic pharmaceutical from Rivka's stash that I might take. I found one called Clonazepam, took two of the capsules, and went to bed.

Chapter Sixteen

After I had destroyed the last of Rivka's 'writings,' I spent most days lounging in bed, staring at the television. The remote zoomed through the channels, my unseeing eyes riveted to the screen.

I stopped showing up at work and eventually lost my job at the lighting store. Not going out meant there was no reason to wash – I could almost smell the fermentation of my own skin but the inertia was more powerful.

Something else began happening, something more insidious than inertia: I was becoming fearful. Everything, it seemed, was making me jittery. Knocks on the door. The idea of leaving the apartment and of being seen by someone I knew. Footsteps down the hallway. Even the sound of running water from the tap. It was as if every cell in my body had been imbued with a nervous energy that was running rampant. And the longer I stayed in bed, the worse it became.

I did have to go out for some essentials – a bit of food, rolls of toilet paper. So after the sun set, I'd venture forth under the veil of darkness. In no time flat I would speed to the corner store, buy what I needed, and come back.

My forays in those twilight hours became more protracted. I wandered around the city aimlessly wearing a hoodie, walking for hours. I found solace with the same group of vagrants who had once allowed me to burn Rivka's stolen clothes. They lived under the Bloor Street Viaduct and I felt alright in their company, they didn't ask questions. Not even my name. I regaled them with stories of my years in the Philosophy Department at the University of Toronto, about how most of my colleagues were worthless and how I had punched out my academic advisor. Swinging uppercut, then a straight jab. I also told them about my writing exploits and that I was on the verge of a big breakthrough. I even talked about golems.

Hiding in the ravine by day, my new friends ventured out only at night, usually to collect beer bottles or else forage for food. They all had their own tales of woe but now treated each other like family, sharing food and drink.

There was no point in sleeping under the bridge since I still had my own apartment. At least for now. But I visited the ravine dwellers as often as I could, that is, whenever my mood allowed. Some nights though I couldn't get out of bed at all; there seemed to be no point. Aside from the ravine, I had nowhere to go. But there were benefits to not getting up. I found that when I lay in bed all day, I didn't have much of an appetite. That saved on food bills.

Sometimes though, my stomach railed against the fasting, rumbling and blowing up precipitously large, like it was about to explode. I would then be forced out of the apartment back to the ravine where I could share a meal. I also began to scavenge through garbage bins in back of supermarkets. "Move the ballasts outta the way first," one of my ravine friends told me. "That way you won't step on them and end up with pieces of glass in the food. That's the best system."

Lettuce, tomatoes, bread, apples, oranges, cantaloupes, avocados, celery, cheese...I found them all. Even the occasional stalk of corn. Most everything was a bit soft or brown or moldy but I didn't mind; it was edible, that was the main thing. On one occasion I found a package of chocolate puddings, a real treat. On another an entire case of extra-virgin olive oil, which I immediately shared with my friends, who took turns mixing it with wine, and then swilling the concoction down.

The problem with dumpster-diving was that there was always lots of competition at the supermarket bins, both human and animal. Vagrants, raccoons. Most annoying of all were the 'freegans,' the dumpster scavengers who never failed to lecture me on the fact they were especially deserving of the food they found. According to them, they weren't homeless but had chosen to live "off the grid," eating and using what had been cast off by others. By doing so, they had in effect disassociated themselves from capitalism and consumerism. They said were living more ethically than I. I knew their rants were disingenuous and convoluted since they were still using gas and electricity to cook some of the scavenged food. And even though they disdained capitalist society, they were undoubtedly benefiting from it, utilizing the fruits of that waste. But I said nothing to them, my inertia was too great and I couldn't argue. Sometimes it was a lot easier not to eat.

This way of living went on for a long time, months even. Then one day an eviction notice for non-payment of rent was slipped under my door. It did mention a thirty-day grace period in which, if I paid the back-rent, I would be allowed to stay. With that notice, a moment of unremitting clarity dawned on me and I realized that I truly had nothing, and that all of my life was one big farce. I was the Ubermensch in a world that didn't matter anymore. Maybe it never did. I walked with new-found purpose into the washroom and removed a small package of Rivka's razor blades that I had kept. There were four small boxes inside, each containing seven blades. I slid one of the blades out and without hesitating, superficially cut my left arm from my wrist to my elbow. When the blood seeped out, fanning out across my arm, I felt a great release and breathed a sigh of relief. Watching the bright crimson tide drop onto the floor, it was as if the earth had turned the opposite way on its axis and spit me out as a newborn.

Chapter Seventeen

I still had money, at least I had that. I could pay the rent, I had just forgotten to do so. I was back on E.I. and Rivka's stolen jewelry beckoned whenever I needed it. It's just that I was despairing all the time. I didn't know what would become of me. Each time I entered the bathroom, the blood that lay spattered throughout reminded me of who I really was – a big fat zero. And I was too broken to clean it.

One of my bridge friends told me about a whole forbidden city of homeless and derelict people, living in tents and makeshift shelters and eating by campfire. It was called Tent Haven and located down by the waterfront. I thought I would check it out. So one evening I rode my bike on Jarvis Street down to the lake. There I found it, a multitude of coloured tents. I wandered in as if I belonged and no one said a word. Dozens of empty cough syrup bottles were strewn on the ground, as were an assortment of needles. Orange flames emanated from steel barrels, as far as the eye could see. I wondered how it was that the cops hadn't shut down the place. Surely they must have known. Maybe on the list of insidious crimes that derailed Toronto, those being committed at Tent Haven were pretty low.

Carnival City, that's what I called the place. I returned each night and quickly found out that most everyone had a

lunar mind that veered off into indecipherable conversations. Many were stoned or drunk. Some mentally
unstable, like Edna. When I first met her, she ran her hands
down her body in quick jerky motions, as if trying to brush
off some imaginary insects.

"Do you know who I am?" she asked.

"No."

"Let me tell you something. I used to be somebody."

She jabbed her forefinger into my chest for emphasis.
'SOMEBODY. GOT IT?"

"Yes, I understand," I said in a mollifying voice.
Almost at once, I could tell what sort of person I was dealing
with. She reminded me of someone, although I couldn't
quite recall.

"Then I started collecting things. I couldn't throw anything away. Bottles, bottle caps, bits of paper, used paper
cups, old magazines and newspapers, pencils, half-eaten
bagels, empty pill bottles, broken toys, cracked planters,
used books, movie ticket stubs, every receipt, clothes that I
had outgrown, shoes with the heels worn down, rusty pots
and pans, socks with holes in them, blankets with holes in
them, hair that came out in the sink, lint from the dryer,
crooked nails, straight nails, pieces of cotton, candy
wrappers, empty shampoo bottles, empty cereal boxes,
empty detergent boxes, old food cartons, dead bugs, used
dental floss....anyway, there's a lot more but you get the
idea. I couldn't move in my own apartment. There was no
place to eat. I used to eat standing up. Nobody ever came
over, I wouldn't let anyone. I didn't want them to think I
was crazy."

"Why are you telling me this?"

"Because you think I might have brain damage, that's why."

"I don't think that."

"Don't flatter me. You're such a liar."

I should have walked away but didn't. As disgusted as I felt about a homeless woman who was wearing a tattered pink terry-cloth bathrobe and with her hair in curlers, I also felt sorry for Edna. Maybe she had been a somebody at one time, although I doubted it. But now she was just pathetic, a shriveled-up shrew. There was something else: I was...well... lonely, and wanted to talk to someone. Especially to someone who wasn't drunk all the time like my friends under the bridge.

"Maybe I wasn't too well then but now it's different," she said. "I'm alright now. But I'll tell you, it was a long road. A psychiatrist from the Department of Health came over to the apartment, the first person ever. I think the landlord sent him. So this guy brought some boxes in and said he wanted me to organize things. *Organize*, just imagine! I knew what he was up to. That organizing was nothing more than preparing me to get rid of my stuff."

"Why did you keep all that junk anyway?" I asked.

"Excuse me, but it wasn't junk, as you call it. Everything I kept was special. Had its' own special texture. Everything felt unique to the touch. Some things smooth, others rough. Some things round, others square. Some things paper, others metal. Every time I touched something, it felt like I had almost...hmmm... anointed it. Made it sacred, you know. Can't explain it better."

"Anointed?"

"Yes. What of it?"

"Who did you think you were? Jesus Christ?" As soon as the words slipped out, I knew it was a mistake.

"You are one pig of a man. You think you're better than me, don't you?"

"Maybe I am." Again, a wrong choice.

Edna stared at me without saying a word. One eyebrow arched high, the mug screwed up tight as a drum, hard and frank. It was a familiar peer. Then I remembered. It was the same sort of maniacal look that often beset the face of that other nutbar, Brenda Bumblegate. Yes, the kooky b-movie lady.

"You're a piss poor excuse for a human being," she excreted.

I didn't need that. I started walking away but Edna ran after me in her high-heeled shoes, almost stumbling on the stubbly, rock-hard ground.

'Wait, don't you want to know what happened with the psychiatrist?"

If there was one thing I came to realize about the people at Tent Haven, it was that they may have been down-and-outers, but they were for the most part harmless. I stopped and listened; the story at least, was mildly entertaining.

"Well, so he came in with these boxes labeled *Hard, Medium and Easy*," said Edna quietly, seemingly more at ease now that she had an audience again. "Hard to throw away, easy to throw away, and things that were in the middle, not hard, not easy – medium. When we started, I put everything into the Hard boxes. He then tried to convince me that some things in those boxes, a few things, could be moved into the Medium boxes, things like hair, bugs, lint. But I couldn't bear to part with anything. This guy just didn't get it. When I was about to put something in the Hard box, he would grab hold of my hand and move it to the Medium box, trying to get me to drop it there. I thought he was crazy, a mad fool. Why did he think that my own hair meant nothing to me? And bugs are so interesting to touch, they're not like anything else."

I furrowed his brow but remained silent. Why was I wasting my time with this lunatic?

"Don't make faces like that."

"Sorry."

"Good, so now let me finish. As I was saying... hmmm..." Edna paused for a moment. "I forgot what I was saying."

"You were talking about the Hard, Medium and Easy boxes. How the psychiatrist tried to make you move things from the Hard box to the Medium box."

"Ah...yah, yah, you're right," she said, suddenly remembering. "By the way, do you have a cigarette?"

I pulled out my pack of Gitanes and gave Edna one.

"Can I have another?"

"Sure."

Edna took a long drag, blew a tight spiral into the air, and continued. "So there I was and this shrink guy – I forget his name – was holding my hand over the Medium box, shaking it, forcing me to let go of whatever I was holding. He was much stronger than me so he was able to make me drop things. He was a brute. That was his idea of getting me to learn to organize. But every time things went into the Medium box, I started crying. It was so hard, I can't tell you."

Edna started mumbling under her breath. "So, what was I telling you?"

"You were describing how the psychiatrist forced you to put things in the Medium box."

"The Medium box. Now I remember. Anyway, every night when the guy left, I would take things from the Medium box and put them back in the Hard box. So in the morning when he came back, there was hardly anything left in the Medium box."

A spasm rocked Edna's right hand.

"You OK?"

Edna laughed nervously. "I got a touch of Parkinson's. Body's out of control. Does what it wants. Strange how things work out."

"What's strange?"

"I always used to do want I wanted. My brain had its own desires which I always followed. We were buds. Now my body is doing what it wants. Except I can't follow it like I did my brain. It's like it's separate from me. Get my drift?"

"I get your drift." I didn't but it made no difference.

Edna picked up with her story. "So that shrink guy got really upset with me. Said my only hope was to get electro-shock treatments down at the hospital where he worked. There was something in my brain that needed to be zapped with electricity. They'd done work like that with criminals and alcoholics. People who just couldn't get it together. He assured me I wouldn't feel a thing; they'd give me lots of drugs. Sedating stuff."

"Did you go?" I asked.

"No, I didn't want them to zap me. I was a somebody, you know. I didn't want them messing with that, then I'd be a nobody. So I thought that if I could find a job, he'd get off my case. The only reason he got interested in me at all was because I was collecting disability insurance from the province. Couldn't work because of my habit of collecting things."

"So you went to look for a job?"

"Yah. I went down to the local employment agency. They asked me what skills I had – did I have computer skills, take shorthand...stuff like that. Well, I couldn't do any of that. But I did know how to save things. I was pretty good at it. They didn't really understand but it didn't matter. I found the perfect job – filing in the office for an activist organization that was hell bent on saving the redwood trees."

Edna was rambling. The story was going nowhere and I was getting tired.

"I think I have to go now," I said.

Edna grabbed hold of my arm with her reed-like fingers. "Don't go. The rest of the story's pretty interesting."

"Make it quick."

"OK, so there I was, working in the office. I got started in the filing room but the problem of saving things started all over again. I couldn't throw anything away. The filing room got quite messy. Became like my apartment. You couldn't move and I couldn't file anything anymore. I also couldn't find anything."

"Did they fire you?"

"Nah. Some of the leaders in the group decided that since they liked my commitment, they would just find me a more suitable position."

"Where?"

"I couldn't really work in the office, anywhere indoors actually, that's where I ran into trouble. That's when we came up with the idea of working outside, with the trees."

"You planted trees?"

"No, better than that. I lived in a tree. Up a redwood. About one-hundred-and-twenty-feet up. Lived there for a year."

"You lived up in a redwood tree for a year? Like fuck you did."

"Sonny, I sure did. Just to stop them tree getting cut down by loggers."

I was full of wonderment that anyone could concoct such a story so I stayed on to listen and see what other crazy verbiage would spill forth from the woman's mouth.

"We need them trees," Edna said. "For the animals, birds and plants. Salmon lay their eggs in the forest streams. Just imagine if all the redwoods were gone? What would happen to all the black bears and foxes? What about beautiful plants like rhododendrons and wood sorrels? Seems to me you wouldn't see none of them woodpeckers either. Not only that but there'd be a lot more earth slides without the trees to hold the soil in place."

Edna took another drag of her cigarette and exhaled deeply. "And it's not just in the forests where we need more trees – it's in the cities too. If you walk down a main street in any big city you'll see those skimpy decorative trees growing out of planter tubs. A long time ago, cities had lots of large trees lining the downtown core. Elms, sugar maples, oak. Beautiful canopies. They're good for cleaning the air and they cut down on noise levels. The problem is that when cities start to grow, things like sewers and buried cables and that there begin to take up space underground. Them tree roots gets all constricted. And then above ground, you've got telephone hydro lines."

The more I listened to Edna, the more I began to think that she knew an awful lot about what she was saying. Maybe I had misjudged her. Maybe there was a modicum of truth in what she was saying. Still, it seemed preposterous, the whole business of living up in a redwood. Maybe she was just repeating something she had read in a book. A child's story about living in a tree, a book of fiction that lodged in her disturbed brain. I just couldn't tell.

"Didn't the loggers try to get you down?" I asked.

"Yah, you bet. They sent people up a few times. Didn't come all the way up but close enough to insult me and threaten me with lawsuits. They used floodlights and loud sirens. Once they had a helicopter fly over the tree. That wasn't the worst part though."

"Not the worst part?"

"No, the worst part were them rainstorms. I had to hold on to the tree for my dear life. The funny part was that I always felt I'd be ok because I knew the tree would take care of me. I really developed a relationship with that tree. She knew I was there to protect her and so she did the same for me."

"So if all that was true, why did you come down?" I said. "And by the way, how did you get your food?

"So I'll answer the last question first. One of them guys in the office, he was an engineer. He made this pulley system, so everything came up and down in a bucket, like this." Edna pulled on imaginary ropes. "Now as to why I came down...well, that's another story. I guess you can say that I made my point. The logging company would've got a lot of bad press if they had a cut that tree down, especially after all the media attention. The other thing was that I was getting kind of tired up there. I had this bad chest cough that wouldn't go away and my lower back was sore a lot from sleeping on a thin mattress. It was just time."

I snatched the second cigarette from Edna's hand and sprinted away. It was like that there down by the lake. Everybody had a story, made up or not. It was just up to you whether you wanted to believe it.

Situated so close to the water, it was desperately cold at Carnival City and my teeth chattered constantly. Only when offered a slug of some cheap booze did my body warm. On one occasion, too drunk to bike back to the market, I bedded down for the night in a tent. Someone put their arms around me, a man. He embraced my body and I could smell the stink coming off him. And yet, I didn't mind. I was cold and it was actually nice to be held. In the morning, I was so stiff from having slept on the rock-hard ground that I could barely walk. I was also famished and sat down with a few others to a breakfast of oatmeal with sliced apples and peppermint tea. It was as good a meal as I had had in a long time.

But as nice as that was, I always returned to my own place in the Market. Taking a cue from my ravine friends, I only left my apartment in the evenings. While they hid during the daylight hours under the bridge, I did likewise. I slept much of the time during the day, I didn't see any reason not to. I just wanted to live peacefully for the rest of my life. No hassles, no mistakes. I was going further underground and that's what I craved.

But periodically, I did show up at Carnival City. Something struck me whenever I came and that was that the rate of attrition was significant. People came and went all the time. Some died, undoubtedly, and others simply wandered off to shelters or any other place they could keep warm. Now that the trees had divested themselves of their leafy coats and the silver moon came out early each evening, glinting like a piece of ice in the night sky, I couldn't blame anyone for seeking refuge indoors. The hardy fools who remained at Carnival City had to huddle closely together around fires, passing around bottles of booze. One vagrant who caught my attention was a guy called Ragman. He had a perpetual stoop that came from years of unattended scoliosis, so he told me. He revealed he had once been six feet, two inches, now... five feet, ten inches. I estimated he was somewhere in his mid-fifties although one might easily have taken him for perhaps a decade older, what with his leathery skin and white hair.

I didn't know his true name...everyone simply called him by his nickname. I asked him about it and he told me that he had long ago been in the *schmata* business in Montreal, selling men's clothing. When I pressed him further about what went wrong, he clammed right up. Someone however, told me that he once had a wife but that she ran off with another man. Some butcher who sold kosher meats. Apparently, that led him straight to the bottle. I didn't know if the story was true or not but I must say that I was intrigued by Ragman. He wore a black yarmulke and I'd often see him standing off in the distance, muttering some prayers. I knew enough about the Jewish faith to know that when he did so, moving his rail-thin body to and fro, that he was davening. But instead of the Wailing Wall in Jerusalem, he was facing the Gardiner Expressway in Toronto, Ontario, and I wondered how a man who was obviously so pious could maintain his faith in light of his abysmal circumstances.

Something else about the man piqued my interest. He seemed to have some sort of busy life. He would leave Carnival City almost every morning and only return late in the evenings. Of course I was back in the safety of my own bed every morning but someone – the same nameless person who told me about his marital breakup – told me of his comings and goings. I decided to not go home one day but rather follow him; why not? I had nothing better to do.

I had the temerity to tell Ragman to wake me up early since I had to make my way to school for an exam. It was a dumb move but I couldn't think of any other lie to spout off as to why I should have to be up then. Fortunately, Ragman didn't think anything of my request and shortly thereafter, at the ungodly hour of 6:15, he roused me from a deep sleep. I wasn't used to being alive at that time of day and my head hurt from the lack of sleep.

"Wait, I'll come with you," I said.

I walked alongside Ragman with my bicycle until King Street, where he hopped on a streetcar.

"Maybe see you later," I said.

"Yup."

It was easy to follow the slow-moving vehicle. I just kept a safe distance back and watched who got off at each stop.

At Bathurst Street, Ragman debarked from the streetcar and went into a flower shop, coming out holding a large bouquet. He then headed into MacDonald's. I peered through the window and saw him enter into the washroom.

Ten minutes passed, and then fifteen. When finally he emerged, I was flabbergasted. The man had changed from his grubby clothes to a suit and tie, his hair neatly combed. He carried the flowers in one hand and the black leather gym bag he had brought with him in the other, which I assumed now contained his regular clothes.

Ragman resumed his travels by taking a bus north on Bathurst. It continued quite far and at times I almost lost it from sight, especially climbing the steep hill north of Dupont Street. I pedaled as quickly as I could, my breath forming vapour clouds in the frigid air. When finally he got off, it was right at the Holy Blossom Temple, an old, stately synagogue just south of Eglinton Avenue.

That was the end of it; it wasn't possible to follow Ragman any further when he walked into the synagogue. I wasn't dressed for whatever occasion it was and moreover, couldn't risk being spotted by him. So I waited outside… and waited. My attention though, was diverted to the black limousines that began pulling up, each with little flags marked 'FUNERAL' attached to the hoods. People dressed in solemn black clothes piled out of the cars and walked into Holy Blossom.

After about two hours, the mourners came out. Black, black, a sea of black. They came out solo and in tandem, holding hands and embracing shoulders, weeping and consoling. They stood around in nervous circles, shifting their weight from foot to foot. As more mourners joined in, the circles got progressively bigger. No one seemed to be leaving.

Ragman was in plain sight. He moved obsequiously from circle to circle, kissing cheeks and shaking hands. He seemed to know everyone and everyone knew him. I noticed that he no longer carried the flowers. Presumably he had given them away. I was at a loss to truly explain anything. I had never seen this side of Ragman before, social and seemingly normal.

After a while, the group of mourners started to disband. People shuffled through the parking lot into their cars, Others walked down the street and disappeared around corners. I hoped Ragman would walk away on his own so that I could continue tailing him but it was not to be. He sidled into a long black convertible along with five others. The car started up and promptly left the lot.

It was the damndest thing. I just didn't get it. Sure, I knew Ragman was Jewish but had no idea he knew so many people. Others of his faith. Especially now that he was, let's face facts, a down-and-outer. It suddenly dawned on me that I might find some answers if I snooped through Ragman's tent.

I high-tailed it back to Carnival City. Standing in front of Ragman's inauspicious green tent, I made sure no one was looking and then darted in. The place was crammed with stuff. Lamplights, a propane stove, fire extinguisher, stacks of newspapers, bags of clothes, a few loaves of bread, cans of baked beans, organic carrots, a stop sign, three typewriters, computer monitors and printers, a laptop, books, a complete stereo system (receiver, tape deck, CD player, speakers), bicycle tires and tubes, boxes of assorted chocolates, a walkman, a walkie-talkie set, 35mm camera, cat carrier, empty jars, tennis rackets. Everything lay in piles, stuff on top of stuff, years worth of collecting. The only things that gave any indications of Ragman's Jewish faith were three ornate mezuzahs and an equal number of menorahs. I had seen a mezuzah on Rivka's door and thought it strange that she would have one; I had always associated religious artifacts with ignorant people who needed a crutch, who couldn't take responsibility for their own lives. But Rivka was an intellect and should have known better. If Rivka was a believer, then that one slender piece of metal inscribed with verses from a holy Jewish book, should have offered her some security. Solace even. But it was obvious that it hadn't.

In addition to the assorted junk, Ragman also kept quite a few newspapers. I saw that the only sections he had kept were those devoted to the Birth and Death Notices. One ad, circled in red ink, drew my attention.

Francis Patricia Kopelman
November 25, 1952 - October 30, 2012
On October 30, 2012, Francis Patricia Kopelman passed suddenly from this life into a place of peace. Scholar, pianist, mother, her memory will forever be held by her husband Allen, daughter Ruth, sister Cheryl Bickford; many aunts, uncles and cousins; colleagues and many friends. Services will be held at Holy Blossom Temple…

I stopped reading. So Ragman knew a Francis Patricia Kopelman. I wondered whether Ragman had ever mentioned her before and concluded that he hadn't. Upon deeper consideration I realized that that meant nothing – Ragman barely revealed anything about himself. No one knew much about the type of life he engaged in outside of Carnival City. Maybe he was friends with the deceased. Maybe she had even been family.

I picked up another newspaper. It too was from the Birth and Death Notices. I scanned the listings until I came across yet another ad that had been circled:

John Michael Solomon
September 22, 1918 - June 14, 2012

It is with deep sadness we say goodbye to John Michael Solomon, known to his friends and family as 'Solly'. To say that Solly lived life to the fullest would be an under-statement. He embraced life and infected all those who had the good fortune to know him with that same spirit. An avid sailor, world traveler, philosopher, mountaineer, musician, he played the harmonica and keyboards in his jazz trio with the same aplomb that saw him scale Everest.

In a loving partnership of 55 years with his wife Rebecca who passed away in 1988, Solly thrived in the company of his children and grandchildren, friends and colleagues. Solly was cherished by those who knew him: his wife Rebecca, daughter Caroline, son Charles, sisters Irene Baltsch of Ottawa and Heidi Travers of Norfolk, Virginia, granddaughters Kathy, Brenda and Gwendolyn.

Services will be held at Holy Blossom Temple...

I put the newspaper down and picked up another and another after that. Each was the Birth and Death Notices and had at least one death notice circled, some two. I rifled through more stacks of papers. They were all the same, going back years and years.

I decided to follow Ragman once more and again the adventure took me back to Holy Blossom. So he was attending funeral services there. But why? Surely he couldn't have known all these people. There were tens upon tens of circled newspaper death notices. Was he simply crashing the services for the heck of it? It couldn't be that simple. There had to be some motive that I wasn't clueing in on. Paying for all those flowers must have cost Ragman a fortune. No one in their right mind would pay out that kind of money for a stranger. But maybe Ragman wasn't in his right mind.

There was another theory that I turned over in his mind, one which I more readily accepted. As bizarre as it seemed, leaving behind Carnival City to attend services, Ragman perhaps was walking straight into something much more hopeful. I couldn't help but notice that the deceased's were fairly accomplished people – scholars, pianists, world travelers, philosophers. That meant they probably had a circle of friends and family who were similarly accomplished, people who held regular jobs, who weren't drunk all the time. Sure it was a bit of an assumption but it didn't take a great leap of faith to believe that Ragman had latched onto something positive. And there was something else. Even though the services Ragman attended were events where the deceased's friends and family would quite obviously not be at their best, that may actually have worked to his benefit. The pall of grief that hung over everything like a shroud reduced things to a level he could readily relate to, even prosper in.

But I was only guessing. As I thought back to the image of Ragman going off in a car with fellow mourners at the synagogue, it occurred to me that he looked awfully comfortable, like he had known those people for years. I saw him drape his arm across another man's shoulders and with a hankie, wipe away the tears from a woman's face. It was apparent that Ragman was reaching out with loving tenderness, way beyond the confines of dismal Carnival City. Perhaps going to all these services was giving Ragman some meaning to his otherwise hopeless life. I knew that unless I asked him though, I would never know for sure. And I never would ask him. For after the two outings in which I played like Sherlock Holmes, I decided not to go back to Carnival City. It was getting too cold down by the lake and as pathetic as my life was, I didn't see it getting better hanging out with derelicts. As depressed and dopey as I was, I was at least cognizant of that.

I had not been at my apartment for a few days and when I returned and sorted through the stack of mail, mostly bills but quite a few flyers, I saw a letter from The Toronto Star. I knew it could only be bad so I threw it out without opening the envelope.

Chapter Eighteen

As unlikely as it may have seemed, the entire Ragman episode gave me some hope of my own. I realized that anyone could be tailed. Anyone could be found out. No one's secrets were safe.

Of late, while not following a derelict, I had been thinking of Solange. There was a simple reason for that: she was the only person in a long time that had shown any interest in me.

I had probably been too hasty with the woman, judging her based on the company she kept. The problem was that the two times of late that I had biked by the Second Cup on Eglinton at the hour I knew she normally was there, she wasn't.

I hadn't actually been sure whether I would have gone in to the coffee shop or not had I seen her, but I just wanted to know she was still around. That some things remain the same. And of course, if I had taken the plunge and walked in, I don't know how I could have explained my absence. Nor my decrepit appearance. I was pretty good at making things up though and undoubtedly would have come up with something.

I googled Private Investigators. The whole cloak and dagger business was way out of my line of experience. All I knew about it was through the Detective Columbo TV series, in which Peter Falk played a bumbling P.I. And even in my current unfocused state, I realized that was simply fiction. But I was pleasantly surprised to find out that a Sheila Suskind worked out of an austere office space on Dupont Street in the Annex, next to a dry cleaning shop. Right at street level, the place was nothing much to speak of – inauspicious to say the least, there was no sign on the door and only two chairs and a black and white wall clock with overlarge numbers, the kind I distinctly remember from grade school. Tick tock, tick tock, went the second hand.... I had only just walked in and the sound was already driving me crazy, like it was ticking down the last seconds of my life. Behind a desk piled high with papers sat Sheila Suskind, the simple black nameplate with white lettering giving her away.

"Come in Mr. Pringle," she said at once, extending a hand. "I've been expecting you." She was much more petite than I would have imagined. I suppose I had been expecting someone big and burly, like Ruth. As for me, I hadn't shaved in quite a few days and my days at Carnival City still plagued me – my clothes were rumpled, my black hair matted and unclean. I was still a mess.

"I usually work on a contingency basis," she said straight off.

"What does that mean?"

"It means that you pay for certain expenses as I go along, like gas for my car, photocopies, phone expenses if long distance calls are required...things like that. But you don't actually have to pay for my services unless I find the person you're looking for. And get the information you need."

"And how much will this contingency basis cost me?" I said.

"$1,000 in this case. You gave me some preliminary details over the phone so I'm somewhat aware of how much work is required." Suskind leaned far over the desk. "Can you afford that, Mr. Pringle?"

"I can afford that," I said assertively.

And I could. I had the money and if necessary, could hawk some of the jewelry from Rivka's dwindling stash.

"But what if you don't find her?" I continued.

Suskind stared at me with steely-blue eyes. "I always find them," she said. "But, in the unlikely event that they elude me, you will only have to pay for my expenses."

"Ok, that sounds fair. Anything else?" The clock was driving me crazy and I had to get out of there.

"There's a $250 deposit."

I signed the prepared contract, wrote out a cheque, and after Suskind and I went over everything I knew about Solange, bolted out the door before another second could tick off.

★

Suskind was as good as her word. Four and a half weeks later, she called to say that I owed her the remaining $750. And that I wouldn't be disappointed. Like she told me previously, she always found them out.

I couldn't bear even a single moment in her office and so I asked whether we could meet at a coffee shop. She agreed and came down to my neck of the woods, meeting at Wanda's Pie in the Sky on Augusta Street, simply Wanda's to everyone local.

"The best pies in town," I said. Extolling the virtues of something as trite as restaurant fare was not in my nature but I was excited to meet with Suskind and hear what she had to say. "I'll buy you one."

"I was hoping you'd say that, Mr. Pringle."

I came back with two pieces of apple pie and two coffees.

"Before we get started, Mr. Pringle, I should tell you that Solange says Bonjour."

I blanched, I must have. I could feel the blood rush from my face.

"Relax, I'm only messing with you, Mr. Pringle. I never reveal my clients."

The panic abated, I poured sugar into my coffee and pretended to be nonplussed about the ruse.

"But I will tell you one thing, Mr. Pringle. You're a total fuck-up, you really are. Now I don't know exactly why you asked me to track down Solange Depardieu but I will say this. If you are interested in her, which I suspect you are, then you shouldn't let that girl out of your sight. Accept her love because she's a keeper and could be, if you let it, the best thing to ever happen to your miserable life."

I put down my cup. Why was this bitch giving me a lecture? She didn't know me, didn't know one godforsaken thing about me. She was just a stupid P.I. who probably didn't have the smarts to cut it in school. When all else fails, become a snoop.

"Excuse me..." I said abruptly, trying to show her that I was in charge. "You know nothing about me. **Nothing.** So if you want to get paid, I would dispense with the derogatory comments and just tell me what you know about Solange."

Suskind smiled knowingly.

"I always check out my clients, Mr. Suskind. Rule No. 1 of the trade, don't take any job for people you know nothing about. I don't work for shady people." She took a long sip of her coffee and continued. "Now I wouldn't exactly call you shady. No, but what you are is a fuck-up, just like I said. You'd be surprised to know how much dirt I've found out about you, about your little dust-up with your academic supervisor, the many jobs you've been fired from or left, your continual collecting of benefits from E.I. Other things too. Oh, I know all about you, Mr. Pringle."

Suskind was a first-class bitch. The fact that she had checked me out made me want to spit in her face. Grudgingly, I held my tongue. Now that the cat was out of the bag about my past, there was no going back. Her checking up on me was horrific, wretched, abysmal, spiteful…any one of another half dozen adjectives. But I still needed to find out about Solange and in a steady voice that belied my hatred for Suskind, I told her so.

The contemptuous woman sitting opposite took a slice of pie into her mouth, rolling it around on her tongue. "Mmm, excellent," she enthused.

"So what do you have?" I repeated. "I'm paying you a lot of money."

"Mr. Pringle, there's a lot you should know."

"Then go ahead. God."

After Suskind told me that she had befriended Solange, she revealed piles upon piles of information about the French woman's life. So much, in fact, that it left my head spinning.

Chapter Nineteen

Solange Gabrielle Depardieu was born in the southern French city of Marseilles in the year 1971. She was the only child of Sonia and Emile Epaul, whose union was one of a handful of interracial marriages in France in the 1960's. It was a marriage not without its share of problems. Emile had a tenuous relationship with work, likening it to slavery. And since his ancestors in St. Domingue had been subject to the degradations of the slave trade, working the sugar plantations (or so he said), he would have none of it. *"Work makes a man feel like he's all chained up,"* was his favourite saying.

It turned out that it wasn't only work that chained Emile up – marriage made him feel the same way. *"A man's got a right to a little freedom now and then."* And freedom for Emile was Amaud's Cafe, a topless go-go nightclub where girls in skimpy G-strings danced right at your table. It was there that he felt unshackled, where he could act on his soul's longings. And what his soul longed for at the darkened bar was a whole lot of fine brandy mixed with an equal helping of E-Z sex. *"Names that starts with an E and I'll go right up to the Z's - I'll have all them, ladies. And I don't mind the A's to D's neither."*

If there was one thing that captured Emile's interest –
aside from the goings on at Amaud's – that thing was
baseball. Growing up in Montreal, Quebec, he had been
touted as a can't miss big leaguer, a whopper of a man who
could not only hit the ball a mile but also run. He had been
clocked at 4.56 seconds in the forty-yard dash and could
bench press two-hundred-and-sixty-five pounds. He could
steal bases and throw with the best of them.

At fourteen, he attracted the attention of most of the
major league scouts. He was on his way to a full scholarship
at any one of a number of universities in the U.S. – the truth
was that he had his pick – when his life went spinning wildly
out of control. One cool September evening, he made the
terrible mistake of trying to pick up the girlfriend of a
neighbourhood gang member. That episode led to him being
ambushed by a group of thugs who beat him bad. They
whacked his knees and ankles with baseball bats and
blackjacks until every bone had been shattered into
eggshells. That was it. At seventeen, Emile's career was over.
It took the doctors three operations to set everything straight
and with all the pins and bolts and metal plates holding him
together, Emile may just as well have been the Tin Man
from Oz. He had that much chance of ever playing again.

After years of rehabilitation, he managed to clang along,
but he could never run properly. The whipping left him a
big uneducated man with no future, an ex-jock, one with a
bad attitude to boot. He sulked and fell heavily into drink.

Things went from bad to worse for Emile. His mother,
fed up with his rowdy behaviour, set him adrift. Nearing
twenty, without any emotional attachments and without a

job, he resorted to criminal activities. He began by stealing car stereos. In time he moved up the illegal ladder, pinching muscle cars and later on higher-end autos, Mercedes' and Fiats. That made him a pile of money. Had he stayed right there, a fallen star with a penchant for stealing luxury cars, he may have been alright. But baseball had given him an inflated ego and now that he had a taste of the good life, he thought he could do better, much better.

His undoing came when he fell in with a gang of professional house thieves, slick cat burglars who could slip unnoticed into an occupied house and come out quietly on pitter-patter feet, armed with bags of jewelry, silverware and priceless paintings. They gave Emile a chance and one was all he needed to slip up. His problem was that he was no cat burglar. He was just too large to slip by unnoticed. Moreover, with his bum legs, he could barely walk properly. Scaling anything like a balcony, which was a routine part of the business, was for him a nightmare. He might have been able to pull himself up using the sheer strength of his upper body but in cat burglar circles, that wasn't considered good technique – too much grunting and groaning, far too much noise. What Emile really needed, what he didn't have, was a dexterous and nimble lower half.

The night he was apprehended was particularly windy and rainy. He was on the job in Westmount, a wealthy English-speaking enclave and slipped on a second-floor railing, landing heavily in a patch of petunias below. The noise attracted the attention of the homeowners who heard the swear words maudit and merde that he was muttering. They also saw him limp away from the property. Since there weren't very many six-feet, three-inch, French-speaking mulatto men around with distinctive limps it was only a matter of time before the authorities zeroed in on Emile.

In prison, he was visited by women from the local Roman Catholic Church, who prayed for his redemption. Since he had nothing to lose, he prayed right along with them. There was little wrong with talking to the Lord, especially if it meant a little time out of his cell block.

One of the women with whom he struck up a particularly good rapport was Sonia Carpentier, a pious white woman who impressed upon Emile that he must give his life over to the Lord, that by doing so he would find everlasting happiness. According to Sonia, there were no hopeless people on this earth, only poor souls who had lost their way because they forgot their place in life, forgot that God rewards those who believe in him.

Sonia would read Emile passages from the Bible. It became their weekly practice. Her favourite quote was from Deuteronomy 31:6: *"Be strong and courageous. Do not be afraid or terrified because of them for the LORD your God goes with you; he will never leave you nor forsake you."* Emile wondered who those people he might be terrified of were, but he kept silent.

Sonia revealed to Emile that one sin leads to another and by continuing to sin, man becomes blind to his wrongdoings. That, she explained, was what had happened to him. He had strayed from God but she continued to emphasize that there was always hope. It was never hopeless. If he would only let God take control of his life, things would turn themselves around. Since he realized that he had made a fine mess of his life, Emile reasoned that God could do no worse. So he prayed along with Sonia and said it was ok for the Lord to take over.

Once a month the prison would allow the women from the church to bring in food. Set out on a communal table in the dining hall were cabbage rolls, dumplings, turkey sandwiches, crab dip, bean soup, and lamb. Sonia got to know that Emile's favourite meal was beef brisket with gobs of mashed potatoes, corn on the cob, finished off with apple pie and ice cream. It delighted her to see him eat. She had never known anyone to like her food that much.

For two years, Sonia continued to preach the word to Emile. The arrangement worked fine and Emile told her that when he got out, he would continue his relationship with God; now that he had finally found something that worked for him, he wasn't about to give it up. In an awkward and tender moment he revealed to her that he felt much the same way about her. She blushed and knew that she had finally met her match, a man who was devoted to the good Lord as much as she.

He was released a full nine months early. His new-found attitude had endeared him to the warden and he was let off on good behaviour, on the proviso that he check in with his parole officer once a month. With that arrangement in place, Emile Epaul hobbled out of jail a new man.

Physically, they were an odd match. Noreen was 5' 4", somewhat small-boned, with fine wisps of blond hair that was neatly pinned at the back of her almond-shaped head. She wore oval, wire-rimmed glasses and no make-up at all, not even at festive church socials. During the hot, dog days of summer she favoured long prissy flowered dresses that fell to her ankles.

Everything about Emile was large. He wore size fifteen shoes and carried close to two-hundred-and-thirty pounds on his six-feet, three-inch frame, although he liked to say that fifteen of those pounds didn't belong to him – it was just the metal embedded in his legs that weighed him down. His hands were huge – he could hold five baseballs in them. Aside from the granny-like reading glasses that he lifted from a drugstore before his conversion, there was nothing small about Emile. Nothing at all. Certainly not the wandering tongue he stuck into Sonia's mouth during one of her visits.

Five people attended the wedding. Neither Emile nor Sonia had much family to speak of. Emile had been brought up by his mother, his father having absconded with another woman when he was six-years-old. He had one brother who hit the rails at an early age and whom Emile hadn't seen in ten years by the time the wedding rolled around. Emile had no idea if he was still alive and in any case, had no way to track him down.

As for the bride, Sonia had been an only child. Both her parents were killed in an auto accident when she was three and she was shuffled off to her only living relative in Canada, her mother's sister, one Auntie Emm, whose social activities revolved solely around playing the organ at church on Sundays and organizing church picnics.

Emm had her own problems. She was diagnosed as an obsessive-compulsive who had a morbid fear of germs. She made Sonia a pair of plastic wraps out of Saran Wrap for his feet and made her wash his hands exactly six times before a meal.

By the time she was seven, Sonia's hands were raw and bloody and she had difficulty holding a pencil. That would have been a problem had the child gone to school, but Sonia never did. Emm didn't believe in schools and homeschooled the girl.

When she was fourteen, Sonia escaped from Emm's asylum in northern Quebec. She was offered a ride by a trucker who was transporting a load of sheep. It was the first time Sonia had ever touched an animal and she was so enamored with the softness of the wool, that she slept in the back with them, snuggled amidst the fleece.

"I can take you to Baie-Comeau," the driver said in between chews of tobacco. "I've got a buddy there who's goin' to Montreal. Got some of them free range chickens to deliver. If ya wanna go with him from, you can go with him. He's goin' to Montreal, like I said."

The ride from Baie-Comeau with the chickens was not as pleasant. They roamed freely in the back of the truck.

"Not allowed to keep 'em in cages," said the trucker. "That's why theys called free range. There was no room for Sonia in the front since the trucker used the remaining seat for his slobbering Bull Mastiff dog. "Travels with me everywhere. Good company. Drools a bit but that don't matter, he don't bite."

The chickens squawked constantly, bitter old hags. They defecated on the girl and pecked at her raw hands until they started oozing blood. Their feathers flew into Sonia's mouth and ears.

She was let off in Montreal and wandered the streets of the Old City, foraging for food in back alleys. She became a street urchin, an uneducated dirty girl, one who was bound to live in abject poverty, bound to taste life's bitter handouts. She begged daily and felt the cold constantly. She was loveless and unemployed, unemployable too. Another victim. End of story.

But astonishingly, saviors arrived for the girl. They promised to take care of her needs. They offered her food, a home, and a chance for a better life. It was the ladies of the Roman Catholic Church who rode to the rescue on their bibles, which Sonia readily latched onto.

Following the marriage, Sonia and Emile decided they needed a fresh start. Marseilles seemed ideal. It was a French-speaking city and far away from all the nonsense that had plagued them in Quebec. Moreover, Sonia had a distant cousin living there.

It was an easier transition than they imagined. Sonia paved the way, visiting her cousin who ended up sponsoring her. She then found a two-bedroom apartment in the first arrondissement, near Marseille's Old Port. It was an ideal location for Sonia, given the close proximity to the city's many churches; she could easily walk to Augustin Chapel and St. Vincent de Paul Church. Close by was the outdoor fish market, open daily from 8 am – 1 pm, and that pleased her immensely, knowing that Emile loved seafood. It got so that Sonia obtained the secret from the various fish mongers about how to prepare Marseille's famous Bouillabaisse, the very savoury fish soup. Turbot, Monkfish, Scorpion Fish, Sea Robin, European Conger – she came to find out that the more fish added to the stock, the better.

How exactly the French government got it wrong was a mystery. For when Sonia started the process to bring her husband to the country, they classified him as a "resident alien of extraordinary ability," an immigration category reserved for athletes, celebrities, scientists, and someone "highly extraordinary in their field." Since Emile was now an ex-athlete with a criminal record, the faux-pas was astounding. Nonetheless, it got him into the country in a hurry and he quietly settled into the two-bedroom apartment, laying low and determined not to make waves.

For the first two or three years, the marriage moved along nicely. Both Emile and Sonia were happy simply not to be alone. They attended church every Sunday and in the summer, the sermons were followed by afternoon picnics where the contented couple would just laze about in the mid -day sun, soaking up the ambient heat of the day. Emile preferred those days to all others. He had gotten a job as a mechanic trainee and although he liked the money, he found that all that bending and kneeling was bad for his legs. He would often come home dog-tired and needed Sonia's gentle massages to revive him. But Sundays were different. He could do nothing all day long and that suited his weary body just fine.

In the fourth year of marriage, their daughter Solange was born. It hadn't been an easy pregnancy for Sonia. The baby moved and kicked day and night and it was made all the worse by Emile's unwillingness to help out. Sonia found herself toiling daily in the hot kitchen, whipping up humongous meals to quell her husband's enormous appetite. She also continued to work tirelessly on behalf of the church, spreading the word of God to all who would listen, and many who wouldn't. She felt pushed to the limit and in continual need of rest, but it was never forthcoming. Her lack of attention to her own needs seemed to have compromised her heath – when Solange was born, Sonia had difficulty producing enough milk and the baby had to be bottle-fed.

Despite Emile's disdain for anything related to kitchen duties, he was, generally speaking, a good father and husband. Although he couldn't tolerate changing Solange's diapers – he said it made him want to bring up – he did his best for his family. Although physically broken up at the end of each working day, he continued on with his mechanic's trade, pulling in decent money which he turned over to his wife for managing. He even had dreams for his daughter, dreams that he had once had for himself. When Solange was four, he'd go outside and play pitch and catch with her. For his daughter's fifth birthday, he bought her a plastic baseball glove and bat. "Never too young to get 'em started," he would tell Sonia.

And so it went. It was good. It was steady. It was what it was. That is, until Solange's eighth year, when Emile started to slide. He missed a few Sundays at the church and then a few more, instead going to a bar to watch a game...football or baseball, it didn't really matter. Quaffing a few brews and enjoying a game with the boys seemed to be what he needed. Something was happening to him, something he couldn't readily understand. His old ways seemed to be simply catching up with him.

He began complaining – about his wife's food, about his job, his co-workers, his daughter's behaviour, about the apartment, about the rainy weather which he said made his legs arthritic, about his being mulatto and about how life had given him a raw deal. He denigrated everything and everybody. But the thing that upset Sonia the most, that caused her the most concern, was his growing disenchantment with the Lord. She told him that although he may not have made great decisions in the past – which is perhaps what had led to his current deep-seated unhappiness – if he would only put his trust once more in the Lord, then his path would be illuminated. God forgives, now he had to do the same.

In spite of his wife's gentle words Emile went on complaining. He began wearing a bandanna around the house. "It's got to do with my roots," he would say, although he never explained further. He added that a white woman could never understand.

One night after work, he happened upon Amaud's Cafe. The rest is history. He liked everything about the place, from the psychedelic strobe balls that hung from the ceiling to the heavy rhythmic beats of the reggae and funk music that emanated from overlarge speakers. The other patrons were similar to himself, surly outsiders of one sort or another who were generally dissatisfied with life. The go-go dancers were fine and better still were the assorted alcoholics and liars, women who had seen better days and listened to his tales of former glory while sidling up close to his large body.

He started missing work, a day here and there. Then two days in a row. Despite his wife's urgings, he wouldn't get out of bed. And when he finally did, he would sometimes give her a back-handed slap for her nagging and head straight for Amaud's, where he would spend entire days.

Sonia missed having her father around. The old Emile that is. The non-complaining Emile. The one who bought her comic books and double-bubble gum and chocolates. Who would lift her high in the air and spin her around and around like a whirlybird. She couldn't understand why her dad didn't like anything anymore, why he wouldn't play baseball with her. Why he didn't seem to like her.

One night Emile didn't return home. The next day Sonia went looking for him. She looked all over town, even venturing into Amaud's where she was met with a silence so overwhelming she was sure the people there must have known something. But they didn't, or if they did, at least they didn't let on. Where Emile went was a mystery. He just vanished. And that was the end of that.

Meanwhile, Sonia had a daughter to look after. She took a job as a chambermaid at a hotel to make ends meet and relied upon the women of the church for emotional support. She was a good mother to Solange but her natural tendency was to smother the girl. She was overprotective to a fault. Her daughter had to tell her where she was going to be every minute of the day and was forced to come right home from school, no exceptions. That made it difficult for her to maintain friendships but she didn't mind too much. With her father gone, she understood that her mother was the only family she had left. That was how it stayed until the day Sonia died.

Her death was most unusual. She was found by a fisherman face down in the waters of the New Port, a bible in her skirt pocket and Emile's old bandanna around her neck. The coroner said she had slipped and fallen on a rock and most probably hit her head before drowning. The cause of death was listed as an accidental drowning but if the truth be known, the autopsy had been performed haphazardly, in a slip-shod manner. With her death being somewhat unusual, a more thorough coroner might have checked the undersides of her fingernails for DNA to see whether she had fought off an attacker, if in fact there was an attacker. Or perhaps whether there was semen in her vagina. He may even have given the odd bite marks on her neck a bit more attention. But he did none of those things. Actually, since the police quickly determined that no one had any motive to murder Sonia Epaul, not even Emile – who was no longer around in any case – foul play was not even considered by them nor the coroner, leading to the unremitting conclusion that you can't find what you don't look for.

Chapter Twenty

For the forty or so minutes that it took Suskind to tell the story, I didn't say a single word. I was flabbergasted by the vast amount of information she had accumulated during such a short period of time. It just seemed inconceivable that anyone could dig up that much detail about a person's background. I wondered how she did it...I simply had to ask.

"It's a good question, Mr. Pringle, but I should tell you that I'm not quite through. There's more. Much more. However, I think what you owe might not quite cut it. Imagine, $1,000 for an entire history. Plus exacting detail about where to find her. Doesn't seem to make much sense, don't you think?"

"You're a scammer!" I shouted it loud enough that a few people at adjacent tables turned my way. I took a deep breath and lowered my voice. "And, I signed a contract. Doesn't a contract mean anything with you?"

Suskind took the very document out of a briefcase. "In fact, I have it right here," she said. "Hmmm, let me see." She scanned the contract as if she were reviewing it for the very first time.

"Don't be an idiot," I uttered.

At once she put the piece of paper down. "You're going to regret you said that, Mr. Pringle."

It was becoming abundantly clear that I was dealing with some sort of weird modern-day Mata Hari, a woman who operated not as she appeared and who had no compunction about sticking a shiv up my spine for the sake of a few more bucks. And that's what she wanted, I had no doubt – more money for her services.

"It says right here," she continued, now holding the contract up to eye-level, "that *the $1,000 fee might be altered if the scope of work is deemed to be excessive. This is at the agent's sole discretion.*"

Suskind slid the contract across the table at me. "And I'm the agent," she said. "And you, the client. It's all in the fine print."

I began reading. I must dutifully admit that I hadn't read the contract. Why would I? I had no reason not to trust Suskind. Now, with each word that I perused, it became clear that she was the very sort of shady character she said she didn't do business with. But it was all there, in mind-numbing black and white.

"How much?" I said, after I had finished.

"Another $1,000 would do nicely."

"That's blackmail," I spat. "and you know it."

"Just part of doing business is what I call it."

If the café had been empty, I would have strangled Suskind. Her neck was there for the taking. But instead, I took the contract and very deliberately and slowly tore it in half.

"Like I already said, Mr. Pringle, it's all about regret. And you are so going to regret what you just did."

Without saying another word, I stood up and slammed the door on my way out.

My apartment beckoned. I just wanted to lie down and forget things. But when I got there, I saw that the narrow flight of stairs leading up was occupied. Two young men were balancing a massive leather sofa up, trying desperately not to be crushed.

"Hold your end up more," the guy at the very top said.

I was concerned that the guy at the bottom end was going to tumble backward into me. He seemed to be losing his grip. As it was, there was no getting to my place. I moved a few steps back and waited.

It was like watching a Laurel and Hardy movie. The two movers kept on giving each other instructions that turned out badly. Both wanted to be in charge of the operation and each step forward was a misstep; the sofa wouldn't fit around the corner so they tried lifting the sofa on its end…then it was too high for the ceiling. "Maybe we should just cut it in half," said one.

"Yah, you wouldn't say that if it was your sofa," countered his friend.

After some twenty minutes or so in which the movers fumbled and bumbled their way up the stairs, taking a chunk of the plaster from the wall with them, the deed was done. They sat down exhausted onto the sofa, huffing mightily and holding their heads.

"Fuck, I can't believe we made it."

"If you had only listened to me, we would have made it much quicker."

That started a whole new row where name-calling became the order of the day. I couldn't tell the two apart; they were slope-shouldered lanky youths in their late teens with identical shaggy-dog haircuts that covered their eyes. They blew gusts of air upward to remove the hair, only to have the strands fall back. The only difference that I could see was that one was wearing a Che Guevera t-short and the other an overly large checked lumberjack shirt.

"Is this for Bumblegate?" I said.

"Who's Bumblegate?" said the Che Guevera guy, eyeing me suspiciously. "And who are you?"

"I live just down the hall."

"Uh huh."

I realized that after the Suskind episode, that I felt a need to talk to someone. Anyone.

"Mind if I sit down?"

"Take a load off, dude," said Che.

I sat between the two. "I see you're wearing a Che t-shirt," I said. "Do you even know who he was?"

"Dude, are you my like history teacher or something? Of course I do."

"So?"

Che sat up straight. "He was like the leader of a revolution. *Re-vo-lu-tion* as they say in Cuba," he said, putting a heavy accent on the last syllable. "He was backing the Sandinistas because they were oppressed."

Lumberjack guy chimed in. "Like man, you are so out of it. He was backing the Federales, not the Sandinistas, you jackass."

Another round of vicious name calling began, punctuated by bursts of fists that bounced off each other's shoulders. Seeing as how I was caught directly in the line of fire, I interjected: "Hey, hey, calm down!" I nudged them back to their respective corners of the sofa.

No question, I was sitting in the middle of two clowns. But who were they anyway? I didn't really care much, but I was curious. Still, I tried to keep the conversation going.

"You guys must be in school, I take it?"

"Yah," said lumberjack guy, exhaling deeply.

"What're you studying?"

"The same thing," he said.

"And what's that?"

"Video gaming. We're gonna be designers."

"Centennial College, that's where we go," said Che, now much calmed down.

I thought it would be a good idea to advise them of my interest in Camelot. It wasn't.

"Camelot?" smirked Che. "That is like so fuckin' old. "Dude, nobody plays that anymore."

"I have to agree with my lame brother here," said lumberjack guy. "That technology is like hundreds of years old. It is so crippled."

I wasn't sure what he meant by that but understood that it wasn't good. Suddenly Che took out a joint and pointed it at me. "Want to join?"

"Sure."

We passed the fag around and as I inhaled deeply, a new sense of calm washed over me. The Suskind fiasco slowly started fading.

"So what do you do?" asked Che, his head lolling back.

"I write books."

"Like on paper?"

"Yes, like on paper."

"Dude, that is so passé," said lumberjack guy. "Nobody reads books anymore. Soon it'll go like the way of Pig Latin."

"You mean Latin?" I said.

"No, I mean like Pig Latin. Do you ever hear anyone speak it anymore?"

In a twisted way, he had a point.

"The problem with books," said Che, sounding very professorial, "is that after you read the first page, there's like another three hundred pages of the same after that."

"Yah, he's right," said lumberjack guy. "Nobody wants to read that much. Nobody should have to read that much. If you can't make your point in one-hundred-and-forty characters, like on Twitter, then you should shut up."

Che clapped his hands. "Yep, there's no question." he exclaimed. "You see, because man, even if you somehow feel the need to go over that limit, you can stop! Put in emoticons."

"I don't know what that is."

The brothers looked at each other and sniggered.

"Like from the 17th century, dude, "said lumberjack guy to his brother.

"I know. Such a wanker." Che pulled on his t-short. "Even this guy would know. And he was born way long ago, before you."

"But he's dead."

"Yah but when he was alive, I bet you he would know."

"So tell me."

"Emoticons are graphics to express how you feel. You ever see those happy faces on computers?"

I nodded.

"That's an emoticon."

Lumberjack guy took over. "Man, you don't even need words like in your text. You can say everything you want to say just by putting in those emoticons. Everyone will know what you're getting at."

I stood up. "It's been a blast fellas, but I have to go." I hesitated for a moment. "My name's Karl, by the way. And oh yeah, before I forget, what about this couch? Are you delivering it for Bumblegate again?"

The guys looked at each other once again and shook their heads. "Like we said, we don't know who that is," said Che.

"The old lady who lives in that apartment," I said, pointing. "Brenda Bumblegate."

"Oh her," said Che. "She died a few weeks ago. Me and my brother here are moving stuff in, kind of gradually. We've already been in three weeks now."

I was stunned. Bumblegate had died? When? And why hadn't anyone notified me? I asked the boys if they knew.

"The landlord said he knocked on your door many times," said lumberjack guy, "but that you never answered."

"You should always answer your door," added Che. "Then people will know if you're home or not."

I walked into my apartment and crashed onto the bed, arms and legs spread eagle. It made sense now that I thought of it. Although I had heard knocks in the weeks gone by, I was cocooning at the time. I never answered. And with all the time I had spent with my friends under the Bloor Street Viaduct or at Carnival City, I hadn't been in the apartment much of late. Still, the death struck me hard. It's not that I cared in the least for the woman, it's just that you always expect things to remain the same. And unfortunately, they never do.

That evening, instead of heading out to visit my ravine friends, I decided to treat myself to a meal. I was feeling so out of sorts what with the Suskind caper and with Bumblegate's death and concluded that I needed a good chow down. And there was no better place than the Country Style Hungarian Restaurant on Bloor, near Borden Street. I had been going there for years, whenever I felt stressed. The waitresses were always friendly with me, the portions humongous, and the prices in line with my meager budget. The place was perpetually busy with a mixed crowd of older Eastern Europeans, young students, and artists. I always brought a book to keep me company but rarely read. It was simply enjoyable to be there, watch people, with there being absolutely no pressure to eat quickly and get out.

The food at Country Style was standard East European fare. Stick-to-your-ribs goulash and schnitzel. I loved the fried potatoes, the pickled beets, and the cabbage rolls with dollops of sour cream. On this occasion though, I ordered the Chicken Paprikash over a bed of dumplings. For dessert I had the apple strudel.

I sat in my seat, hands clasped behind my head, completely sated and at peace. I felt so much better than when I came in. And why? Simply because of food? Yes, it was like dining in someone's living room. My parent's, maybe. Exactly like a time warp.

The feeling of equanimity all ended rather abruptly when I made the unwise move to open the envelope that I brought with me. It was another letter from the Toronto

Star, but unlike the first one, this I kept. The content was straightforward. It talked about how they had done some due diligence with regard to their short story contest and discovered that my story Starchild had been previously published. The third place winner would be moved into my second place slot and the fourth place finisher, who had obviously been out of the awards, would slide to third place. There would be a retraction of my story in an upcoming edition of the newspaper. The kicker however, was that I was to immediately pay back the $2,000 they had given me. There was a due date for the return of the money. Legal action would be instituted if I failed to do so. It was not what one might call a friendly letter. Hardly, it was rather pointed.

The paprikash suddenly sat heavy in my stomach. I considered a retort to The Star, saying that as how they had failed to check on matters, that they themselves were equally culpable. As culpable as I. In that regard, I would be willing to pay one-half, $1,000. I turned the idea over in my head but gave it up. I knew I had no chance. I gave the waitress a $2 tip on my $17 meal and headed out the door into the night.

Chapter Twenty-One

There were knocks on my door and the phone rang but each time I answered, no one was there. I would run to the door or pick up the phone rather quickly and...nothing. I peered down the hall to see if the dopey brothers were up to no good but their apartment door was closed. On one occasion, I did hear footsteps traveling down the steps and chased after them. But it was too late; whoever knocked had vanished. These were disturbing episodes but not nearly as upsetting as when I came home after a day out and discovered that my apartment had been ransacked. Nothing was taken but everything was in a mess. Drawers had been pulled out, the contents of which were spilled onto the carpeting. Food littered the kitchen floor. The toilet was stuffed with copious wads of toilet paper, necessitating that I extract everything by hand; it was gross, to say the least. In the bedroom, my pillows had been cut wide open and the foam within thrown about. The bed sheets were balled up into tight knots.

I considered calling the cops, but didn't. What could they do? There were no leads, I knew that. With the exception of Rivka's jewelry, which I hid beneath a wonky floorboard in my closet, I had nothing of any value that a thief might want. Moreover, except for some of Rivka's pharmaceuticals, nothing was missing. It was theft and vandalism perpetrated by amateurs, pure and simple.

But as I thought about it long and hard, it became obvious that I had been targeted. After all, I lived on the second floor above a variety store. If someone were interested in simply vandalizing properties, there were many in the Market that was easier pickings at the street level. I also wondered how anyone had gotten into the place. Unless you had a key or picked the lock…

I went downstairs and looked closely at the keyhole. I could detect tiny scratch marks on the metal and that was all. Simply the result of wear and tear. The keyhole itself looked intact. It was obvious – if someone got in, they did so because they either had a key to the door or else someone let them in.

Back in the apartment, I began the onerous task of cleaning up. This was so much worse than when I cleaned Rivka's hovel. This was my place, after all. My privacy had been invaded. Worst of all was when I ventured into the washroom. Many of the blades that were streaked with blood still remained and on the bathroom mirror someone had written in lipstick: C U T T R E.

I needed more money in a hurry. I had to pay back The Star pronto. I didn't need any more hassles, certainly no legal action. So I took some of the last few items from Rivka's stolen jewelry down to the pawnshop on Church. This time, I was determined to get the exact sales price of the goods. I added them up – $1415.00.

"I'll give you $ 1175.00," said the pawnbroker. "Not a penny more."

"I know for a fact that this jewelry costs $ 1415.00 and that's what I want. And not a penny less for me, sir."

Although I had done business with this same guy before, I noticed that today he was eyeing me somewhat suspiciously. "You've been bringing this stuff in on a regular basis," he finally said. "So I have to ask you – where are you getting it?"

"I don't see why that's any of your business," I said.

"Wait right here."

The pawnbroker retired to a back room. I could hear the unmistakable sound of a rotary phone's wheel turning. Such a dinosaur. I walked behind the counter and leaned my ear to the door.

"Yes, he's here right now," I heard the pawnbroker whisper. "I'll try and keep him. He's selling more jewelry."

I didn't hear the rest of the conversation. I scrambled out of the store and ran as fast as I could north on Church. I didn't stop until I reached the Gay Village, just north of Wellesley Street. I bent over at the waist, my hands on my knees, trying to catch a breath. Drops of perspiration dotted my forehead.

I walked slowly up the street, my frozen hands deep in my pockets. I hardly spent any time in this neck of the woods. There was really nothing for me here. There was an organic butcher shop called Cumbrae's that I would have liked to frequent, if only I'd had the money. There were lots of bars, coffee shops, restaurants, and plenty of guys wearing leather and sporting big black moustaches and beards. If my sexual orientation had been different, then maybe. Nonetheless, as I made my way up Church Street, I felt safe, like I was amongst others who perhaps had been felt like outsiders once in their lives. It was a difficult feeling to articulate but it didn't matter. I could walk with ease and not worry, that's all that was important.

And still I did have worries. I needed to get rid of the jewelry I was carrying – a gold bracelet, a diamond pendant necklace, and a watch. I fingered the items in my pocket and removed the Gucci watch. It was still firmly ensconced within its case where a small card outlining its properties was attached: *U-Play Collection, Black-plated Stainless Steel Bezel...* I stopped reading. Such bullshit, $650 for a watch that simply told time.

I figured that I should try another pawnbroker. I briefly considered that I might take out an ad in Kijiji or Craig's List but quickly nixed the idea. The entire transaction, from putting the ad in to waiting for the appropriate buyer to show up, would take too long. I needed the money right away.

I returned home and googled *Pawnbrokers Toronto*. I found one on Dundas Street West, in the Junction area. That was perfect, away from the downtown core and Church Street. I couldn't be sure that the cops weren't searching the streets for me; I felt certain that the old man in the pawn shop I had just been to had indeed called them. Maybe he just got suspicious, maybe the cops had notified the pawnshops in the area to be on the lookout for stolen goods. Who knew? But I couldn't take another chance.

I took the Bloor subway and got off at Keele Station. There I took a bus to Dundas Street. Before I entered the pawn shop, I took the watch out of its case and picked up a small stone from the ground, which I used to put a tiny scratch on the watch face. I figured that might remove suspicion. It worked. I pointed out the flaw to the shop owner and advised him that the jewelry belonged to my deceased brother and sister-in-law. Tragic. Murder- suicide. I got $1125 for the lot and didn't bargain a cent higher.

Later that evening I wrote out a cheque payable to the Toronto Star and mailed it off, enclosed within was the letter they had sent me. I added no comments. Then I headed out to the ravine under the Bloor Street Viaduct. I just wanted to drink myself silly with my friends.

I still had some money and a few pieces of Rivka's jewelry. But soon I would run out. Certainly I had no cash left for the likes of an Ingrid, which was a shame. All I could do was think about her nightly, and satisfy my urges that way.

The phone calls and knocks on my door continued. As time went on, I began to ignore them. I'd just lie in bed until they went away. I'm not saying they weren't discon- certing – especially when they happened in the middle of the night – but I understood who was responsible. Now I knew. I also knew that unless I made good on the contract, they would not end. Or perhaps they would morph into something worse, like my getting the shit beat out of me. I couldn't take a chance.

So a few days after the sale of the jewelry, I headed to Suskind's office and offered to pay up. Not quite the $1,000 that she said, but a negotiated figure. I started at $500 and inched up to $550, $575…increments of $25. Then $50.

When I hit upon $750, we sealed the deal. I despised her but also realized she held the key to something better in my life, like another chance with Solange. I wrote her a cheque for $1500, the $750 owing as part of the original contract, plus an additional $750 as part of the trumped-up and bogus contract. We amended the contract to reflect a final price of $1500 and this time I read every single word. Every fucking word.

Chapter Twenty-Two

Four days later I met with Suskind at Starbuck's on Bloor Street, kitty-corner to Jarvis Street. I purposely gave it a few days, just to see if the insane phone calls and door knocking would stop. They all did.

We sat at a table near a window and watched as a photographer took pictures of a bride and groom across the street. They were kissing, hugging, and mugging for the camera. On one occasion, the groom carried the bride in his arms across the street. It was an inordinately warm winter day, suitable for such frivolities.

"Ever have those taken of you?" said Suskind.

"What do you mean?"

"Wedding shots. Have you ever been married?"

I poured two creams into my coffee and stirred. "You know so much about me, why don't you answer that."

"You've been missing out."

"How do you figure?"

"It's part of life. As you philosophers say, an experiential part of living."

Great. Now I was being given a lecture from a P.I., something I didn't need in the least.

"I'm not suited for that sort of thing," I said huffily.

"You'd be surprised at what people are suited for."

"Look, I'm free and that's all I care about."

"So you're free?"

"As a bird."

"And what exactly are you free to do, Mr. Pringle? You have no job, no family, no responsibilities, nothing."

"If you want to know the truth, I have none of the sludge that bogs people like you down. If I want to say that the moon is made of green cheese, I can do that. Or if I profess that five plus seven equals one-hundred-and-five, I'm at complete liberty to do so. "

The P.I. crossed her arms defiantly across her chest. "I suspect, Mr. Pringle, that you just spout out these handy little phrases from time to time but that inwardly, you don't believe a word of it. Of course, you would never admit to it but I have no doubt it's true. At some point, everyone is answerable to someone. And we're all answerable to ourselves."

Suskind pushed her business card across the table at me.

Sheila Suskind, M.A. Psych.

Private Investigator

That explained the attempt at playing Freud. But I wasn't impressed. If anything, my disdain for the woman grew. Psychology wasn't nearly as difficult a discipline as Philosophy. And the universities were churning out garden-variety M.A.'s in Psychology all over the place. The fact that she had a job following people around was proof.

"My impression," continued Suskind, "is that your world is very small. That you exist within a three or four kilometer radius in the city and rarely venture beyond that.

And the reason you wanted me to track down Solange is because underneath it all, you're desperately unhappy with how tiny that world is. Finding her may open things up for you, at least that's your hope. Your salvation."

If I had had a gun, and knew how to operate it, I would have shot Suskind in the space between her eyes, right then and there. It wouldn't have mattered that other patrons in the café witnessed the massacre. In fact, I would have gladly led the police to the body.

I didn't want to engage any further in this psychological profiling. I hadn't paid Suskin $1750 for that. So I simply said: "Enough. Just get on with it."

"Ok, it's all about Solange. I get it. That's what you really want to talk about." She took a sip of her coffee and said: "Fine. Here's what I can tell you." Then she began where she had left off.

"After her mother's death and with her father nowhere to be found, Solange was put up for adoption. She lucked out, ending up with a fabulous family in Loir et Cher, about one-hundred- and-forty kilometers from Paris. Jean-Pierre and Geraldine Depardieu. They had inherited a farm in that region but that is another story, which I shall get to.

So before Solange's arrival, Jean-Pierre had been an account executive at Publicis Groupe, an advertising agency in Paris. The money was superb but the hours long and the pressure high. On those occasions when he would visit his uncle's farm in the Loire Valley, his stays never failed to evoke in him pangs of discontent with his present life. He suspected that things could be so much different, if only he had the courage to make a change.

Geraldine was no less busy in Paris. Blinded from an accident during her youth, she taught residents Braille at the Hopital Quinze-Vingts during the day and pottery at night at a school for continuing education. An expert potter for many years, she had struggled against her innermost desire to give up her day job and become a full-time artist. The problem always came back to the same thing – money. Artists are the working poor, her family would always tell her. There was something else. She was fiercely independent, whether because of her handicap or not was difficult to say. But she railed against any notions that she was any less capable than others, any less able to be financially secure. That meant two jobs and long hours. Even when she married Jean-Pierre, she staunchly refused any suggestions that she should give up her day job and concentrate on her pottery. Her husband's salary would have easily allowed her to do so but she would absolutely have no part of it. So she toiled at the two jobs but inwardly wished she could concentrate all her efforts at the potter's wheel."

At this point, I interrupted Suskind. "Is this all necessary?" I said. "You're giving me tons of information that I probably don't need. Just like the last time. And in fact, I've heard some of this from Solange herself. We're not exactly strangers, you know."

Suskind looked at me as if I were the devil incarnate. "Don't you want to know what kind of woman Solange is? Where she's from? How she was raised?"

"I'm not sure."

"The other thing you should know, Mr. Pringle, is that women only reveal to men what they know they can handle.

My suspicion is that the stuff Solange fed you was pabulum because that's what she thought you were capable of ingesting."

"Fuck." I banged my closed fist lightly on the table.

"Just let me finish, Mr. Pringle. Because I suspect that after I tell you what I'm about to tell you, that you'll be running into that woman's arms. At least that's what you should do."

Suskind was so daft that I couldn't bear arguing with her. I went to the counter for another coffee and sat back down with my brew, waving my hand for her to carry on.

"When the farm came their way after the sudden death of Jean-Pierre's uncle, Jean-Pierre and Geraldine couldn't believe their good fortune. Of course they were devastated by his premature demise but never had any inkling they were in his will. It was as if the man was looking down at them from heaven, lighting their path. They had always adored him and looked upon his joie de vivre and carefree lifestyle with envy, envy that was borne of their own desires, their own unfulfilled longings. As I mentioned, they too had long wished they could summon up the courage to make the necessary changes to live in a more harmonious arrangement with their own souls."

I interrupted once more. This time because I was curious.

"I forgot to ask. How did Geraldine end up blind?"

"Nice. Now you're interested, Pringle. I have your attention. Look, the story is that when she was six years old, she had been standing at the bottom of a garbage chute in an apartment building when someone threw a bottle of acid down. Not only did the acid blind her but she suffered terrible scarring, mostly around her eyes and mouth According to Solange, one doctor told her she should be thankful she was blind, the scarring was so bad. Imagine saying that to a little girl."

"I guess," I mumbled.

"Solange told me that over the years, Geraldine had a lot of corrective surgeries. Magic hands worked on her. A lot of good doctors. But the skin around her eyes was pulled tight, waxy, like it had melted. Nothing could change that. And interestingly, she had an eye made of glass. A blue one I'm told, to match her other, unseeing eye. Just for cosmetic reasons."

The thought of having a glass eye made me nauseous. How would you put it in? Take it out? Clean it? I didn't dare say as much. To filter the thought from my mind, I did ask what the couple looked like.

"Jean-Pierre about six feet in height, a few inches taller than Geraldine. Both have olive skin colour with and full lips. And now that they're on the farm much of the time, their normal uniform is a pair of jeans, work boots that are scuffed, and plaid shirts that look like retreads from the Sally Ann. Actually, Solange tells me that when she visits – which is quite often – she dons that same gear. No pretentions in their little slice of land."

"And how old?" I surprised myself, I was becoming a regular Chatty Cathy.

"I guess they'd be in their mid-sixties now."

"And how old is Solange?"

"Thirty-seven. It's a good age."

I wasn't sure what Suskind meant by that last comment but let it slide.

"So back to the story. The farm that the Jean-Pierre and Geraldine inherited is spread over two and a half acres. They have a quaint sign attached to the front gate that says: L'amour vainc tout. Know what that means, Mr. Pringle?"

"I'm not up on my French," I sniffed.

"It means 'love conquers all.'"

Sentimental crap. But as with the glass eye episode, I held my tongue.

"Anyway, so they run it pretty much the way it had always been run; that is to say, not in the manner of your typical farm. Jean-Pierre's uncle had been an artist and the farm was a place to paint and revel in solitude and nature, his Walden Pond. You do know Walden Pond?"

"P-l-e-a-s-e," I croaked. Suskind was so annoying.

"The only real change to the place is that Jean-Pierre and Geraldine put in a rather extensive organic vegetable garden. That and the dozen chickens in the barn give the farm some semblance that it is being run by farmers. But nothing could be further from the truth. They're city people, Paris born and raised. I should also mention that Solange has a horse there. A 3-year-old mare called Blondine. That's her baby. She loves riding her through the countryside and sometimes takes kids from the city to the farm to ride as well."

"What kids?"

"Well you know she teaches and sometimes some of the older kids from the school visit. But she also volunteers at a school for children with mental challenges. And it's those children who come. They ride the ponies – Blondine is too high for them."

I hadn't known Solange volunteered. I wondered why she never told me.

Suskind nodded at me and continued: "So inheriting the farm made it easier for Jean-Pierre and Geraldine to change. Both gave up their day jobs and started in new directions. Geraldine concentrated her efforts on setting herself up as a full-time artist, obtaining an agent, contacting galleries, doing exhibits, and generally getting her work out for public viewing. She had a kiln installed on the farm that allowed her to work out of the house. She still comes into the city one afternoon a week to teach pottery. And, as if all those changes weren't enough, she also began to supplement her artistic salary by starting her own line of jams and jellies.

As for Jean-Pierre, quitting his advertising job was perhaps a more traumatic move. It meant giving up a full-time salary in order to go back to school and work on a master's degree in art history, his first true love. But I guess you can say that after some soul-searching, they both determined that they could live without Jean-Pierre's big salary and still live well. In fact, they could live better, more peaceably. Through diligent investing they had managed to put away a tidy sum of money and since there was no mortgage on the farm, they knew they could make do. The final step was to well up the courage within to make the final break. Once they did however, they knew there was no turning back."

"Jams, huh?"

"*Tante Mathilde: Confitures et Gelees* – that's the name. Pear-honey, fig, plum, of course strawberry. Oh, and uh, blueberry-lime, grape, and rhubarb. Seven in all. I hear the business is thriving."

"Nice, if you're into that sort of thing."

"Anyway, it's an eight-room farmhouse. Five cats now share the place, mostly strays who wandered in and never left. Chickens roam freely in the barn next to two Shetland ponies named *Gloria* and *Mollie*. And then of course there's Mitch, Geraldine's seeing-eye dog. Golden retriever. And, oh yes, Blondine."

"A regular menagerie."

"I notice a little disdain in your voice, Mr. Pringle."

"I'm not really into animals. They need attention, and I have no such paternal instincts."

"*Paternal instincts?* Huh, that's a strange term to use. You mean, you have to take care of them, is that what you're saying?"

I wasn't about to answer Suskind. She wanted to trip me up, it was obvious. So I just waited her out, my arms folded across my chest.

"Ok, look, I brought all this up because you should know that after Jean-Pierre and Geraldine settled into the farm, they thought about adopting. I don't know the entire story about why they didn't have a child of their own, but it's not important. The point is that they were ready for an addition to their family and that's when they adopted Solange. It was serendipity, you might say. The timing was perfect at both ends."

Suskind appeared pleased with herself. A slight smile curled her lips. She then excused herself and retreated to the washroom.

I looked absently out the window and contemplated the story to date. Suddenly I wasn't sure that I really wanted to meet up with Solange once again. For one, I had time against me. More to the point, I wasn't really sure I could offer her anything. She had had a rough go of it at first, just like me. But she had come out the other end a fine human being. Salt of the earth. Whereas I...well, who was I kidding?...I was a rogue.

Suskind returned.

"Maybe that's enough," I said.

"Mr. Pringle, you haven't received your money's worth," she said emphatically. "There's not much more but you should really hear the rest."

My heart felt heavy, like it was weighted down with rocks. And Suskind's insistence that I keep my ears open only served to make it worse. It was like she was my shadow, following me around and making me ingest the cold reality of my situation. And yet...and yet...the woman did not see it the same way. For as soon as I told her to begin, she said:

"I can sense you're despairing, but don't. Solange is a grand human being, but a human being all the same. Like many of us, she's looking for love...it's something that's eluded her."

"Don't despair? Is that what you said?"

Suskind rested her elbows on the table and stared at me. "Yes, because people who go out of their way to contact others usually do so for reasons of the heart."

There was no arguing with this psychopath. She seemed to read my mind, the low-life.

"How would you know she's looking for love?" I said, trying to shift the conversation away from me.

"Because she told me."

"No boyfriend?"

"No. Ah, but she was married a few years back. Would you like to hear about that?"

"Why not…" I said quietly.

"Well, about fifteen years ago, Solange found the true love of her life. He was a Lieutenant with the National Police, situated in Paris. Their daughter – Angeline – was born the following year. By all accounts, it was a wonderful marriage. Of course Solange always worried about her husband's job. She worried that when she kissed him goodbye in the morning, that that would be the last she would see of him. Now, as it turned out, her fears were misplaced. But only slightly. For you see, Mr. Pringle, he did die. Not on duty as had been her concern but rather in a car crash. The driver who caused the accident was going the wrong way. He was drunk. It happened along the Autoroute du Soleil, a rather ironic name for a highway."

"Like I told you, my French is bad."

"It translates to Highway of the Sun."

"So Solange must have been inconsolable."

"You don't know the half of it, Mr. Pringle. Because her husband was on his way to see his in-laws in the Loire Valley, Jean-Pierre and Geraldine. Solange was busy and stayed behind. But he had a passenger with him. Two dead in the car."

"You mean…"

"It's true. Their daughter died in that accident."

I had nothing to say. The story exhausted me. I couldn't bear to hear another word.

"That was roughly seven years ago, Mr. Pringle," she continued. "Nobody ever gets over those sort of things. You just manage."

I shrugged.

"So Mr. Pringle, here's what you should know. Solange is back in Paris."

"What?!"

"She went back a few weeks ago to take of some business. But once again, don't despair, because she's returning for another six months. She loved it so much here that she asked her school for a further leave. She really wants to improve her English."

"When is she back?" I asked.

"Shortly. I'll call you."

"Not so bad, I guess."

"Before she left, Solange was going to school four days a week at the *Hansa Language Centre* on Eglinton Avenue, just west of Yonge Street. She lived with an English-speaking family in the area and cared for their two kids the days she wasn't at school. And during the days when she wasn't at Hansa, she went out for lunch with her ESL friends to *Hannah's Kitchen*. It's a café on Yonge Street, just south of Eglinton. They'd usually arrive at 12;10 or so. Every day during the work week except Thursday. I imagine that routine will continue when she returns."

There wasn't much else to say. I wondered how Suskind had obtained so much information, and so I asked her. Her answer was somewhat murky, mumbling something about having her own way of doing things. Undoubtedly she had managed to befriend Solange and garnered her trust. That was a given. Throughout the telling of the story, I actually got the impression that Suskind had grown fond of Solange. It was nothing I could put my finger on, just an intuitive sort of thing. She did say that there were plenty of police and court records regarding Emile and Sonia. And oh, that the murdered woman had kept a diary, which Solange read.

I began writing out a cheque for the remaining $1500 when Suskind reached across the table and touched my hand. "It's only $750," she said.

I looked at her askance.

"I never meant to actually charge you more than the original contract price. I just wanted to know that you were serious about locating Solange. That your intentions were good. Like I mentioned to you earlier on Mr. Suskind – *I was only messing with you.*"

I didn't understand any of it. Especially when Suskind once again pushed her business card in my direction. "If you ever want to talk…"

Chapter Twenty-Three

I don't know what caused me to do it, but as soon as I returned home, I looked carefully at the lock on my front door. I was no forensic expert but could have sworn that the keyhole had been widened considerably. It almost looked as if someone had jammed a screwdriver in there.

I walked about the apartment, contemplating what I might do. Briefly, I considered playing Camelot. I hadn't done so in a while but my interest now was almost non-existent. It might have had something to do with goofy Che and his brother, telling me I was playing an ancient game. More likely though, it was because I felt preoccupied by Suskind and all she had revealed. I had grown up reading about investigators like Sherlock Holmes and Jane Marple, and Suskind was not in the least like them. She had called me a 'fuck-up' and no one had ever said that to me. Well, Aaron had in a roundabout way but that was so very long ago. I also wondered if I wasn't getting myself into a hole, one I wouldn't be able to extricate myself from. Or rather, one I could, but at the expense of someone else.

I stopped pacing. I stood in the living room and gave the apartment the once over. It was a dump. Clothes were piled everywhere, dust had accumulated on surfaces, spider webs dominated some ceiling corners, the windows looked dirty, dishes were stacked in the sink. In the washroom, the floor was littered with razor blades.

The bedroom, with all of the pill bottles, looked like the refuge of a mad pharmacist. After the break-in, I had done what I could to restore order. But I had only taken care of the bare basics. My place was becoming as bad as Rivka's.

It was too much. I picked up the first piece of clothing. Then the second. And on it went. At first I did so laconically, like someone recently roused from sleep. After a few hours though, I increased the pace and with that, the apartment began taking shape. It was odd though, the feelings that a clean living space engendered in me. Because as I looked about, I came to the somewhat disturbing conclusion that even though I had initiated a massive clean-up, that the best I could do wasn't much at all – I really was residing in a pretty dismal apartment. 39- years-old and I was still living much as I had when I was a student. A threadbare existence. Nothing had changed, not really. The realization, one that slapped me in the face like a cold rag, was that I had always lived in a circus, complete with thinking machines, freaks, has-beens and underachievers. But moreover, I came to the conclusion that I was no longer the great performer. The days of performing mental gyrations, jumping from Plato's cupped hands onto Nietzsche's shoulders, a neat trick, just seemed inadequate.

I sat down at my computer, the very one I had purchased with some of the proceeds from the book sale. It had cost $199 and was refurbished from a computer store on Spadina Avenue, just north of College Street. Windows 7, Microsoft Word, High-Speed Internet Access...I didn't need anything else.

I hadn't been on Facebook for quite a while, not since I started accumulating 'friends' on the site because of my literary success. Now I saw the real carnage from my theft. The retraction that appeared in The Star had been posted directly onto my home page. The headline screamed out: *Toronto Writer Plagiarizes Story.* There were plenty of comments from those cyber friends of mine and sufficed to say, not one was supportive. They slandered me, calling me a slimeball, a disgrace to the human race, a piece of gunk that sticks to the bottom of your shoes. It went on and on. Some suggested that I be burned in a cauldron of bubbling oil, or flogged. One person wrote that I should do the right thing and hang myself. I had no idea humanity could stoop that low.

★

Gusting winds blew falling snow against the frosted window of my apartment. Looking out, I saw a solitary pedestrian walking backward into the face of the tempest, muffled and silent. The streets had been bleached milky white. Cars were parked haphazardly into mounds of snow, abandoned. I watched as the phantom pedestrian turned a corner and was gone from sight. Despite the inclement weather, I desperately needed to get out. Just take a very long walk. I might go mad otherwise.

From Kensington Market, I ventured east on College Street until Yonge Street. From there I walked north. It took me about fifty minutes until I made it to Eglinton Ave., where I stood looking in the window of Hannah's Kitchen. A panhandler sidled up to me, asking for spare change. My standard line in response to being asked for money was to tell people to get a job. But this time I reached into my pocket and pulled out all the coin I had – eighty-two cents.

I placed my forehead on the icy window pane of Hannah's and stayed a long time, exhausted, shivering. The restaurant was closed but I envisioned Solange and her friends sitting at a table. Laughing, enjoying each other's company. And there I was, the outsider, separated by a pane of glass.

I took the subway back. I couldn't walk, I was too tired. When I arrived at the apartment, two burly Metro Toronto cops were there to greet me. Right in front of my door. It was apparent they had been waiting for me and their presence made me nervous. Extremely so. I was not unlike my uneducated, primitive parents – leery of people in law enforcement. That aspect had been drummed into me at an early age by my mother and father. Roma, again. And although I was educated and much more cosmopolitan and worldly than they ever were, I couldn't divest myself of that inheritance.

The men introduced themselves and flashed badges. Detectives. They were each big in stature, over two-hundred pounds by my estimate, and I felt somewhat puny next to them with my dripping-wet one-hundred-and-fifty-five pounds. They asked to come in.

Rivka Howard. Pills, Stolen goods. My pawn shop escapades. And my theft of the stories! I thought about how I would explain everything. Maybe I could plead guilty, throw myself upon the mercy of the courts and get a reduced sentence. Maybe plead insanity.

"This won't take long," said one of the cops. He had a great handlebar moustache that looked as if you could hang two kettle handles from, one at either end of the upsweep.

"Can I see your badges again?" I asked flippantly. I wouldn't take shit from them, no fuckin' way. As big as they were, I knew my rights.

Only the handlebar guy obliged. The other, a stout man with a bull neck, simply looked pissed.

Detective Graziano Quilico.

"My father was a big boxing fan," said the detective, putting his badge away. His buzz-cut hairstyle was a throwback to another era.

"He loved a boxer by the name of Graziano. That's how I got my name. Everyone calls me Gracie but it's short for Graziano."

I gazed attentively at Gracie. What was with the small talk? If he wanted to arrest me, he should have just gone on with it.

"So what can I do for you?" I asked Gracie. I didn't look at the other cop.

"How long have you lived here?" he said.

"A few years."

"Have you had a break-in lately?"

"Actually..."

"What did they take?"

"Just some proscription pills, that's all. They made a mess of the place though."

The bull-necked cop stepped forth. "There are some new tenants, I'm told. Two brothers. Do you know them?"

Suddenly I was beset with a sense of horror. My mind raced. I quickly put two and two together.

Grace and his partner went on to explain that they had been looking for Paul and Andy MacFarlane for a long time.

They were pill-pushers, the worst kind of drug dealers. Barbiturates like pentobarbital were contaminated with a fungus. Caffeine was added to Ecstasy to enhance the latter's effect. Amphetamines were cut with chalk and talcum powder. It was all in the name of increasing margins. The drugs were clearly inferior and had taken two lives.

Since I wasn't the suspect, I could relax. I told the men about my encounter with the brothers.

"Have you seen them since?" asked Gracie.

"No but..."

"But what?" said Gracie.

"Someone's been knocking on my door and phoning me. Then when I answer, no one's there. I thought at first it was someone else, but no. So I wonder if it's those guys."

"That's how they operate," said Gracie. "They do that to see if you're home. If you are, and they make your life miserable enough, you'll want to go out. Then when you're gone, they walk right in and help themselves to anything they can find in your place that is of value."

I showed the Gracie and his partner the keyhole on the front door.

"Yup," said Gracie, examining the hole in detail. "It's been tampered with."

"That's the MacFarlane's handiwork," concurred Gracie's partner.

There was nothing to hide, nothing to fear.

"Did you report the break-in?" said Gracie.

I shook my head. "I don't have anything of value. And I don't have insurance."

"So nothing was stolen?" probed Gracie.

It was too complicated to divulge the story behind the pills, so I simply confirmed that the guys had made a mess but stole nothing.

"If I see them, I guess I'll call you," I said.

"You won't see them," said Gracie's partner. "They've already packed up and left. They only stay at an apartment for a few weeks. Maybe a few months at most. Then they take off."

"We're always a day or two behind them," said Gracie.

I was handed business cards. *Detective Grazinao Quilico. Detective Theodore Longworth.*

"If you remember anything else, call," said Gracie.

"There's nothing else," I said.

I flopped onto the couch as soon as the coppers left. I took a deep breath and closed my weary eyes. C-U-T-T-R-E. I should've known the bastards couldn't spell. Twitter twits.

Chapter Twenty-Four

When Suskind called to tell me that Solange had returned and resumed her normal activities, my heart leapt with joy. I was terribly anxious to see her once again but nerves got the better of me. Every day, just as 11:30 am rolled around, my hands got clammy and my stomach churned, twisting itself into knots. So I stayed put within the Market and went out to grab a coffee at the Moonbeam Café instead. One day morphed into another and before I knew it, two weeks had passed.

I couldn't go on this way and so before I knew it, I was on the Yonge subway heading north to Eglinton. Which is where I got off. There before me was Hannah's Kitchen. I checked my watch. It was 11:54. The timing couldn't have been better.

I found a corner seat, dumped my knapsack onto a chair, and ordered lunch. Sheppard's Pie, a garden salad, and chicken rice soup. I didn't have a book with me so while the food was being prepared, I darted outside for a newspaper – Now Magazine. I didn't want Solange to think I had come into the café especially for her; it was far better to pretend to be engaged.

The café was teeming with the lunch hour crowd. Every so often, in between nibbles, I would lift my eyes from the newspaper and scan the crowd. No Solange. I looked at my watch. 12:22. Then I checked the date in Now. It was Thursday! The only day of the week she didn't frequent Hannah's Kitchen.

I asked for a doggie bag and left. As I rode the subway, I realized the excursion hadn't been a total disaster. I had worked up the gumption to go to the restaurant and wait for Solange. Pretty simple then, I would try all over again the next day, when I was certain she would be there.

Instead of going straight home, I got off at Yonge and Bloor and started walking east to Sherbourne Street, where I knew there was a Goodwill. As a general principle, I didn't buy clothing from second-hand shops. I had had enough of that growing up, when my parents would drag me to the local Salvation Army store. I remembered row upon row of wrinkled, shoddy, hand-me-downs that were ten years out of style. And the harsh fluorescent lighting always made me blink. Sometimes I thought I could smell the stench coming from the unwashed fabrics.

As a result of my aversion to used clothing, I had exactly four dress shirts, four t-shirts, three pairs of pants, one winter coat, one spring jacket, one pair of running shoes, one pair of casual dress shoes. I didn't wash the clothes often so it was always a challenge to find something that was clean enough to wear.

But something lured me to the Goodwill store. If I'm honest, I would say that it was the prospect of meeting with Solange. Not only meeting with her; rather, the idea that we might see each other on a regular basis. That thought gave way to the fact that I simply needed more clothing.

In front of the Goodwill store, a large crowd had gathered. I made my way closer and saw that a fight was taking place. The two combatants had struck classic fighter poses and were circling each other slowly. They were just kids, fourteen or fifteen perhaps but the look in their eyes was unsparing – they were dead serious about inflicting serious damage.

Members of the crowd seemed to be egging the fighters on, crying out loudly in a language I could not understand. The pugilists were clearly Filipinos and I assumed the hurled shouts were in their native language.

One of the boys was considerably larger than the other. He stood at least a foot taller and was much more stout, almost pudgy. The other boy was wiry, thin, but I could see by his small but bulging biceps that he was in better shape. And that was quickly borne out: he threw the first punch, a left jab that the larger fighter easily blocked with his massive paw. But that was followed by a feigned left and then a looping right. It caught the larger boy flush on the nose, drawing blood.

This was Ernest Hemingway/Morley Callaghan all over again. Having had a strong interest in the many artists and writers who lived in 1920's and 30's Paris, I once read about their legendary fight. Hemingway was the much larger of the two men, an avid outdoorsman, a hunter and fisherman. But Callaghan was the more experienced boxer, and considerably faster. He darted in and out, throwing lightning-quick jabs, eventually knocking his opponent down. For his part, Hemingway became infuriated at the referee, insisting that he had let the telling round go an extra three minutes.

But there would be no extra time added on here. There was no referee, no timekeeper. This was all out mayhem and there were no rules.

The big kid wiped the blood from his nose and tried to get his opponent into a headlock, barging in like a bull. At the sight, I felt incredibly tense, as if I myself were fighting. And then I did the most incredible thing. It was so unlike me, so out of character, that there was no way to rationally explain it.

I waded right through the crowd and directly into the melee, trying to separate the two kids. "Hey, hey, break it up!" I shouted. "Cut it out!" Stupidly, I assumed that because I was an adult, they would listen to me.

I didn't see the punch coming. It connected at the corner of my right eye, causing scorching pain. Instantly, I dropped the plastic bag I had been carrying, the leftovers from lunch. I could feel the warmth of blood as it cascaded down my face. I staggered away.

In the subway, I bought a packet of Kleenex from a very frightened vendor. She dropped the change onto my bloody hand, careful not to touch it.

I could feel the eye swelling. I was dripping, dripping, and went through the entire packet of tissues trying to staunch the flow. With each passing minute, I felt increasingly faint and can't say I was unhappy to see the two subway employees. They made me sit down and then called the paramedics.

At Mt. Sinai Hospital's emergency room, I was seen by the triage nurse who made me hold a cold compress to my eye. I waited in a chair and watched a sea of sick bodies parade before me. An unconscious, pale-skinned red-headed girl of about ten years of age was brought in on a stretcher, her panic-stricken mother running alongside. They zipped right past, quickly attended to by a doctor. I didn't want to know. I also heard a man in blood-stained pants say that he had been swinging an axe when it misfired; the missing thumbnail-sized piece of flesh was packed in an ice bucket and carried by the man's son, who was standing alongside. Then an obviously drunken sod was warbling some long-forgotten song; he stank like a sewer. And on it went…

Forty-five minutes later I was stitched up and given a tiny envelope containing half a dozen Tylenol # 3's for the pain.

I walked back to the apartment. It wasn't very far and I didn't need anyone staring at me on public transit. In the washroom, I surveyed the damage. My right eye was purple and red and half-closed, a fine line of black-threaded stitches extending out from the corner. I looked like a boxer who had gone the distance. I packed some ice cubes into a plastic bag and held it to my face. Then I carefully lay down on my futon bed.

I considered that I should call someone, just to commiserate. But there was no one I could reach out to. On the night table, I spotted Suskind's business card. I picked up the phone and began to dial. But when I heard Hello, Sheila Suskind here, I hung up. A few seconds later, my phone began ringing and I let it continue on. I closed the thick curtains and lay silently in absolute darkness.

Chapter Twenty-Five

The worst part about getting whacked is that it was so unnecessary. I didn't have to stick my nose into other people's business. Especially when those people were hell-bent on murdering each other. But I did and paid the price. Especially as it related to Solange. Now I was in no shape to meet her. As the days went on, the skin around the eye turned a kaleidoscope of colours – black, yellow, dark gray, chestnut brown. After five days, I went to a walk-in doctor's clinic and had the stitches removed.

In the bathroom mirror, I surveyed the damage. My eye had mostly reopened and the deep, blood-infused colours appeared faded, leaving only a shade of pale yellow, like Dijon mustard. It was good enough. Time was running out and I absolutely had to return to Hannah's Kitchen.

The next morning I woke early and went for an espresso and biscotti at the Moonbeam. Then I returned to my place. I noticed the door to the apartment down the hall – the one that had been occupied by Brenda Bumblegate and the Macfarlane Brothers – was slightly ajar. I went to investigate.

A woman was on her hands and knees, sorting through a large cardboard box. She was surrounded by many boxes, a virtual cardboard fortress. I vaguely recognized her although couldn't quite place the face. I knocked softly. "Hello, I saw the door open. I just live down the hall."

The woman came toward me, hand extended. "Wow, I can't believe it."

"What can't you believe?"

"You're Karl Pringle. My old T.A. I'm Beverly. Beverly Holt."

Now I remembered. Beverly had been one of my students. As part of the PhD program, I had been required to teach two classes a week to first year students. Six hours a week.

"This is so weird," she continued.

"What's weird?"

"I never would have imagined that you'd be living in the Market. I always pictured you as more of a middle-class kind of guy. You know, like near Danforth Avenue."

Gentrified Danforth. Greektown. Yuppies pushing strollers, Golden Doodle dogs. Fair-trade furniture. Hot Yoga. Organic this and that.

"No, I'm here. Actually, I've been living in the Market quite a long time now."

Beverly gazed at my right eye. "What happened there?" she asked.

"Stupid accident. I got up in the middle of the night to make some tea, didn't see where I was going and knocked into a door." I clapped my hands together for emphasis. "Smack."

"Oh gosh. I hope you're ok."

"Fine. It looks worse than it is."

Beverly went on to reveal that she was now enrolled on a part-time basis in the Graduate Program at the University of Toronto, having switched her major from Philosophy to

Fine Arts. "It's where my heart is," she said. "I love sculpture, drawing with charcoal. Constructing things, composing things, you know. Actually, next summer I'm planning a trip with a few classmates to Paris. It has such a rich history in the arts, as I'm sure you're aware. We'll be visiting the Louvre, the Mussee d'Orsay, the Georges Pompidou Centre, so many places."

"Great." I paused and surveyed the clutter in the apartment. "I guess you're moving in?"

"Yup. I've been looking for a place for awhile. Rent's good, location the best. I think I lucked out."

I extended my own hand. "Well, I can see you're busy, Beverly. I'll let you go. And actually I have to get ready; I'm meeting someone for lunch." I turned to go.

"Wait."

"Yes?"

"I'm wondering what you're doing these days, Mr. Pringle. You know, I once heard a story about you and Aaron Feldstein. Maybe it was like one of these urban myths. Just rumour and innuendo. Of course that was a long time ago."

I always knew this day would come, when I would be faced with confronting my desultory past. I just didn't think it would happen a few feet from where I lived.

"I'm a writer," I said without a moment's hesitation, skirting the Feldstein issue.

"You're a writer?"

"That's what I said."

"Wow, what do you write?"

"I freelance for magazines. Stories about urban affairs mostly."

"Amazing."

"I also write some fiction," I blurted. "For little-known literary magazines, but I'm also working on a novel."

"Again, amazing. I should read some of your work."

"Sure. Not a problem."

"And so what about you and Aaron?" said Beverly, persistent. "They say you put him in the hospital. That's why you were dropped from the university."

I fell silent for a time to consider my answer. "Aaron and I had a falling out, it's true," I said at last. "But you know how things get convoluted as time goes on. It's like that old children's game of Broken Telephone. Say 'hello' to the first person and by the time that word gets passed on to the twelfth; it comes out 'hell is a hole.' You can't win."

"I see," said Beverly. "So you're basically saying that it really is one of those urban legends."

"That's what I'm saying."

And that was that. I told Beverly I would be right back and emerged from my apartment carrying a bottle of Pinot Grigio. "Welcome to the neighbourhood," I said.

She gave me a warm hug. "I always thought you'd make a great prof. Your class was so interesting. Too bad you didn't continue in the program."

Before heading out, I considered what book I might bring with me to the restaurant. I absolutely had to pretend to be reading when Solange walked in, there was no other way. I settled on Perfume, by Patrick Suskind. Again, *Suskind*. It was a strange and disturbing tale to be certain, about a depraved young perfumer who attempts to create the quintessential perfume by murdering women and lifting their scent. Yet, the story was set in 18th-century Paris and I thought that if nothing else, it could be a topic of conversation.

I took the subway north on the Yonge Street line, just as I had done the week before. At 11:45 am, Hannah's Kitchen was bustling. There was no getting around that; there were many businesses in the area and at the lunch hour, one couldn't expect anything less.

I ordered the vegetable risotto with salad and cream of mushroom soup. Nice and light. I sat at a corner table. The food was hot and hearty. Not quite up to Country Style fare but good all the same. I ate with gusto and quickly realized that I hadn't had a decent meal in days, subsisting almost solely on coffee, muffins, bearclaws, and various other desserts. The shock of the eye punch had somehow thrown my entire system into some weird state where I just hadn't been very hungry except for sweets.

At 12:03 I took out the novel I brought and began reading. It was strange. Very strange. The main character Grenouille, had no personal odour but his sense of smell rivaled that of a bloodhound. I had read the book on two previous occasions and found it to have a bizarre, captivating hold on me, like I was reading about the life of my doppelganger. Born in a cesspool of a food market to a mother who abandoned him, it appeared the protagonist had no chance. And so contemptuous was he of his fellow man that he retreated to a cave for seven years, far removed from the smell of humans. As I was leafing through the pages that I once knew so well, I realized that this may not have been the best of books to bring along. Even the Paris connection now seemed tenuous in light of the utter bizarreness. So I slipped it into my knapsack and resumed eating, grabbing the Business section of the Globe and Mail from a nearby rack.

As a rule, I never read about business. Why would I? I knew nothing about mutual funds, stocks, and the like, principally because I never had any money to invest. Well, and also because the sorts whose lives were immersed in the trade of making piles of dough seemed unsophisticated to me, not at all interested in the arts or matters of the mind. I did know I was oversimplifying but they disturbed me, those money-mongers with their perfectly coiffed hair and expensive suits that they wore like badges of honour. Moreover, they were, well, like what donut boy had said… psychopaths, interested only in their own well-being, irrespective of who they trampled en route to the top My mother coveted what they had and it led her straight to an early grave.

Fortunately, I didn't have to read long. Solange saunter-ed in, surrounded by a gaggle of laughing and shouting friends. I quickly picked up the newspaper and stuck my nose inches from the page. My heart thumped, I thought it would burst forth from my chest. I didn't dare look up.

A few minutes passed. Nothing happened. I gave in and snuck a peek. She was still at the counter. And then it happened.

"Karl?"

"Solange. I can't believe…"

"It has been such a long time." She smiled. I had seen that smile many times in the past few months. Now it was real, brighter than I had imagined. I stood up. Solange put her tray down and we embraced.

"Karl, you remember my friends, maybe." She swung her arm out to encompass a wide swath of about ten or so people. They all nodded or offered perfunctory waves. "Yes, we're going to have lunch. You can join us, please."

The group moved three small tables together and I took a seat. They immediately started up with their cackling ways but this time I didn't mind. I was just glad to have the opportunity to see Solange and very shortly we fell into our own private conversation.

"It's shocking to see you here at Hannah's," she said.

"My publisher is in the area."

"Ah yes, your writing. But Karl, your eye. It looks bruised." It appeared to me that she was about to reach up and finger the area, but she didn't.

"I accidentally walked into a door," I said, and repeated the same far-fetched tale I had told Beverly.

"Mon Dieu, what a mistake. Maybe you should keep a light on."

"I know. Very dumb."

"And how have you been, Karl? I was disappointed you never called back. J'estais tres triste."

I looked at Solange beseechingly.

"Ah yes. It means 'I was very sad.'"

"I just got so busy, I'm sorry. With school and my publisher, there have been so many deadlines, so many demands." I went on to feed her some cockamamie story about how my publisher was trying to groom me for success by creating a public persona, even going so far as to possibly give me a nom-de-plume. "It's all about image, creating a brand," I said.

"Creating a brand?"

"Yes, 'branding' is common for most artists these days. It's a step-by-step process and really takes awhile to get everything right. They try and change your private personality and give you a more, shall we say, 'interesting one.' Well, at least interesting to the public. It's all about selling. Selling your book, selling the movie you're in, selling your product, selling you as a brand. And who knows, maybe even changing your name."

"I like your name already – Karl Pringle."

"Yes, me too, Solange. But I have to play the game for the publisher."

"This means your book, the one about golems, is going to be published soon."

"Yes, soon."

"You must tell me so that I can buy a copy."

"Of course. Of course."

I didn't exactly relish telling Solange a pack of lies but the truth was way too complicated. And ugly. She would also be long gone by the time I had to account for myself so I figured no harm was done. All I was doing was creating that proverbial brand for her right now. The most appealing one I could imagine. Really, I just wanted to spend time with her until she boarded that plane once again. And now that I was inches away, I realized that I desperately wanted to fuck her.

Chapter Twenty-Six

I found an envelope on my doorstep. The return address simply said 'Beverly.' Inside was a picture, one I had never seen before. It showed me lecturing to a group of students. A note from Beverly simply said that she had taken it with her cell phone and thought I might want to have it. I did. I tacked it to the front of my fridge and spent quite a bit of time gazing at it. That was me, years ago. I looked confident, gesturing with my hand to something I had written on the blackboard. There was a smile on my face. I was wearing a brown tie and my gray Herringbone tweed jacket. My favourite jacket. For a brief moment I wondered whatever happened to it, whether I still might have it. But then I realized I had thrown it out shortly after the Feldstein debacle.

★

There were things to do before Solange came over. Yes, she had agreed to come for dinner, as unbelievable as that seemed. I had to give the apartment a thorough cleaning once again. Maybe get a vase and fresh flowers. Something bright, like tulips. As luck would have it, there was a florist on Baldwin Street, right in the Market. And I also had to cook. I had told Solange that I made a pretty mean lasagna, so that was on tap. Of course I had to explain to her, quite unsuccessfully mind you, how the word 'mean' played into the business of cooking up beef lasagna. She understood the normal meaning of the word but was stupefied by the context in which I had used it. I explained it was an idiom, similar to the phrases 'break a leg,' or, 'kicked the bucket.' That only made things worse. Solange's English was quite good but she just didn't get English-language idioms yet. Still, it was all in good fun, I was simply thrilled to have the woman coming over.

Lasagna and salad. Wine. Dessert was asking too much from my limited culinary skills so I bought some Hungarian Dobos Torte from Country Style, a decadent cake filled with layers of chocolate buttercream and topped with a caramel glaze. A classic dessert.

On Sunday, two days after meeting with Solange at Hannah's Kitchen, I began preparing the lasagna. She was coming over the next evening and I didn't want to have any surprises with a botched meal hours before. That turned out to be a wise move. I had rarely used the inside of the stove, instead simply using the two burners on top. When I tried to turn it on, it didn't. I would have called the landlord for help but didn't really know how to contact them; it was an obscure numbered company. Someone from the company always picked up my rent cheque the first of every month from my doorstep; that was the extent of our involvement. So I did the only thing I could think of: I scooted over to Goodwill and purchased a toaster oven. Fortunately, it was in working order and the rest of the food preparation proceeded without a hitch.

The very last thing I did was box all of the stuffed animals that had belonged to Rivka. I'm not sure what Solange would have thought about all the furry creatures littering the apartment but I didn't want to take a chance. And I had to admit that the glassy-eyed doll above the toilet looked a bit creepy. I had kept the whole lot in the open during the book sale because I thought it might be a nice touch, and bring in more sales. But having the collection about when I was trying to impress a woman was another thing altogether.

I'm not sure what Solange was thinking when she showed up wearing a short black dress and a white silk blouse. I know what I was thinking about however – I wanted to rip her clothes off the minute she walked through the door and took her winter coat off.

She kissed me on both cheeks and produced a bottle of French Shiraz. "Very beautiful wine for beef," she advised. I showed her around the apartment although in truth there wasn't much to show. I concentrated on the many books in my library and also the photograph that Beverly had given. "This is me in front of my class, taken a few years ago," I boasted. "I was teaching a course on ancient philosophy. Plato and Aristotle."

"The Greeks," she said. "I know them a little. Socrates spent much time in that market, the agora, lecturing to anyone who was willing to listen. And sometimes to people not so willing to listen." Solange let out a hearty laugh and I quickly followed suit.

As the evening progressed, we talked about many things, my parents, her family, the school she's teaching at, the Philosophy program I was enrolled in, her hobbies, her interest in the English Romantic poets, how she's enjoying Toronto. I asked whether she's related to the famous French actor, Gerard Depardieu, and she replied that sadly, she was not. She did not speak of her late husband or daughter, or her birth parents, instead referring to Jean-Pierre and Geraldine as 'her parents.' She was particularly curious about how my novel ends. Fortunately, I was in a position to tell her. After the whole Rivka charade had died down, I secured a copy of The Puttermesser Papers from the library and read it through.

"As I told you, Solange," I said in a clear voice, "these golems become too difficult to handle after a time. Then you must put them down. Back to the earth they go!" I pointed downward with my forefinger. "But first the golem in my story is brought forth to help the protagonist, the main character. Her name is Ruth Puttermesser and she's a small-time lawyer in N.Y. Nothing is going right in her life and the golem helps her in many ways. For instance, Ruth becomes the mayor of New York City. And she finds love."

"Wow, you have an imagination. It's wonderful. I think you are very talented."

"I think everyone has some talent," I said modestly. It's just that some people don't foster their talent."

"Foster?"

"Yes, it means to nourish the talent. You know, to work on it all the time so you become very good at it."

"Ah yes, now I understand. And now I have something to tell you. I don't tell many people."

"Ok."

"In France, we have a show on the radio – *Le Monde Etrange* – that always has very strange topics. Things like vampires and ufo's and maybe even golems, like you write about. I listen to it any time I can. It's so interesting. The world is very big and unusual."

"*Le Monde Etrange?*"

"*The Strange World*. Yes, I love that show. You know, if I could, Karl, I would like to go on an expedition one day into the jungle and find some creatures. Or maybe even create some creature...like some mad scientist."

"Wow, I never knew, Solange."

"Science is very interesting. But *mad science* is much better."

The lasagna was a big hit and we each had a second helping. She was right about the Shiraz – it really was the perfect accompaniment to the beef lasagna. And the Dobos Torte was to die for, simply irresistible; after tasting it, Solange said I must absolutely take her to Country Style to try the rest of the food.

The dinner was interrupted on one occasion by a knock on the door. It was Beverly.

"Oh, I didn't know you had company," she said, offering a sincere apology. "I thought you might have wanted to grab a coffee."

"Next time, maybe."

I closed the door and Solange turned to me. "Is she your girlfriend?"

"No, just an old student," I said.

"She likes you. Women know such things."

"I'm not interested."

"In French, 'girlfriend' is 'La Petite Amie.'"

"So no *Petite Amie* for me."

"Ah non? That's a shame." A hint of a smile appeared on Solange's face, and she took a sip of her wine.

All of this, the food, the conversation, the wine, the friendliness I showed Solange, was leading to the moment that I leaned in closer and kissed her. At first she seemed hesitant, almost unsure. I thought she might bolt from the apartment, she seemed that skittish. But after I withdrew following the initial kiss and told her some lame joke that we both laughed at, she relaxed and began to enjoy the affection. I stuck my tongue deep within her mouth but she gently pushed on my chest. "Not yet," she said, and I obliged.

★

That was the start of it. During the work week, Solange and I saw each other on Tuesdays and Fridays. Usually I would join her for lunch at Hannah's Kitchen. I didn't much care for her assortment of worldwide friends but tolerated them for her sake. I regaled the group with my short stories... Rivka's stolen short stories. Now that I had fully convinced Solange of my literary prowess, it was a given that I should hold court in the restaurant; her friends were fascinated with my command of the English language and with my imagination. On one occasion, someone asked me how I come up with my ideas.

"I daydream, "I replied. " I know if I tell you I lay on the couch with my eyes closed, you'll think I'm taking a nap. Or maybe I'm just lazy. I'm not, I'm really letting my mind wander. It travels around the world picking up new experiences."

I didn't see any harm in playing the entertainer. There was no possible way for any of them to find me out.

On Saturdays and Sundays we found time to explore the city. The family she boarded with was particularly lenient, allowing her much time off. The weather had turned, warm gales from the south signaling the end of winter. It brought with them smells of animal droppings and damp pine needles. Here and there patches of yellowed grass could be seen beneath the retreating snow.

We went hiking in the Rouge Park, where we saw a family of beavers frolicking. Seemingly at every step Solange would point out some earthworm or spider or field mouse and tell me that the park's floor was teeming with life. Life upon life, as she said. She lifted a rock and showed me the slugs and ants that resided underneath. At a pond, she revealed the water skidders that slid on the surface. Having grown up in the city, it was all rather new to me and had I been with anyone else, chances are that I would have been annoyed. I had never understood the attraction about nature and would rather have spent my days on a restaurant patio than commuting with the creepy-crawlies that inhabited the forest floor. To be certain, carrying a heavy backyard while trekking along trails held no interest for me and paled in comparison to having a cappuccino or espresso while reading a book in a café. There were secrets that nature held, ones I would never be privy to, and that was just fine with me. Besides, I had enough bugs in my own place. But now it was different. Walking with Solange made me want to understand the beauty and magic of things that were foreign, the hills and rivers, the insects, birds, and animals.

I brought Solange to the top of the CN Tower where she jumped on the glass floor, while I stood a good distance back. Looking down at the ground through a glass partition some eleven hundred feet high was not my idea of fun. But Solange reveled in it, moving her arms and legs like imaginary car windshield wipers while on her back. Making snow angels.

I rented a car for one for excursions out of the city. We drove to Niagara Falls, Stratford, and the quaint Amish village of St. Jacobs. There, we visited studios and galleries and famer's markets. We picked up jars of jam and jelly for her return to Paris. I noticed Solange carefully scrutinized each and every jar for ingredients. "My parents will love these," she said.

More than almost anything, Solange loved music and dancing. She could do it all – Jitterbug, Ballroom, Swing, Salsa, you name it. She had taken many dance lessons throughout her life and could move with the best. And that is precisely what she did – move. She told me that dance allowed her to let go, dispense with the mundane chores of the everyday. While I learned to accommodate her on her many interests, this one I couldn't. My body always felt firmly rooted to the ground, like I was wearing shoes of cement. To appease her, I would accompany her to nightclubs. But when she pulled me on to the dance floor, I froze. She danced circles around my stationary body, vamping and mouthing the words to songs I didn't know. I tried waving my arms but became aware that I must have looked like a chicken flapping its wings, and so I stopped. But that didn't deter Solange. If I wouldn't, or rather couldn't dance, she would bounce away from our table and find a group of similarly-inclined women on the floor. Rhythm, sweat, the beat of the drums. They were in a zone and there was no entry for me, the man who had always been more attuned to the mind than anything else. Certainly more than the body. I didn't mind sitting it out, I loved watching Solange dance. But on one occasion, a man asked her to dance. She looked at me, I nodded, and away she went. They danced quite a long time. He was very adept, very slick, with all the right footwork. He dipped her, lifted her, and even flipped her in the air. I saw them laughing and my heart skipped a beat, I could barely breathe. My jealousy was almost unbearable but I just had to take it.

That one episode aside, I was having a blast. A blast: a word that had never appeared in my lexicon before. I did all these things for Solange but it was her enthusiasm for life that motivated me, that brought something out that I never knew existed – joy. Her motto, explained in a mix of English and French and hand signals, was that *you will never again be as young as you are today.*

We became lovers. I lusted for her daily and when not there, had to satisfy those urges myself.

If I had been a different sort of person, I might have heeded Suskind's words and never let her go. Maybe gotten on to my knees and proposed. But I wasn't. I was me, Karl Pringle, full of contradictions and insecurities, carrying around an entire Louis Vuitton set of heavy emotional baggage. I may have been an ok boyfriend but was definitely not marriage material.

And despite knowing that, I really didn't want to let Solange go. I understood, yes I knew, that I would never find anyone as good for me as her. She was so caring, so nonjudgmental, that it made me feel that I could do anything in her presence. Be more than what I was and let go of my checkered past. Every day I hesitated, unable to decide between who I was and who I aspired to be. During my worst moments, I wondered what Solange saw in me. Even when she told me that she thought I was handsome, very smart, highly creative, caring, I had a hard time believing her. I thought that if only I could embrace her vision of me, then maybe I could escape my fate. And all of this against the background of an hourglass that was running out. Only months remained before *ma petite amie* would be leaving for good.

As it turned out, a new complication was thrown into the mix, one I was hardly ready for. Solange came over one evening, a night she usually reserved for the family she was staying with. She appeared especially solemn and unsteady, like she would collapse from the weight of her burden. I offered her a drink of something warm, a tea or hot chocolate, but she asked for a glass of wine instead. She reached for my hand with both of hers and stared me straight in the eyes.

"I'm pregnant," she said.

Chapter Twenty-Seven

It was my fault. I should have worn protection. It's just that I wanted to know her completely, warm flesh on warm flesh, deep within. Stupid, I realize. And yet, I felt I should be gentle with myself. Not overly critical. The woman had brought out feelings in me that I never would have imagined.

I had only one piece of jewelry left. It was a ring valued at $1625. Diamond band with burnished brown 18k gold. I was never one for jewelry, thinking it to be adornments worn by the very vain, but had to admit this was a stunner. Elegant. I had been saving it for when I needed another infusion of ready cash. Now I did the unthinkable; I got down onto one knee and offered Solange the ring. She gasped, and cupped her hands around my face.

"Karl, please get up."

"Solange, I'm serious."

"We need more time, Karl," she said. "We must talk."

"At least keep the ring." I put it on Solange's left ring finger.

"Oh Karl. Please hold it for now." She put the ring into my palms and closed my fingers around it. I could see that she was blinking back tears.

I made Solange tea and toast and blueberry jam. I had been a wordsmith my entire life but now had none. I didn't know what to say, didn't know what to do. Now that I had a moment to collect myself, I realized I didn't want to marry her and be a father. I had no instinct for those things, I just didn't want to lose her. But in the overall scheme of things, that meant nothing. Nothing. Solange was looking for love, just as Suskind had told me. And the only sort of love I had ever known my entire life resided in school, with books and imaginary characters. Even if my dearest told me otherwise, I knew I really had nothing to offer her.

"The baby, Karl. I'm going to have it. There is not so much time left for me."

I nodded. "Yes," I burbled.

"Soon I will be thirty-eight. Not much time at all." Solange then went on to tell me the story I had heard before, about her marriage and the family she lost. "I was buried after that," she said. "My heart, my soul. I will never forget but can move forward. Life is always about moving forward. There is nothing else."

The words dried up for Solange after that. We spent the rest of the evening just holding onto each other. She took the ring from my hands and put it onto her baby finger. Unlike when it fit snugly on the ring finger, now it moved around and around. "It's a better finger for now," she whispered. "And I can have the size changed."

We met the next day and the day after that. Weeks passed. Although Solange realized it wasn't the right time to make any commitments to me, she also knew that she couldn't leave. Not yet. So she called her parents and told them the news. Then she called her school and asked for yet a further 4 months leave. Circumstances had changed, she told them. Extraordinary circumstances, although she didn't elaborate further. Seeing as how she was a long-term employee, the leave was granted.

For my part, I made a concession as well. I gave up my writing persona. I told Solange that the book deal with the publisher had fallen through. Artistic differences was the way I put it. Money, the print run, editing, royalties, we just couldn't agree on terms. As ironic as it sounds, I fed Solange this lie because I wanted, as much as possible, to divorce myself from all the lies I had previously told her, the ones I had used to artificially inflate myself. Her response was that it was a great shame, seeing as how talented I was. And that I shouldn't give it all up, there was a publisher out there who would love my work and with whom I would get along with especially well.

"And besides," she continued, chopping some onions and green peppers for the spaghetti and meatball dinner we were preparing, "this golem story of yours is so unique. It could even be true."

"What do you mean?"

"I loved this idea so much. So I did some research. Many books. And then I went to see a rabbi."

"You did what?" I stopped stirring the pasta.

"Yes, a rabbi. He had a long white beard, and a tall hat, like someone from a funeral house."

"Undertaker."

"Ah *oui, c'est ca.* Un-der-tak-er."

"Except that a rabbi isn't an undertaker, Solange. He's a religious Jewish man. You shouldn't be fooling with people like that." I shook my head.

"What's wrong?" she said.

"You're pregnant, there's so much to think about. And you go around looking for rabbis because you're curious. That's unbelievable."

"Are you upset?"

"Don't you see, it's ridiculous. Like I said, you can't go fooling around with people like that."

Solange shrugged her shoulders. She obviously didn't know what I meant by 'fooling' but since I had repeated myself, she obviously knew I meant business. To be honest though, I didn't understand myself what I meant by the word, or rather by the entire phrase 'people like that;' what exactly I was trying to imply. All I knew was that it seemed silly of her to seek knowledge from a rabbi at this time.

"I love learning," she countered, "especially unusual things. And I told you about that radio show I always listen to. It's maybe a side of me you don't know too well, yes? For example, in France there is a very famous story about a terrible animal called The Beast of Gevaudan. Ah, I call it an 'animal' but some people say it was only part animal, and maybe part man also. Or maybe part 'something' that we don't understand. This story was in the 18th century and it happened in Gevaudan where there is a lot of mountains. This beast killed over a hundred people and ate many of them."

"Oh Solange." I couldn't help myself.

"Yes, Karl? You would change your mind if this thing, this animal, bit you, I guarantee."

"Oh Solange."

"So the beast was like a wolf," continued Solange, now totally ignoring me, "but much bigger, like a cow. It had a red tail and big, big shoulders. Mostly it was walking on four legs, but sometimes on two. One person said it had the hands of a man, but except it was covered all with fur."

I had nothing to say.

"But you want to know about the rabbi, am I right, not so much the Beast of Gevaudan?"

I shook my head slowly.

"I went looking for this man quite a long time ago, after you first said your story to me."

"That was a long time ago," I finally said.

"Yes, Karl, it was."

"So, who exactly did you see?" I said.

"I saw many rabbis but they all looked at me like I was very strange. Some even laughed and said golems were fairy tales. But then I went to one who had very much knowledge about the Kabbalah. You know this Kabbalah because you told me about it. The Zohar too."

I continued slowly stirring the pasta but said nothing.

"It took me a long time to find such a man," she said. "It was almost like looking for a golem itself."

Solange laughed but I remained silent. Where was this going?

"I wonder if you're being pregnant is making you do odd things." I put the spoon down and stroked my chin. "But of course, you went to see this man before you were pregnant. Still, we have to talk about 'us', about the baby. That's more important than chasing rabbis. Besides, like some people told you, there's no such thing as a golem."

Solange laughed once again, this time with more verve. She popped a baby carrot into her mouth.

"You think I have a craving for pickles and for golems, because I'm pregnant? For crazy things? Non, I can assure you. Not yet, anyway."

"Ok, ok. I'm sorry. Now tell me. I'm all ears."

"All ears?"

"An idiom, Solange. It means *I'm ready to listen*."

"Bon. This rabbi, his name was Mr. Bilchen. Well, Mr. Rabbi Baruch Bilchen." Solange pulled a business card from her purse. "Ah, oui. Mr. Rabbi Baruch Abraham Schneerson Bilchen."

"Schneerson? That can't be a real name. No one calls their son 'Schneerson.'"

"Yes, it's very bizarre I know. But he told me his name was from a very famous rabbi. A rebbe, he called him."

"Rebbe? I have never heard such a thing."

"Me too. Me too." Solange became highly animated at this point and I wondered what this rabbi, or rebbe rather, had told her.

"But in the Hassidic Jewish world," she said, "a rabbi is called a rebbe. No where else."

"So who was this very famous Rebbe Schneerson?"

"He was like the messiah. Some people say he will come back from the dead. This is very interesting."

"Why is it interesting, Solange? Why? It's just silly talk."

"*Ecoute*, I am on your side. But you don't understand, Karl."

I didn't understand, huh? That was a new one on me. And Solange was going to educate me on people rising from the grave? What a joke.

"After the Second World War, Rebbe Schneerson built up again Jewish communities around the world. Am I saying this right?"

"Well, undoubtedly Jewish communities had been devastated by Hitler and his allies. So yes, you're saying it right. Also I would think that in Russia, especially after communism, that it too would be a place where Jewish life was affected."

"Exact," said Solange, pointing her forefinger at me.

"So anyway, Solange, you were saying that Schneerson is thought to be a messiah, that one day he will come back from the dead. I want to tell you that if you believe this..."

But before I could continue, she went on to say that Schneerson was similar to the Golem of Prague!

"Uh, huh. Can you explain that please."

"Oui mon amour, I'm not lying," said Solange. "But look, everything is ready now." She waved her hand across the table like a magician in the midst of a card trick. "Spaghetti, salad, meatballs, cheese, bread, wine. Let us sit and eat a little and then we can talk. Schneerson can wait for a moment."

She was right of course – Schneerson could wait. I had to give it to her, preparing a meal was, for her, akin to a great feast. It didn't matter how simple the meal was... everything was managed with great care. Eating was a ritual

– putting out a tablecloth, good dishes and cutlery, even lighting a candle. I never knew how intricate a role food could play in our lives, how important it was for one's well-being. Before Solange I always ate in a hurry, on the run, cramming as much food down my gullet as I could afford. For the most part, I only ate take-out, and not very healthy take-out at that...MacDonald's, Wendy's, KFC. At home I prepared...and I use that word loosely...TV Dinners, Kraft Dinner, sandwiches of sliced meats, peanut butter (often eating straight out of the jar), cereal (especially Captain Crunch) and my absolute favourite, hot dogs. Mostly, I munched on chips, chocolate bars, jelly beans, yogurt-covered raisins. I hardly knew what a vegetable was. Only at Country Style Hungarian Restaurant did I ever eat anything that resembled real food. But, I was happy with my diet. Sure the food was bad for me, but it was quite delectable, and cheap. Even if something was a bit off, I could smother it with packets of ketchup. Yes, the liquid red nectar, sweet, savoury, good for what ails poor people.

However, and much to my own amazement, I now became quite an adept cook. The mini- toaster oven didn't hold much promise for cooking deep dish meals and so I asked the proprietor of the variety store downstairs for assistance with the apartment's oven. It turned out that all that was needed was someone to take a match to the pilot light. So now that it was working, I began preparing roasted turkeys and chickens with baked potatoes, stews with beef cubes and assorted vegetables that simmered for hours. On the stovetop, I became somewhat skilled at soups—chicken, barley, mixed bean, and pea. Desserts were still in the exploratory stage and I messed up muffins, cakes and pies on a regular basis. Too much flour, too little sugar, not enough yeast, things didn't rise, the dough tasted bland, all that and more. Still, I did turn out an awesome apple crumble pie on one occasion and peanut butter chip and oatmeal raisin cookies on others. I used recipes, my blueprints for success, and chopped and diced, sautéed and braised. I wasn't afraid to try my hand at new foods and the idea that I might fail never entered my mind. I loved cooking for Solange and got enormous satisfaction knowing she was enjoying my creations. I'd look into her sea-blue eyes, staring at them as she ate. I'd watch her smile. It was a happy dream.

Aside from my wretched diet, there was something else that I parted with – the razor blades that seemed to periodically show up on the washroom floor. Those, and the pharmaceuticals. I just couldn't afford to have Solange stumble across either. But with her at my side, I just didn't seem to have any use for the pills and certainly not for the sharp steel. Fortunately, I had never cut myself very deeply and the scars healed up nicely; I was grateful that Solange never noticed. And lest I forget, the same disinterest I showed with the pills and blades extended to my long-time faithful companion – *Camelot*. There was no way to explain it other than to say that I now turned my interest toward other things. Like my looks. Ah yes, my looks.

The truth was that I never took any real interest in my appearance. My wardrobe consisted of a rag-tag assortment of clothes picked up at Goodwill, Value Village, and the clothing-donation box at the corner of my street that I found myself occasionally rummaging through. My socks never matched, my pants were from too short, sometimes too long, sweaters had holes. What did I care? I had always been a philosopher, a man of mind, so taking an exacting interest in my looks didn't compute. Besides, I wasn't sure that fashionable clothes and a proper haircut (I cut my own) would change anything – I was a tall, gangly sort, with flattened hair and a cowlick at the very top that absolutely refused to be tamed…it stood straight up like a mini, wind-swept twister. I had the same pair of black glasses for so long, at least 20 years, that they had come back into fashion. I had to thank Harry Potter for that. But it was my 'look,' the absent-minded 'academic,' and I accepted it. In that sense, I was very much like Aaron Feldstein. Aaron knew, as I did, as my classmates did, as all the great philosophers did, that appearance is deceiving. Put me in those nice clothes, and one person might suggest I was handsome. Yet a second would say that while I was well turned-out in my fine duds, I was nevertheless ugly. Which to believe? Why would one perspective be any more real than the other? Put me under a giant microscope and the texture of my clothes, of my face, my hands, arms, and the like, would differ from what could be perceived by the ordinary eye. Texture, I concluded – of clothes, of skin, of anything really – is ambiguous. A far better philosopher than me – Bertrand Russell – confirmed as much with an ordinary brown table, proving that both colour and texture were doubtful, subject to interpretation, remarking that the colour of the table changes as one walks around it. Certain places on the table would reflect more light and appear as a brighter shade of brown than some other places where the light did not shine. The colour of the table therefore, could never be certain but rather would be entirely dependent on the position of the observer and the way the light shines on that table. Anyway, I guess that accounts for why I never cared about clothes, it's all relative. Ok, well, I never had any money to buy anything nice, that too.

But now I dispensed with Russell and tried to make myself look, well...as presentable as I could. I went to Hair Cutters for an $8 haircut; it was better than cutting my own hair. I shaved and bathed regularly and even managed to tame the cowlick with gel. Lots of it. As for clothes, I found that if I took my time to carefully select them from thrift stores and the clothing-donation box, I could look decent. And now I washed everything I bought; previously, that was not the case – I would simply put on the clothes, which led to a few nasty cases of flea bites. To complete the picture, I even bought an iron. And so in the 'selfies' Solange was so fond of taking of the two of us, I scrutinized myself very carefully and was surprised...I had to admit, I looked pretty good...and it didn't take a microscope.

Of course, of paramount importance was that I now had a lover and my life became devoted to her. I thought about Solange constantly, the one firmament in my otherwise dismal existence. I even went so far as to ask her to move into my apartment. She declined though, saying that it was better for the moment to remain with her Canadian family. They had graciously allowed her to stay on and she was quite comfortable in their house.

If there was one regret I had regarding my relationship with Solange it was that my parents never got to meet her. They would have adored her, I have no doubt. She lovely girl, is what my mother would have said in her broken English. And while both my parents were quite set in their ways, I believe Solange might have changed them, the same way she was changing me. She would do so just through her indomitable spirit, where everything she imagined was possible, even without a lot of money.

I had this habit, you see. At the end of each meal, I liked something sweet. Usually cookies. Solange found that to be deplorable. I would take a cookie, usually an Oreo, and dunk it in a glass of milk. Oftentimes, I would hold it underwater a little too long, and drown it. The soggy cookie would sink to the bottom of the glass and I'd have to remove it with a spoon.

"Ecch," said Solange, her face all scrunched up.

"You know that's what I like," I said, fishing for the remains of the Oreo, like I was scavenging for sunken treasure.

"So North American. Nobody in France does such a thing."

"We're not in France," I said, and smiled ironically.

"I will now close," said Solange, placing the palm of her hand across her eyes.

"You should see what happens to Captain Crunch cereal when it gets soggy. It's worse."

"Ecch."

I reached across the table and lowered Solange's hand. "Tell me about the rabbi," I said.

"Oh my God, Karl. You make me crazy. But OK, I will tell you." Solange took a deep breath and continued. "So Rabbi Baruch Abraham Mendel Schneerson Bilchen told me that the Golem of Prague was a very helpful monster, that he worked in Rabbi Loew's synagogue cleaning up. Sweeping the floor or dusting."

Now here was a genuine problem. How could I tell my beloved that she was a gullible fool if she truly believed such a tale? I would have liked to say that Shneerson Baruch, or whatever his name, was probably an escapee from a mental institution. Of course I didn't say any of those things.

"Oh Solange, you can't believe that," I said softly yet deliberately.

"You had to listen to this rabbi, Karl. He knows things. He said that it is possible to construct such a monster, even today. That the Golem of Prague is like Rebbe Schneerson because they are both not dead, only resting. The Golem of Prague is resting in the attic of a synagogue in Prague, just waiting. The same thing with Schneerson, just resting, waiting for the right time to come back. I told you, this rabbi thinks Schneerson is the messiah."

Oh brother. I stood up and carried my dishes to the sink. I ran the water and squirted liquid detergent all over. The bubbles formed, overtaking the dirty dishes. I wanted to dive right in, I really did.

"The golem in Prague had the name Josef."

The words wafted to my ears. I recalled the name from my research. I needed another Oreo cookie. Nietzche, Schopenhauer, Plato, and now there was Schneerson and Josef the monster. The witching hour was officially here.

"So-lange," I said, stretching out the syllables for effect. "So-lange." I turned around to look at her. What was I thinking? Was the rest of my life to be immersed in this craziness? Who knew what other wild ideas were brewing in my beloved's brain?

"Yes?" said Solange, tilting her head to one side and giving me a look that suggested she was not insane. And, and…I had better not infer as much.

"When I first met you and told you about the Golem of Prague, you looked at me like I was a nut. Do you remember? I even told you about the Zohar and how that rabbi and his son stayed in a cave for 13 years and studied the Torah. And what did you say?"

"That of course he would study because there is not so much else to do in a cave."

"Precisely. You were making fun of it. Making fun of the whole golem story."

Solange sighed. "Sometimes in life things change, Karl. Before I met Rabbi Bichen, I was interested in this whole golem story, just because, as I told you, I love learning new things. Better still are strange new things. But after Rabbi Bichen explained to me that the Golem of Prague was a true story, that Josef existed and helped the Jews, I started to change my mind. Not right away you know. But later, after he showed me. Have you never changed your mind?"

"Oh, Solange."

"Karl, he showed me one! More than one! Golems! Just small ones, maybe 4 feet tall. He made them himself from the mud and stuff from Lake Ontario, that's what he said. He took me down the steps in the synagogue. Very deep, we were walking forever. And it was dark down there, like night…"

I held my head with my palms. "Oh God." It dawned on me then that my sweet babboo was a naïve girl.

Solange headed for the front door of my apartment.

"No, no, I didn't mean it, Solange," I said, hurrying to catch up with her. I held her arm. "You have to understand this sounds so crazy."

"You think I'm crazy?"

"No.

"You think I'm, making this up?"

"No."

"Then will you listen to the whole story before you make a judgment?"

"Yes, yes. Of course. I am so sorry. So sorry." I ushered Solange back to the kitchen table and pulled the chair out for her. I would have to listen now to the whole decrepit tale…what choice did I have? – the woman was carrying my child.

She took a long sip of wine. "You're lucky, Mr. Karl. I once murdered a man because he made fun of me. I cut up the body and buried the pieces at the beach. Late at night. Nobody saw. The perfect crime."

"How did you do it?" I deadpanned.

"Sex. I blindfolded him and tied him up. Then a big butcher's knife." Solange held the imaginary knife by the handle with both her hands and plunged it deep. "AEIIIIEGH!"

I laughed. This burst of eccentricity was so fresh and unconstrained. I liked it even more when Solange threw her arms around me.

'So anyway," she said, picking up the story without missing a beat, "Rabbi Bilchin led me down these stairs. Everything at the bottom, bottom, bottom, like we were going to …"

"Hell?"

"Yes, my sweet. To Hell." Solange took a deep breath. "But you know, the steps, these were made of wood, very old, every step was like 'creeeaak'… 'creeeak. Like a warning to stay away. So, if I think about it, maybe not to Hell but probably to someplace not so good."

I could have done without the sound effects but took a seat at the table and let Solange continue with her story.

"He had a lighter, that was the only light. So dark, big shadows, I thought I would fall. Then he finally turned the light on, it was like a little miracle after so much black. I was never so happy in my life to see the light! But the smell was very bad, like alcohol, something sweet too, like licorice, and some things I couldn't know. Very strong, maybe some cleaning fluid or something, what you find in a hospital, except ten times stronger. But I couldn't believe my eyes. Never mind the smell, it was my eyes that were burning." Solange hesitated. "Is this the right word, Karl, that my eyes were 'burning'?"

"I know what you mean, Solange, so just continue." I was going to throw in a 'oh brother' but thought the better of it.

"So my eyes were burning at what I saw. All these animals…they were all stuffed!"

"You mean the rabbi was a taxidermist?"

"Now this word is far too hard for me, but yes, just what I said – stuffed bodies. Because he told me that was his hobby, his passion. Of course he loved his religion but this was something else he also loved, I could tell. His big collection. There was a red fox, butterflies, squirrels, deer, a cat, a few bats, fish with sharp teeth, so many animals. There was also skeletons of things I did not understand, not human but I think not animal…maybe something in between? I couldn't tell. All these dead things, but somehow not completely dead. It was like the Rabbi wanted to hold onto their life, do you know what I mean, Karl? And there was paintings, very old ones, from another century, mostly from circuses that showed people who were deformed…very fat lady, two men, twins, who were joined together, a man with a head like an elephant, a very small lady, like my finger." Solange held up her forefinger.

"I was very nervous by all this," she continued, "especially when he showed me some hair in between two pieces of glass…he said it was from Joan of Arc. French people know of this Joan…she heard voices."

I was going to tell Solange that not only French people knew of Joan, but held my tongue.

"And also a piece of bone," she continued, "how you say…cartilage…from a knee, he told me. And a brain floating in a terrible solution – it smelled so bad, Karl, you can't imagine."

Solange became visibly upset as the story progressed and I held her hand, not daring to reveal to her that the rabbi must have been a complete lunatic. For certain a rogue rabbi who knew no bounds. I wondered who else was aware of all this. The big question is why he would reveal all this to a complete stranger. That much I could ask Solange, so I did.

"I think it really had to do with the golem, Karl. As I said, I went to many rabbis to see what they knew about such a monster. Finally I got to Bilchin. I think he's a very lonely man. He's a rabbi, yes, but with not too many people in the audience."

"In the congregation."

"Yes, that's why I mean. Only a few old, old men. I saw them, they were moving back and forth, praying, whispering. No young people, that's for sure. So I think this rabbi was very happy to show a young person his collection. I mean, it's not illegal, right Karl?"

I had to wonder how a rabbi would come up with a lock of Joan of Arc's hair. Maybe he was just lying. He probably was.

"No, I don't think what he showed you is illegal, Solange. Just very, very unusual. Weird, actually. No true rabbi would be involved in such things."

"Yes, I know. He told me he had been kicked from a regular synagogue. So he had to start his own." Solange hesitated. "Oh, mon Dieu, I forgot to say that there were many statues also. They were of dragons, and snakes, and gar...garga.."

"Gargoyles."

"C'est ca – gargoyles. And they all had their mouths open, like this." Solange opened her mouth as wide as possible and tilted her head slightly to one side. She looked grotesque and I hoped I never again saw her in that pose. But she got her point across.

"He's a collector for sure," I said. "The mouths are open because the water would come from a spout through them."

"When the moon is out, the light shining on their faces, these creatures must look very terrible. Very terrible." Solange glanced skyward. "And then he showed me the golems. On tables. Real ones for sure. On the forehead was some lettering I did not know. The rabbi said it was from the Hebrew alphabet."

"There's no such thing, Solange." I couldn't help myself, but how did I ever get it so wrong? Knucklehead. Here we were, my girlfriend and I, having a civil conversation, and now I had to go and open my big mouth.

"Excuse?" That look. Worse than the grotesque one a few minutes earlier. The eyes narrowed, the lips pursed, I could see her right hand balling into a fist. It all spoke of someone very strong-headed who, once they took hold of an idea, wasn't about to let go of it.

"It must be just a piece of art work, Solange. Like maybe made of paper mache or something."

Wrong again.

"You are so upsetting me so much, Karl Pringle! I touched it! Like this!" Solange made a stabbing motion with her forefinger. "It felt like pig. Rubbery. Not like paper mache, Karl Pringle!"

She never called me by my full name so I knew Solange was angry. But that only served to stir something deep within and made me wonder. She was utterly convinced of the existence of some mythological creature. What else did she believe in, I wondered…unicorns? mermaids? Bigfoot? Maybe she had spent too much time listening to that Le Monde radio show. Sheesh.

A thunderstorm suddenly moved in, the air crackled with electricity, and the rain, whipped by heavy winds, pelted the windows. Solange and I sat on the sofa and looked out, safe within the confines of my tiny apartment but aware that Mother Nature had effectively trapped us inside. I didn't mind, I was with my lady. My pregnant lady who believed in kooky things, including me, maybe the kookiest of all things. Me, the failed philosophy guy, the failed writer, the failure at just about everything. As I reached for Solange's hand, it felt so strange that I had managed to pull the caper off. It came to me then, this song by the band Talking Heads – Once in a Lifetime. Yes, about the man who has a beautiful wife and a beautiful house, and he wondered how he got there.

So we sat there, the two of us, and not a word further was spoken about the rabbi and his creation. Words, words, words…always my lifeblood, and now there were none. But still, I did wonder whether the golem smelled like pig's grease. I also realized that even smart people could be duped by a trickster. Joan of Arc – what a hoot!

I looked over to the table. There was still some Oreo cookie at the bottom of my glass, sunken treasure. But I let it linger in its bliss, slowly disintegrating. I couldn't tempt fate, lest I wake up from the dream.

All the things Solange and I had done over the past while cost me a small fortune. I was running out of money. My two credit cards were nearly maxed out, I had no jewelry to hawk, no job. Because I simply stopped showing up at my last job, I wasn't eligible to collect E.I. The only source of money coming in was the princely sum of $599 a month from Welfare. The one saving grace was a $2500 bond that my parents, as poor as they were, managed to squirrel away for me. It was my only safety net and I was always reluctant to cash it. Now I had to. There was no way out though – I needed to work. While I didn't mind, I just didn't want to be stuck in another dead-end situation. I wanted a job that was viable, where I could use my faculties and one in which Solange would have been proud. But the odds were against me, I knew that. I was almost forty and with only sales jobs and academic achievements on my resume.

I began as a trainee in the claims department of an insurance company. The phone rang nearly every minute. Someone was unhappy about the repairs to their car, the settlement offered on their break and enter claim, the contractor who was late arriving to fix the water damage in their basement, even my tone of voice...this, that, and the other. The person who was in charge of my training seemed to abscond for large periods of time and so every day I tried to muddle through thirty to forty new pieces of mail on my own. I lasted eight days.

My next job was as a taxi driver. The city roads were congested and I hated driving for long stretches with no passengers. I tried parking in front of a few hotels, hoping to get some decent fares to the airport but the doormen directed customers to airport limousines instead. On one occasion, an inebriated man threw up in the back seat; I had to clean up. On another, two punks got into the cab, one in the front and one in the back. I took them seven blocks and they got out without paying. I wasn't about to chase them. I lasted five days.

I tried other things. Pest-control technician, for instance. But I quickly realized that sleuthing through houses looking for rodents was making me physically ill; I felt nauseous all the time. Three days. A better option was working in a hardware store. At least for four days. The problem was that I had no interest whatsoever about any of the products. I couldn't tell the difference between a ball-peen hammer and a tack hammer or understand why anyone would want either of those things.

In the short course of a month, I was becoming an aficionado of exes. Ex-taxi driver, ex-insurance claims clerk, ex-this, ex-that. It was a joke, or should have been, but I didn't see it that way. Trying all these jobs with no luck made me feel worthless, and I could sense that I was slipping back into old patterns of thinking where the world was a stinking quagmire, populated by unthinking drones.

So quite on the spur of the moment, I went to see Suskind. Just to talk, as she had once proposed. I couldn't reveal all of my job failures to Solange but felt a strong need to unburden myself to someone. Anyone. I hadn't forgotten the endearing moniker the woman had saddled me with – a 'total fuck-up' – and how she had messed with my head. But she was smart, I had to give her that.

Unlike the previous two times, this visit didn't last as long. I met her at her office. For some reason, I didn't mind the clock...I seemed not to be bothered by it. I told Suskind about my relationship with Solange, that she was now pregnant and a regular fixture in my life. I also revealed all of my recent job tribulations and how I was somewhat desperate for a steady source of income.

It didn't exactly come out of the blue when Suskind said she knew all about the relationship, that Solange had told her as much. I did know that the two had forged some sort of bond when she the P.I. was working for me. I just didn't know the extent of the relationship and whether it had continued. Now I know that it did.

"As I explained to you last time," Suskind said, "Solange will be the best thing that ever happened in your life, Mr. Pringle. You shouldn't let her go. But you…"

"Me what?" I was readying myself for the verbal onslaught that I knew was coming.

"You will have to change."

Suskind's remark wasn't delivered with the type of venom I had anticipated. In fact, I found her manner almost to be gentle, unlike the way she dealt with me previously.

"You don't have to be the same thing your entire life," she continued. "It's entirely possible to change."

"I am changing," I protested. "Just being with Solange is doing me a lot of good."

"That's great. But go a step further. You can actually reinvent yourself, Mr. Pringle. I've seen it done. Let me ask you this: Do you think your present self has served you well up to now?"

It almost seemed that this was a trick question. After all, to answer properly meant that I would have to actually know myself. And furthermore, what did that mean? Exactly what was I to know about myself?

"Don't overthink the question, Mr. Pringle," continued Suskind, as if she could read my mind.

"It's not easy," I said.

"Then let me answer it for you: Dante. *The Divine Comedy.*"

Suskind looked my way with big, searching eyes.

"Heard of it. No expert, that's for sure."

"In the middle of the journey of our life I came to my senses in a dark forest, for I had lost the straight path."

I knew this was written hundreds of years ago but it sounded curiously like new-age gobbledygook. I told Suskind as much.

"I knew Dante's quote would elicit that sort of reaction from you, Mr. Pringle. That's why I brought it up. To prove a point."

I opened the palms of both hands beseechingly and shrugged my shoulders, as if to say: So what is that point?

"I'll get to that in a second," said Suskind. "I do want to tell you that Dante was talking about sin and how such a life is consumed in darkness. The forest of course represents that dark place where one might be lost."

"Are you suggesting I'm a sinful person?" I was about to add 'you twit' at the very end but backed off.

Suskind placed her palms together and brought them precipitously close to her nose, like she was praying.

"I read all about you in the Toronto Star," she said solemnly. "How you stole a story and passed it off as your own. That made all the rounds in the media. You were pretty famous there for awhile, Mr. Pringle."

"Oh." I suddenly felt extremely fragile, like I might splinter into a thousand little pieces.

"I should say, infamous, rather."

"That's probably a better word," I said.

"That was a moment of indiscretion," said Suskind. "You're not always like that, I'm sure. But the point I'm trying to make is that there are aspects of your personality that don't help you. They hinder you. And if you have any hopes of staying with Solange, you should make some real efforts to alter them. That's what I'm saying."

"Sometimes I think I've done all the changing I can," I said, musing. "I have long thought that a person's personality is forged during childhood, adolescence, then maybe in one's twenties. After that you're stuck with what you've got. Maybe you can change just a bit, but that's about it."

"I don't believe that," said Suskind. She went on to talk about how genetics plays a major role in shaping personality and to some extent, those aspects may be fixed. But that there were many elements of a person's essence, many different traits. Beliefs and values could be changed and as a natural consequence one's personality. Above all, she tried to emphasize that I should be more accepting of others, that I shouldn't assume my personality was the only right one. Because doing so had gotten me into a cocoon of isolation. Moreover, that intransigence was a hallmark sign of fear.

I didn't say anything more, just listened intently. For I didn't get the sense that Suskind was gunning for me; just the opposite, in fact – it seemed she was trying to help. Before I walked out the door, she told me to do good by Solange, that the two of us – or rather, given Solange's pregnancy, the three of us – could make a great team. I should have told her about Solange's strange beliefs, wanted to in fact, but decided not to. No one would really believe it anyway.

Chapter Twenty-Eight

Solange was always telling me how much she loved learning English. She thought the world of the teachers at Hansa, whom she considered to be wonderful, caring people. So after careful consideration, I enrolled in a school that taught people to become ESL teachers. It was a five-month program, two evenings a week. There was also a two-week practicum where prospective teachers would be placed at schools for hands-on teaching. There were other institutions I could have chosen, ones that offered certificates in a matter of a few weeks. But this one was well-respected and moreover, they allowed me to pay the $600 tuition in three installments. When I told Solange, she went on hugging me for what seemed like days. Of course, it wasn't the answer to my financial woes – I still needed to find immediate work – but it was a positive step. It was interesting too, being in an English-language teaching school. I had assumed I would breeze right on through but I was greatly mistaken. I quickly started realizing how little I actually knew about the English language. Progressive Verbs, Subjunctive Verbs, Restrictive Relative Clauses, Relative Adverb Clauses that Modify Nouns, Interjections, Correlative Conjunctions, Present Perfect Continuous Verbs, Gerunds, Infinitives – I didn't have a clue about what any of those entailed. Of course, I had used most if not all of them in daily speech and writing, but never realized it.

The course also focused on how to prepare a lesson plan, something I was somewhat familiar with given my T.A. experience. But this was different – role playing, using music, books and photos to teach grammar skills, social chat, listening activities to understand pronunciation…all of that was new to me. Having taught Nietzche was no help at all in this environment.

We all took turns preparing those plans. Classmates served as guinea pigs for those presenting, advising whether the lesson was comprehensible. How it might even be made better. The instructor gave us complete leeway and so the very first lesson that I cobbled together was entitled I'm Being Stopped! On paper, it looked like this:

LESSON PLAN
I'M BEING STOPPED!

OBJECTIVE: Students will be able to identify the reasons why a policeman might stop their car and then have the ability to plead their case to that officer or to a judge.

NECESSARY SKILLS RELATED TO THE LESSON:
Speaking/Writing
Creative thinking
Ability to interact as part of a team member
Ability to interpret data
Ability to conjugate the verbs 'to be,' 'to have,' 'to do.'

Familiarity with the auxiliary verb 'can.'

TENSES REQUIRED OF STUDENTS TO
COMPLETE THIS EXERCISE:
Simple Present
Simple Past
Present Perfect Continuous

VOCABULARY REQUIREMENTS:
Red Light, Speeding, Stop Sign, Stop, Slow Down,
Illegal U-Turn, Wrong Way, Road, One-Way Street, School
Bus, Car, No Left Turn, Drinking, Traffic Light, Weaving,
Crossing Guard.

PREREQUISITES:
Students should be familiar with basic rules of the road
and the Simple Present, Simple Past, and Present Perfect
Continuous tenses.

I divided the class into pairs and prepared index cards
that I gave them, a set to each duo. On the cards were
examples of the required tenses as they related to the topic of
having their car stopped by a policeman. So, this is what was
written:
Simple Present of 'To Be'
   I Am/He Is/They Are
   Example: I am a very good driver.
Simple Past of 'To Do'
   I Do/He Does/They Do
   Example: Yes, he did drive the bus.
Present Perfect Continuous
   Has/Have + Verb + ING
   Example: I have been driving for six years.

There were many such index cards, each with more verbs and with accompanying examples. Then I wrote on the backboard a simple dialogue exchange between an officer and a driver who had been stopped:

Officer: Can I see your license please.

Driver: Did I do something wrong?

Officer: Have you been drinking?

Driver: I have not. Why do you ask?

Officer: You were weaving all over the road.

I divided my classmates into pairs. Then they started interviewing each other, asking, *Did you see that stop sign? Can you name five reasons why a police officer might pull your car over? Did you know there was no left turn? Were you drinking?*

Each student within the pair was then assigned the role of either the police officer or the driver. And after a few minutes, I reversed the roles. I had them talk about how they would explain their weaving to the officer. Then to a judge. Role playing was a large component of the communicative practice that the school espoused and I was determined to get it right. Sometimes I felt just plain embarrassed about being involved in such simple game-playing but then I'd think of Solange and carry on with greater zeal.

There was special emphasis placed by the school on learning to be empathic. It was drummed into us from the start that immigrants learning a second language will encounter many problems and that we, as teachers, should be aware of that. For instance, learners from other countries often have difficulty pronouncing *th* sounds, primarily because those sounds generally do not appear in most languages. We were also taught that Chinese Mandarin is for all intents and purposes a tonal language. So a word like 'ma,' for instance, can have different meanings, entirely dependent on where the emphasis is placed by the speaker. In the third tone, 'ma' translates to 'horse,' in the first 'mother,' in the second 'hemp,' and so on. If all that weren't confusing enough, we learned that Chinese learners tend to be passive during group talks, so it was likely no help would be forthcoming from them that might shed light on their difficulties.

On the other hand, Spanish students have more of an advantage than their Chinese counterparts simply because so many English and Spanish words are similar. But nonetheless, they too encounter difficulties learning the language. English has twelve vowels and eight diphthongs, while Spanish has only five of each. I had never heard of a diphthong before I started at the school; to me, it sounded curiously like something very exotic one might order off the menu at a Vietnamese restaurant. But I found out that it's a gliding speech sound that begins with a vowel and then gradually changes to another vowel within the very syllable. In effect, two vowel sounds pronounced as one syllable. For instance, the oi sound in toil would be considered a diphthong. So too would the ei in eight. We were told that the word comes from the Greek *dipthongos*, di translating to 'double' and *phthongus* meaning 'voice' or 'sound.'

As a result of the inherent differences in the two languages, Spanish students often have difficulty distinguishing between words like "ship" and "sheep." Or "full" and "fool." And they often add an "e" before "s" at the beginning of certain words, especially consonant clusters. So a word like 'scrap' becomes 'escrap.' They simply find the "s" at the beginning of the word difficult to pronounce. Ah, the romantic language of Spanish. Like all romance, fraught with problems...but certainly open to wonderful possibilities.

Whether it would be language issues such as intonation, grammar, spelling, pronunciation, or more cultural aspects like shyness or trying not to appear foolish by asking questions, we came to understand that learning a new language for newcomers was no walk in the park.

Ah yes – not wanting to appear foolish. While it may have been the bailiwick of certain students, it also applied to me. For when I was taught how to give a simple grammar lesson on correct pronunciation of th, much to my chagrin, I had my fellow classmates rolling in laughter. I had to position my tongue between my teeth as I prepared to sound it out, then pull my tongue in as I pronounced the sound, allowing air to escape around it.

For some reason, I just couldn't do it. Maybe it was nerves but every time I tried, I seemed to literally spit. Saliva went tumbling out of my mouth like a cowboy expectorating into a spittoon. Of course I could easily pronounce words like *thicket or thrush*; it's just that I did it in my own inimitable way – no exaggerated wagging of the tongue. The whole affair was terribly embarrassing and I was aware I made a complete fool of myself. I laughed at my own ineptitude but secretly, I hated having anyone laugh at me. I found that part of the learning process especially daunting, the whole idea that it was perfectly acceptable, even encouraged on occasion, looking like a silly fool. Apparently, many foreign students loved it. Just as they loved games and role-playing, putting a human face on the teacher helped them relax and feel more confident about learning.

In short, it was a tour de force through the wonderful and sometimes wacky world of language. I might mention that I didn't mind my fellow students at all. Like me, I found they were a bit older. They all had undergraduate degrees from a diverse range of disciplines and many were in the program for the most altruistic of reasons – fully intending to give back to the community by volunteering their time once the course was over. Whatever the motivations, we were all in the same boat.

Finding a full-time job was proving extremely difficult. I was competing against people much younger than I, ones who often had relevant experience. I didn't want to go back into sales, that was a given. I sent out literally hundreds of resumes but got nothing. A big, fat zero.

My luck changed the day I happened to be walking past High Park. The west end was another area of the city I rarely went. I was only in Bloor West Village visiting a French pastry shop Solange was so fond of. I bought a few baguettes and fine pastries and decided to walk back. Along the way, I noticed a sign tacked to a bulletin board at the entrance to the park. It said that Parks & Recreation was looking for part-time help. To apply within. So I did and much to my great amusement, I got the job on the spot. It so happened that the administrator who interviewed me – Istvan Bartus – had been a friend of my father's. Another Roma, but one who had done exceptionally well for himself.

It was laughable. I knew absolutely nothing about taking care of grounds. And yet, in some ways, the job suited me. Istvan allowed me to pick my own hours of work and the three days of the week I wanted to work so I chose the evening shift, starting at 6 PM and finishing close to midnight. I was to prune, weed, roll sod, trim the hedges, plant, empty trash cans and pick up branches and garbage. If it rained, which it often did in the spring, I had to gather up all the worms I could see and deposit the whole squirming lot into a paint can on Istvan's desk. I never found out why nor did I bother to ask. The public washrooms had to be cleaned and all graffiti scrubbed from the walls. There was a swimming pool that I was to keep an eye on, making sure that kids didn't scale the fence for a quick dip. The training period consisted of two weeks, after which I was on my own.

One perk that came with the job had to do with the allotment gardens. For a flat fee of $30.00, the public could rent a plot of ground. They weren't terribly large, about twelve feet by seven feet, but for the avid gardener they would do nicely. They were also much coveted, with long waiting lists. I was no gardener but Solange surely was. And because I was now an employee of Parks & Recreation, I was able to secure a spot of my own at no charge.

The arrangement worked out perfectly. I was in school two nights a week and working three. I could meet with Solange during her lunch hours at Hannah's Kitchen and we also had the weekends to ourselves. Saturday mornings we ventured to the allotment gardens.

Plant low crops on the east, tall ones on the west, advised the old man who worked the plot next to ours. *That way the morning sun will warm the soil.* He certainly looked like the real deal – coveralls, straw hat, rake in one hand, trowel in the other. And according to Solange, it was sound advice. She planted carrots and potatoes to the east and peas and tomatoes to the west. She also found space for zucchinis and kale.

One evening I arrived home at just after 1 AM to find Beverly waiting for me. She had a bottle of wine and was sitting comfortably in a lawn chair right outside my door. Seeing me approach, she raised the bottle in the air. "Cheers, mate," she warbled in a mock Aussie accent. She had clearly been drinking.

"Beverly, what are you doing here?" I said, with just a hint on annoyance in my voice.

"Don't be upset, Mr. Pringle. I just couldn't sleep and thought we could have some of the Pinot Grigio you gave me. I never opened it."

"Just call me Karl," I said. "But that aside, we're not in class anymore."

"OK Karl. How about a little nightcap then?"

It may not have been the best decision to let her in. She was wearing a pair of very skimpy black gym shorts and a white halter top that clearly showed her nipples.

"I thought you could tell me about your writing." Beverly immediately foraged in the kitchen for a wine opener, as if she owned the placed.

"Top drawer," I said.

She brought out two wine glasses from the cupboard and joined me on the sofa. "I love wine, don't you?"

"Just one drink. Then you have to go."

"One drink it is, mate."

Beverly did the pouring and we clinked glasses.

"To health," I said.

"To us," she replied.

Beverly peppered me with questions about my writing – which magazines has my work appeared in, what was my novel about, did I have any writing mentors, where do I get my ideas from. They came at me from all angles but I was just too beat from working to make up any lies. So I evaded and stickhandled my way around each question. What I did notice was that with each question, she moved a bit closer.

"How's the wine?" she said, a bit breathless. She leaned over and blew softly into my ear.

What I did next was unthinkable but I put my arm around her shoulders and pulled her toward me; I may have well have asked her to move in. We kissed. Long and passionate. I put my hand on her breast. I was getting excited and before I knew it, I had taken her hand and was leading her to the bedroom. Then I stopped abruptly and ushered her straight out the door.

"I can't," I said, exasperated.

"Feel your desire," she replied, and tried to squeeze back in.

I barred the way. "Beverly, I'm in a very serious relationship. I just can't." Then I shut the door and slid the deadbolt in place.

Chapter Twenty-Nine

Solange had insisted that I get a cell phone. She wanted us to be able to reach each other at a moment's notice. I hated the twits who walked around yapping loudly on their phones, subjecting me to their inane conversations about what they were going to have for dinner that night, trivial details of their appalling lives. So I held my nose and bought one. The most basic phone imaginable - $29.95 for 200 minutes a month. No texting, no picture-taking, no internet access. For Solange, I would do anything. It turned out to be prophetic. Because on an evening when I was working at the park, using a pressure washer to remove some graffiti from the outer brick of a washroom building, she called.

"Don't be upset, Karl," she said.

Starting a conversation that way was tantamount to giving me a good swift kick in the balls. It could only be bad. I immediately turned off the washer.

"I'm in the hospital," she continued. I could hear her crying.

"Solange, what's wrong?"

The next voice that appeared on the line was that of Mrs. Sutherland, the woman whose house Solange was staying in. I had met her on a number of occasions and was someone I was quite fond of.

"Karl, it's Joan."

"What is it?"

"You should get here as fast as you can. Solange has lost the baby."

I left the pressure washer right there on the ground and sprinted to Bloor Street, where I hailed a cab. My stomach was in knots, my mind was racing, and each red light we stopped at seemed interminable. The driver started the usual small talk about the weather but I shut him down at once, telling him to just drive as fast as he could.

At the hospital, I took the stairs two at a time. In the room, Solange was surrounded by June and her husband and the two kids. June was holding Solange's hand when I walked in. There was nothing to say, not really. I just embraced my girlfriend and held on, kissing her madly on both cheeks.

"I'm sorry," Solange said at last.

"No. no. There's nothing for you to be sorry about." I held her at arm's length and looked at ma petite amie. She was as beautiful as ever. Pale, clammy, but still beautiful.

A short time later, a nurse walked in and asked us all to leave; the doctor wanted to run some tests. In the hallway, I corralled him, a black stethoscope hanging loosely around his neck.

"What happened?"

"Are you the husband?"

"Boyfriend."

"Most miscarriages occur during the first trimester," he explained. "Women in Solange's age bracket have a one in four chance of miscarrying. But we don't always know why they occur. It's sometimes related to age but not always. Often there are chromosomal problems, a damaged egg or sperm."

"But there were no warning signs," I said.

Joan was standing nearby and interjected. "Actually, she was having some really bad back pains lately. She had also lost a few pounds. Maybe five or so."

"Those could be signs," said the doctor. "Now if you'll excuse me."

"What are you going to do to her?" I asked.

"We had to do a procedure called a D & C to control the bleeding and prevent any infection. It's fairly routine but we like to monitor her. You can come back tomorrow."

The doctor put his hand on my shoulder. "I'm sorry for your loss," he said.

Joan and her husband invited me to the cafeteria for some food, a tea or coffee, but I declined. I just wanted to be alone.

As I walked out of the hospital, I thought about the doctor's edict: likely a damaged egg or sperm. I concluded that it could only have come from my side. Solange was as healthy as a horse, from good stock. Whereas I had come from the underbelly of European civilization – Hungarian Roma. Silently I cursed my parents. Even from their graves they were tormenting me.

We held hands and went for walks. Solange's pain was palpable; I could sense it in every pore of her body. It wasn't anything she said; rather, it was what she didn't say. She didn't talk about the baby, not about her school friends, she didn't say much at all. On occasion, she would mention her kindergarten students and how much she missed them. And her horse *Blondine*. Or the newspaper *Le Monde* and the magazine *Paris Match*. Most of all she missed her parents.

It shouldn't have come as any great surprise then, when she put both my hands in hers, held them to her cheek, and said that she was returning to France.

"You can't go," I implored.

"My heart is broken," she whispered. "Mon coeur est brise, there are no other words. So you must understand that I want to be close to my real life. I must."

"I don't understand. Real life? Am I not real for you? And so, what about me? What about us?"

"I love you. But it's not enough."

"Of course it's enough," I said. "We can try again."

"No."

"Just that – no?"

"Yes, just that, Karl." Solange turned to look into my eyes. "You are such a good writer, you have forgotten. Maybe you should resume your work. Put your energy into that."

How could she say that? I let go of her hands. Let go of the woman I cared about, the only person I cared about.

The days that followed her departure felt like the end of days. I tried to continue on – I went to school, kept my part -time job. But I was empty, emotionally crippled. My heart was heavy as a sack of bricks and I found myself just going through the motions. I would climb into bed and think of Solange. Only her.

This went on for weeks, and with each one that passed, I felt more hopeless. On one occasion, I visited the allotment gardens and saw that all the vegetables Solange had planted were withered.

I spent hours walking aimlessly through the streets, locked into myself. I met no one's eyes and no one met mine. I felt no connection to anyone, like I was an alien just landed. If I could have lived in a cave at the side of a mountain, I would have done so. Then I thought: Why not? Why not leave the city for a time and live off the land? If nothing else, it might make me forget my misery. And I needed a vacation from my life. So I arranged with Istvan to take some time off and took a bus to an area roughly three hours north of Toronto, where the terrain was especially hilly. How did I know where to go? Simple, I googled it.

Having slept poorly the night before, I was already tired when I boarded the bus. I read a book of short stories by Gabriel Marquez throughout the trip and seemingly in no time flat, the bus opened its doors and let me out. The rain, which had accompanied us throughout the trip, streaking the windows, had not let up. As soon as I debarked, I was pelted and the wind whipped my face. The other two people who left the bus, a middle-aged couple, immediately ran into a building and so I was left alone in the middle of a dirt road. I hiked up my backpack, filled with fruit, three bottles of water, some wine, sandwiches, and started to walk out of the Godforsaken little village. On top of my backpack was a rolled up sleeping bag, one that I had once purchased at a garage sale but never used. With my eyes stinging, my glasses runny with water, it was near impossible to see. I squinted and noticed hills in the distance. That was my destination, why not?

I put one heavy foot in front of the other. And the longer I walked, the greater the incline became. Although I couldn't make out my surroundings, there was no question but that I was walking uphill. Each step was an effort and it was like I was trudging through a bowl of jello. My shoes became muddy and I was soaked through and through. Every few minutes I stopped to try and get some bearing, but it was no use…I couldn't see even two feet in front. For some inexplicable reason, the face of Aaron Feldstein sifted into my frazzled brain and I found myself standing face-to-face with the slimeball. I reared back and knocked him to the ground with my fist. Immediately my body tensed up and as I kicked him a good hard one in the ribs, my breathing became laboured; I paused to catch a breath. What was this? I was miles and years removed from Aaron and yet here he had come back to haunt me, on a winding country road, in the middle of nowhere. Worst of all was that Aaron, bleeding from the nose and mouth, was looking up at me from his prone position, smiling ironically. Mocking me. Then he quickly vanished.

When finally the rain abated somewhat, I found myself standing close to a gaggle of Holstein cows. Chewing their cud, they stared at me as though I were insane. And maybe I was. A city boy born and raised, standing in the middle of a farmer's field. I had wandered off the main path. I made a face, sticking my tongue out and opening my eyes wide as saucers, but except for a solitary 'moo,' there was no response from the animals. Cold and miserable, I squeezed some water from my hair and then cut a swath through knee-high grass, jumping a small barb-wired fence.

I shivered uncontrollably but found that if I picked up the pace, I felt somewhat better. I had never jogged my entire life but there I was, sliding over the terrain like a long-distance runner. So I continued jogging and scanned the countryside where I might bed down for the night. The sun was setting and I needed to rest...all this exercise. It occurred to me then that perhaps I had made a grievous mistake. The question was philosophically evident to even the simplest minds: What exactly was I doing in this remote region, surrounded by farmer's fields and grazing cows, when I had my own bed in the city?

There was no one around, of that I was fairly certain. I had read that this area was prime hiking territory but at this time of year, newly removed from the dreaded winter and still quite chilly, not to mention muddy, it was only rarely traversed. I veered from the dirt road I was walking on and proceeded to my left, where I began to climb over sheer rock face. I could have stayed on the dirt road, but no, that was too easy. And 'easy' had never been part of my world. My wet shoes slipped time and again as I scaled upward on hands and feet, sending a small avalanche of gravelly rock downward. Fortunately, the incline wasn't all that steep and I was in no danger of falling.

And then I found it. A cave. Well, sort of. Not the deep limestone type that one studies in high-school geography class, full of stalactites and stalagmites hanging from the ceiling like icicles. Hardly, it was more like a shallow burrow dug by some large animal, a bear perhaps, and only a few metres deep. But for my purposes, it was perfect. A place to bed down.

I removed two peanut better and strawberry jam sandwiches from my backpack and sat down on the dirt floor of my cave to have dinner. I was famished and ate quickly, gobbling up the food. I wasn't exactly warm – my clothing stuck like a second skin to my body – but at least I was protected from the elements. It was still spitting rain and as I looked down into the valley below, I could make out a solitary fox scampering along a hill.

After swilling down the remnants of Beverly's wine, I let out a long sigh and my body relaxed. This wasn't so bad after all. The view was good, the company fine, and best of all was that nobody knew where I was. Like Ragman, I could assume a second, inconspicuous life. Karl Pringle, earth man. I rolled out my sleeping bag to let it dry and stayed sitting for hours, doing absolutely nothing but gazing into the distance and looking at the still-falling rain.

But then a strange thing happened. The longer I stayed stock-still, the more my brain started to wander. And it dawned on me that I had indeed made a fine mess of my life, that Suskind was absolutely right – I was a major fuck-up. My chest constricted and as the sun had now completely receded and I was awash in blackness, I was overcome with loneliness. Abject solitude that was unremitting and which bore down and covered me like a shroud. Was this how I would spend the rest of my days, alone? I had to lie down. I carried the still-damp sleeping bag toward the interior of the cave and slipped between the covers, pulling my legs into a fetal position, my hands beneath my head. I could hear the rain falling and was very glad for the sound. It lulled me to sleep.

In the morning, after having slept well, I woke with a burning desire to empty my bowels. The ground was saturated with dew and the rays of the sun shone brightly. Birds soared overhead in lazy swoops. As I left the cave and veered off onto the main path, I could see the cows grazing peacefully down below in the pasture where I had been. The chimney of the farmhouse was billowing lazy grey smoke. I saw a couple of black squirrels and I felt incredibly enervated by the entirety of my surroundings…any doubts I had had about what I was doing in the countryside were now gone. I felt that much better after I relieved myself in a wooded area. Only then did it occur to me that I had forgotten to bring toilet paper. So I reached down for some withered brown leaves from the ground and did the best I could. Then I used water from one of the bottles for a thorough wash. Not a great job then but what the heck, there was no one around.

I hung my sleeping bag and clothes from tree branches to dry out and returned to my cave to have breakfast. Another couple of sandwiches, this time baloney and ham with sliced tomatoes, and a healthy bunch of carrot slices. Sitting there in my underwear, I felt considerably better than I had the previous night. Looking down at the valley, I noticed railroad tracks, a smattering of farmer's fields, and in the distance, the small village where the bus had dropped me off. After the long winter, I could smell the impending renewal of nature, with vegetation inching through the soil. It was an 'earthy' sort of smell, there was no other way to describe it. A smell of mud, grass, tree bark, leaves and dew.

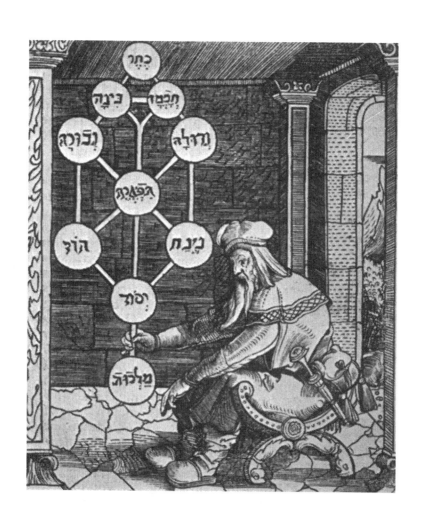

Then my eye caught sight of something glinting in the sunlight. I descended carefully from my perch and walked over. Hidden behind a phalanx of fallen branches was a very small cast iron charcoal grill. Undoubtedly left by campers, the discovery left me dumbfounded. There were briquettes of some sort in the grill; I had seen ones made of charcoal before but these looked curiously like peat moss. I noticed a crack in the grill but I didn't care.

I carried my find back to the cave and searched my knapsack for the lighter I always carried with me. I tried lighting the briquettes; they sparked but wouldn't catch hold, there was too much moisture.

Moving away from the cave, I upturned the grill and laid out the briquettes next to a tree where they could dry. The sun was shining brightly and I knew in a few hours, all the dampness would be gone.

I grabbed hold of a low-lying tree branch and let out a little shriek as I hung. Just because I could. It was glorious, I had nothing to do. I was as far removed from my not-so-glorious city life as could be. I could be anything here – a writer, movie director, big hullaballoo. Of course, there was no one to lie to but today it didn't matter.

A train rumbled by and I hid behind a tree. I was still in my underwear and peeked out, venturing a wave with my right hand. A short, Queen-like wave. Nothing ostentatious. OK, so maybe I wasn't exactly like the Queen. But this was my space now, and I lorded over it.

Days passed and I had almost run out of food. Only a couple of sandwiches remained. I considered going back to the city but liked being out in the country by myself so much, that I decided against it. Sure I had things going against me, like no change of clothes, no food, no toilet paper, no shower…but with the exception of the food, those were all minor inconveniences.

I watched a rabbit hop on by and thought about how tasty it might be. I could kill the little varmint and roast it. By this time, the peat had dried and I found I could easily light it. So I had a stove. All that was missing was something to fry up.

I decided right then that I might as well have a decent meal. So I followed the little rabbit into a forested area, where I lay low behind a boulder. He was cute, I had to admit, but it didn't matter – now it was all about survival.

I stayed behind the boulder until the rabbit moved into the shadows of the trees, a tangle of intertwined limbs. Big mothers that they were, the trees leaned their wooden bodies heavily toward me, obscuring my vision. If I didn't know better, I would have thought they were protecting the rabbit. I stood up, had a look behind some trees and not seeing any sign of the hopping critter, retreated back to my cave.

The next morning I woke to the sounds of something rummaging through my knapsack. A wolf! All black, with streaks of tangled auburn fur down its back, it was now eating the last of my peanut butter and jam sandwiches. I lay still, not daring to move, and just watched. If it was a wolf, I might be next on its menu. Feeling incredibly vulnerable within the confines of my sleeping bag, I thought the better of remaining quiet; perhaps doing so wasn't the best idea. I didn't know though…this was nature, and really, what did I know about nature?

I needed to let the intruder know I was in charge. The alpha male. I was about to yell out when the animal slowly made its way over to me and put its cold nose up against mine. Christ. I closed my eyes, my heart beat wildly, and waited for the worst. But then it licked my face…once… twice. I opened my eyes and saw that the creature had rolled onto its back, its legs sticking straight up into the air. I took a chance and started rubbing the belly. Would a wolf really ask for a belly rub? As little as I knew about nature, I concluded that probably not, that this had to be a dog.

I could feel every rib; this was one skinny pooch.

"Hey, you," I said. "Who do you belong to?"

I got onto my knees and patted the dog's fur, my hand getting stuck in the burrs. "You need a bath, Mister."

The dog, who had the appearance of a medium-sized mutt with no clear lineage, a mutt, closed its eyes meaningfully upon the remark and resumed licking my face. Its tongue felt like sandpaper.

When I had had enough face licks, I gently pushed the dog away. Its spindly appendages unable to maintain the weight of its body, it quickly dropped onto the ground like a stone and lay at my feet. It was abundantly clear that it needed a lot more food than peanut butter sandwiches.

"I think you've been on your own a long time," I said. "Just like me. I wonder if you have a name, huh?"

The dog opened its mouth as if to speak and I fondled its snout.

"How about I call you *Gorky*? You kind of look like a Gorky to me."

I dressed and walked down to the railroad tracks, Gorky following close behind, doing his best to keep up. A train passed, I lowered my pants and mooned it. What did I care?

There was nothing wrong with doing that…who hadn't seen a bum before? Then I skedaddled back up the hill to the cave and hid deep inside, shivering with excitement; I really was free to do anything I wanted. When the next train passed, I took off all my clothes and hung once again from the tree branch, with only my shoes on. I jerked my legs back and forth in wide arcs.

"I know this might seem strange to you Gorky," I said, "but I'm a free spirit and I do exactly as I please. You have no problem with that, right?"

Gorky let out a tiny yip.

"Thought so."

My stomach was rumbling and I suspected so was Gorky's. I made a half-hearted attempt to look for the rabbit, but it was nowhere to be seen. Having a mangy dog at my side was certainly a detriment to catching something to eat. More than likely Gorky would have wanted to play with anything I tried to catch.

There were plenty of squirrels scampering about but I wasn't about to eat one, they looked like giant rats. Gross. But at a little creek I found two green frogs lazily reposing on a rock, basking in the sun. I took my shoe off and bonked them, one after another. Again and again until they were flattened out, Gorky looking on passively. I scooped the pieces to the grill and started the briquettes up, searing the food, blood and everything else, until it was all crisp and golden. Then I ate it, tentatively at first, but then with gusto. It was actually pretty good, tasting much like chicken. I handed a chunk to Gorky, who gobbled it down.

I was still hungry so I went looking for the rabbit. But again the little bastard was nowhere to be found. So I thought I would check out the farmer's field – surely he had chickens or roosters. I put on all my clothes and Gorky and I walked back down the path until we came to the barbed-wire fence that I had previously jumped. I carefully lifted Gorky over and cautiously slid between rungs of the wire. We calmly walked past a dozen cows but they seemed to care not in the least. Gorky though started fidgeting, rearing up on his hind legs.

"You have to be quiet here," I said. And it struck me at that instant that Gorky had never barked. He had let out a single yip, but not a bark. Not once.

Just as I suspected, there was a chicken coop near the house and when we entered through the wooden doors of the barn, fowl flew hither and yon, their feathers catapulting into the stale air. I set my sights on the smallest of the bunch and while Gorky sat on his haunches and watched, I made a lunge for it. It squirmed madly in my arms and tried to peck at me.

"Piece of shit!"

So I wrung its neck. It was simple. A quick twist and it was all over, the thing fell dead in my arms. I opened the barn doors and stuck my head out. Gorky did likewise. When I was sure no one was around, we made a mad dash back to the fence and then up the path to my hideout. I looked for a rock with a sharp edge and proceeded to remove the chicken feathers as best I could. Blood squirted everywhere but after a few minutes, I had in my hands some semblance of a chicken we might eat. All I had to do was fry it up. I lit the peat and blew on it until red hot embers appeared. Then I carefully laid the bird onto the grill and with Gorky following at my heels, walked back to the creek to wash myself.

Every day after that, Gorky and I snuck into the barn where I proceeded to steal a bird. Some days two. And sometimes even eggs. On one occasion someone came in and Gorky and I hid behind a bale of hay. My heart beat madly and only when the barn door was closed was I able to breathe again. Good 'ol Gorky…he just kept watch and not a whisper came from his mouth – he was the perfect foil.

Unnerved by the episode, Gorky and I did not return to the barn but instead scoured the countryside for something to eat. I found more frogs and killed an entire colony without a thought.

I found some berries on bushes.

"These might be poisonous," I said. "What do you think, Gork?" I held a handful in my palm and let my companion sniff them. Gorky licked his lips and that was good enough for me. We gobbled them up. My big find that day however was the bunny that had to this point eluded me. I saw it hop behind a boulder and ran after it. I bent onto my haunches and reached into my pocket, pulling out some berries that I held in my open hand. Unbelievably, it crept forward. It didn't seem at all scared. I couldn't believe it, I had real power. I slowly picked up a large rock with my free hand and brought it down hard on the animal's head. There was a loud 'crunch' and the thing dropped dead at my feet. For good measure, I whacked it a couple of more times, dismembering one of the legs. Gorky stood passively throughout, looking on in awe.

I brought the rabbit back to the grill where I skinned it. There wasn't much peat moss left to light so I used twigs and some pages from the Garcia book I had brought along. It took hours to cook through but when the meat was a toasty golden brown, Gorky and I ate heartily. I couldn't believe a rabbit could taste that good. I licked my fingers and when I saw Gorky licking his chops, I laughed out loud.

I sat back against one wall of the cave and with the back of my head firmly cradled within my open palms, my companion's head in my lap, I considered that things were very good indeed. It had now been 10 days since my adventure began and I was in a much better frame of mind than when I left the city. I even thought that perhaps I could extend the vacation for quite some time, weeks, months maybe.

And now, feeling as good as I was, there seemed many possibilities. Even in writing. Sure I had messed up the Rivka stories but that didn't necessarily mean I was a bad writer, or that I couldn't write. I could, if only someone gave me a chance. And it struck me that the very bad press that I had received might actually work in my favour. I was a known commodity after all with notoriety. Some publisher might take a chance on me, knowing any book I wrote might sell. I was a curiousity to be sure but I wouldn't be the first time a writer who found himself in that position. Wasn't that James Fry guy in a similar situation? Yes, the more I thought of it, the more I realized things were looking up. Even the prospect of going back to the city didn't seem too bad at all. Of course, there was the added complication of what to do with Gorky, but one thing I knew for sure – I couldn't leave him to starve in the countryside.

The next day, bright and early, I took handfuls of berries and with Gorky at my side, waited patiently for the train I knew would be coming. It arrived regularly and by now, I knew the schedule. So when it passed, the sound of the rail cars clacking in my ears, I reared back and flung the berries at the windows. They landed with 'splats.' I could see passengers pointing at me and I dropped my pants to reveal my backside. Screw them. Were they so much better than me? I should hardly think not.

We trudged back up the hill and I got myself together, washing in the creek. The time seemed right to pay a visit to the village. I drank some of the water and then cleaned up Gorky as best I could, using my wet comb to smooth his fur. Gorky shook all over like an outboard motor. Then we slowly walked back down the hill to the little village.

"You and me, Gork. You and me. We're not going anywhere yet, but soon."

In a convenience store I bought some dried pepperoni, cheese, rye bread, olives, paper plates, water, and a large bag of kibble.

"New in town?" asked the storekeeper.

"Just camping out with my trusty companion here."

I looked awful, I'm sure, and I smelled, so what? People accepted you more readily when you had a dog, and the storekeeper threw in two cans of dog food.

"Promotional giveaway," he said.

"Thanks. Very nice of you."

Back at the cave, Gorky and I settled down to enjoy our feast. I had never seen an animal eat like that...no sooner did I finish filling a plate with kibble than Gorky gobbled it all and looked up at me with doleful eyes; the poor kid, he had probably gone weeks, months maybe, without having anything substantial to chow down on. To spice things up for him, I added bits of cheese and pepperoni into his food.

As a habit, after a meal Gorky and I would go for a walk. I would sometimes throw a stick for him to fetch but he never did chase after it; it was painfully obvious that he had never learned to play. The poor kid.

We returned to the farmer's field. An intoxicating smell of warming strawberry pie wafted to my nostrils. I could see Gorky sniffing the air as well. We bypassed the barn and instead made a beeline to the stone house, where I knew the smell was coming from. I stood on tiptoes and looked in through the crack in the window. There it was, a couple of pies cooling on the wooden kitchen table.

"Smells nice, huh Gorky?" I whispered. "Bet it tastes even better."

There was no one in the kitchen and I thought that if I opened the window just a bit more, I might be able to sneak in and grab them. I don't know what came over me, it was sheer madness.

But I just thought that since things were going my way of late, that I could get away with it. I slipped my fingers underneath the window sill and began to push the window open. Suddenly, I could hear a woman's voice and I started at the sound.

"Can I help you?"

It wasn't exactly a question. Not really. It was more like an accusation, one tinged with rancour. I readily accepted that, I wasn't about to make excuses, especially as I saw the woman standing with a pitchfork in hand.

"Me and my dog here, we're just hungry," I said. With that pronouncement, Gorky walked over to the woman, his ears pinned back and his tail forming little concentric circles in the air.

"Well, this dog is sure skin and bones," said the woman, stroking Gorky's fur. "You been stealing our chickens, haven't you?"

"Yes."

"Come inside."

The woman was wearing a red kerchief , worn jeans, and a faded red and white checkered shirt that ended in a flowered apron. She lowered the pitchfork and opened the front door. Gorky and I followed through the threshold into a large and inviting living room, a fire glowing in the cast-iron hearth.

"Have a seat."

I made myself comfortable in a wooden rocking chair and Gorky, ever obedient, sat at my feet. The woman, who I took to be in her late sixties, perhaps older, remained standing.

"Now then," she said, her dark eyes giving me the once-over like I was a common criminal, "how do you intend to pay me back for all the chickens and eggs you stole?"

I took out my wallet and offered her everything inside, a grand total of $ 28.35.

"Do you know how much each chicken costs?"

"No idea."

Just then, a calico cat wandered into the living room and upon seeing Gorky, arched its back menacingly. Gorky simply watched the feline with searching eyes but didn't move.

"Her name's Repunzil. And what's your dog's name?"

"I don't know. He's not exactly my dog. He just came into my little camp and has been hanging around. I call him Gorky."

"Gorky? That's a strange name for a dog."

"There was a writer by the same name."

"I have no time for reading," said the woman dismissively.

I could smell the sweet aroma of the pies and it made me salivate.

"What's your name?" asked the woman suddenly.

"Karl. Karl Pringle."

"Well, Karl, I'm Hilda. We don't get many strangers around here this time of year and when we do, and if they want to rest their bones, we let them stay a night or two. But when they steal from us, that's a different story…"

"I was hungry, that's all," I reiterated. "I'm sorry. I didn't mean you any harm. I came from the city and didn't bring enough food with me. I'm really not used to camping out."

"You coulda knocked on the door, all friendly like, and me or my husband woulda helped you out."

"Where is your husband?" I wasn't sure if this was an appropriate question or not but out it came all the same. I leaned forward toward the hearth and rubbed my hands vigorously; they were cold and stiff anyhow.

"Buying some livestock at an auction. Morty won't be back until late."

"Anyway, I have money back in the city," I said. "I can send it to you when I get back to Toronto."

The offer seemed to satisfy Hilda. She asked whether I was hungry, didn't wait for an answer, and ushered me into the kitchen. Gorky followed and ignored the swipe Repunzil took at his rear-end.

Pots and pans hung from hooks in the kitchen ceiling and the pies now looked as delicious as they smelled. Hilda fed both Gorky and myself large bowls of chicken stew from a cauldron that was on the stovetop and cut for me generous slices of black bread which I slathered with butter. The stew was brimming with chicken, potatoes, onions, carrots, peas – I had never tasted anything so exquisite and between mouthfuls, told Hilda that she was an amazing cook. She seemed to take great delight in watching me eat and as soon as I had finished one bowl, she said:

"Are we almost ready again?"

I nodded and very quickly my bowl was filled.

Hilda was a genuinely warm person. I don't know why, but she reminded me of my own mother. I hadn't thought of my mother in a long time and doing so made me sad.

"Where are you camping out?" she asked, as she doled out a slice of strawberry pie. I was stuffed, which wasn't surprising given that I had had cheese, bread and pepperoni earlier that day. But the pie looked too good to pass up, the rich smell so alluring, I just had to indulge.

"In the hillside," I said in between mouthfuls. "I found a cave."

Hilda joined me for coffee, strong and black, with a dollop of brown sugar. It was just the right way to end the meal. I sat back, my belly swollen, my mind at ease, my spirit sated. All I could say was 'oh my,' which I repeated twice. I looked down at Gorky. He had eaten three bowls of stew and was now curled up on the floor, sound asleep.

"You can stay the night," said Hilda. "Normally if people want to bed down, we charge $40."

"Like a bed and breakfast."

"Exactly. We have plenty of room. It's just Jack and me. But no one normally comes this time of year."

"I don't have $40 with me," I said.

"So if I let you stay, you'll owe for the chickens plus the room."

"I can't complain."

"I'll show you your room," said Hilda. "You don't want to sleep outside - it's gloomy and damp this time of year."

"Very kind of you," I said.

We let Gorky sleep it off on the floor and Hilda drew a bath for me. I never took baths, considered them a luxury I couldn't indulge in, and yet here I was, ready to slip into one.

"One for you and one for your dog," she said. "When he wakes I'm going to scrub him good. To get all the dirt off."

I stayed in that bath for a very long time, letting all the scum and grunge of the world dissolve. And when I emerged, Hilda had Gorky in his own bath out in a shed. Using a long-handled scrub brush, she untangled all of the messy fur. Water flew everywhere and a small puddle accumulated on the ground. Gorky remained silent throughout, looking down at the soapy water in resignation. I could see him anxiously swallowing and licking his lips, over and over.

"I don't really know how you got to be in such bad shape," barked Hilda, "but from now on, you'll be looking like a respectable dog."

When the water had turned black as coal, Hilda lifted Gorky out of the tub and wrapped him in a big towel. She produced from her apron a treat of some sort that she let Gorky snatch from her palm. It worked – he appeared especially mollified at that point and if I didn't know better, I could have sworn that a smile creased his elongated face.

The cat, who had followed us from the main house, sat transfixed, purring, and only moved when Gorky gave himself a massive shake, spraying Repunzil.

We went inside the house once again and by this time, the sun was setting. I was glad to be inside this warm, inviting house; it was so much better than being outside and for once, I didn't mind the company. I even offered up some tidbits of a real conversation.

"I was in school a long time," I said, as I stretched out before the roaring hearth. "I should have worked, but I never knew what I could do. Really, the only thing I was good at was philosophy.".

"Philosophy doesn't put bread and butter on your table. Only hard work does."

She had a point.

"So what are you doing now?" she said.

"Well, I think there's a job at High Park in the city. Kinda like a landscaper."

"That wouldn't hurt. Working the land builds character. And it'll build up your constitution."

By now, I desperately wanted to tell Hilda more about my life. About Aaron Feldstein. About Solange. I trusted her but something held me back and I just couldn't.

"So I'm going to leave in the morning," I said. "Go back to Toronto. And when I get there, I'll send you the money I owe."

"Keep your money," said Hilda. "But I think I should keep Gorky here. She'll have a lot of space to run around and Morty and me will make sure she's fed right proper."

"You mean…?"

"Yes, we'll have to rename Gorky. Maybe Jilly. She's no boy."

"Wow. I had no clue."

"Trust me. I know."

And who was I to argue with her?

I never did meet Morty. By the time I woke and had breakfast of pancakes and scrambled eggs, he was already hard at work driving a tractor. I looked out the kitchen window and Hilda pointed him out. There he was in the distance, a tiny speck against the horizon.

As I was about to leave, I put my arms around Gorky and gave her a hug. I didn't want to let go. She smelled so clean, and looked so happy. Never a peep from her, what a great dog. Tears streamed down my face. Hilda was right though – the dog was better off on the farm.

"Here, take this bag," said Hilda.

"What's that for?"

"Lunch. Meats and vegetables."

Hilda kissed my forehead and I embraced her. She really was like my mother.

"I'll come back," I said.

"Come whenever you like."

I walked out of there and waved as Hilda and Gorky stood in the doorway. I noticed all manner of tools leaning against the barn, rakes, a mower, sickles and shovels. I turned around to survey the countryside that had served me so well, making me feel better about myself, and my throat constricted.

People on the bus going back to Toronto gave me a wide birth and no one sat next to me. I don't know why, I certainly didn't smell bad or anything like that. Even the driver looked at me as if I were some sort of farm animal.

So that's the way it's going to be, I thought. *Fine.*

But maybe it was just me imagining, I don't know. It didn't matter though, my trip to the countryside had been an unqualified success – it not only made me feel good but it also allowed me to figure things out. And the one unremitting conclusion I came up with was that the entire Solange affair had been a complete waste of time. Yes, like it or not, it really had been. Like I had always said, women brought forth fear in me, and other utterly useless emotions. Things always ended badly with them. They always left. Even Gorky. I wasn't cut out for relationships because I was a thinking machine. A finely-tuned thinking machine; it's something I couldn't ever forget. Hilda may have been right when she said Philosophy didn't put bread on the table, but I never had a say in the matter. Not really, I was born to think. And I could still use my brain to great effect – I could write great stories, I was so sure, and be a fabulous success that way. Right, I could do it. Now I felt certain I could.

Chapter Thirty

I expected that Istvan would keep my job for me but he hadn't., he hired someone else. I told him about Solange, just to see if I could sway him, but even that didn't work.

"I'll keep you in mind if something turns up but you have to understand that I didn't know when you were coming back," he said.

"That's the best I could hope for," I said. I laughed good-heartedly and shook his hand.

Then I went to see Ragman at Carnival City. I just needed to talk to someone. I had felt so self-sufficient in the country, didn't need anyone at all, and now, back in the city, that all seem to be evaporating.

I found Ragman sitting on a large rock near his tent, looking into the distance, like he was contemplating the secrets to the universe. "Any ideas?" I said.

He eyed me suspiciously. We had never actually been the best of friends.

"What ideas?" he said. "What do you want?"

"I know what you do," I said. "I just don't know why, or how. Care to explain?"

"No."

"Oh, that's the wrong answer."

"Not to me it's not."

"Just tell me why you go to all the funerals. I give you my word I won't tell anyone."

"Your word is crap. He began walking away but I followed and grabbed hold of his skinny arm.

"Tell me or I'll make this hard for you."

"Let me go! I have to daven."

"You can pray later." I twisted his arm even further.

Ragman tried to squirm away but I held on tight. When it became apparent to him that my persistence was not to be denied, he stopped trying to get away and instead ushered me into his tent.

"If I tell you, you have to promise you won't tell anyone," he whispered.

"I won't tell a soul."

"So it's like this," he said. "I'm a…"

Ragman fell silent and immediately turned downcast, his forehead wrinkling dramatically.

"You're a what?" I said. "Spit it out."

"A thief," he whispered.

"You, a thief? Ha! I hardly think so. You're just an old feeble Jewish man."

"You doubt me."

"Of course. You're a harmless old coot."

"Then you're in for a surprise. Come, I'll show you."

"Where are we going? I don't have time for games."

"You have all the time in the world. Just follow me and you'll see."

So we left Carnival City and traveled to College Street West, to a warehouse with rented storage lockers. Ragman took me inside the building. He looked all around before opening a wide locker with a key. Inside was a cache of goods – flat screen TV's, computers, iPods, fur coats, leather jackets, electric bikes, motorcycles, kitchenware, perfumes, pottery. I had never seen anything like it.

"What is all this stuff?"

"Mine. All mine."

"You stole it?"

"Technically, no. But yes, it's stolen."

He then led me to another locker and opened that one. There was even more stuff. I ogled original paintings by Miro, Degas, and Dali. Jewelry spilled out from a small box that Ragman overturned.

"See this?" he said. "It's worth a small fortune."

He sat down on the floor and held his head. I looked through the bracelets, watches, broaches, and rings. Since I had had my own escapade with fine jewelry, I knew this was not cosmetic, it was the real deal, rightly worth thousands upon thousands.

I shook my head. Nothing was adding up. Here was an old man with oodles of treasures at his disposal, and yet he lived like a pauper, with copious amounts of junk in his tent. And what exactly did he mean when he said that 'technically' he had not stolen the goods but that 'yes', they were stolen.

"So why do you live at Tent Haven?" I said. "Are you nuts? You could be living in Forest Hill or The Bridle Path. Someplace tony and exquisite."

Tears started to form in Ragman's eyes. "Take what you want," he said. "It means nothing to me now."

"Really? If that's what you want," I said. I grabbed a fistful of jewelry and stuffed it in the pocket of my pants. Then I did the same with the other pocket until both were bulging. "OK, I'm good. Thank you. You're a nice guy after all, Mr. Ragman."

"Actually, my name is actually Jack. Jack Howard."

"OK Jack. But I think you have a lot to explain."

We sat on the dusty floor of the locker. I fingered the stash in my pants and felt incredibly happy at the touch. All mine now, my way out of poverty.

"Just don't tell anyone," said Jack.

I crossed my chest with my forefinger.

"I had a happy marriage, so I thought. But my wife left me for another man. Some butcher guy. A guy with blood on his hands and his smock. Imagine. I fell apart after that. I couldn't handle it."

I bobbed my head up and down. "I know what you mean," I said. "Women."

"So I took to drinking. We had a young daughter who I loved dearly and after the split, she went to live with my ex. I could only see her weekly and it was just too much for me. I had to get away, even if it meant leaving my daughter behind; I was a drunkard, she didn't need to see that.

We lived in Montreal and so I hopped on a Greyhound bus to Toronto."

"Interesting story, Jack. I feel for you."

"Tent Haven was the first place I came to because I had no money. Anything I had I gave to my good-for-nothing wife. Lawyers, you know…I spit on them. Anyway, people accept you there at the lake no matter how hard you've fallen."

Jack was turning out to be more articulate than I'd imagined, a highly intelligent man. I was about to prod him for more information but it wasn't necessary – he was a dam ready to burst; he needed to get the story off his chest.

"So you see," he continued. "I've lived at Tent Haven ever since I left Montreal. It's been a long time."

"But what about all the stolen stuff? And the funerals?"

"Ah that." The story that followed was almost un-believable and if he hadn't been sincere in its telling and even shed a few tears along the way, I might have thought it was all poppycock. But it wasn't, it was the honest-to-God's truth.

Living away from Montreal and hiding out at Carnival City, Jack lost touch with not only his wretched wife but also his beloved daughter. The divorce was not amicable, with his wife accusing him of child molestation. The judge believed it. His daughter was too young to know her own mind and had been swayed by her mother to repeat lies, lies she told the judge. Jack had to sell his clothing store and handed over the proceeds to his wife. Everything he had. That's when he took to drink and ended up at Carnival City. The story would be tragic enough if it ended there, but it continued on. Four years later, his wife died of cancer and the daughter was on her own; she was also without much money because her mother hadn't ever worked and went through nearly all of Jack's funds. By this time she was in her late teens and got it into her head that she should know her father. The very man she had inadvertently disowned when she was a child. It took a lot of digging on her part but finally she tracked Jack down. And she took the bus to

Toronto and like a ghost from the past, stood in front of him. Except he was in no shape to be a loving father — he was destitute and a drunken sod.

But seeing his daughter evoked something deep within him. It killed him that when they finally reunited, he smelled so bad that his daughter wouldn't even hug him. So with the help of AA, he fought through the booze and haze and swore to her that he would be the kind of father she needed. He just needed a bit of time. And it was during that period, when his daughter returned to Montreal, that he hatched the idea of going to funerals. He figured he was too long in the tooth to actually do an honest day's work, that no one would hire him, so he devised a plan to become a thief. Not the best sort of example for a daughter who he hoped would eventually look up to him, but he would sort that out later. Right at that time, he needed to land on his feet. And to do that, he needed money.

He thought stealing from the rich was the way to go. Surely the quickest. But how to do it? He had never before stolen anything. So he started perusing the newspaper death notices. He figured that with the family away at a funeral, the house belonging to the deceased would be empty. And he was right. All it took was a little ingenuity on his part, a little digging as to where the house was. He also had to ingratiate himself to the dead person's family and friends at the funerals and visitations. He always had a story handy, one he had devised before meeting with them, and it usually was that he was friends with the deceased in grade school or high school.

"Why did you have to go to the funerals?" I interjected. "If you knew the house was empty, why didn't you simply break in?"

"Ah, very good question. You see, if I was at the funeral, I could never be mistaken for the thief. It's as simple as that. Besides, I didn't have any technique for breaking into houses, that was beyond me. I was, let's just say, the mastermind behind the entire caper."

"I get it now. You recruited professional burglars to break into houses you knew were empty, right?"

"Well, not exactly burglars. Just one burglar. And it wasn't that clear-cut. You see, I didn't need this guy to do the actual break-ins. I only wanted him to teach my protégé the tricks of the trade."

"Your protégé?"

"Yes, someone I knew. You see, because while I was making sure the involved parties were away, she would enter into those empty homes. I knew it wouldn't take much if my protégé was well-trained. It really was the perfect caper."

Jack went on to discuss how he only targeted people he suspected of having money, people who were well-educated, who held down decent jobs, who had homes in good neighbourhoods. And so, with just a few phone calls and clandestine meetings with shady people, he was able to secure a top-notch burglar who could teach his protégée what she needed to know, how to pick locks, get in through locked windows, disable alarm systems, cut holes through roofs.

"Ah, so you were all set up," I said.

"More or less."

"Why more or less?"

"At first, I fully intended to hire this burglar to do the break-ins. It would have been the two of us. But there was a problem. My daughter wanted to come to Toronto to be close to me. I told her the time wasn't ready yet, that she should wait. But she wouldn't listen. She was very impetuous and as soon as she knew I was sober, she hopped on a Via Train. Showed up right at my tent once again. This time we hugged. Well, I couldn't very well let her live with me – that's no place for a decent young woman, as you know. But we both had very little money. Hard to get a decent place in the city that doesn't cost a fortune. The best we could do was get her a small apartment in a run-down building."

"Doesn't sound bad, Jack. I mean, maybe not great, but not terrible either."

"Oh, but it was bad. That building was full of roaches, and scary neighbours. Very scary."

Jack held the sides of his head between his palms. "Such a mistake. Such a mistake."

"You can't undo the past," I said.

"Yes, that's so. If only I could though. If only I could…"

I watched as the faraway look on Jack's face took him to other times, other places. I didn't say anything and let him linger until he was ready to talk further. After a time, he sighed deeply and came back to the present.

"My daughter enrolled in university while I continued to sober up and get clean. It's an ongoing process, you know. Being an alcoholic is like that, a life-long process. Anyway, when we were both somewhat more settled, I told her of my plan to dig us out of the hole we were in."

"What did she say?"

"I was surprised. I thought she might be really upset and try to talk me out of it. But she wasn't, she actually liked the plan. I guess she was worldly enough even at her young age to know that money is hard to come by. Also, she loved me, that was the bottom line. She wanted me to do well and pull myself out of poverty. I think she agreed more for my sake than hers. But she saw us as a team – Bonnie and Clyde, maybe."

"So what happened?"

Jack shook his head.

"My daughter enrolled in school and I started the process of working my way into funerals. It took a bit of time but soon we became that team we had talked about, schemed about – I would attend the funerals and my daughter would break into houses. ..she became the protégé. She was perfectly trained by the burglar. It wasn't hard at all. If anything was amiss, if someone from the funeral was unexpectedly on their way to the home, I'd phone her and she'd get out of there. It worked perfect. We started accumulating all these goods, which we stored here in these lockers. Just to take the heat off and prevent any suspicion; it was better than putting all the stolen goods into her apartment. So, we continued like that for quite some time, going to funerals, visitations, wakes, and breaking into more and more high-end homes. My daughter became expert at not only breaking into the houses but also shops. Commercial stores. She had become so good at what she did, she expanded her role as a thief and started stealing from high-end stores. She could beat any safe, any alarm system."

"So what happened?"

"She started losing it. And you know, I should have seen it coming. All this stealing ate at her. She was a sensitive girl. To cope, she started doing drugs...sedatives, anti-depressants. And her clothes, oh my God. She had always been such a colourful dresser; but now, she only wore black clothes, like she herself was going to a funeral. Anyway, I know she wanted to please me, that was the bottom line. It came at the expense of her own psyche though. I guess that's the word – psyche. I tried to help but I didn't know what to do – we were in so deep. By then, we had accumulated a locker-full of goods. And she also kept some stuff at her dingy apartment. Mostly clothes."

"Why didn't you guys just stop all this nonsense? Call it a day and be happy with what you got?"

"Yes, I know. But it was more complicated than that. Because the burglar who taught my daughter saw what we were doing and wanted in. I should have realized it would be difficult to have him not notice. Every time we stole something, he wanted his share. More than his share. I had paid him for his services but that wasn't enough. So he blackmailed us. When he saw what we had accumulated, he wanted us to continue and give him a big cut. He said that if we didn't, he would alert the police to the locker...and to us, obviously. We had no choice but to keep on with the entire charade just to satisfy him. He made us continue on, I tell you. And you don't want to mess with guys like that, I can assure you."

Jack started tearing up once again. "I didn't know what to do. We had all these goods but they just sat in the locker until we figured things out. But we never did. My daughter deteriorated, taking more and more drugs. And I started drinking again."

"So what happened to your daughter?"

By this time, Jack was in the throes of an all-out bawl. I had never seen a man lose his composure like that. "She died," he finally uttered. "A drug overdose."

I don't know why I did it but I reached out to grab Jack's hand, which was cold and clammy.

"I'm sorry," I said. "That's a terrible story."

Jack exhaled deeply, sniffling. "Even after she died, I continued going to the funerals. I wanted to stop, I really did, but I was pushed beyond my limits. Because the burglar decided to step right into my daughter's shoes, and so while I continued to play the sympathetic old friend, he did the nasty part of breaking and entering. My dead daughter's shoes. Her shoes. So I continue on even to this day because if I don't, the scoundrel will advise the police."

"My oh my." I considered what Jack had told me and told him that if the guy ratted on him, he would implicate himself.

Jack wiped the tears from his eyes. "I guess so, but I can't take the chance. I don't want to end up in prison. But you know, all the davening I do down at Tent Haven, I'm praying for the soul of my daughter. It's the least I can do."

"There's one thing I don't get," I said. "When she died, why didn't you step forward to claim the body? Because I know you didn't."

Jack could barely speak. He whispered that he couldn't, he absolutely couldn't. There were stolen goods in his daughter's apartment that might have led the police straight to him. He was only trying to protect himself.

"And how did you find out about her death?"

"She didn't pick up when I called. So I went around and saw the police in the apartment. There was a whole bunch of neighbours standing around and I just blended in. I found out that way, by asking what was going on in the apartment." Jack blew his nose. "I know, I know, it's terrible. I deserved to die, not her."

There was one more thing. I just had to ask. "Do you know anything about a group called The Underclass?"

Jack wrung his hands and his brow furrowed up. I had obviously struck a nerve.

"Bastards," was all he said.

"Why do you say that?"

"When my daughter started stealing," said Jack rather slowly, "we both thought it would be for the short run, until we got on our feet. But then there was that burglar…"

"Right. You said that, Jack. The guy who taught your daughter how to steal."

"That's the one."

"The guy who wanted in on your take otherwise he was going to rat on you."

"One in the same."

"So what about that guy?"

"His name was Michael Watson. A big slob of a guy, but a helluva thief." Jack shook his head scornfully. "You'd never know it by looking at him, I'll tell you."

Michael Watson? The name rang a bell but I couldn't quite place him.

"Anyway, he ran that organization The Underclass and he influenced my daughter terribly," said Jack. "Put all sorts of ideas in her head about having the right to steal from rich people. She was fragile to begin with and yes, I'm to blame for having gotten her involved in all this stealing in the first place. But I'm telling you, Watson and his group pushed her right over the edge. Even gave her some drugs. I've heard they're bad. Unclean, mixed with stuff. And it was his doing that she started breaking into stores. He forced her. He wanted a piece of that action too."

By this time, Jack was thrusting his forefinger at me accusingly.

"I'm not him," I said.

"Right. Right. I'm sorry. Just talking about the past makes me a little crazy."

"I get it, but it's not good enough." I stood up and reached into my pockets, pulling out all the jewelry and putting them back in the box.

"Maybe the next time you daven, Jack," I said, "you should do so for your own soul." And with that, I departed the warehouse, leaving the old Jewish man sitting on the ground and crying.

It struck me then, quite out of the blue, that the stories people tell are never as simple as they appear. That they are interwoven into the lives of other people, and are highly complex. It also dawned on me that like it or not, we're all inter-connected. I understood it all now, and although I knew Jack was responsible for a life, had actually been the catalyst for the demise of that life, I was grateful to him for connecting the dots.

The first time I sat down to play Camelot once more, it was like returning home all over again. I was back in Albion and being threatened by Morgana...I needed a sword in the worst way. This is where I belonged, in this fantasy realm. To hell with reality! Camelot was so much more interesting, and safer for someone like me. Here I could reign and be my true self. I was almost content, that was saying something.

So I settled into a routine of playing Camelot, sleeping in late, and going out for walks late at night. The days held no interest for me, but the nights were full of intrigue. Where possibilities existed. Of course, those were only forged in my mind and had no basis in reality. Still. Still. So it was only then, under the veil of the night, that I pulled open the heavy curtains in my living room and let in the light of the streetlamps.

I tried to write. Really I did. But I sat down at the computer and found that I couldn't get past the first few paragraphs. I'd read what I had written and throw it out. I knew good writing from bad and this was definitely in the latter quality. It's not that I didn't have any ideas; I had a head full. In fact, I thought my own life story might be of interest. But I found I just couldn't write in an interesting way. Nothing flowed, I couldn't turn a sentence over. I tried mixing it up, using both the present and past tenses, first person and then third. Nothing. So with each failure, I felt myself sinking and would slump my head against the computer desk. It was sheer agony, nothing less, and old feelings of worthlessness began to emerge. I thought my brain would explode and I found I had to nap often during the day to keep myself sane.

The one thing that kept me going was Beverly. She came over. Many times. Two animals in heat. The sex was rough, the floor of the apartment littered in the morning with empty beer and wine bottles and condoms. After, she would ask me about writing - she wanted to try her hand at it. I told her the most important thing was rewriting. Revise, revise, revise. Polishing the work until it shone like a cut diamond. I explained to her that she should write what she knew about, that all writing was, at least to some extent, autobiographical. I went on and on. "And don't aim for the stars," I said. "Start small, try to get your work into literary magazines. Not The New Yorker. My first story was with a very small magazine in northern Ontario, I don't even remember what it was called. It was a general interest magazine. Oh, one last thing: when you think the story is good, let it go. You have to know when something is finished." I told her the story of Joseph Grand, the character in Camus' *The Plague*, who has ambition about writing the perfect novel but can't get past the first sentence. He wanted to shock the world with his writing but that first sentence never was quite good enough to do so. Standard stuff. I felt good about lying to Beverly regarding all that I knew about literature and writing, my successes, and how I managed to climb to the top. There was nothing left for me but to lie.

Chapter Thirty-One

It so happened that one day, at the ungodly time of 10:15 in the morning, there was a knock on the front door. That was followed by two others. Hard, solitary knocks, with long pauses in between. Who knocked that way? It was those pauses that startled me and caused me to get up out of bed and answer.

Solange?

Numbed by shock, flabbergasted, I dropped my head and flung my arms around her. I stayed holding her a long time, uttering Oh my God, Oh my God, over and over again. With my arm around her waist, I escorted her into the living room.

"Please sit," I said, my eyes moist. I could barely see.

But she stood.

"Solange, please." Briefly, I held her cheeks in my palms. She blinked but remained standing, almost rigid, as if at attention. I wiped my eyes with the back of my hand and looked at her carefully; she appeared glassy-eyed and it struck me that she might have been repelled by my appearance or perhaps the smell – I hadn't washed or changed my clothes in days; looking down at my feet, I could see two giant holes where my big toes emanated through my socks.

"I'm sorry," I said. "I thought you were gone. I haven't been taking care of myself, as you can no doubt tell." I kissed her forehead. She now wore her hair in long bangs and I had to move her hair to the side. It was an unusual look for her; normally she wore her blonde hair up, off her face.

That's when I noticed it. The strange markings. I took a step back.

"What the..."

I cautiously ran my fingers across the markings, which looked like hieroglyphics. Solange remained unmoving, barely registering anything, certainly not my touch. With only the occasional blinking, she appeared like an automaton.

I took a deep breath. "What's going on?"

But there was no response.

"They decided to make my novel into a movie," I said. "We should go out and celebrate."

Nothing. I was sure she would laugh, jump up and down, maybe even kiss me. But Solange, or whatever it was that stood before me, did not react.

"Oh no..."

I had to sit down, I felt faint. Nothing in my life had prepared me for this. How could it? Myth and reality were now intimately intertwined. Myth and reality! Studying philosophy had always been for me, a search for the truth. But myth was an alter-reality, and I had no context.

Then, quite suddenly, I thought that perhaps Solange was having me on. It had to be. She was just getting back at me for all the derisive comments I made about Rabbi

Bilchen. I stared at that goofy, faraway look of hers, the bizarre writing on her forehead, and began to relax.

"OK, Solange, I get it now," I chuckled. "I get it." I pointed my forefinger at her. "You're getting back at me and honestly, I don't blame you. So smart. Come sit down." I patted the cushion on the sofa. Then I grabbed hold of her wrists and squeezed lightly. My fingers sunk deeply into the flesh and I immediately let go. What was this? I squeezed again, harder this time...there was no bone structure, her skin felt almost rubbery, like I was squeezing baking dough.

I started crying. When I composed myself a few minutes later, I went through the thing's pant pockets. I found a note:

Dear Karl, it began. *Now you have it, your own personal golem! I know you are lonely because I am gone and so I thought I would give you a gift. Of course I had to go to Rabbi Baruch Bilchen for help, so you can say the gift is from both of us.*

The golem looks like me. I thought this was best. Sometimes when people are alone it is nice to have something to remind them of the past. You would not want a golem who looked like Albert Einstein, correct? There are certain advantages to having a female golem, as you will see. However, as with anything that is good, there is usually something not so good. I am sorry about this, but there is no way to fix it. I think your golem, the name is Simone, cannot speak. That is the bad part. I think you know from your own research that golems are not able to talk. There is also the Hebrew lettering on the forehead which maybe does not look so great, but you cannot erase it. Do not try. If you do, you will kill Simone. That lettering brought her to life.

There is something else. Simone will not do anything by herself, by her own will. Of this I am almost certain. You must always command her. This is easy to do. You can speak the name of God first, and then tell the golem what to do. But you must not call God by his actual name, the Rabbi advised. You must only call out HaShem, which Bilchen said translates to 'his name.' This keeps you separate from God and in this way, you acknowledge his eternal presence. Humble. So you can say, 'Simone, in the name of HaShem, I ask you to wash the dirty dishes in the sink.' One more thing, my dear. I must tell you that if you misuse the power of the golem, it will be very bad for you. Very bad indeed. Misuse...that's a word the rabbi explained to me. Now I can use it in conversation. So, always use Simone for good, never evil, that's the important thing.

I miss you.

Love,

Solange.

So now I knew. I studied the figure before me. With the exception of the hair, it looked exactly like Solange. I suspected Solange had the golem wear her hair in bangs so as to hide the Hebrew lettering. Even the clothes the golem wore resembled those from Solange's wardrobe. And maybe they were. Perhaps Solange had simply outfitted Simone with some of her clothes.

A haunting silence settled over the apartment. I could feel it in every fibre of my body. I was in the presence of another being but I felt quite alone. Scared too, and then suddenly angry. I mean, why would Solange stick me with a cheap copy of herself? Did she really think I was so shallow as to accept this imposter, one who couldn't speak at that? With Solange, I came to understand how important communication is in a relationship. Why, I even buckled under and bought a wretched cell phone, the calling card of the masses. Now all that gone and I was faced with a lifeless copy. If Solange had really wanted my happiness, she would have come back in person. And then I thought: This entire episode was just another example of what my German philosophers colleagues would call weltschmerz, the agony of realizing the world wasn't meeting my ideals. Unfortunately, it never has.

My instinct was to run away. Run from this madness. But I stayed. Call it curiousity – I realized that not many people get to take part in a Grimms' fairy tale.

"Hello," I said to Simone. I used the small flashlight on my keychain and shone it in her eyes. They looked lost, staring into the unfathomable distance. Maybe she was pining for the far shores of Lake Ontario, from where, undoubtedly, Bilchen had constructed her.

I need to rest, I thought. I lay on the couch and stared at Simone, who remained standing. Then I closed my eyes and before long, drifted away, probably out of sheer anxiety and exhaustion. When I woke, Simone, like a bad dream, was still there in all her otherworldly glory. She hadn't moved a muscle.

So I was stuck with a cheap copy, there was no doubt. I wondered what Solange meant by saying that there were 'certain advantages to having a female golem. As far as I could see, there were none. It was like having a dog; with all due respect to Gorky, you had to walk the animal two or three times a day, pick up after it, feed it, bathe it. Who needed the headache? I had no idea if any of those same type of responsibilities awaited me with Simone, but I suspected as much.

I thought of other things, like what would happen if I stuffed Simone in a closet and left her there. Or if I let her loose in Kensington Market; undoubtedly, with that glazed look in her eyes and the fact she would not move (unless I ordered her to), the police would pick her up. At some point, she would be subject to a psychiatric evaluation. And the diagnosis would be that she was catatonic. Mute as well, perhaps the end-result of drugs or some catastrophic traumatic event. She would be shuffled off to a mental institute where the doctors would pump her full of drugs to get her responsive. And would the drugs have any effect? If not, what then? Simple. Big Pharma would step in and in conjunction with the head doctors, create a brand new pill, a very expensive one at that, to cure whatever it was that ailed Simone.

But truly, I didn't know what I was now saddled with. I was just making all sorts of inferences. Ok then, if I didn't know, there was one person who did – Rabbi Baruch Bilchen. I had to seek him out and ask him what the hell he had created.

I looked at Simone. She was alive, obviously, but seemed half-dead. Alive and dead at the same time, that was interesting. It reminded me of a physics class I once took where we talked about the famous Schrodinger's Cat thought experiment. Such a paradox. It took place a long time ago. In 1935 to be exact. And it was that Erwin Schrodinger, a physicist, who said that if he were to place a cat inside a sealed opaque box along with a radioactive sample, a Geiger counter, and a vial of poison, there would be a 50/50 chance that an atom in the radioactive sample would decay and emit an electron. If it did, the geiger counter would sense that and smash the vial of poison. The cat would then die. On the other hand, if that atomic particle didn't decay, the cat would live. But this would not be known until the box was opened. In the interim, the cat would exist in an indeterminate state…the possibility that it was dead, the possibility it was alive. Two simultaneous but contrary states being true. So now, here in front of me, was a real life example of that alive-dead state in the form of a golem.

It struck me as I ogled Simone that perhaps I wasn't so much different. Of course I was alive, but at various times in my life I had been a somnambulist, a sleepwalker. I couldn't deny it, I had slept away large chunks of my life.

I thought I would try to command the golem:

"Simone…er…HaShem," I blurted clumsily, before retrieving Solange's note. "So again. Simone, in the name of HaShem, I want you to go to the fridge and make me a sandwich with whatever ingredients you can find. I'm hungry."

There was no response. It was like the Golem's batteries were dead.

I diverted my attention away from Simone and did what any normal person would do when saddled with a golem – I googled its creator.

Rabbi Bilchen was the head of the Aaliyah Syngagogue. To say it was a full-fledged synagogue in the manner of some of the more traditional synagogues in the city, like the Holy Blossom Temple where I followed Ragman to, would be stretching it. I learned that Holy Blossom had roughly

6,500 members and was located in the heart of a Jewish enclave – Bathurst and Eglinton. Aaliyah, on the other hand, was a ramshackle cottage in the west end of the city, at the end of a dirt road far removed from the road, close to a meat-packing plant. And it was there that I decided to go. Right then and there.

As I walked to the front door, the stench of newly-slaughtered animal carcasses turned my stomach. The front lawn was overgrown with weeds and as I made my way along the cobblestone pathway, I wondered exactly what sort of synagogue this was. It was partially hidden by a raft of clinging vines, like something out of an old Victorian gothic novel. I assumed that this was a synagogue that surely couldn't have been many patrons, the location and smell being such a turnoff. Equally disturbing was a sign posted on the front door – Buns of Steel, 8 PM. Buns of steel? I swatted at a wasp that was buzzing my head and stepped inside.

Four men were kneeling on mats, their foreheads flush on the floor. What? Since when did Jewish men pray in such a manner? They didn't. The men were clearly Muslim, I could see by their white prayer caps, Abe Lincoln-like beards, and long white robes.

I turned to go, this was too weird. But suddenly a man, who couldn't have been a day under seventy, wearing a yellow yarmulke and a Jewish prayer shawl, appeared near the pulpit. His fluffy beard was as white as the driven snow and he had long, stringy hair to match, sticking out from beneath a tall black hat. He motioned to me and I followed him into a room. When he turned the light on, I could see we were in a kitchen, surrounded by an assortment of hanging kitchen utensils and pots. There were unwashed dishes piled high in the sink.

"You musn't disturb them while they're praying," said the man. "It's a sacrilege. Salat is done five times a day. What's the matter with you?"

I looked at the stick-thin man who was now talking. Scolding might have been the more appropriate word, and I didn't like it. The veins in his pencil-thin neck held up a very angular face. In fact, he was all angles, a walking quadrilateral. He reminded me of Ragman, except he wasn't. The Wizard of Oz's Strawman perhaps. What was it with religious Jewish men though, didn't they eat? Or did their constant devotion to a God cause them to forget to nurture themselves?

"I'm Rabbi Bilchen," said the thin man, extending a limp hand. "Why is your hair so shiny?"

"Gel, but that's not your business."

"Hmpphhh."

"Buns of steel?" I said, changing the subject. "Muslim men? Is this really a synagogue?"

"Of course," said Bilchen. "Of course. We have to pay the rent, you know. Anyway we can. So we allow a pilates class to hold their sessions here." Bilchen tapped his rather decrepit rear-end. "Buns of steel, you see."

"No I don't."

I stood looking at the scrawny Bilchen and wondered whether he was a real rabbi.

"Anyone who has good intentions and money can rent our space," he continued. "We're all for equal opportunity.

It's the same for Muslims, the Jains…anyone who needs a place to worship. You can say we're an Interfaith type of synagogue."

"Not a real synagogue then. Just a place that incorporates a hodge-podge of assorted religions and events."

"Hodge-podge. Hodge-podge," mumbled Bilchen to himself. He turned away and slipped around a corner, completely out of view. Did he want me to follow? I couldn't be sure but I did anyway.

Down a rickety wooden staircase we went. It was completely dark and the stairs creaked miserably with our every step, like it about to buck us off. I held on to a wooden railing for all I was worth. At a certain point, Bichen took out a Bic lighter and turned to address me. "Why are you following? Who are you anyway?"

'You know a woman called Solange?"

"No."

"What do you mean no? She told me all about you, how the two of you created a golem in her image. In fact, the golem is in my apartment. Her name is Simone."

Bilchen fingered his beard. "I see," he said laconically. "I see."

"Look," I said, "I'm here because I want to understand about this golem. What it can do for me, how to use it. Can you teach me?"

"Teach me, teach me," parroted the rabbi, throwing his puny hands in the air. "Everybody wants something from me." He continued down the stairs and with each one we traversed, the smell became more despicable, like a combination of formaldehyde and yes, just as Solange had said, licorice…sickly sweet. I felt like gagging. If I thought the smell at the front of the synagogue was wretched, this was so much worse.

At long last, we descended into the basement where Bilchen turned the light on. I was astounded by the sight of stuffed animals – a red fox looked as though it was ready to pounce and up above, hanging from a wire, a great horned owl, looking especially severe, appeared poised to jump on my head, claws extended. Then a leopard was about to take an imaginary swipe at me. An unfinished sea lion with very long whiskers had wire and white cotton sticking out of its great belly. Of particular interest was a large aquarium, its sole occupant either dead at the very bottom, or else simply resting.

It was a long, slithery-looking thing, not exactly a fish, with the appearance somewhat like an eel…but not quite. In fact, it looked like nothing I had ever seen before – an elongated dish rag maybe, a slippery, unformed thing…a blob.

"I see Charlie has caught your interest," said Bilchen, rubbing his decrepit hands together.

"Charlie?"

"Yes, I name all of my friends here. See that beaver over there, munching on a tree branch? That's Topo. And the baby deer standing in the corner, Mildred. The giant tortoise is called Grassy because when he was alive, he loved to munch on tall grass."

"Where did you get all this stuff?"

"That's not something you have to know."

"So what about Charlie?"

"He's a siphonophore. Don't think about putting your hand in the aquarium because Charlie will give you a nasty sting."

"I had no intention of doing so. Are you a fool?"

"Look, Mister...Mister..."

"Pringle."

"Look Mr. Pringle, if you're going to slander me, an esteemed rabbi, you can just leave now."

An esteemed rabbi? What a riot.

"I'll continue then," said Bilchen, shaking his head sadly at my insolence. "Charlie is not just one creature, he's a whole colony called a 'zooid.'"

"I never heard of that," I said.

"I'm not surprised." At that declaration, Bilchen appeared to puff out his chest. "So you see, Charlie is composed of dozens of these zooids and each one has a special function. For instance, one will be responsible for feeding, another, swimming. And yet another for fending off predators."

"You wouldn't think there'd be many predators," I said. "Charlie looks like a piece of trash."

Bilchen snuck a quick sideways glance at me and ignored my last statement. He went around petting each stuffed animal, talking to them affectionately. For Charlie, he sprinkled into the aquarium some flaky green-coloured food and all at once, a portion of the zooid, the rear end, sprung into action and gobbled it up. It really was alive, this very strange creature.

I turned to a frozen-solid cottontail rabbit that caught my eye. "This is highly unusual," I said. It wasn't the bunny itself that was so odd as its placement in back of a coyote – it looked as though it was pursuing its natural enemy.

"You're right," said Bichen. "Edith here was chased her entire life. From the air, by hawks and owls. From the ground, by coyotes, skunks, weasels, foxes. But in death, I wanted to give her a chance to turn the tables. No longer prey, but rather predator."

"Predators and prey exist only while alive. Now they're just animated figures."

"Predator," said Bilchen, once again ignoring me. "Edith the predator."

Rabbi Bilchen was one strange dude. If he couldn't tell the difference between reality and fiction, he was nothing less than deluded. So I brought it up again, the very reason I had come.

"Golem," I said. "Simone."

"Back to that then, are you?"

"I have the golem at home and you're the only person who can help me."

"Only person, huh?"

"Yes, as much as I hate to admit it."

"Only person, only person..." Blichen went on muttering and smiling wryly, as if that declaration caused him great joy.

"I suppose I could try and contact my old girlfriend Solange but we've lost touch. Better to leave things in the past."

"Wise boy," said Bilchen. He escorted me through the dank basement past a myriad of terrible-looking gargoyles, and then finally to a large oak desk, where he unraveled what looked like an architectural blueprint. Except what I stood looking at was no building, as one might have thought, but rather the very intricate outline of a being, complete with veins and muscles, internal organs, the whole works.

"This is Simone," said Bilchen proudly. "On paper anyway."

It was then that I noticed on the image the same strange hieroglyphics that appeared on Simone's forehead.

"Why do you need that?" I muttered, pointing.

"To make her real of course."

Bilchen went on to tell me all about golems in Jewish history, how they have been used to vanquish oppressors, how their strength was unparalleled. I knew much of what he talked about, except that it became readily apparent to me that there was not a shred of doubt in his mind that these creatures were tactile, alive and spirited. You could touch them, interact with them. Myth? No damn way, not according to Bilchen.

"In the early morning light of the 18th and 19th centuries, Jewish men throughout Europe would walk with their donkeys and collect not only things, but also fragments of everyday life. A turn of phrase, a chorus from a long-forgotten song...nothing escaped these men." Bilchen lifted a forefinger: "These were the only ones who could see a utilitarian value to the refuse that others threw away."

The rabbi cleared his throat and continued: "Largely ignored and scorned by the rest of society, they added value by carting away garbage and also by remembering little idiosyncrasies...jargon, songs, just like I said. Those songs and such they placed with great reverence into their other carts, the garbage-strewn cart of their minds, piled high. Maybe later, another decade perhaps, they would unravel them, the forgotten phrases. Collecting the garbage of course was how they made their money. But then the industrial age took over and sanitation improved. Suddenly, there wasn't as much garbage to pick over. In Paris, for instance, an entire underground sewer system was built. Where were these garbage pickers to go?"

I wondered why this crazy rabbi was telling me such an outrageous tale. Despite his excellent command of language, this was poppycock. What did I care about 19th century Paris? And really, who did he think he was talking to, telling me about recovering phrases and jargons? Did he think I had just fallen off a turnip truck? I held up a hand to signal him to stop the nonsense right there but he didn't.

"A golem named Schmuel carried each and every one of the garbage pickers and their donkeys to safety."

"A golem named Schmuel carrying people to safety? I don't think so. And why did they need to get to safety anyway? Garbage pickers? Get real, Mr. Bilchen, you say outrageous things."

"You should get real. Yes, a golem did do that, exactly what I said. Many people blamed these garbage pickers for the poor sanitation, for the disease and terrible smells that were rampant throughout the city. Even for poisoning the water. Why? Because they were Jews. There was a lot of anti-semitism, just like today. So the people formed lynch mobs and were ready to do away with these Jewish men."

Now I was no scholar concerning Paris and its history but I'm certain I would have heard about a golem named

Schmuel saving a group of Jewish garbage pickers. Totally absurd. But it didn't really matter what I knew, or even what I thought. It was easy to see that Bilchen was hell-bent on educating me about the outstanding attributes of the Paris golem.

"So Schmuel carried these poor men and their animals high into the hillsides, away from the mobs. Then, after Schmuel had killed a few of the more unfortunate members of the mob with his bare hands, the Jewish garbage pickers came out of hiding and took up residence in Paris. Of course, they all had to find new work."

"Why did he have to carry them?" I asked slyly. "Why didn't they just walk?"

"Because their carts were so full there was no way they could have climbed uphill with them!"

That was it. I spun on my heels when suddenly the nutty rabbi called out:

"Best not to leave. Don't you want to know about Simone? I'll show you details of the blueprints."

I stopped at once and stared at Bilchen. "You're mad," I blurted. "There, I said it."

"Just an opinion, and a worthless one at that. But remember, if you leave now, you'll never unlock the secrets to your golem. And woe will be your plight, let me assure you."

I walked slowly back to the madman.

"The rag men were paupers and outcasts…just like you, Mr. Pringle."

"Excuse me?"

"You heard me," said Bilchen, adjusting his yarmulke as though he were readying for a fight.

If there was one thing I learned from the Aaron affair, it was that it was best to pick your battles very carefully. I could have slaughtered, annihilated the dufus, but…not a word did I utter. Not one. It was just as well too. Because my attention wandered to a long wooden table where I saw assorted body parts – a brain, what looked like a liver, eyes, bones, even a hand. A cornucopia of creepy grossness.

"Oh my God!"

Bilchen slid over to the table and picked up what looked like a meat cleaver. "This here is very good for hacking through bone. You wouldn't want to use it on a brain however, especially if you were looking for the Corpus Callosum."

I was shocked – there was dried blood all over the table.

"No, you would want to use a much finer instrument, like this." Bilchen picked up a very slim knife from a silver surgical tray.

I was beginning to feel unwell, queasy. What with the obnoxious smells in the basement and the sight of body parts, it was all becoming too much. It was like some strange scene out of an Edgar Allan Poe novel. All that was needed was for a black cat to emerge from behind a wall.

"Plastic parts, I guess?" I whispered hopefully, and sat down. A solitary drop of perspiration hung precipitously from the tip of my nose.

"No sir, not plastic."

"Animal?"

"No sir, not animal parts."

I dabbed at my face. Slimy stuff came out of my nose and I started coughing. "I don't suppose you're going to tell me where you've gotten the body parts from," I said.

"No sir, I'm not. But I can tell you what I use them for."

At least there was that, an explanation that would probably defy any rational explanation. I was certain that it would be an explanation that went right into the heart of golem lore.

"You see," continued Bilchen, "there has always been a problem with golems. They become too unwieldy and have to be destroyed. And they are beasts. Unthinking brutes."

I knew this from my own research, and had even brought it up with Solange.

"And the fault always lay with my predecessors," said Bilchen. "With the rabbis."

"Rabbis?"

"Yes, with the rabbis," reiterated Bilchen. "With the rabbis."

This declaration seemed to bring about a sense of ennui in Bilchen; he sighed and took a seat next to me.

"The rabbis had no knowledge of anatomy and physiology. That's why the golems failed. Well, one of the reasons anyway. If they had only been schooled in biochemistry and the way in which bodies work, they might have created a more perfect specimen. One that might pass for something close to a human being."

"But we're not talking about a human being, you realize."

"Dumb, dumb," said Bilchen, mocking me. "Didn't you hear what I said: close to a human being...that's what I said."

Despite the lunatic I considered Bilchen to be, he still appeared to have the answers I needed. And so I couldn't very well turn away from him, not with a golem in my living room. So I stayed and waited for him to finish his story. Which he did.

"And so now you know," he said, after about 10 minutes.

So I did. And what I heard was this: rabbis constructed golems solely from the mud and clay of riverbanks or lakes. Given that, they were bound to fail. Why? Because soil contains great power. The strength of Gaia. To understand, we need only consider the type of upheavals that earthquakes and volcanoes are capable of. So a traditional golem will harbour all the power of the soil. Is it any wonder then that these creatures will run amok at some point?

"I never thought of that," I said.

"There's more of course. But have a close look here," said Bilchen. He picked up a scalpel and very carefully dissected what looked like very tiny balloons. A clear thin fluid seeped out. That was it. A small geyser erupted from deep within my gut and I spewed bile all over the floor. Some of it splashed on Bilchen's black shoes.

"Look what you've done," he snorted. "Just look at what you've gone and done!"

Acid had made its way up to my throat and, unable to speak, I waved my hand, signaling my sorrow.

"What am I going to do now?" said Bilchen, quite panic stricken. "I have to give a speech later on. For God's sake."

"No harm done," I finally sputtered, handing Bilchen a Kleenex with which he could clean his shoes.

Bilchen looked down and considered the state of his shoes for quite some time. When at last he had come to the conclusion that all they needed was a good wipe, he got down onto one knee and went about the task. His black fell off and he quickly scooped it up, kissing the brim and reurning it to his angular head.

"That was alveoli," he said. "Air sacks in the lungs where carbon dioxide and oxygen are exchanged." He continued wiping. "But I wouldn't expect you to know anything about that now."

"You could be right," I said quietly. Really, I just wanted to get on with things and not argue with the nut.

A stippled, grey-coloured body part lay next to the alveoli. A brain, it was rather obvious, I had seen pictures in magazines. "You see here," said the rabbi. "Look, let me show you." He cut through the centre and then pried apart an almond-shaped structure. "The amygdala," he said.

"Never heard of it."

"Why would you? Here, touch it. Feel the texture."

Given how I was feeling, I preferred not to, and said as much.

"Don't be a baby."

Bilchen held all the cards so I did as I was told and ran my finger along the smooth amygdala. I could feel my stomach churning once again but this time, literally willed my insides to quiet down.

"See the little white things that look like stones?"

I stared closely at the tiny pebbles and even gingerly picked one up in my fingers.

"This is the amygdala of a golem." Bilchen picked up a second brain and like the first time, cut it down the middle with a fine knife. "Here, now look at this one." In quick order, he dug his thin fingers into the interior and pulled

out the amygdala. This time, there were no fine stones to be
seen

"From a human," he explained.

"Where do the stones come from?" I asked. "And what
do they do?"

"They're not really stones," said Bilchen. "They're
protein deposits that have hardened. But they interfere with
messages to the brain. So they cause hallucinations,
fluctuations in alertness, sometimes even tremors. And
golems become very rigid and walk in slow, shuffling
movements. Like lumbering zombies."

"Protein deposits?"

"Yes, they develop because golems are made of mud and
clay, as I told you. And the mud and earth is a perfect
breeding ground for them. Protein deposits like it hot and
moist."

I had no way of knowing whether what Bilchen was
telling me had any validity. From what I could tell, he was a
certified whack job. Maybe he was making the whole thing
up.

"How do you know all this?"

"You ask too many questions, Pringle. Let's just say that
I needed to find out why golems continually failed. So I did.
I'm as handy with a scalpel as I am with the Torah."

The longer I listened to Bilchen, the more it dawned on
me that here was a man who had an overabundance of what
the ancient Greeks called 'hubris.' Way too much ego. He
just seemed to have an answer for everything. That was all
confirmed to me when he suddenly and unexpectedly got
down on his knees and started praying:

Baruch Bilchen

She-amar

Haolam

Baruch hu

"Are you going to keep me in the dark?" I said.

"Nope. For now you shall know who runs things. What I said was: "Blessed is Bilchen, The one who creates, The world, Blessed is the awe-inspiring process.""

"What are you implying?"

"Implying nothing. I'm saying that I can create things. Wonderful, unique things. Like golems. Flawless and gem-like."

What a twit. But again, I had to stay and extract the information I needed – taking him to task for thinking he was a god was no way to do it.

We moved through the basement to a wooden door and out onto a field with grass that was just as overgrown as the front yard. We continued walking to a small shed that was camouflaged beneath a bow of willow trees. I could hear a brook bubbling nearby. Up overhead a very large bird circled the shed. Bilchen removed a key from his pocket and, looking around carefully, turned the padlock.

I was startled by the sight. Table upon table rested bodies, covered to their necks with white sheets. Bilchen uncovered one of the creatures. It was small, maybe four foot tall. And clearly unformed – the face was nothing more than a mass of pasty, white…well, not quite flesh, more like clay, or some such material. There were no features – no nose, mouth, eyes. It looked like the type of aliens one sees on late, late-night science fantasy movies.

"These aren't ready," advised the rabbi. "Not yet."

"All golems?"

"Yes, at my beck and call."

"But these don't look like anything except lumps of clay. And Simone looks like a real woman. Like my old girlfriend. How did that happen?"

The rabbi contemplated for a moment. "You're delving into uncharted territory with questions like that. State secrets."

"Just tell me."

"Very well. I had to extract from Solange a vial of her blood, containing her DNA. I injected that into my creation and produced a replica golem in her image. More than that, I cannot say."

I went from table to table and ogled the creatures. Then I poked and prodded them. Remarkably, their skin felt much like human skin. A bit spongy perhaps, but not that anyone might notice. Except that just like Simone, there was no bone structure. Press harder, as I did, and it was like pressing down into a doll. Then I noticed that cards were affixed by string around the big toes of each golem; I could hardly miss it since the feet of the creatures plainly stuck out from beneath the sheets that covered them. I read names like North Korea, China, and Libya. And the prices, oh my Lord, anywhere from $ 7,500 to $ 15,000.

"You're selling these to rogue nations, right?"

"I won't lie."

"You don't know what those places will do with the golems. Probably nothing good I'm sure. You have no ethics."

"Ethics, schmethics."

"Christ. You really are something else. And you're making a ton of money here."

"Yes, but it's dangerous work. If some authority like the FBI finds out who made the golems, I would be in big trouble."

"But I know."

"Yes, but you won't tell anyone. No one of any importance anyway."

"How can you be sure?"

"Well, who would believe you? Try going to the police and telling them your story, about a rabbi who makes golems from the mud and clay of Lake Ontario. Go ahead. I dare you."

He had a point that I couldn't contest. But I did wonder about why, if he was making so much money selling golems, he had to rent out the synagogue to non-Jews, even to the 'buns of steel' people.

"Hodge-podge. Hodge podge! You ask too many questions, Pringle. Look, the money I make from selling my creations goes into my own retirement fund. I've been dismissed from many synagogues and could never hold a job for very long – they didn't like my delving into the mystical aspect of Judaism. So I didn't have savings…until I starting constructing golems."

It struck me then that Solange must have paid Bilchen for his services.

"She did," said the rabbi. "But how much is confidential. Good luck to you trying to guess."

This was all very good and I had learnt a lot, but there was still the small matter of the golem in my apartment. Why was she so inert? Why didn't she take instructions?

"Like I said, you ask a lot of questions," said the rabbi. "So this'll be the last one I'll answer. Then I must go. Give your golem two tablespoons of apple cider vinegar mixed with honey. It seems to do the trick, the golems become more animated, more humanlike, and of more importance, no longer destined to fail. They really spring to life."

"Apple cider vinegar?"

"Yes, ACV for short. I had very painful knees for awhile. Then I read that ACV helps to dissolve the calcium deposits in knees. So I tried it and it worked! Then I figured it might work for protein deposits in golems and I was right."

The rabbi looked at his watch. "Now I must go. I have a lecture to attend."

"What's it on?"

"I call it: **The Creation of the Cosmos and why Everyone has it Wrong.**"

Of course. Of course. Why was I not surprised?

Bilchen led me by the arm back up the rickety stairs and before I knew it, I was standing once again in the kitchen. We hurried past the pots and pans and the Muslim men who were still praying. Finally, I stepped out the front door, and took a deep breath. The sickly smell of newly-slaughtered animals filled my nostrils. My head began spinning and my stomach started acting up again. I had to make a conscious effort to put one foot in front of the other and begin the hike to the subway. On the sidewalk, I took one look back where Bilchen stood in the doorway, smiling and adjusting his top hat: "Remember, Simone will now only take commands from you. You are her master. I instructed her to get to your apartment but that was the extent of my telling her what to do. Good luck, my lame friend. You'll need it."

"That's it? You call me lame and wish me good luck? What kind of person are you?"

"Better than you, that's for sure. But look, there's one more thing. You must never use the golem for nefarious purposes."

"Why not?"

"Because these creatures are created with goodness. Purity. If you do anything to destroy that, your life will fall to shambles."

My life is already in shambles, I thought, as I turned my back to the rabbi and hurried up the street.

Chapter Thirty-Two

Back in the apartment, I found Simone just as I had left her – her mouth slightly agape, standing dumbfounded in the middle of the living room. I figured I had nothing to lose and opened the bottle of Apple Cider Vinegar I had bought on the way home, mixed in a bit of honey, and poured a spoonful of the concoction down Simone's mouth. The transformation was instantaneous and astounding. Frightening even. She wiped the fluid that had trickled down her chin with the back of her hand and her eyes brightened. She looked all around the room, taking everything in, and yawned, her mouth as wide as a cavern. She appeared to want to speak, mouthing something or other, but a look of fright crossed her countenance when nothing came out.

"Golems can't talk," I assured her. "But don't worry, now that we've kick-started your metabolism, it looks as though you'll be able to do many more things. Interesting things." I held the bottle of ACV up to eye level – *Apple Cider Vinegar with the mother inside* – it read. I had no clue what 'the mother' meant but it didn't matter…as long as it worked.

I made some lunch – grilled cheese sandwiches with potato chips – and served Simone. Would she eat? I had no idea. I held my sandwich to my mouth and took a bite, showing her. Then I chewed.

"Simone, in the name of HaShem, I want you to start eating."

So she did, tentatively tasting the food, swirling it around her palette as if to gauge the texture. Once she had assured herself that she could in fact eat, she swallowed.

"Good, Simone. Good."

She was hungry enough, downing two sandwiches in great big gulps. I had no doubt that if I had served up a couple of turkeys with all the stuffing, she would have polished them off in no time.

"Simone, in the name of HaShem, I want you to slow down your eating," I said. "Don't chew so quickly. There's no rush. And there's plenty more of that where it came from." I put a couple of more pieces of bread and cheese on the skillet and pressed down with a spatula, turning the browning sandwiches every few seconds. When ready, I placed them onto Simone's plate and dumped another bag of BBQ chips into a large bowl in front of her.

"That'll be the last of it, Simone," I said. "But you sure know what to do with food." I laughed and Simone nodded, acknowledging what I had said. It was totally amazing, mind -blowing really.

After she had eaten what I put in front of her, she opened her mouth to say something:

"I'm still hungry, Master."

I put my fork down. What was this?

"Can you say that again?" I said.

"I'm still hungry, Master. I can go for another bag of chips."

"In the name of HaShem, stay right here," I said, rubbing my hands with glee. "I'm going to the store to pick some up."

"I can come with you, Master."

"Of course you can! Of course!"

Simone looked at me askance.

"Ummm, in the name of HaShem, of course you can! Of course you can!"

So I walked arm in arm with my golem to the local 7/11, glancing every few seconds at her. My, she was such a beautiful woman! The spitting image of Solange. I noticed a few guys looking at her. At the store, I bought 4 bags of BBQ chips, a tub of chocolate chip ice cream, and 2 bottles of Cream Soda pop.

"What is that, Master?" asked Simone, looking as I extracted bills from my wallet.

"Money," I whispered, as the storekeeper snuck a quick peek at my companion. "I should allow you to look and feel these bills. Just in case you ever use them."

Simone remained silent.

"Ok, forgot. In the name of HaShem, I order you to feel these bills." I handed her two tens and a twenty.

"Master?"

"Yes, Simone."

"From now on, I would suggest that it is not necessary for you to mention the name of God all the time when you want me to do something. I get it."

"Huh. That is so interesting."

We got out of there before the storekeeper could ask us any questions. With his mouth wide open, he looked like an inert golem himself.

Outside, Simone noticed people looking at her. And asked me about it. Well, not exactly all people – only the guys. Now here was a problem: how to explain to a golem that men were lustful, and that she was pretty. A natural, volatile combination. When I didn't answer, Simone took matters into her own hands, yelling at a male passerby: "What are you looking at!"

"You've got a real winner on your hands," came the retort, aimed directly at me. "Arm candy. Dumb as a door-knob."

In the apartment, Simone snacked on the chips and ice cream and watched Bugs Bunny and Fred Flintstone cartoons, often yelling at the TV whenever a villain's intentions became obvious. I didn't feel at all uncomfortable with the arrangement – I watched her watching TV and simply thought I was lucky man...after all, what guy wouldn't want his own a living, breathing golem? One who would do whatever he wanted. But there were more pressing questions that I didn't know: What *exactly* would she do? And not do?

I decided to put her to the test.

"Simone, come over here and kiss me. On the lips."

"Yes, Master."

She kissed. Oh, and how she kissed. It was deep and passionate, and her tongue slipped around my mouth, as if she were searching for long-forgotten artifacts.

"That's enough," I said, gently pushing her away. Now that I got the inter-locking lips agenda out of the way, I dreamily contemplated what else I might do with Simone. But there was time for that later. Right at this time, I realized I was still hungry, and made myself a couple of those scrumptious grilled cheese sandwiches. I always felt hungry when I was elated. Simone looked over to where the bread was browning and her nostrils flared, taking in the smells. I knew it would be impossible to deny her and made an extra sandwich for her.

"Here, try this, Simone." I drizzled some honey over her toasted bread. She took a bite and her eyes opened wide.

"Yummy."

"You have quite the vocabulary," I laughed.

In short order, Simone and I became constant companions, and I slowly started forgetting about Solange. We went shopping together, took in movies, and enjoyed bicycle rides around the city. All of these things were new for her. She was like a newborn making her way through a strange and exciting world. Her eyes strikingly wide at the simplest things – squirrels climbing a tree, streetcars rumbling along tracks, a toaster popping up bread. She was amazed with escalators, and tried scooting up those going down. She could do it of course, she was as agile and strong as anything in nature. I taught her things – how to pedal a bike, swim in a pool, even feed the pigeons. Every hour of every day was an adventure. I gave her certain firm commands, such as not to talk in a movie theatre, and not to say a word to men who gave her the look. And I explained to her exactly what that look entailed, what they had in mind. I don't think Simone blushed, not exactly, but she batted her eyes and was slightly taken aback. "That's human nature for you," I told her.

While all this was going on, I didn't sleep with her. The temptation was there, but it didn't seem right – we were just getting to know each other. And while she looked exactly like Solange, she wasn't her...she was something else entirely, another type of being, one that I really didn't get. So each night I ordered Simone to sleep on the couch in the living room. I primped her pillows, covered her with a couple of blankets, and brushed her lips lightly with mine. "Now sleep until 9 o'clock in the morning," I said. "I'm not getting up before then."

"I will try, Master. I'm not exactly sure but I am a little sleepy."

"You're not sure, are you?"

"I've never felt sleepy before."

It was strange, I must admit. I didn't realize golems slept, or ate, defecated, or even spoke. To the best of the knowledge I had acquired through copious amounts of research, they didn't. But then, the golems I read about didn't have Rabbi Bilchen as their creator. To that end, every morning, I gave Simone a tablespoon of ACV mixed with honey.

If there was one thing that was disconcerting about the golem was that she did almost everything to excess. She loved ice cream, but a single cone wasn't nearly enough. Nor were two cones. She ate and ate and ate. I asked her to cook and bake and when she was done, there was usually enough food for a week. A stack of pancakes for breakfast meant a mound that was piled two feet high, like a tower of Jenga blocks, the kind I had seen in store windows. What was to have been a single pan of lasagna for dinner ended up being four pans of lasagna. When we watched a movie at home, Simone popped enough popcorn to feed an entire theatre. I quickly learned that I had to curb Simone's excesses, give her very explicit instructions on how much to cook, how much to eat, even how quickly, or rather, slowly, to ride a bike. Literally everything.

Still, I took those excesses as simply a part of the learning curve for a newly-created golem. What did strike me as more disturbing however, was when Simone asked me why I never went to synagogue. The question came out of the blue – we were sitting enjoying a meal at Country Style Restaurant (Simone particularly enjoyed Wiener Schnitzel and dumplings and beet salad) – when she brought it up.

"Well, I'm not Jewish," I replied. "If I had to go anywhere, I'd go to a church. But I'm not religious, so even that is out of the question."

"That's a good answer, Master," said Simone, and she went back to her meal, calling the waiter over and asking for another beet salad.

"Wait a second," I said. "You just sprung that on me. You have to tell me more – where did you come up with that idea?"

"Well, I don't exactly know what a church is, Master, but I do know what a synagogue is. It's inbred into my DNA. I can't help it, I was created by a Jewish holy man who studied the ancient Jewish books of wisdom. I know I don't have parents like you that brought me to life and that I was brought forth from the mud of a lake....that's how I was born onto this earth. Still, even without parents, I know there's a creator."

Simone went on eating but I couldn't. Here was an issue for me – a religious golem. That complicated matters. I myself was an avowed atheist. I thought I would see just how religious she actually was, how deep her faith was.

"I see what you're saying," I said, picking at my bowl of sauerkraut, "but what do you think I should do at a synagogue?

"Pray."

'And just who should I pray to?"

"Your maker."

"I don't believe in that, Simone."

"Oh, but you should, Master. Just as I have a maker, so do you."

"Your maker is Rabbi Bilchen. Should I pray to him?"

"You're very clever, Master, I can tell. Trying to trick me. But Rabbi Bilchen brought me to life from the soil, but he didn't create the soil. Something else did. The ultimate creator."

"How do you know there's an *ultimate creator?*"

"I just know certain things, like I said. Master, maybe I am not very good at understanding how a radio works or why an escalator changes direction sometimes, but I do understand the universe and how it works, how it came about."

"Nietzche, Marx, Bertrand Russell, John Stuart Mill... they were all atheists. Not exactly stupid guys."

"I don't know these people, Master. But it doesn't matter what they said."

"Everything on earth came about by accident. We had all the right chemicals for life. There was no need for a maker. Evolution took care of the rest. All those guys I mentioned believed that."

"But if everything was an accident, then even the thoughts of those people you mentioned..Mill and Russell and all, all their thoughts are just by-products of that accident. So you can't believe in what they say, Master, because it's all just chemicals and accidents. Why should you believe that what they've said is true? You shouldn't. There's no reason to do so."

I didn't want to argue with her. Nothing felt right about doing so. I just wanted to enjoy a meal at my favourite restaurant, with my favourite golem. I was schooled in philosophy, and Simone, she was just a creature made of mud and clay. What did she really know?

"Simone, I'm your master, right? And you're always supposed to take instructions from me, correct?"

"Yes, I was designed that way."

"Good, so I'm instructing you to never bring up this subject again. Never talk about a maker of the universe, never ask me why I don't go to synagogue, never question my own personal belief system. That's the way it's going to be from now on. Do you understand me?"

"Yes, Master. Would it be ok if I ordered another Schnitzel?"

It was bound to happen but I dreaded it all the same. Each time Simone and I left the apartment, I tried to make sure I didn't run into Beverly. I'd stick my head out the door and when she wasn't around, I instructed Simone to quickly follow me into the hallway and down the stairs. On one occasion however, as we bounded back up the stairs after a morning out, Beverly was coming down.

"Good morning, Beverly."

"Morning, Karl. Morning ------"

"*Simone.* Beverly, this is Simone."

"Morning, Simone."

The golem looked at me quizzically.

"Simone, Beverly is an ex-student of mine. She lives down the hall."

Again, Simone looked at me, slightly askew. She understood that something was expected of her but she didn't quite know what.

"Karl, can I talk to you privately," said Beverly, breaking the awkward silence.

"Of course, of course."

I led Simone into the apartment, instructing her to wait. When I returned to Beverly, she was shaking her head sadly.

"That is one strange woman, Karl."

"She's from France. Her English isn't that good."

"Don't give me that."

"It's true, I'm telling you."

Beverly took out her apartment keys from her purse and dangled them in front of me.

"I can't," I whispered, touching her arm. "Simone is here for a while."

"You loss," said Beverly abruptly, bounding down the stairs and out the front door.

Inside the apartment, Simone stood waiting. Without prompting, she said: "She likes you. Golems can tell these things."

Meeting Beverly was bad enough. But running into P.I. Sheila Suskind while I was out with Simone was light smashing head on into a train. It was made all the worse because the day was particularly windy. Normally, Simone wore her hair in soft bangs, which Rabbi Bilchen had purposely styled to effectively hide the strange lettering on her forehead, the lettering that I googled and came to understand meant 'Life' or 'Truth.' In Hebrew, the four letters formed the word 'Emet.' But the day Simone and I ran into Suskind, the wild wind fluttered the golem's soft hair, revealing the lettering.

Suskind stood stupefied. "Oh my God, Solange. I thought you went back home. Oh my God." She leaned forth and hugged Simone. The gesture was not returned and it was then, as she pulled back from the stiff and erect body, that she noticed the lettering. "What the…"

I explained it. Or tried to. A new fad. It was all the rage. A temporary tattoo that people in France were into. Of course, Simone didn't say a word, not even after Suskind ran her fingers over the letters.

"Isn't that right?" I said, careful not to mention my golem's name.

"Yes, Master," came the monotone reply.

"Master?"

"Yes, you know, Master and Servant. An old song by that English pop group Depeche Mode. We love it. Sometimes I'm the master and sometimes Solange here is the master. We switch roles all the time. Like I said, a master and a servant. It's all good fun and games."

Suskind looked at me as though I had escaped from an insane asylum. She knew I was lying to be certain but still, she glossed it over. But she had to ask my golem a question. She just had to.

"But Solange, why are you here?"

Simone turned to me, as if to extract the correct answer. Much to my surprise however, she took it upon herself to reply, quite suddenly in fact. It was clear from her first few words that she was about to tell Suskind that her name was not Solange. Oh, I could see it coming so I quickly interjected.

"And so, my love has returned to me," I said rapidly, waving my arms about. "We're going to try and work it out. Yes, we are. There are obstacles to overcome, but I'm sure that with time…"

I didn't finish. I felt flummoxed, and the back of my neck turned hot and damp.

Suskind looked Simone over. I could tell what she was thinking, that something wasn't not right. That something was terribly wrong in fact. It was obvious - not a hug, not a smile? Not even an acknowledgement? After all they had been through?

So there we stood on Bloor Street, the three of us, not saying anything, not knowing what to say. And then, quite abruptly, we were two. For Simone bolted away. I had never seen anyone run so fast and as I watched the golem jump over high fences and finally turn into a tiny dot in the distance, only then did it dawn on me that she was truly a monster, with unimaginable powers.

Personally, I had no use for Suskind, and now it was apparent that neither did Simone, who must have sensed that Suskind was at a loss. How very perceptive of her.

"I've got to go after her. She's an emotional wreck these days."

I left the bewildered P.I. to chase after Simone and as I did, I could hear Suskind call out after me, saying she wanted an explanation.

"You'd better have one too, Pringle."

Chapter Thirty-Three

I was losing control. My brain wasn't functioning the way it had in the past when I was a graduate student and a thinking machine. Now my thoughts were muddled and nothing seemed to make any sense. It was like I was living in the Bizarro World of DC Comic Books, where everything was inverted from the real world. Where Superman and Lois Lane were chalk-faced, strange versions of their real selves on Earth. I mean, a golem in my life? A girlfriend from France who lost my child? A private investigator? A drug-addled dead woman whose work I stole? Let's get real. But real it was, despite the fact that my reality was spinning out of control.

There were other things too. Solange had been all wrong about Simone. Perhaps Bilchen had not told her that with a bit of ACV, Simone could actually talk. And the whole business of ordering Simone around by invoking the name of HaShem, that was all wrong too; it was becoming increasingly apparent that with each new day, my golem was becoming more and more independent – she almost seemed not to need anyone to tell her what to do. It appeared that she had a fully-functioning brain of her own. Maybe even her own will.

When I finally found Simone after she had run away, she was cowering in a bus shelter a few blocks away, shivering. She had obviously made a conscious decision to stay in the open where I could find her. She was so smart, she really did want to be found. We walked slowly back to the apartment, my arm wrapped securely around her shoulders.

After Simone told me she had run from Suskind because she could sense what the P.I. was thinking, that she was nothing less than a fraud, and that I was lying, I took up smoking again. I hadn't smoked in a long time, not since that debacle with Rivka Howard, but now I couldn't help it...I needed something to calm my nerves. How could a golem, made of clay and mud, 'sense' someone else's thoughts? The idea made me very nervous. What if Simone could sense my thoughts? What if there ever came a time that she would have to be 'killed,' as Solange had once said? Would she be able to sense her own upcoming demise? That someone was planning her death? If so, wouldn't she rail against anyone or anything that wanted to return her to the earth? And the damage she could do to that person...oh my.

All of this, the whole business of being saddled with a golem who had her own mind, an intuitive one at that, was borne out one evening when I lay in bed and called out to her. I had showered, stripped down to my undies, and waited anxiously under the covers. I hadn't mentioned anything about making love but yet, it was certainly what I had in mind. And so, the answer I received in response, that she was too engaged in watching a TV show, was flabbergasting. I threw on my bathrobe and walked into the living room. There sat Simone on the couch, her feet up on the coffee table, munching on a bowl of potato chips, and watching TV. She was laughing, watching the old I Love Lucy show." That Lucille Ball," she chuckled. "What a goofball."

That episode, while it was enough to cause me great pause, appeared to be a one-off. And I was glad for that. For aside from the cigs, I really did need something else to ease my tension. So almost every night, I ordered Simone to take off all her clothes and lie next to me in bed. I would run my hands up and down her supple body and I must admit I was duly surprised at how soft it always felt to the touch. I should have worn protection but I figured I was in no danger, she had just been newly-erected erected from the mud...could she really be carrying some sexually-transmitted disease? Hardly likely. I did wonder, albeit briefly, whether she could get pregnant, but thought that that too was unlikely...golems were only born through the magic of crazed Jewish holy men, not from sexual intercourse. So I hoped anyway; the last thing I really needed was a tiny hybrid rubbery-like baby running around the apartment, one with inordinate strength and an appetite that could not be quelled.

After a few hours of sheer pleasure, I would roll over on to my side, completely worn out.

"No more?" Simone would say.

My pat answer was: "No. I'm sore and tired."

"Sore and tired?" Simone would contemplate the words but it was apparent she had no context for them...she could have continued for days and even weeks.

"Go to sleep now, Simone. And we'll talk in the morning."

"No more?" she would ask once again.

"No more. Now sleep."

"No more?"

"Pretend you're tired."

"Yes, Master."

After those lovemaking evenings, I always woke in the morning with deep scratches on my back and chest, like some animal had clawed me. During the trysts, I had only been vaguely aware that I was being massacred. But on one occasion, I was now in so much pain, that I had to go to a walk-in medical clinic for treatment. When asked what had happened, I told the truth, that my girlfriend liked rough sex.

"I'm not going to tell you what to do," said the doctor, "but you could get seriously hurt this way. As it is, you'll need a few stitches." When I removed my pale-coloured shirt, I could see the blood that had seeped through in spots and stained it.

When I returned to the apartment, battered and bruised, Simone asked to go to the synagogue. She wanted to say a prayer to her maker and wanted me to say one as well. So we went. I almost told her that she was disobeying me since I had told her in the past never to mention religion again. But I couldn't lecture her, I could barely move and pain seared through my woeful body. I took a couple of Percocets and ambled slowly in back of Simone, who was skipping along, trying to avoid cracks in the sidewalk.

I had never been to a synagogue before and found the experience unnerving. I suppose we should have gone to a reform synagogue but Simone was adamant that we attend services at an orthodox one, saying a reform place wouldn't serve her purpose, that it wasn't 'real.' I hardly knew what was real or not so it hardly mattered. And when I asked Simone to explain further, all she said was that God didn't reside in reform shuls, that those places were only there to appease Jews that didn't care about religion so that they might not feel so guilty about having forsaken their maker. They were woeful non-believers. How Simone knew all that, I had no idea. I didn't press her though and simply assumed that like the whole region bit, 'it was in her DNA.'

At the synagogue, we were allowed admittance only at the very rear. I grabbed a skullcap from a cardboard box and so did Simone. Up at the front I saw a group of old men who resembled Ragman. They swayed back and forth on their heels like crazed automotons. It was surreal, but nothing compared to when Simone joined in their movements.

"What are you doing?" I said.

"Shhh…" The old man next to us put his thick forefinger up to his mouth.

"Later, Master," she whispered, and continued swaying.

The man, sporting a long grey beard, kept his finger to his mouth, as if paralyzed. He looked at Simone and then all at once brushed the hair from her forehead, gasping. "Golem?"

I nodded. There was no point in lying, I could see that the old man would not be dissuaded, he somehow knew the truth. I just hoped he would not rat us out.

We sat down, then stood. Sat down, then stood. Up and down. Up and down. All that movement was hurting my scratched-up back. Not to mention the headache I was getting from surreptiously eyeing the old man. And when it was all over and we hurriedly exited the synagogue, blowing past everyone, I felt totally defeated. Not only did I not understand a single word that was said, but Simone seemed to be particularly joyful. She bounced up and down on the sidewalk and told me she was particularly grateful for having given thanks to her maker.

"Your maker, Rabbi Bilchen?"

"Oh, he just brought me forth as I told you. He didn't make the soil and…"

I interrupted her at that point, telling her to shut it. I had heard all this before and didn't want to listen to all the balderdash about her maker again.

Still she kept on. "But I think, Master, that you didn't give thanks to your maker."

"That's right, because I'm an atheist."

"What is that?"

"Someone who doesn't believe in a maker."

"But Master."

I turned angrily to look at Simone. Now this was too much. "Didn't I tell you never to bring up the subject of a maker again? Didn't I tell you?" I felt a searing pain in my back and stopped to catch my breath.

"Yes, Master," said Simone, her head downcast.

I brushed the hair from my golem's forehead and kissed the Hebrew lettering. I didn't want to be angry with her so it was the least I could do.

Suskind left a couple of voice messages on my home answering machine, but I never returned them. With Solang out of the picture, I cancelled my cell phone plan and threw the piece of intrusive junk into a trash can.

Just as Solange and I had made small excursions out of the city, so too did Simone and I. In Niagara on the Lake, we walked the main street and entered into Just Christmas, a year-round store devoted to the holiday season. Simone was enthralled by all the sparkling trinkets and lights and after I explained to her what exactly Christmas entailed, she squealed with delight, saying she could hardly wait. She threw her arms around me and the bill of the Toronto Blue Jays baseball cap I had bought for her in Toronto brushed up against my forehead.

"Wait," I interjected. "Christmas has been cancelled this year. I'm sorry."

Simone withdrew her arms and her body started to shrink backward.

"Why?"

Her downcast face overwhelmed me.

"No, no, Simone. I was just joking. Just joking."

"Joking?"

So I explained. But Simone's face didn't change.

"No more joking, Master," she said. "I don't like joking."

"OK Simone. No more jokes."

We went on a wine-tasting tour (she was so enamoured with the flavour of wines that I had to buy her an entire bottle, which she consumed in one sitting...without getting the least bit tipsy!) and bought jars of homemade jam. Jam...it reminded me of when Solange and I had bought some in St. Jacobs and so it briefly elicited sadness. But

Simone's enthusiasm was so infectious that I quickly forgot my old flame. She was like a newborn, my golem, everything was wondrous and exciting and it rubbed off on me, banishing my normal ennui. Even when she lifted a rock to inspect the insects, just as Solange had done, I only thought of the current moment.

Despite all that, chasms of doubt penetrated my being at times. My mood sank and it was through sheer willpower that I carried on during those uncertain periods. I had always assumed that a life of the mind, as I had enjoyed throughout my university years, was the path toward a pure, fulfilled life. But now I saw that I was wrong. It wasn't anything at all, that life, but sheer illusion. It was far more important, more fulfilling, to share experiences with someone. Live the more experiential life. Both Solange and Simone showed me the way. And I had that now, but with a golem! A creature derived from the mud and clay. And one that was taking me to task because of my unwillingness to believe in an omnipotent being!

During those moments of doubt that bubbled to the surface of my frazzled mind, I wondered whether life was worth living. Whether it had ever been. In the long run, everything dissolved into nothingness…my parents, school, Solange…

One morning, I purposely hid the Apple Cider Vinegar from Simone and watched as she slowly started to become inert. Her eyes rolled to the top of her head and her mouth opened wide, a long winding rope of spittle eked out and dropped onto the floor. I don't know why I did it. Power maybe, just to remind myself that I was in control. Or spite perhaps, because I could be that sort of person. But I was just curious, really. I wanted to see how my golem would react without the magic elixir. Not well, as it turned out. Not well at all.

Chapter Thirty-Four

I called Istvan again. He was a Roma, part of my tribe, and maybe my only hope. I really needed money in the worst way.

"You're lucky, Karl. I fired your replacement. He just didn't work out."

"Good. I can't say I'm upset."

"Well, you're honest, I'll give you that. But tell me you won't ever abandon the pressure washer without locking it up. Am I right about that?"

What an asshole. Didn't he realize what I had been through? "Never," I said.

As the days progressed, I tried to maintain some semblance of normalcy, dragging myself to work or to school. I hadn't actually dropped out of ESL school, but now I was really far behind. The school allowed me ample leeway after I told them about the Solange affair. There was no real reason for me to continue, now that Solange was out of the picture. But I did anyway...my classmates weren't bad sorts and I almost felt I owed it to my old flame. And if I had to work, toiling away during the shadowy hours approaching midnight was alright. There were fewer people around. On a couple of occasions I even brought Simone with me. But for the most part, I enjoyed being alone. Sometimes, when my work had been done, I'd lie down on the cool grass and look up at the stars. Then my thoughts invariably drifted to Solange; I didn't want to think about her, it just happened. I wondered what Solange was doing, who she was with. One thing was certain, she would be happy, as she always was. I remembered the game we used to play, Solange called it the 'Happy Game.' She would approach me on those days when she sensed my melancholia to be at its zenith and give me a great big hug, practically lifting me a foot off the ground. Then she'd say: Are you happy yet? If I equivocated or said no, she'd dig in for a second round of hugging. This went on until I had no choice but to be happy. She'd ask me for a smile to prove it and when I finally agreed, we'd both burst out laughing. It was a child's game but that's how she lived – with the unbridled joy of an infant at play. Amongst her many endearing qualities, the ability to live life to the fullest and with happiness was perhaps her greatest.

Away from the park and not surprisingly, I sometimes drifted to Hannah's Kitchen. Not often, just on a number of occasions. I just wanted to see the place we had been and to remember things. I would sit there, nursing a coffee, watching the parade of people sift through the front door. I always brought a book and tried to read, but it was no use. No damn use. I would stay until my coffee got cold, my eyes misted over, my throat constricted. That's how it was until, until I couldn't stay any longer and stumbled out the door.

I found myself wanting to get out more and more. Leave Simone behind and simply stroll. Yes, jaunty strolls, with no destination in mind. There was a Latin phrase that I liked – *Solvitur ambulando* – which translated to 'solved by walking.' I felt that, that everything could ultimately be solved if one walked long enough. Even my wretched life. Because even though I had Solange's doppelganger as my constant companion, she wasn't human. I tried not to think about that but oftentimes I couldn't help it – living with a golem made me feel like a fraud. Like my whole life had come down to this. One failure after another until I was saddled with something less than human because…that's what happened to people who couldn't hack it.

One night, while walking along grungy Parliament Street, a woman asked me for a smoke. I handed her a cigarette and as she stood smoking, told me that I looked lonely. That I could use some company. I looked around, to my left, to my right, and when I saw that no one was there, I walked with her into an alleyway.

"How much?" I said.

"Depends what your pleasure is."

Her blouse was sheer and her nipples were showing. My eyes narrowed and my anger suddenly bubbled to the surface. For an instant, I tried to repress it by turning away, but it was too strong, I felt overwhelmed. Before I knew it, I was hitting the woman with my balled-up fist, drawing blood. She let out a scream of shock and fought back but I hit her harder still, until she lay unmoving on the pavement. Her eyes were shut, her face bloody and swollen, but she was still breathing. I bent down low to smell her perfume. It reminded me of the Chanel No. 5 I found in Rivka's apartment. My head swirled. So exquisite. I inhaled and was suffused with lingering gossamers.

"Serves you right," I whispered. "Maybe next time you won't wear such a provocative blouse." Then I stood up and rushed off to a corner of the alley to heave.

In the apartment. I soaked my bloodied and raw hands in warm water.

"Master, what happened to you?"

Gradually the shock of what I had done began to come to the fore and my body shook all over. Simone held me tight and slowly, very slowly, I began to breathe easier. I tried dabbing Polysporin over the abrasions and cuts but my hands were still quivering and I made a mess.

"Here, let me do that, Master."

She was careful with me, using a Q-tip and then wrapping the cuts with gauze. The blood came through the white material, turning it crimson. I needed something to soothe the anxiety I felt over what I had done. But there were no longer any mood-altering pharmaceuticals in the apartment, none at all, so I drank from a bottle of white wine, the one Simone and I had brought back from Niagara on-the-Lake. I took two aspirins and then went straight to bed. Simone followed and held me tight but it was so constricting that I had to tell her to loosen up.

"Make love, Master?" she asked. "Maybe it would make you feel better."

"Not tonight," I said. "Roll over and go to sleep."

I tossed and turned much of the night as the image of the woman I had assaulted came into my mind. She had fought like an animal, and the fear was evident in her eyes. The funny thing is that had she relented, I might have let up. I had a sharp pain on my right side, just below the ribcage, and it made my nervousness worse. I got up at 3 am to google the malady and was alarmed to find out that it usually meant liver damage. So I took two more aspirins and washed it down with more wine. Thankfully, I fell into a deep sleep.

In the morning, I looked at myself in the mirror. There were red marks all over, like a tomcat had gone wild with its claws and used my face as a scratching post. There was nothing I could do about the mess, I would just have to hole up for a few days while the injuries settled down.

I removed the bloodied gauze from around my hands and had a closer look. So too did Simone.

"What exactly happened to you, Master?"

"Hurt myself at work," I said. "Some tool. It's a dangerous job."

"On your face?"

I didn't answer.

"I think you should go to the hospital, Master. I know hospitals are for humans who have hurt themselves. I saw it on a TV show. Want me to come?"

"You're sweet, but no."

I didn't go. I had to – the woman had somehow bitten my hand and broken the skin during the assault – but didn't. The police would be called. But I was in so much pain, my head reeling, I simply had to get treatment somewhere. So I went into a nearby walk-in clinic.

"It was a bar fight," I told the doctor. "I'm not a violent person but the guy was all over my girlfriend. I was worried about her safety. Anyway, I didn't think the injuries were too, too bad. The pain though, it really hurts."

"You're lucky you came when you did," said the doctor. "You were starting to lose circulation."

I was given a tetanus shot and stitches closed the wound. Gauze was wrapped around and around my hand and I was handed a couple of Tylenol # 3's for the pain.

Back home, I made bowls of instant oatmeal and sliced banana for both Simone and myself, eating absently with my mouth half-open. I had no strength to chew and I only ate a wee bit, throwing the rest into a garbage bin. But Simone fished it out, eating it all. Then I drank from a quart of milk; it had been in my fridge a very long time and had soured but I didn't care.

★

After a few weeks of working and going to school, I stopped everything. Just didn't show up anywhere. What was the point? Like just almost everything else, it became too much of an effort. Istvan left a number of messages on my answering machine but then gave up. It was so much easier to sit on my decrepit rear-end and beg for money. Others I had once befriended did it; it was easy. For once in my life, I wanted something easy. Not straining my brain with Nietzche, not toiling at jobs that were beneath me, not dealing with girlfriends that pulled my emotions every which way, not giving instructions to golems. Nothing, just nothing.

So I made a crude sign on a piece of torn cardboard: PLEASE HELP. BRAIN SPENT, ARMS HOLD NO ONE, HEART BROKEN. ANY SMALL CHANGE WILL

DO. I knew it would get attention, I knew how to pull people's strings. Arms that hold no one, a heart that is broken...of course, of course. People were so predictable, so malleable, I could get away with it, there was no doubt.

I set up shop in the St. Andrews subway station, the heart of the financial district. Four hours a day at rush hour. When the suits came by, I pressed the door open for them. Karl Pringle, their own personal butler. They stopped to look at the sign, just as I knew they would. Many dropped coins into my Starbuck's coffee cup and walked on, but a few stopped to talk. To those who did linger, I told a version of the truth, that my beloved was gone, dead. Cancer. It had ravaged her once-beautiful body. It all became too much for me, my heart far too heavy. So I dropped out of the school where I had been a PhD. candidate in Philosophy. I had been doing T.A. work and was a rising star destined to become a prof. Now nothing. Again that word – nothing – it served me well.

"You're not nothing," various passersby said. "Just give it time."

I opened my eyes wide and gazed upward gratefully, like I was praying to my maker...hah! "Anything will do," I said. "You're so kind." I said that over and over again.

In no time at all, I had good coffee to drink, delicious muffins that people gave me – banana, bran, blueberry. Sometimes even sandwiches. Those I put in my backpack and kept for dinner. A few words of encouragement were offered, which, in my mind, I discarded immediately...they had no value. But the change, how it flowed, plentiful manna from heaven. Of course, not everyone viewed my presence on the floor with equanimity.

"Get a job," I was sometimes told.

"I have one," I would spit back. "I'm a beggar."

Better yet was this exchange: "You've made your own bed, your own choices that led you here. You have no one to blame but yourself."

And I would shout after them, my words roiling through the subway halls: "Free will is an illusion! Things happen over which you have no control!" Then I shut up. I wasn't about to engage in an argument about free will versus determinism. Or limited free will and limited determinism. I just wanted to make a point, to let the fools know I couldn't be bested, that I was one smart dude. Not your ordinary vagrant.

Still, as crazy as it sounds, for perhaps the first time in my life, I felt somewhat content. Things had simplified and now, without my doing a thing, I was getting my just rewards. Why shouldn't I get things just for being me? I was so much brighter than most, gifted. A philosopher's job is only to consider the nature of being, not to teach English to foreigners, not to trim hedges and empty other people's trash cans.

Ah yes, the language school. Before I dropped out, I thought long and hard about whether I should I have continued. I have no doubt, none at all, that had Solange been around, I would have soldiered on. But it was work being there. And now...let it all come to me without effort, my arms that hold no one are wide open.

Chapter Thirty-Five

I walked alone along the streets in the most wretched areas of the city, St. James Town being my favourite. There was a lot of public housing in the area, many men's shelters, and hordes of miscreants working the streets. Wherever one looked, chaos appeared ready to take hold. A fight. A bum pleading for money. A mother screaming at a belligerent child. Someone being thrown out of a bar. I got swept up in the maelstrom, my brain whirring from all the commotion.

The woman was only a teenager, belying the gobs of black eyeliner and blood-red lipstick. We spoke, briefly. "Twenty-five dollars up-front, the rest when we finish," she said. "I'm no charity worker."

"Fine with me," I told her. "I don't expect anything for free."

She led me through a dismal tavern and up winding stairs to a small room. She unzipped her skirt, then removed her blouse. Suddenly I felt terrified and had no idea what I should do. I swallowed hard and remained standing, fully dressed. The woman looked at me with disbelieving eyes. "One of those, huh," she said, shaking her head. "I should have known. A mama's boy." She pointed a crooked finger. "Look, I ain't no social worker."

Mama's boy? That's what you're saying. So I hit her. My fist against her jaw. She fell backward against the bed and screamed. Blood- curdling, her eyes now wide with fear. I set upon her at once, biting at her stomach and breasts, drawing blood. The blows reigned down, one after another, I couldn't stop.

She kicked at my groin, which caused me to double over. Then she reached for a buzzer on top of a night table. That was it. Very quickly, I was jumped by two burly men who burst through the door, pummeling me with fierce punches of their own. My mouth spurted blood, my eyes ballooned and started closing, the world receding into a tiny speck. Somehow, I managed to squirm free and made a mad dash down the stairs. They followed, I could hear the clatter of their footsteps, but I was running for my life. It was no contest.

In my apartment, I collapsed onto the sofa. Mama's boy, huh? Mama's boy. The words assaulted my ears. I squeezed my eyes shut and my whole body began to shake violently.

"Master! Master!"

My golem. She meant so well, what a gal. Without my saying a word, she curled up with me on the sofa.

After laying there for what seemed like hours, there was a loud knock on the door. At first I imagined it was the brothers. Them again. But then I heard the shouting.

"Toronto Police! Let us in!"

I stumbled to the front door and threw it wide open, gesturing with a magnificent sweep of my arm.

"You got me," I said.

As they were putting the cuffs on, Simone ran toward the officers. She lifted one up by the throat and pinned him against the wall. His partner put Simone in a choke hold from behind but she forcefully bumped him off with her rear end and then kicked him so hard in the groin I thought his entrails would come out the other side. He moaned and was still. But Simone wasn't through. She punched both officers with closed fists and some of their teeth spewed out, like a volcanic explosion.

"STOP!" I commanded.

All at once, Simone, her eyes wild and crazy, slowly moved away from the strewn men. I looked at her and felt distinctly afraid; this was the very first time I had ever witnessed her brute strength. She was bent on mayhem, utter destruction, and the unconscious police were the end result. There was blood and teeth all over.

I collapsed back onto the sofa.

"Oh my God," I said to myself.

"Yes, exactly. Your creator should know what you're up to," said Simone, seizing upon my words. "I am so glad you now see it my way."

I moaned time and again. *What am I going to do?* I thought, but I had no answers.

I sat on the sofa, dripping snot and blood and contemplated my next move. I needed to think it through. Meanwhile, Simone prepared banana bread in the kitchen. Of late, she had developed the habit of listening to the radio and singing along with the pop music. So as she swirled the batter, she crooned at the top of her lungs:

Shake it up, shake it up...up...up...up...

I didn't care much for pop music, didn't know the stars, but the Taylor Swift song, that much I knew...I had heard the song many times. The poor woman, Ms. Swift, would have cringed hearing Simone's off-beat rendition. Indeed, for some reason, my golem was a half-beat off; it was as if she needed a second or two to assimilate the music before attempting to sing along.

For some reason, that made me feel slightly better, the klutzy singing. But as I looked at the unconscious bodies of the police officers, their chests rising and falling, I realized I was in big trouble.

"How about some French Toast?" I called out to Simone. For some reason, the sticky sweetness appealed just at that moment.

"I'm making banana bread, Master."

"Can you put that aside, Simone, just for now? I can really use some French Toast."

"Of course, you are still my master, Master."

As Simone whipped up the food, I walked slowly into the washroom and attempted to wash the blood from my body. Seemingly, I was bleeding from every orifice – my mouth, ears, nose. My face looked like I had gone 12 rounds with a prizefighter, it was so swollen.

I dabbed at cuts with hydrogen peroxide, each one stinging like crazy. I bloodied toilet paper and towels, making a big mess in the sink.

"Ready, Master."

I emerged just as my golem was placing a huge stack of French Toast precariously on the table. Before we chowed down, I told her what to do in case one of the officers was to wake.

"Hit him a good one at the side of the head until he loses consciousness again."

"Yes, Master."

French toast with plenty of sticky syrup was just the thing.

"Very tasty, Simone."

"Thank you, Master. I was hoping you would like it. Especially because you had another accident at work."

My face was throbbing. I got an ice pack from the freezer ice and held it to my face with one hand, while I ate with the other.

"Let me do that, Master."

Simone held the pack to my face. She pressed it to my flesh for a few seconds, briefly lowered it to allow me to eat, held the pack to my face, lowered it, and so on. And she herself somehow ate, nothing could slow her down. Just then, I noticed that one of the officers was stirring and I mentioned it to her. With no hesitation, she walked right up to the man and punched him viciously three times so that he groaned and went right back to sleep.

"There, we don't want them bothering us, Master. Not while we're eating. They're very rude, Master." She held her fork in mid-air, contemplating. "But who exactly are these guys, Master? And what do they want of you?"

"They're bad men, Simone. They wanted to rob me."

"Rob?"

"Yes, take something very important away from me."

"What, Master? What exactly?"

"My personality."

So we left it at that. But I told Simone to bodily park the two dumbbells in uniform across the road somewhere in an alleyway. When she had finished eating, she lifted them up like they were as weightless as marshmallows and draped them along each shoulder. I watched from the window as people on the street gave her a wide berth and stared with disbelieving eyes. Then she slipped into the alley and was gone from sight for a few minutes. When she returned to the apartment, she told me that she had placed the two officers on top of a mountain of black garbage bags in the back of a restaurant.

"I had a feeling that's where you might want them put, Master."

For the next few hours, Simone very gently tended to the swelling on my face and even made me some soft boiled eggs and toast when I told her I was still hungry. She drew a hot bath for me and washed my aching body all over with a soft washcloth and soap. It wasn't so bad being washed. Not at all. In fact, all the care she showed me made me realize I actually needed her, even if she was only a golem.

The next morning I layed in bed and waited. But the police didn't come for me, as I suspected they would. I was all ready to give myself up, but nothing happened. So I went outside with Simone to where she had dumped the officers to have a look but they weren't there. A trail of blood was clearly evident on the ground. Of more immediate interest was a large metallic dumpster. I took a nose-dive in and

Simone followed. Very rapidly, we emerged with two cantaloupes, a loaf of rye bread, three tins of sardines, half a dozen tomatoes, four bananas, and many cans of dog food. The bananas had been thrown out in a small wooden box that said Imported from South America and with the exception of a few brown spots, appeared to be perfect. I couldn't figure out why they had been thrown out. And the cans of dog food had expired 'best before' dates, but so what? They were still good, I was sure. I wasn't exactly certain what I would do with them but as I looked over the ingredients – beef and chicken by-products, wheat, ground yellow corn, bone meal, animal fat, natural chicken flavour, dried beet pulp, brown rice, amongst assorted other items that only had letters to designate them – I realized that in a pinch, eating dog food wasn't going to kill me. Nor Simone.

"Simone," I said, as we emerged from the alley. "This is all good food but now I would like some cheese. Assorted cheeses like Swiss and Provolone."

"I don't know those cheeses, Master. We have only eaten sliced Kraft cheese."

"You'll be in for a treat then. All you have to do is go into that cheese store over there and steal some."

"Steal, Master?"

"Yes, steal, Simone. It means to take things without paying for them."

"How do I do that, Master?"

"You'll have to make sure no one is looking at you. Then you put them under your blouse, walk out, and come back to the apartment. Just make sure like I said, that when you're in the store, nobody sees you putting the cheeses in your clothes – that's important."

"Yes, Master."

"Now don't take too much cheese, one bar of each will do."

"Yes, Master."

So while I continued to explain the intricacies of shoplifting to Simone, I took the dumpster food from her arms and made my way slowly up the stairs leading to the apartment. As luck would have it, Beverly was coming the other way.

"Where's your weird friend?"

"That's some greeting," I said. "No hello, no how are you? And besides, she's not that weird."

"You're all bruised and cut up."

"Accident at work. I'm hurting."

I should have expected it, I guess. Beverly leaned in for a kiss and I reciprocated. Before I knew it, I had lost control, catapulting down a road I knew I shouldn't go.

"Condom," she whispered.

"I don't have a condom," I said.

"Doesn't matter," she said.

So I walked right in, nice and moist. Slow and then fast. Ecstasy. But then I heard pounding on the front door.

"Just ignore it," said Beverly.

That would have been fine had the door not been knocked over, completely torn off its hinges.

"MASTER!"

I was in the middle, what could I do? So I continued, yes, I did.

"Go home, Simone! Now!"

She did so, except she was carried me with her. She just lifted me bodily off Beverly, dripping and exasperated. For good measure, she slapped Beverly so hard across her face that it drew blood from her mouth.

"OK, down now please." Simone dumped me on to the sofa in my living room. I would have expected her to simply place me down but instead it was a ceremonial dump, like she was depositing a sack of potatoes. If I didn't know better, I might have thought she was upset, jealous perhaps. But how could that be, a golem to have its own emotions? I should have known by now that I wasn't dealing with just any golem.

"Here's the cheese," she said tersely, handing me two large chunks. $10 apiece, she had saved me $20 I didn't have.

"Ok, grilled cheese sandwiches, with salad, coming up," I said deferentially, still panting. "Dessert – bananas and cantaloupe. You just relax and let me do all the cooking."

I was stark naked and ran to the bedroom to put on clothes. I certainly wasn't going back to Beverly's top get the ones I left there, Simone might have killed me. I put on underwear, socks, a Bob Marley t-shirt, and a pair of jeans. I took a deep breath and returned to start lunch, buttering slices of bread and cutting the cheese. Simone sat in the living room, her arms crossed, watching my every move. To say I was a bit scared was an understatement, I was petrified, although I couldn't exactly account for it...well, maybe being torn to shreds by an angry creature with inordinate strength was the reason why. Was she really angry? There was no question because she told me as much.

"I'm angry at you," called out Simone.

I noted she did not call me 'Master' any longer. She didn't have to explain why, I understood perfectly, well... had she been human. But she was a golem. A golem! Was it really possible that she had emotions like jealousy and anger? I guess it was. Bilchen had created an uber-Golem, one capable of human-like behaviours, there was no question. So I diverted my eyes from Simone's glaring stare and concentrated on slicing the bananas... I had to make the perfect lunch.

Chapter Thirty-Six

For a few days, Simone and I had coffee at a donut shop on Bloor Street, across from The Royal Bank of Canada. She loved the powdery jam donuts, deliberately smearing the white powder over her lips until she looked like a clown. She would ogle herself in the chrome napkin holder and burst out in laughter. But I was there for more serious pursuits, like staking out a bank. I wanted to rob it and get myself out of the dreadful hole I found myself in. I found out that Saturday morning was when the bank carried the most cash; at exactly 11 am, Brinks security guards came for the cash that had built up during the entire week. So I had to get there before then. And I had no doubt that the money was safely ensconced within a safe, somewhere in the back of the building. But it was simple: I didn't see why it would be any more difficult than putting a gun to the teller's head – that's all it would take for them to open the combination.

I considered the scenario long and hard. I wasn't a hardened criminal and certainly had never handled a gun before. But there were advantages in stepping out of my comfort zone...like cold hard cash, something I was in dire need of. My life could be so much better if only I didn't have to worry about finances. Things had derailed to the point where I was hardly employable, I knew that. The future looked incredibly bleak. And perhaps if I didn't have to concern myself with money, I wouldn't have bashed those women. I hadn't given the matter much thought but maybe, just maybe, I'd be a different person with wads of cash in my pants. But without some financial stability, well, who knew what the future would be like. So the way I looked at it was that pulling off the heist was my last chance at respectability.

But could I actually pull it off, robbing a bank? I concluded I could but that the gun business was out...that I couldn't do. Not a real one, anyway. It didn't matter though, I had a golem at my disposal. A creature with incredible strength, who could frighten anyone into submission.

We needed outfits. Disguises. So Simone and I went to Goodwill, the very store where I had once dumped Rivka's belongings. Rivka...a name from my past. I ruminated that it was she who was responsible for the mess I was now immersed in. Damn woman.

At Goodwill, we found exactly what we needed. There was a Mr. Penguin costume for me and a Catwoman one for Simone. Complete with capes, face masks, we were characters straight out of a Batman movie.

"Stuff left over from Halloween, I guess," I told Simone. "Brand new though, still in the packaging."

She stood in front of a full-length mirror and twirled round and round. "I can't believe this, Master. I look completely different." She squeezed my arm with excitement. "You say this is from a movie? I have to watch it. We have to watch it together, Master."

"Better yet, Simone. We'll use these costumes in real life. It'll be like we're characters from the movie."

I couldn't tell her what I planned, she was so innocent. In time though, in time. And besides, she had already gotten a taste for stealing. First cheese, and now cash. What was the difference?

"Master?"

"Yes."

"Ssssss." Simone took a swipe at me with her claws, dangerously close to my Mr. Penguin mask.

"Don't do that, Simone."

"Catwoman, that's who I am. Ssssss." Again her extended fingers swiped close to my face, almost connecting with my elongated penguin nose.

"Now look," I said, exasperated. "This is no time for tomfoolery. Got it?"

"I don't know what 'tomfoolery' means but I think I understand. There will be a time and place for acting like we're in the movies, right?"

"That's right," I said, removing my mask.

"Master?"

"Yes, Simone?"

"Can we go home and watch this Batman movie?"

I decided I would use a fake gun. A water pistol. I just needed it for effect. I found it at a toy store on Yonge Street and it looked exactly like the real deal; it was even named after the Glock handgun...a *Glock Water Express Pistol,* able to squirt water at fast speeds. Quick reloading capacity.

It was all I needed. For Simone I bought an Uzi Sub-Machine Gun.

"It has an open bolt," said the sales clerk, a young girl with studded eyebrows and an oversized lip ring who was chewing a big wad of gum and who looked no older than 18. It was ridiculous, what could she possibly know about machine guns?

"It's a semi-automatic," she said, blowing a large bubble that popped loudly. "It was modeled after the true-to-life Israeli Uzi."

"I don't know anything about Israeli Uzi's."

"Trust me."

"How much is it?"

"$49.95."

"That's expensive! Man oh man."

"A real Uzi will cost you thousands and they'll have to do background checks."

So I bought it, just to get out of there. The last thing I needed was a lecture on Uzi's from a teenage girl.

"Would you like the extended warranty with that, sir?"

"It's a water pistol."

"I have to ask, sir. It's my job."

So I walked out with the replicate Glock and Uzi. When I got home, Simone was totally immersed in the Batman Returns movie which I had rented for her, so much so that she didn't even acknowledge me.

"Good afternoon, Simone."

"Master, I'm watching," she whispered, putting a forefinger to her lips. I tiptoed into the bedroom and lay down, the guns at my side. I just needed to escape from all this madness.

★

Over the next few weeks, Simone and I continued to stake out the bank. We just watched the comings and goings and ate our donuts. Simone continued to act silly, smearing her lips with donut powder. Every time I saw her do it, I was reminded of Solange. The latter had been so full of joy, so full of life, and Simone was no different. She was borne of Solange's DNA, so how could she be any different? And looking at her with those crazy powdered lips, I wondered what I was getting her into.

At home, we practiced. I made Simone walk up to the counter and demand all the cash. She would say: "Hand over all your cash. Don't you dare ring any alarms, if you know what's good for you." Then she would point the Uzi at the teller's head, aim right between the eyeballs. If the teller didn't direct Simone to the money, including the safe, she was to smash her hand against the counter, shattering it. Anyone seeing that would no doubt be frightened out of their wits. As for me, I would stand a good distance back and survey the scene. Make sure no one ran out and that there were no funny tricks. First though I would shout out was: "This is a bank robbery. Everyone down on the floor!"

The Saturday of the heist came and went. I was a jumble of nerves and couldn't muster up the courage. But the following Saturday, everything changed. For some unknown reason, my nerves steadied and Simone and I went to the donut shop at 10:15, where we casually ate donuts and then changed into our Mr. Penguin and Catwoman costumes.

"Follow me!" I ordered Simone, and we darted across the road and into the bank, guns drawn.

"THIS IS A FUCKING HOLDUP!" I shouted at the top of my lungs. "EVERYONE DOWN ON THE GROUND! NOW!" I waved my Glock high in the air.

The damned security guard, the very one I had seen a million times before, did not follow my orders. He stood up instead. I was going to pistol whip him but thought that my plastic gun might explode upon impact. So I told Simone to knock him out. One punch against the jaw, that's all it took. He crumbled to the ground in a heap.

"He's an old man!" someone shouted from a prone position.

"Shut up! Shut up!" I screamed. I had a quick glance; it was true – the guard was really old, not a day under 70 from what I could see. Too bad, all he had to do was listen to orders.

"Simone, go to the counter and do as we planned." As soon as the words slithered out of my mouth, I realized the error of my ways. I had called my partner in crime by her name! Now everyone heard it. Shit.

Not that it mattered to my golem. She acted perfectly and performed just as we had rehearsed. The frightened teller, a middle-aged woman, started handing over tens and twenties, which Simone stuffed in a canvas bag.

"Now the safe," said Simone. "I'm the Catwoman." She lunged forward and whipped her hand, fingers extended, within inches of the woman's face. "Sssss." We hadn't rehearsed that part and I was chagrined beyond belief. The less said, the better. Of course she was the Catwoman. Everyone could see it; from the black mask with the white whiskers to the pointy ears gracing the top of her head, all the way down her slinky black leather bodice, no one would think otherwise.

"On…only the man…manager has the combination," stuttered the teller. "And, and, he's not here right now."

Simone turned to look at me.

"You know what you have to do."

"Of course, Master."

With one earth-shattering crack, the counter splintered. It caved in right where she put her fist, and all the computers and pens and brochures on the long counter made a swan dive into the abyss. And all the fifteen or so people laying facedown on the ground covered their ears at the sound. No doubt they thought a gun had gone off. It was truly frightening, the strength Simone possessed. People screamed Oh My God over and over.

It was then that I heard it. The unmistakable sound of a child crying.

A little girl was among those on the ground. She was lying next to her mother and shaking uncontrollably. She had blond hair with pigtails and a yellow flower was entwined within. But those pigtails…amidst the carnage, I suddenly remembered that that was just the way Solange had often worn her hair.

I had to get out, we had done enough damage. I also noticed the teller staring straight ahead at Simone's forehead and realized the mask Simone wore didn't cover her entire face; her forehead was clearly exposed. It was the sprint across the road to the bank that had undoubtedly pushed the bangs of her hair to one side.

I ran forward and grabbed Simone by the wrist.

"Let's go," I said hurriedly.

Simone ran alongside but then abruptly stood still for a moment, surveying the wreckage. I pulled at her arm but there was no moving her.

"I'M THE CATWOMAN!" she shouted. "SSSS!" She took imaginary swipes through the air and started laughing uproariously.

Once again I grabbed hold of her wrist. "Let's go. Now!"

There was no stopping us. We ran like crazy people on drugs, dodging cars and flinging aside pedestrians. One woman, pushing a stroller, fell heavily into a garbage can. We finally beat it into an alleyway, where we disrobed and dumped the guns and costumes into an empty wooden crate. Simone so loved her getup that she didn't want to leave it behind; I had to convince her we would get another the next day.

And that was that. My career as a bank robber was over. Our take – $625.00. Not bad for a morning's work but not great. Not great at all.

The following day, there must have been 6 of them, a whole battalion of police officers who broke down the front door and cuffed me. I supposed Beverly had called the police, or maybe it was the two brutalized officers Simone had dumped unceremoniously in the laneway who reported the matter. Or maybe someone had followed us from the bank the previous day. No matter, I was done for. It was fortunate that Simone was outside, shoplifting once again. We had already devoured those two blocks of cheese…and wanted more. I thought about what she might think when she would arrive home and find the place empty, signs of a struggle very obvious. I did struggle, kneeing one of the city's finest when he put me in a headlock.

"I can't breathe," I gasped.

"You'll have plenty of time to breathe in lock-up," he said.

"Where's your girlfriend?" another asked.

"Screw you. I was alone."

"A regular Bonnie and Clyde. We'll get her."

The guy they locked me up with was a regular head case. Sammy Santana was his name, so he said. Truly certifiable. He told me he had once knocked a guy cold with a guitar. His daughter's guitar. His daughter's boyfriend. Then he started strangling him with one of the strings, until his daughter made him stop. So he pulled the guy's ear off instead, literally tore it until it dangled in place.

"Why did you do that?" I asked.

"Made her preggies," he answered. "And I would do it again. But this time I would finish the job."

Did I want to hear all this? Even be near this lunatic? Especially when he asked me whether I had ever done it with a man before.

It took two days before I was seen by a judge, who, because I was a first-time offender, let me out on bail. $500. I had that much from the heist, but it was supposed to go toward the rent. No matter, I wrote a cheque and would worry about paying the landlord later. I just felt fortunate that I hadn't been arrested for the bank job, that the coppers hadn't put two and two together. Especially because one had referred to Simone and I as 'Bonnie and Clyde'.

Back in my apartment, I found Simone unconscious and curled in a fetal position on the sofa. I immediately rushed to get the ACV, carefully opened her mouth, and poured some down. She blinked a number of times, as if awakening to the world, and then sat up, seemingly none the worse for wear.

"Hello Master. I seem to have fallen asleep." She yawned deeply, stretched her arms, and then hugged me. Hugged me!

"I'm glad to see you too, Simone," I said, carefully pushing her off after she went on embracing me for what seemed like an eternity.

"Make love, Master?"

"Not right now."

"Cook something for you, Master?"

"Not right now. I need to take a shower."

"I can come into the shower with you."

"OK. Just give me a minute to wash off the grime, then you can join me."

So she did, in all her female golem glory. I soaped her up and snuggled against her body. Then I entered her time and again. Who was I kidding with all this petty theft and bashing of women? – I had everything I needed right here. There were only three things that were amiss – no job, no money, and those damn charges...resisting arrest, assault.

I had no food, other than three more blocks of cheese that Simone had pilfered, including Gorgonzola. There were also 3 rotten apples on the counter, so I mashed them, grated the cheese, put in a bit of olive oil, and threw sea salt on top of the whole shebang until it became edible. I paced the living room and realized that I had all of a week of freedom remaining. For it was then that I had to return to court for sentencing. That was not appealing so I considered taking a bus back to my cave where Simone and I could hole up – no way could they find us in such a remote area. Simone might actually like it there, out in nature, although I suspected she would not have harmed any frogs or rabbits. And taking her to meet my farm friends was out of the question. I would have liked to see Gorky but unfortunately, the whole thing didn't seem like much of an option.

"What are you thinking about, Master?" said Simone, a towel around her hair. "More lovemaking maybe?"

I made a mental note that she was a machine and could go on forever. But I couldn't.

"Let's eat," I said. "Apples and cheese. My own recipe."

As I munched away, I noticed Simone ate with zest. With incredible zeal. As she always did. Nothing fazed her. But I didn't have much of an appetite, I had so much on my mind. Maybe I should have just tried to write once more, that might have helped with the burden. So after the meal had been eaten, I sat in front of the computer and made a concerted effort to write, yet again. But I didn't have a single original thought. Not one. It was killing me, not being able to write. It wasn't like I had writer's block. Not really. It was more like any creative juices I might ever had had, however few they might have been, absconded, replaced by haunting thoughts. Those thoughts permeated my essence and I realized that if I were to die, no one would care. Only my golem. Only her...a creature made from mud. I placed my forehead on the desk.

"Something wrong, Master?"

"Nothing, Simone. Nothing."

"You're the best writer in the world, Master."

The world wasn't poetic, it wasn't just. It was an organism that throbbed and beat to its own chaotic rhythm, one that for the most part excluded me. It was a world hell bent on anarchy, on entropy, where every plan was capable of being thwarted. Even love was a ruse; there were no soul mates, no salvation through giving of oneself to another. Intimacy was a joke, meant to expose vulnerabilities. Human love was replaced with a golem's love.

It took all of my will not to succumb to these thoughts and I realized the only thing that would help me get through all this would be if somehow I could return to my former glory as a writer of fiction. And there was only one way to do that – steal.

I had destroyed all of Rivka's writings but I did keep the literary magazines I found in her apartment. So I perused them to see whether I could use an idea from a story. Any story. And when I say 'use,' I meant only to steal the idea, not any of the actual writing. Right. Hah. That was the intention but I knew I was kidding myself. OK, so I would steal some of the writing. Not all, anyway. Mix and match. *Hodge-podge, hodge-podge,* as Bilchen was fond of saying. A few sentences from one story, others from another story. Despite my previous experience, the stories in the literary magazines were pretty obscure, I knew that. It was highly unlikely that I would be found out twice. The problem as I saw it was that I needed time, and that was something I was running out of.

Chapter Thirty-Seven

Five months. That's what I got. The judge said that I had a propensity for violence. He ordered that I partake in anger management classes once I got out of the slammer. It may not have appeared too harsh in light of what I had done but all things considered, it would have been preferable had they thrown away the key – I was a lost soul.

I returned home under supervision to get a few things and to tell Simone.

"You're going to prison, Master?" she asked.

"Yes."

"What is that – prison?"

"That's where they put the bad guys."

"But you're not a bad guy, Master!"

I took Simone's hands. "No, but sometimes good people do the wrong things."

"I can help you change, Master."

Maybe she could. Maybe she could. But that wasn't the point. The fact of the matter was that I would be away for some time and Simone couldn't exist without me. I had to put her down, and said so.

"You want to kill me, Master?"

"It's not exactly like that. It's more like I'll be returning you to the soil. That's where you came from."

She slapped me across the face, so hard that it drew tears. My escort, a burly 6'4" or so hulk of a man, stepped forward, but I held him back with one hand and shook my head. "No," I said.

Then Simone was gone. A blur out the front door.

My cellmate was named Loco. He was too. If I thought Sammy was bad, this dude was worse. He told me he was a full-patch member of the Rock Machine motorcycle gang but I doubted it. To me, he looked like a biker wanna-be, maybe a small-time hood. Big paunch. Thick arms and legs. Tattoos. But you could never tell, I found out right away. He would often give me the once-over without blinking, like he was sizing me up as to whether he could take me. I couldn't risk it, he might have been truly crazy. So I told him I shared his aversion to people, they were almost all moronic. "Women are the worst," I said. "They make you crazy with lust and then leave you." Loco liked that and nodded his big head, the same one that he could occasionally bang against the wall. Back and forth...back and forth...knock knock, like a woodpecker...day in and day out. Sometimes he drew blood. Then tasted it. I told him that if I had the chance I would live on an island in the South Pacific...alone. Just me and some palm trees. Or coconut trees, whatever grew there.

However clever I tried to be, it wasn't enough. I couldn't play the game long enough. For one thing, I had to share a toilet with Loco. No privacy. He would intertwine his huge fingers and stare at my genitals. And when he went, it was all gas and mind-numbing groans. Hands to the head, eyes closed. Shits that were seemingly orchestrated, drawn out like one-act plays. Standing to pee, he would sometimes miss the bowl. There were puddles all over the floor and the guards gave me a mop and pail to clean up.

When Loco wasn't banging his head or relieving himself, he would sometimes walk up to me and say: "You like to beat up little girls, huh? That's what I heard. Word spreads fast in this joint. Well, I can beat the shit out of you. When the time's right, just you wait and see." Very methodically, he'd pump his fist into his open palm. Sometimes he'd spit at my feet. "You think you're a bad guy, you ain't seen nuthin'."

One day he would be my best friend, the next he would threaten my life. No matter what I said, no matter how placated I made him feel, he would forget and change stripes. He was a certified nutjob, I was sure of it. I wanted to talk to the guards but worried that might set off my cellmate. Besides, I had no bruises. I also knew they didn't care what happened to me.

This all went on for two weeks, at the end of which I was thoroughly psychologically beaten down. I could no longer speak, I could no longer eat, I could no longer sleep. I was in a dank, stifling cellar, a wasted rat trapped underground. I just lay curled on my bunk and rocked, locked within myself.

I was moved to the prison's hospital ward. I was grimy from going in my clothes, shit and urine all over my legs and bum, so two male attendants carried me to a shower stall and propped me against the wall. The water rained down, thousands of tiny body blows. I couldn't wash, my body had turned to stone. I just stood ramrod stiff and accepted the assault. The attendants yelled at me to clean myself but I couldn't, my arms wouldn't work. Only when one smacked my face with an open hand did I comply. Very slowly.

Everything felt like an abstraction, nothing was real. A psychiatrist was brought in to do an assessment. *Severe clinical* depression was the diagnosis, I heard him tell a nurse. "He won't eat. He spits out every pill. He may be suicidal. Start him on IV. Lorazepam."

I was 'formed,' which meant they gave me a hospital gown and slippers. I suppose they didn't want me running away. *Running, hah!* I could barely lift my legs.

They put me in a stark cell, this time by myself. It was barren and had no windows and even when I was wearing my slippers, the floor felt ice-cold. If only they had put me in my cave…if only… I asked one of the attendants about moving to a better place, something a bit more 'homey.' He laughed. "You'd better get used to it," he said. "This ain't the Ritz."

Shortly after I arrived, the same attendants escorted me down the hall to a large room, as sterile as an operating room. The light was blinding and I had to shield my eyes with the back of my hand. As my eyes gradually grew accustomed to the brightness, I could make out many bodies lying inert on crisp white-sheeted beds. They were unmoving, occasionally moaning. They seemed drugged, long drools of spittle emanating from open mouths.

The sonorous hum of machines permeated the room. That sound infiltrated me, to my very core. It reminded me of a verse I had once read, a verse from George Elliot, the writer. Middlemarch, yes that's it. It was a small miracle that I could still recall. But I had carried it around with me everywhere, for reasons I never could comprehend. *"If we had keen vision and feeling of all ordinary human life, it would be like hearing the grass grow and the squirrel's heart beat and we should die of that roar which lies on the other side of silence."*

My hearing was so acute, it was like listening to the grass grow. To die then of the hum! I managed to prop myself on my elbows to have a better look. Situated on the white-enameled night tables next to many of the patients, the rectangular black machines showed a tangled web of red and black lines, little cobbled hills and valleys that paraded across the screen. But what was even more disturbing was the honeycomb-like cream-coloured wires that sprouted from the heads of the ghouls, the wires in turn connected to the odd-looking machines It gave them the appearance of space beings. I wanted to ask the nurses what it was all about but my ability to control my own body had vanished. Almost as quickly as I sat up I was back down, flat on my back.

Masked doctors in pristine white lab coats came. They moved me from my bed onto a metallic gurney and I was wheeled into an operating room. The room was unnaturally cold. They slipped my body off the gurney onto a table.

"What are you looking for?" I heard one of the doctors say. I didn't understand what he was asking of me. All I could think of saying in response was - *please don't hurt me.* But I couldn't speak.

"What we look for," answered another doctor, "is excitation of large numbers of neurons. The excitation builds and quickly overwhelms any inhibitory mechanisms that hold the neurons in check. And when that happens the brain gets swamped. Cerebral blood flow increases dramatically. We monitor the electrical signals using EEG."

Please don't hurt me.

An IV was put into my arm, just like when I was first brought into the hospital ward, I was told to bite down onto a rubber block; it tasted like chalk and I wanted to gag. A plastic mask was placed over my mouth and jelly was rubbed onto my temples. I could feel something being connected there. Then I was asked to count backward from one hundred…

I woke up back in my cell, strapped onto the bed. A nurse wiped the drool from my mouth and adjusted my helmet. I tried to tell her that my jaw was incredibly pained but no words emerged from my throat; it was like I was sinking in a mud puddle. A short time later, my nose began to bleed.

Two days later, I was jolted once more. For the rest of the day, I was utterly confused and could not remember my name. My limbs ached and again my nose bled.

The following day, as I was being taken from his room, aware of where I was going, I began to cry.

"Life is tough," said one of the attendants. "Like I told you before – you just have to get used to it. This ain't no hotel."

In all, I was given six unilateral electroconvulsive treatments over a period of a week and a half. Interestingly and unlikely as it seemed, I responded fully. Fully! My depression went into remission and I began to eat voraciously. For some reason, I couldn't get enough of ham and cheese omelettes; along with salted chips, I just ate them all day long. I just asked for seconds and thirds. And I slept, sometimes for ten or twelve hours at a stretch. I felt happy, even gregarious. I greeted the nurses with great big smiles.

I was returned to my small cell. Weeks went by, and then months. I did jumping jacks, pushups, ate everything they offered, took my meds, slept or relaxed on my bunk much of the time, tried to engage the guards in idle chitchat. Generally, I was quite happy with the arrangement...it was silky smooth. And then there was an early discharge for good behaviour. Why not? I was the ideal prisoner.

I returned to my apartment. My apartment, hah. For when I got there, the key would not open the door. I spoke to the proprietor of the variety store downstairs.

"Where has you been?" he said. "My wife and I, we was worried."

"I had business out of the country," I said. I still knew enough when to lie.

"You could has told me. Always tells is better than no tells."

"Yes. I'm sorry. It was urgent though."

"Aha, that there girl?"

I hesitated. It was best to be agreeable. I smiled knowingly. Yes, of course, that girl. But which girl was he referring to? And then I remembered...Solange, Simone. Maybe Beverly?

In his very broken English, he told me that I had been evicted for non-payment of rent. The landlord had thrown out nearly all my stuff but that some remained. It was being kept in an empty storeroom at the back of the store.

"Did you ever see the girl?" I asked, as I was led to the rear. "You know, since I was away."

"I keeps to myself, Mr. Karl. It's better that way. You I likes a little, I don't know why, maybe you private so I likes, so...so... I worries."

"Right. I understand. Thank you for worrying."

There were two very withered brown plants. And a computer monitor that had a large diagonal crack. Books too. Bags of them. That was all that was left from my previous life. I pulled apart the thick clear plastic and leafed through the bags: David Hume, Friedrich Nietzche, Baruch Spinoza, Plato, Aristotle, George Berkeley, Immanuel Kant, Thomas Aquinas, Martin Buber. Henri Bergson... there were so many authors. Baruch Spinoza? Such a name! I wondered whether he had been bullied all his life because of it. I opened the books and tried to read. Each word in itself was fairly clear but collectively, the ideas behind them were an utter mystery. It was all too convoluted, too complicated.

There was a thin book by someone called John Keats. I picked it from the pile because there was a pink sticky note attached to a page. The inside sleeve had an inscription: To Karl, my great love. Solange. I turned to the page with the note. Some lines were highlighted in yellow: *I am certain of nothing but the holiness of the heart's affection and the truth of imagination.*

Chapter Thirty-Eight

She had run, then stopped and walked. There was something approaching fear in her but it was a strange emotion, one she had never before known. Nor did she understand why she felt this way. It was late in the evening and the lights of the city twinkled overhead, like a million stars. Stunning, but far out of reach. She was hungry and listened intently for the sounds of crickets from a nearby field. Then she instinctively plucked them off stalks of grass with her hands, one by one. And the fireflies that sparkled against the pitch-black sky were no safer. But she disdained the taste of these insects, and longed for human food. So she wandered about looking for a store, similar to what she had seen in Kensington Market. When she found one, it was no problem to steal the cheese, she had become quite adept. A quick movement of the hand and the block slid between the open buttons of her blouse. For good measure, and because she had become quite enamoured with the taste, she took a jar of black olives. The chimes above the door signaled her successful lift.

As she sat down in a park and ate voraciously, it occurred to the golem that her freedom was an illusion, that she would give it up in a minute if only she could attain safety and security. It was no good being alone and now she understood why she was beset by this very strange and unsettling feeling of fear.

Before she had bolted from her Master's apartment, she had snatched the small bottle of ACV. She understood she needed it, it was her lifeline. Her Master had confided in her one day. Already she was feeling a bit weak and her head was swimming. In a few hours she would expire. She could simply lift the bottle to her lips, it was all so easy...

She was mesmerized by the three men that came upon her. In the morning, there would be the squeals of children playing, but now, at this hour, there was no one in the park. Only the men.

"What do we have here?" one said, and they surrounded her on all sides.

She didn't respond.

They took out a bottle, passed it around, took slugs. Offered her some but she shook her head sadly.

"My Master," she said quietly.

"We're your masters now."

Then they were upon her and tore the clothes from her limp body. They took turns and she did not resist. She could have crushed them, annihilated their puny bodies. But it was better to accede, she knew. Her will had been broken. She could feel herself receding from the world, it was spinning wildly away. Ever so slowly, her flesh began retreating from the bones and coming apart. Strands of her hair, now drenched in sweat, merged with the dust, with the ground, and dissipated, flaking off.

"Look at this," growled the man on top of her, a long cord of spittle slipping from the corner of his mouth. "Something weird on her forehead."

"It doesn't matter," said another, pushing at his friend. "Hurry up. My turn next."

They entered her even harder, with so much force that her body was pushed further into the ground. Folded in half, like an accordion. She screamed with each thrust, but they were screams of relief, she felt no pain.

And when it was all over and the men stood up, they ogled their prey one last time and were afraid. For their victim seemed to be returning to the earth, molecule by molecule, until she was no longer visible and had completely merged from the very soil from which she had arisen.

About the Author

Originally from Montreal, **Jerry Levy** now resides in Toronto, Canada. His short stories have appeared in many literary magazines throughout Canada, the U.S., and the U.K. In 2013, a collection of short stories – Urban Legend – was published by Thistledown Press. He has an upcoming book of short stories entitled Paris was the Rage, which will be published in 2020 by Guernica Editions. He is a regular judge for the Writer's Union of Canada Short Prose Contest and occasionally does a similar task for an organization called Vea'havta, judging short stories from people who are marginalized and who have experience homelessness at some point. He has a B. Comm. Degree from Concordia in Montreal and a teaching certificate (Teaching English as a Second Language) from CCLCS in Toronto. The Philosopher and the Golem is his first published novel. His website can be accessed at: jerrylevy.weebly.com

91023433R00236

Made in the USA
San Bernardino, CA
24 October 2018